Winter Park Publ.

SPIRIT FOX

Spirit Fox

Mickey Zucker Reichert
and Jennifer Wingert

DAW BOOKS, INC.

DONALD A. WOLLHEIM, FOUNDER
375 Hudson Street, New York, NY 10014

ELIZABETH R. WOLLHEIM
SHEILA E. GILBERT
PUBLISHERS
www.dawbooks.com

F

Jacket art by Gordon Crabb.
Map by D. Allan Drummond.

DAW Book Collectors No. 1105.
DAW Books are distributed by Penguin Putnam Inc.

Book designed by Stanley S. Drate/Folio Graphics Co., Inc.

First printing, December 1998
1 2 3 4 5 6 7 8 9

DAW TRADEMARK REGISTERED
U.S. PAT. OFF. AND FOREIGN COUNTRIES
—MARCA REGISTRADA
HECHO EN U.S.A.

PRINTED IN THE U.S.A.

To the memory of my dear father,
John P. Wingert: teacher, adviser, hero.
and
To my living father, Arthur Zucker,
who will never understand me but
is proud of me anyway—
(even when he pretends he isn't).

ACKNOWLEDGMENTS

Mickey would like to thank the following people: Mark, Ben, Jon, Jackie, Ari, and Koby; Sandra Zucker; Sheila Gilbert; Jonathan Matson; and the Pendragons.

Jennifer adds: I would like to thank the following for their encouragement and long-suffering patience—my family, Judy Miller, Beth Nachison, Emily Lovett, Jenny Blackford, Claudia Meek, and all my friends at Sysco Foods. Most of all, I would like to thank my mentor and collaboration partner, Mickey Zucker Reichert. Mickey: without your guidance, I'd still be throwing it all away.

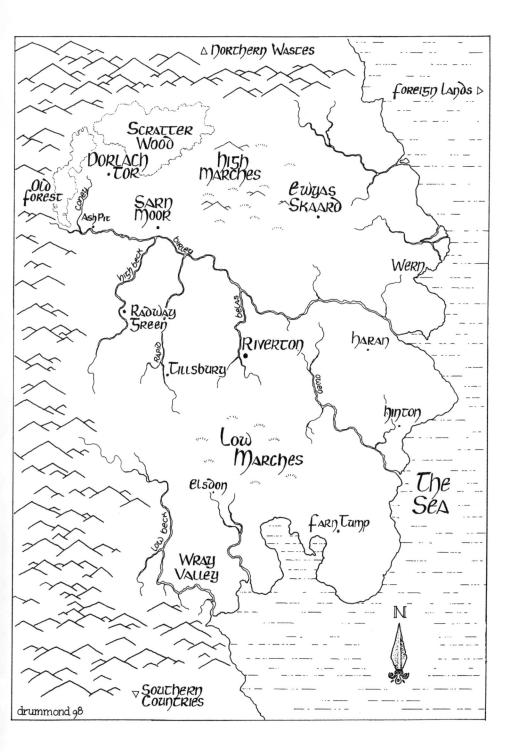

Northern Wastes

foreign lands ▷

Scratter Wood

Dorlach Tor

Old Forest

High Marches

Ewyas Skaaro

Ash Pit

Sarn Moor

Wern

high beck

belas

Radway Green

Riverton

Haran

rapid

Tillsbury

dano

Hinton

Low Marches

The Sea

Elsdon

low beck

Farn Tump

Wray Valley

N

Southern Countries

drummond 98

SPIRIT FOX

PROLOGUE

L ORD Stane lay awake, gazing into the darkness. The turmoil
in his heart chased away his much-needed rest, though he
knew a full day of work awaited him with the dawn. In one short
month he would become a father. He had only that long to ac-
quire the wisdom and compassion of his own father. *I'm not
ready*. The certain knowledge of imminent failure washed over
him. *Not ready*.

His wife, Lady Wylfre, slept beside him in the curtained bed,
her left leg flung over the small of his back. Her big belly pressed
warmly against his side, moving with the silken rhythm of her
breath. The unborn child also seemed to slumber now, though
she spent most evenings in determined attempts to kick her way
into the world.

Wondering if he were the only waking member of the household, Stane lifted his head to listen. In the alcove just outside
their chamber, the whistling snores of Wylfre's old nurse split the
air. One of the two deerhounds at the foot of the bed sighed in
its sleep. Outside, no louder than a whisper, an early April wind
blew over the earthen walls of the ancient fort of Dorlach Tor.

It suddenly occurred to Stane that, between the active baby
and her aching back, Wylfre rarely managed sleep. Raising his
head a bit higher, he peered down at the plaited band of horsehair
around his right wrist. A recent gift from his Horsemaster, the
charm was supposed to draw the discomforts of pregnancy away
from Wylfre and onto himself. He hoped his wakefulness meant
the bracelet worked. If it did, he would gladly tie horsehair
around every part of his body.

Moving with tender caution, Stane propped himself up on his
elbows to admire his lady. In the dim light, Wylfre's strong-jawed

1

face seemed to glow with inner radiance, and her auburn curls appeared black. Seven songs extolled her beauty and proud will, and the extravagant poetry of the High Marchland bards styled her "the Dark Flame of Dorlach Tor." Her right hand rested on Stane's pillow, callused palm up, fingers curled slightly. A powerful hand, he knew, capable of a crushing grip, the hand of a noble lady, the hand of a horsewoman. He longed to press his lips to her palm in a secret kiss but dared not for fear of waking her.

In the morning, Stane would tell the Horsemaster that the charm seemed to work, but he would neglect to mention to Swordmaster Gaer that he had spent the night awake. Gaer tended to worry about such things, and he might see it as his duty to put the new Lord of Dorlach Tor through a grinding afternoon of practice.

Grinning, Stane stroked the new growth of blond hair on his upper lip. Though her idea, Wylfre loathed the mustache. To command the respect of men twice his age, a young lord of twenty summers must look like a war chieftain. Stane's lips matched the perfect curve of a bow, his nose was small and fine, and his long lashes were as golden as his hair. Without the mustache, he did not resemble a fierce Battlemaster so much as a pretty maiden.

Since the death of Wylfre's father in early December, Stane needed to claim his rightful place as the new Lord of Dorlach Tor. His smile faded. No one openly challenged his leadership, but he knew they obeyed him only out of deference to Wylfre. She was their Lady, their law-giver; and he was merely her new husband, an unproven outsider from the Low Marches. It was fortunate, he reflected, that she possessed no brothers to complicate matters.

Wylfre stirred.

Stane held his breath, pinching the strand of horsehair. *Work,* he silently urged the charm. *Work.*

Wylfre opened her eyes. Blinking sleepily, she smiled up at him.

Crestfallen, Stane released his hold on the bracelet. "Awake, my love?" he whispered. "And you slumbered so beautifully."

Wylfre did not answer but reached up to his face. With one

finger, she rubbed the anxious crease between his brows. "You're worried," she said quietly. "What is it this time?"

Stane clasped her hand in both of his and pressed it to his cheek. "Everything."

Wylfre chuckled warmly. "Again?" She propped herself up on one elbow and leaned to touch her forehead to his. Her sparkling eyes filled his vision. "Tell me."

Stane's breath caught in his throat as he gazed at her. *So beautiful.* "I'm just—" Undone by emotion, Stane struggled to marshal his thoughts. "Spring is already upon us, and there's so much left to do."

"Ah," she said softly. "You're thinking about the news from the Low Marches."

Reluctantly, Stane dropped his gaze. Surrounded by mountains, the Marchlands lay between the northern wastes and the highly populated countries to the south. Though always racked by blood feud and war, the Marchlands faced a new threat in recent years. Raiders from the south traveled in ships up the eastern coast and invaded the interior by the riverways. Every spring, the raiders rode the rivers farther north; and the current news from Stane's kinfolk in the Low Marches indicated they would soon breach the High Marches. "Actually," he confessed, "I was worrying about the baby."

Wylfre's smile deepened. "But everything is perfect. Our firstborn will be a daughter. Yes?"

Stane nodded. Men died in battle, many while still young. Women inherited the lands and properties, to insure the continuance of bloodlines. The healer, old Sygil, seemed certain that the ancient passage of Dorlach Tor from mother to daughter would remain unbroken. "Yes," he answered softly. "A daughter."

Wylfre sank back onto the pillows, still smiling. "And she will be born in May, spirit-linked to one of the finest colts in our herd. Yes?"

Following her lead, Stane also reclined. He disliked contradicting his lady, but the spirit-link was not a sure thing. If a human and an animal were born at precisely the same instant, and within a certain distance of each other, their souls merged and they could communicate. A spirit-link was a rare and special blessing of the gods, but he and Wylfre would attempt to force the link to occur. No one, to his knowledge, had ever tried to do such a thing. It might prove impossible. "Maybe."

Wylfre gave a low, provocative laugh. " 'Yes,' " she corrected. She laced her fingers through his and pretended to wrestle him. "Say 'yes.' "

Stane offered no resistance. Mona, Wylfre's cousin in the neighboring fort of Sarn Moor, had borne a spirit-linked child just over a year ago, and Stane understood it was Wylfre's deepest desire to do the same. "Yes, my lady."

Wylfre drew their joined hands to her belly. "And because of the link, our daughter shall never know illness, shall live beyond a hundred years, shall find—"

From the courtyard, a dog barked a warning. At the foot of the bed, the deerhounds stirred and grumbled. Stane lifted his head and held his breath, listening.

Abruptly, discordant clanging rang through the air, the night watch hammering an old, iron cauldron as the alarm signal.

Stane swept aside the curtains and rolled out of bed. Born and raised in the battle-torn Low Marches, he expected the worst.

Moonlight spilled into the bedchamber from a high, narrow window. The air was damp and chilly. Upon the oaken rack on the wall beside their bed, his sword belt hung beside Wylfre's bow and quiver. He pulled his weapon down and strapped the belt on over his night robe, muttering to the goddess of battle an invocation that was also a curse. "Almighty Hepona!"

From the courtyard, a man hailed the watch. Stane could not make out his words through the alarm's din, but he recognized the voice of the Swordmaster, Gaer.

The hammering fell silent. "A rider!" called the watch. "A rider from the south!"

Sarn Moor, the closest fort, lay a half-day's ride to the south, the holding of Wylfre's cousin, Mona. Stane's sense of disaster settled into certainty, and he loosened his sword in its scabbard. To send a rider out in the night, alone against ghosts and the Dark Court, bespoke a dire emergency, and he could only assume the River People had staged a surprise raid.

Moving awkwardly, Wylfre clambered toward the edge of the

bed, her eyes wide and anxious. "Wait for me," she said. "I'm coming, too."

Despite the need for haste, Stane gave Wylfre a hand to her feet. He knew she worried about her kin, and he could not find it in him to reproach her. "My love," he said. "Of course, I'll wait."

The most ancient of forts in the High Marches, Dorlach Tor crowned its steep hill with two concentric rings of earthen walls. Within the inner ring, a rugged outcropping of solid granite rose to the sky like a tower. It took its name, "dorlach," from the ancient word for a quiver of arrows, and it overshadowed the Great House built at its base.

Breath steaming in the cold night air, Stane glanced around the outer courtyard. A thin blanket of dry snow had fallen in the night, and it magnified the light of the full moon. Wrapped in Stane's borrowed cloak, Wylfre stood close, her shoulder brushing his, her face pinched. Around them, the household of Dorlach Tor assembled. Several men wore their swords, and a few women carried their bows. Excited children and dogs scampered among the adults.

One of the great gates stood ajar, open just enough to admit a single horse and rider. Gaer, the Swordmaster, stood by the wall, fully dressed and impeccably groomed. He wore his silver hair long, and his lean face evinced no sign of weariness. With an admiration bordering on envy, Stane studied the urbane and elegant figure. He wondered how Gaer always managed to appear wide awake and fresh from the bath.

As if sensing the young lord's regard, Gaer turned to meet his gaze. A trifle embarrassed, Stane nodded his head in a dignified greeting.

Wylfre also noticed the Swordmaster. "Uncle Gaer," she called. "Over here."

Suddenly smiling, Gaer tossed his cloak over one shoulder and performed an elaborate bow. He was not actually Wylfre's uncle, but her late father's most trusted retainer. A lone wanderer from exotic lands across the Sea, Gaer retained the pretty manners of a foreign court, even after fifteen years in the High Marches. He could sing, dance, and tell a good story. Though not born to the Marchlands, he nevertheless served the goddess of battle with a devotion that earned him the respect of the most hardened warriors. In Gaer's hand, a sword became the very lightning of Hepona.

Gaer strolled to where they stood, moving with easy grace. "My lady," he said in a reverent tone. "My lord."

The night watch, a battle-scarred old warrior named Fawley, crouched atop the outer wall. The sound of hoofbeats pounded the air, and Fawley raised his voice. "Watch out," he called. "Here he comes."

The thunder of galloping hooves grew louder, joined by the jingle of tack.

Stane tensed and wrapped his arm around Wylfre, ready to pull her from danger. The messenger might be one of the Dark Court, those rumored to steal children and pregnant women in the night.

Gaer drew his sword in a smooth, sweeping motion and stepped between Wylfre and the gate. Around the courtyard, other men also held their swords at ready, and the women bent their bows, taking aim.

A tall, white horse hurtled through the narrow opening. Its rider hauled back on the reins. The horse screamed and shook its proud head but came to a plunging halt. Foam spilled from its mouth and flanks, and its sides heaved with every breath; but the horse pawed the flagstones as if spoiling for a race.

Wylfre gasped. "Sea Cloud!" She clutched Stane's arm. "It's Sea Cloud!"

Stane gazed in wonder at the stallion, the pride of Sarn Moor, the last horse in whom the old blood ran true.

From the sheltered paddocks of the inner courtyard, the horses called in answer to the newcomer, high-pitched whinnies of wild distress.

Stane's scalp prickled. The horses of the Marchlands were known in song as the Children of Hepona, and they were stronger, more fleet of foot, and wiser than the lesser breeds. He wondered what Sea Cloud had told them, what news caused them to keen like banshees.

The rider slid from the stallion's back, falling more than dismounting. Mud plastered his hair flat and covered his face, save for his eyes and the tracks made by tears. He cradled his left arm in his right, and his breath was dry panting. He gazed around, seeming dazzled by the torchlight, and took a staggering step.

Moving before anyone else, Stane abandoned dignity and darted to the rider's aid. "Easy," he said. He threw a steadying arm around the youth. "Easy, now. You're safe at Dorlach Tor."

Trembling, the rider stared blankly at Stane. "Dorlach—?"

Wylfre said, "He's hurt. Someone, go bring Sygil."

A murmur passed through the gathered folk, and several young men raced toward the Great House.

Cadder, the Horsemaster, wove his way through the crowd, moving purposefully toward the agitated stallion. Only a few years older than Stane, he stood as solid as a block of granite, but was already graying at the temples. Behind the Horsemaster trailed his four-year-old son, Maddock, clomping in boots a bit too big.

The rider turned erratically, as if he also intended to care for his mount.

"Easy," Stane repeated. "Cadder will look after Sea Cloud." He could only imagine what terrors the rider had faced on his dark journey, and he tried to speak gently. "Give us your news, my lad, while we wait for old Sygil to come heal your arm."

The rider's eyes widened. "No!" he cried out, trying to twist away from Stane. "No, not for me! For little Adan!"

Afraid the fellow would fall, Stane gripped the rider's shoulders in both hands. Adan was the oldest son of Wylfre's cousin Mona, he recalled, just six years old. "Adan?" He kept his tone calm. "What happened to Adan?"

The murmur strengthened, and the folk passed along Adan's name in a rising tone of worry.

Wylfre drew near, her face white and rigid in the moonlight.

The rider caught sight of her and spoke in a breathless rush. "Oh, my lady! For the love of all mercy, lend the skill of your healer—" He broke off in a rasping cough.

At that moment, Sea Cloud roared low in his throat. Cadder stroked the stallion's neck. "Gently, brave one," he said in a soothing tone. He eased his hand around the headstall's cheek piece and attempted to lead Sea Cloud forward. "Steady, now."

The stallion took one step and stumbled, throwing Cadder to his knees. The horse balanced splay-legged on the flagstones for a heartbeat, then collapsed onto his side.

With a desperate cry, the rider ripped from Stane's supporting hands and scrambled to his mount. "No!"

Sea Cloud's legs thrashed, as if he attempted to canter on air. A flying hoof sent Cadder tumbling. With an oath, Gaer leaped forward and carried the Horsemaster's young son from harm's way.

The rider flung himself to the ground and lifted the stallion's head onto his lap. "Get up, Cloudy," he begged. Tears left new trails in the mud on his cheeks. "You can . . . do it. Get up . . . for me."

Sea Cloud sighed, then lay still.

For a long time, no one moved or spoke. Feeling as if he'd just woken from a spell, Stane walked stiffly to the rider and knelt beside him in the snow.

The rider sat with his face averted, one hand crushed against his mouth, shaking his head in denial. "No," he whispered. "Oh, gods, no."

Stane looked at the dead stallion, the bright pride of Sarn Moor, and did not know what to say. He glanced around at the crowd. Cadder slowly got to his feet, his expression blank with shock and grief. Little Maddock clutched the Swordmaster's hand, his face puckered with encroaching tears.

"I tried to hold him in," the rider said thickly. "I tried—" A sob choked him, and he paused for breath. "But he seemed to know Adan needed help. When he smelled Dorlach Tor, he just ran away with me. I tried—"

Stane set a careful hand on the rider's shoulder. "Tell us," he said. "What has befallen young Adan?"

"Horrible," croaked the rider. "Accident." He gestured feebly toward his own forehead. "Horse . . . kicked—"

A cold deeper than the snow seeped into Stane's blood. He

remembered the last time he saw Adan, when Wylfre's father died, and what a consolation the lad had been to Wylfre. Stane's memory presented a picture of Adan with his small hand pressed against Wylfre's belly, feeling the baby kick.

As if given a signal, the crowd shook off its daze and stirred to action. Some clustered around the fallen Sea Cloud. Others ran to bring more torches. Chatter broke out as people speculated about the accident. An elderly woman drew little Maddock away from the Swordmaster, and several men gathered around the rider.

Relieved of his responsibility toward the fellow, Stane climbed to his feet and turned to Wylfre.

The Lady of Dorlach Tor stood as rigid as a post in the court-yard, shoulders tight, arms folded. The wind lifted strands of her hair and tugged at the embroidered hem of her cloak. She looked down at the rider. "When did the accident happen? What time?"

The rider drew his brows together, as if thinking were an immense effort. "Before sundown," he whispered. "Rode all night." His gaze fell again upon the dead stallion. "Sea Cloud." He tried to escape from the men's ministering hands. "My poor Cloudy."

At that moment, old Sygil pushed her way through the crowd. Her face was as brown and wrinkled as a dried berry, but her blue eyes remained shrewd and bright. "What's this about Adan?" she snapped.

Stane looked at Wylfre, since it was her place to speak; but the lady of Dorlach Tor remained silent. Stane nodded toward the rider. "Evidently a horse kicked Adan in the head. They beg you to come tend the lad."

"Huh." Sygil did not sound enthusiastic. She strode to the rider and laid her hand on his injured arm. "You. Did you see Adan?"

"Oh," the rider stammered, "blood everywhere. Blood—"

Sygil made an impatient noise. "Never mind that. What part of Adan's head? Was the skull broken?"

The rider made an obvious effort to think. "I saw—His scalp above his brow . . . laid open like a flap." He gestured to the right side of his face. "And the flesh here . . . like pulp." Two tears rolled down the rider's face. "You . . . you should have heard him. Telling his mother . . . not to cry. . . ."

Sygil's gray brows shot up. "Awake and talking? That's encouraging." She released the rider and turned to Wylfre. "I'll go. There's a chance I might do some good."

Wylfre did not seem to hear her. Stane stepped forward. "Let me send someone ahead of you, so they'll be ready."

The old healer grunted approvingly. "I'll want a cauldron of boiling spring water and lots of clean linen for bandages. And don't let Adan sleep." She turned on her heel and strode toward the house, still talking. "I'll get my bag. Bring my mare to the door when she's saddled. I want to ride before the next quarter-hour."

"Wait," Stane called after her. "This fellow's arm—"

"Broken," she replied without looking back. "Someone ought to set the bone."

Fresh chatter burst over the courtyard as folk began preparations. A young fellow ran to Stane and dropped to one knee. "My lord," he said, eyes shining. "Send me ahead to Sarn Moor. I'm not afraid of the Dark Court, and my horse is the fastest."

Stane could not recall the youth's name, or that of his horse. "Good man. May Almighty Hepona ride with you."

"Thank you, my lord!" He snatched Stane's hand and kissed it, then leaped to his feet and ran to the stables.

Stane turned to the Swordmaster. "Gaer, please arrange an escort for Sygil. I don't want her riding out alone."

Gaer bowed. "My lord."

Wylfre spoke stiffly. "I'm going, too."

Gaer glanced at Stane.

Though dismayed, Stane nodded, as if agreeing. Neither he nor the Swordmaster possessed the right to argue against Wylfre's wishes. "My lady and I," he said carefully, "will ride for Sarn Moor at daybreak." He glanced at the sky, checking the position of the stars, hoping he had provided enough time to change her mind. "That allows about four hours for us to make preparations for an extended absence."

Wylfre looked from Stane to Gaer. "Daybreak."

Gaer bowed again. "I'll see to it." He turned away and began calling instructions.

Stane gestured to the group of men who held the rider. "Take him inside and see to him. Give him a place close to the fire."

Against the rider's protests, the men bundled him in a horse blanket and led him away to the Great House.

Stane turned to Wylfre. She still stood stiff and unmoving, her face like a mask of white stone, her eyes fixed on the dead stallion. Gently, Stane cupped her chin in his hand. "My lady?"

Wylfre sighed as if awaking from a deep sleep and leaned into him. "Oh, my love." She pressed her face into his neck. "What a wicked folly we have contemplated."

Stane enfolded her in his arms and bent his mouth to her ear. "How so?"

"The spirit-link. Had the messenger been linked to his mount—"

The man would have killed himself when his link-mate died. Stane understood her misgivings. A spirit-link prevented illness and extended the lives of those so blessed to span three generations. But if one member got killed, the other must pay the ultimate price. "We knew the risks—"

Wylfre lifted her head. "I thought so. I thought I knew the risks, but now I'm not sure. What doom might we be placing upon our daughter?"

Stane touched his forehead to hers and gazed deeply into her eyes. "It is all," he whispered, "in the hands of the gods."

"The gods." Wylfre repeated woodenly. "It's because of their quarrel that we suffer."

Stane searched for words of comfort. Humankind learned war and poverty when Hepona and Hernis, the divine lovers, became estranged. Some said the deities had disagreed when the goddess created horses, encroaching upon Hernis' lordship over animals. Others claimed the separation occurred when the god invented the bow, thereby challenging Hepona's reign over tools and weapons. Only in a future age, when the Lady of Battle married the Lord of the Hunt, in the time of the Joyous Reunion, would mortals know peace and plenty. "The gods," he said, "also suffer. In life or death, our only choice is to follow our hearts. Yes?"

"Yes." Wylfre returned her head to his shoulder. "Yes, my lord."

After two hours of riding, the entourage from Dorlach Tor left the grassy slopes of their home country and descended into the lowland moors that bordered the edges of the Old Forest. Bird-song filled the air. The sun burned bright in the April sky, melting the snow and coaxing green from the trees and scrub brush. The warmth did not touch the mood that hung over the travelers, however, and the group rode in silence. The coil of anger and worry in Stane's gut tightened with every passing mile.

A lanky woman who never smiled, Anra the Hunt-Keeper headed the line of riders. She held her tightly-curved bow ready, guiding her mount with her legs and weight. Beside Anra rode an armsman, one of the fort's best swords. Stane had learned as a boy that the warm weather often brought more than birds to the Marchlands; with the spring came raiders from the walled settle-ments along the river valleys. And though Stane doubted the River People would make a move so early in the year, or travel so far north undetected, he could not risk complacency.

Behind the leaders rode two bow-women dressed in their hunting leathers. Stane stayed beside Wylfre in the center of the column, and Gaer rode just behind them. Two more bow-women followed, leading the packhorses; and a lone armsman brought up the rear.

Six deerhounds paced alongside the horses. They were not quite a year old, still pups, and Wylfre brought them as gifts for the lady of Sarn Moor.

Stane pretended to survey the surrounding countryside while keeping a close watch on Wylfre. If he stared at her, it would only make her angry; then her pride would never permit her to admit she had made a mistake in undertaking this journey.

Wylfre rode her gray mare with her back rigid and her eyes straight ahead. Stane recalled seeing a similar expression on the face of a soldier with an arrow in his gut. The mare seemed to sense her rider's distress. Her ears flicked back and forth to catch Wylfre's slightest sound, and she stepped carefully.

Stane's mount, a bright bay stallion, also responded to his rider's mood. He snorted with excitement and danced, obviously believing they rode to battle. Stane stroked the stallion's muscled neck and wished the situation were that simple.

The road turned marshy in places, and mud hissed and sucked at the horses' hooves. To the left of the road, a bowshot away, a tiny grove of beech trees stood on a hillock. Stane smoothed down his mustache with his thumb knuckle. The grove could yield drier ground, a good spot for Wylfre to rest. He glanced in her direction, ostensibly checking the position of the sun.

Perspiration ran down Wylfre's colorless face, and her dark brows knotted in pain.

Heart stinging, Stane flung up his arm. "All halt!"

The party reined in their horses, and those in front glanced over their shoulders. Wylfre slowly turned her head to look at him, moving as if it required concentration. "My lord?" Though controlled, her voice carried a note of anger. "Why are we stopping?"

Because I don't want you to die! Stane forced himself to smile pleasantly. "I think Blood Rage picked up a stone." The deliberate lie raised heat in his cheeks. Unable to look Wylfre in the eye, he dismounted from the opposite side and crouched by the stallion's front feet.

Sneezing and snorting in happy greeting, the pups gathered around him. Stane gently pushed them aside and picked up his horse's foot. Aside from mud, the hoof was absolutely clean. "Ah, poor fellow," he said. "No wonder you hopped around like a sparrow."

Blood Rage twisted his neck to watch Stane and nickered curiously.

The Hunt-Keeper trotted her mount back to him. "Need help?"

Caught in the lie, Stane glanced up at the dour-faced woman and wordlessly nodded in Wylfre's direction.

Anra's hard gaze flicked toward the lady, then down at him

again. Her expression remained unaltered, but she gave a slight nod. "Looks bad."

Stane spoke casually. "This may take time. Lead everyone to those trees over there to wait. Let them eat, if they're hungry."

The Hunt-Keeper nodded again and whirled her horse. Trotting back to the head of the column, she raised her bow in the air. "All ride!"

The party ambled off toward the little beech grove, but Gaer hung back and dismounted. He dropped the reins, leaving his mount where it stood, and approached Stane. "My lord," he said in an elaborately courteous tone, "you are a miserable liar."

Stane looked over his shoulder and watched Wylfre's stiff back as she rode away. His heart twisted within him. "Gaer, I—" He sighed and reluctantly met the older man's gaze. "I don't know what to do."

The Swordmaster knelt on one knee beside Stane. "The Dark Flame of Dorlach Tor has left you little choice." He smiled kindly. "Don't blame yourself, my lord. Had you refused to make this journey, she would have ridden without you."

Blood Rage shifted restlessly and tried to pull his foot from his master's hands. Stane set the hoof down. "But she's in pain. I need to—" He spread his hands, unable to finish. He did not know what to do, or what he might say to Wylfre to persuade her to return home.

Gaer shrugged, as if he heard Stane's unspoken thoughts. "Pain lends strength." His tone was gentle and respectful, taking the edge from his words. "Borrowed pain, my lord, only weakens."

"But I love her," Stane protested. "How can I harden my heart against her suffering?"

"Not against her," Gaer explained. "For her." He clasped the young man's shoulder with a fatherly hand. "Your hard heart will become a rock in the wild sea. She can cling to it."

Stane shook his head. "But don't you see, Gaer? She could lose the baby, or she might—" His throat closed, but he swallowed and forced himself to go on. "She might die. I can't let that happen."

Gaer tilted his head. "You can't prevent it," he said softly.

"My lord, even if we were safe at Dorlach Tor, the hand of death could close around her at any moment. She could fall down the stairs, or—"

Stane's pulse raced. He scrambled to his feet, dragging himself from Gaer's grip. "No!" His voice was too loud, and he struggled for composure. "No." Worried that Wylfre had heard his outburst, he glanced toward the beech grove.

The party was dismounting. Two of the women helped Wylfre from her mare. She stood doubled over, as if the weight of eighty winters lay upon her. Stane's heart dropped. Anra strode over to the lady and seemed to question her. He could not hear what they said, but Anra turned and ordered the packhorses unburdened.

Only at that moment did Stane realize he was sprinting toward the grove. He could not remember a decision to move.

The deerhounds loped out to meet him, wagging their tails. They frolicked along beside him as he ran and escorted him up the hill.

Wylfre still stood in a half-crouch, breathing in little grunts. Stane rushed to her and laid his hands on her shoulders. "My lady? I—"

Wylfre raised her head and stared at him without recognition. Blanched with exertion, her face streamed sweat. Her eyes seemed sunken and bruised. Stane's blood shocked through him.

Anra drew near. "The baby's coming, my lord." Her tone was matter-of-fact, as if announcing the approach of a rain shower. "We'll need your cloak."

Stane tore his gaze from Wylfre and turned to Anra. "My cloak?" He knew he sounded like an idiot, but he could not fathom the sense of her words. "The baby—?"

One of the bow-women chuckled. "Be kind, Anra. Our young lord is new to this."

"But—" Stane could scarcely think. "But Wylfre can't have the baby here. Not under the trees."

Old Anra shrugged, but something relented in her eyes. "Best place on the road, my lord. Clean spring water, wood for a fire, shelter from the wind and sun." She nodded curtly. "You chose well."

Heart pounding, Stane glanced around at the gathered women. Their expressions ranged from affectionate amusement to calm patience, but none of them seemed anxious. They all, he remembered, had several children each. They had all experienced what Wylfre endured at the moment.

Stane returned his attention to his lady. Her face was blotchy and sweat dripped from the tips of her hair, but her eyes no longer seemed blind. Beneath the pain, he saw her locked in a monumental effort of will, and he suddenly felt as if he stood in the presence of a great warrior. He remembered Gaer's words, that he must harden his heart for her, make it a rock in the wild sea, a tower of granite in a ringed fort.

Drawing a deep breath of sweet April wind, he reached for the brooch that pinned his cloak. "Very well." He kept his voice low and calm, and he met Anra's gaze directly. "What else do you want of me?"

Anra jerked her head toward the foot of the hillock. "Take the horses, dogs, and men, and wait down there. We'll need every man's cloak."

Stane nodded, though he wanted to stay with his lady. It was forbidden for a man to attend childbirth, since the curses of a woman in travail possessed the power to render men impotent.

Wylfre shook the sweat from her eyes and smiled grimly. "Won't be long . . . my love. . . ."

Though his soul twisted like a dying thing, Stane smiled back. "I'll be waiting." He dried her face with the sleeve of his tunic. "When you want me, I'll be here."

The sun rode high in the flawless sky. The horses kept their heads down, contentedly picking through the rough grasses for tender shoots. The hound pups romped together or hunted for mice.

Gaze fixed on the grove, Stane stood apart from the other men. He listened to their convivial talk, stories about the births of their own children and the children of kin. He resented their good cheer, their stupid blindness to the tragedy that might occur; but he also clung to the hope they offered. Women bore babies every day and did not die. Even babies born before their time often lived and thrived.

No sound but the whisper of leaves drifted from the grove. Stane resisted the urge to pace. He twisted the bracelet of horse-hair between thumb and forefinger, hoping the dread in his heart belonged to her and that she fought her battle with an easy mind.

Gaer approached and stood beside Stane. "My lord?" His tone still held that measured balance of respect and kindness. "We've a skin of sweet wine, if you would like any."

Stane's gut protested the bare thought. "No." He forced himself to look at the older man. "No, thank you. I'll save my drinking for the birth of my daughter."

Gaer made a polite bow. "Yes, my lord."

Stane looked back at the hilltop. The women were hidden among the trees. For all he knew, the Fair Folk had carried them away, and he and the men would turn to four stones, forever waiting for the women to call from the beeches. "It's been hours," he said irritably. "She said it wouldn't take long." Then he realized how ridiculous his words sounded, and he shook his head in self-disgust. "Ignore me. I'm a fool."

"Not at all, my lord," Gaer said smoothly. "It's hard to wait. Now we know a little of what the women must feel, when they watch us ride off to war."

The young lord of Dorlach Tor nodded, finding obscure comfort in the thought. "And neither men nor women can—"

A shriek split the air.

Stane bolted toward the hilltop.

Swiftly, the Swordmaster blocked the way. "Wait, my lord!"

Another thin cry tore the air, joined by the excited bell of a hound. One of the armsmen swore.

Stane whirled.

All six hounds chased a creature through the scrub grass and heather. At first, Stane thought it was a hare, but then he clearly saw its bushy tail. "A fox!"

The hounds closed the distance to their quarry and bore it to the ground. The two armsmen rushed to intervene. The hounds tore at their squirming victim, and the fox screamed again with the voice of a woman.

Stane ran to help. Foxes were the shy little helpers of human-kind. They kept the grain stores free of rodents and made safe paths through the treacherous moors. It was not only considered unlucky to harm one, but a disgrace and shame to those responsible.

By the time Stane and Gaer arrived, the two men had pulled off the hounds. One of the men turned a woeful face to the young lord. "A vixen," he said. "And I think she's carrying young."

The fox lay panting on the ground, blood soaking the fur around her throat. Traces of pale winter color still marked her tail and torn belly.

Sick at heart, Stane prodded the fox's forelegs with the toe of his boot. She made no move to defend herself. "Poor little lass."

Entirely unrepentant, the hounds struggled to break free from the men.

Stane made a sweeping gesture. "Take them away. Tie them up."

"Yes, my lord." Gaer gripped the collar of a lunging hound in each hand, but he managed to sound entirely self-possessed. He turned, hauling the dogs with him. "This way, you misbegotten curs."

The three men trudged back toward the horses, dragging two hounds apiece.

For a moment, Stane stood unmoving, staring down at the vixen. Her entire frame jerked with the rhythm of each gasping breath. The stink of blood and viscera mingled with the musk of fox, fouling the sweet April air. Reluctantly, Stane pulled his dagger. He could not allow the poor creature to suffer, and he wondered if somewhere a dog fox waited for the return of his mate.

The vixen issued a high-pitched whine. Her hind legs thrashed convulsively, and a bloody mass emerged from under her tail. Cursing himself, Stane knelt on the wet ground and raised his dagger. For an instant, the vixen raised her head and opened her eyes, seeming to look up at him. Stane thought he read in the fox's gaze all the wild desperation in his own spirit. Then her head dropped to the ground, and she lay still.

Numb, Stane sheathed his dagger. The sticky lump under the fox's tail squirmed and rolled over. Without thinking, he picked up the newborn kit and dried it off with the sleeve of his tunic. Smoky gray with tightly shut eyes, it lay quivering in his cupped palm. It looked more like a mouse than a fox, its ears folded flat against its head like scraps of velvet. Stane stroked it with his little finger, and it unsteadily nosed around his hand, searching for a teat.

Though familiar with the ways of war since the age of twelve, Stane had never been a man who killed without thought. For a moment, he entertained childish fantasies of trying to save the fox kit. He could keep it warm and take it to Sygil at Sarn Moor. The old healer would know what to do. He thought maybe he could coax one of their deerhounds to nurse it, and the fox would grow up to become the living good luck talisman of Dorlach Tor.

Stane's gaze fell upon the beech grove, where Wylfre fought her solitary battle, and the cold hand of reality closed around him. He knew he had to mercifully end the fox kit's brief life; it would never survive without its mother.

With an aching heart, Stane drew his dagger again. The kit pressed its nose into the crack between his first and second finger, determinedly paddling with its tiny, clawed feet. His throat tight, Stane picked it up by its hind legs and held it upside down. The kit let out a surprisingly loud squeal of fear. Not allowing himself to hesitate, Stane used the hilt of his dagger to club the kit hard on the back of its head, killing it as he would a hare.

The little creature died instantly. Stomach lurching, Stane laid the limp body beside its dead mother. "Sorry," he whispered as he sheathed his dagger. "I'm so sorry."

A shout drifted to him from the direction of the horses. Stane glanced up. Gaer ran toward him like a boy, his silver hair flying. "My lord," he called, his face lit with excitement. "My lord, your lady is asking for you!"

Stane launched himself into a sprint before the Swordmaster finished speaking. He scarcely felt the ground under his boots as he flew past the older man and tore up the hill.

At the edge of the grove, the Hunt-Keeper blocked his path. "One moment, my lord."

Half mad with impatience, Stane stopped. "What?"

Anra put her hands on her hips. "My lady is tired. Don't wear her out."

"Yes, yes!" Stane dodged around her.

Wylfre lay on a makeshift bed of cloaks, eyes closed. Sweat pasted tendrils of her auburn hair to her face and throat. Wordlessly, Stane knelt at her side.

Wylfre's right hand lay on her head, fingers curled.

Carefully, Stane raised her hand and pressed his lips to her palm.

Wylfre opened her eyes. "My love?" Her voice emerged as a squeaking whisper. "Have you seen her?"

Startled, Stane shook his head. He had worried so much for Wylfre, he had forgotten about the baby.

One of the women came forward, carrying a bundle wrapped in his red cloak. "She has your nose and chin, my lord." Beaming, she settled the baby into his arms.

Stane looked down at the tiny stranger, expecting to see a newborn like all others. She was small and bluish, with a strangely-shaped head; but that was normal. He inspected her nose and chin and found the resemblance to his own uncanny. "Almighty Hepona," he whispered. "She does look like me."

Stane glanced at Wylfre and added hopefully, "Maybe she'll grow out of it?"

Wylfre's smile was tired but full of love. "She's beautiful." She leaned her cheek against his shoulder. "You're beautiful."

Stane shook his head but did not voice an objection. He glanced up at old Anra. "She's going to be all right, isn't she?"

Anra shrugged and pursed her lips, the closest she came to smiling. "Probably."

Stane returned his attention to his daughter. Her eyes lay complacently shut, and a myriad of strange expressions paraded across her little face.

An unfamiliar sensation seized Stane. It burned in his chest like unshed tears and stretched his nerves like terror. His heart began to pound. He struggled to breathe. A great love filled him, encompassing and binding together all the other loves in his life, and he knew himself to be changed completely. "My daughter," he whispered, believing his words the most profound ever spoken. "My little girl."

Without warning, the baby's face contorted, and her mouth opened, revealing a tiny red tongue. Her small body went rigid in his arms, and she squealed.

It was exactly the same cry as the newborn fox's.

Horror flashed through Stane.

"Ah," one of the women said indulgently. "Sweet, wee darling."

The baby went limp in Stane's arms.

He gasped for air and bent over his daughter. *What have I done?* A silent cry to the gods welled up from within him, powered by a love strong enough to level mountains. *No! Please. Don't take my little girl!*

The baby inhaled in three hiccuping jerks, then burst into heart-wrenching cries.

The Lord of Dorlach Tor looked up at the bright April sky and let tears fill his eyes. Perhaps some kindly god had intervened, softening the curse his slaying of the fox kit had wrought. It seemed his newborn daughter would not die in his arms. Wylfre stirred beside him, but Stane could not look at her for fear of sobbing aloud. "And what shall we name her?" he asked unsteadily. "This future Lady of Dorlach Tor."

Wylfre laid tender fingertips on the baby's forehead. "Kiarda."

Kiarda. "Blessed gift of the gods." Stane clenched his hands. *A truer name was never given.*

Wylfre placed her head upon Stane's shoulder.

A quivering hope seized Stane, as precious and fragile as the new baby wrapped in his war cloak. If only he might view this miracle as a sign of the Joyous Reunion, a coming age of universal peace. *Please,* he prayed. *Let it be so.*

CHAPTER ONE

TYNAN strode across the yard of trees and lush grass that surrounded the Great House of Dorlach Tor. Wisps of brown hair, curling with perspiration, clung to his forehead and cheeks; and he loosened the lacing at the throat of his linen tunic. Though the late August sun burned down from a cloudless sky, Tynan found the free-moving air much cooler than the heat of the main hall, where the feast continued without him. He brushed the damp hair from his face and hoped no one commented upon his absence. His link-mate was in the yard somewhere, and he sensed the cat was vexed and ready to make his displeasure known.

Tynan sported the handsome, angular features of the noble family of Sarn Moor: a strong jaw, large eyes, and straight brows. But even when worried or upset, his expression always reflected a gentle nature, a rare and soulful sweetness. Forehead wrinkling, the young man paused and swept the area with his gaze, seeking the ginger tomcat.

Tables loaded with baskets of fresh bread and platters of roasted quail sat at regular intervals around the yard. Laughing adults stood conversing in small groups or reclined on cloaks on the grass. Children of every age raced between the tables in wild games of their own invention. Everyone wore festively embroidered versions of their work clothes: full-sleeved tunics, loose trousers, and knee-high buckskin boots. All were Riders of the Marchlands, all kin in some degree, come to Dorlach Tor to celebrate the birth of Lord Stane and Lady Wylfre's fourth child, a son spirit-linked to a foal.

Though concerned about his own link-mate's capacity for mischief, Tynan smiled as he wandered through the yard. He enjoyed noisy family gatherings, and horse fairs, anything that placed him in the midst of people. He loved Dorlach Tor, his second home, and how it seemed to remain changeless in spite of yearly additions and improvements. When the Joyous Reunion of Hernis and Hepona had occurred, and permanent peace came to the Marchlands, Lord Stane had been the first to open trade with the River People. A shrewd and fair-dealing merchant, Stane garnered a considerable amount of wealth for his family, and Lady Wylfre transformed the rough fort into an elegant estate. The orchards, gardens, and vast stables were the settings of Tynan's happiest boyhood memories.

As if summoned by Tynan's thoughts, a dozen young cousins galloped toward him, neighing shrilly. He grinned, recognizing the game. "Oh, no! A stampede!"

A little boy with a smudge of dirt down his nose led the herd of pretend horses. He snorted and charged straight at Tynan.

Feigning desperation, Tynan flung himself out of the way at the last moment. Giggles mingled with whinnies as the herd thundered past.

Still grinning, Tynan straightened his tunic and watched the children run around the corner of the House. He toyed briefly with the idea of joining their play, though he was seventeen and a grown man. More than anything, he wanted a family, a clever and beautiful wife, lots of happy children.

On a nearby cloak, a cousin from the southern fort of Ewyas Skarrd sat with his new wife and baby. "Bravely done, Tynan," he called. "But be careful. Those beasts will yield to no one's hand."

Tynan laughed. "I do believe you're right." The cousin, Badhg, was not much older than him, and he swallowed back an unfamiliar pang of jealousy. *Badhg's married already?*

Badhg's wife beckoned. "Come sit with us, Tynan. Badhg tells me you're spirit-linked to a cat. I'd love to hear all about it."

"And I'd love to tell you." Tynan felt shabby refusing such a gracious invitation. "But I'm afraid I must find my link-mate. He's out here, somewhere, and on the verge of causing trouble."

She pouted but kept her tone sweet. "Later, then. I'll look forward to it."

Tynan bowed. "My lady." He turned and strode away, feeling

rude. He did not know how to talk about the bond he shared with the cat, and most young women of his acquaintance were resentful when he put his link-mate's needs before their wishes.

Another husband and wife stood at the wine table, laughing, with their arms around each other. A courting couple strolled by. Barred from touching by the strict traditions of the Marchlands, they each held an end of a horse-hobble festooned with bright ribbons; but their gazes mingled freely.

Tynan sighed and glanced away, then spotted his oldest brother standing beneath an oak tree. Adan of Sarn Moor was not a handsome man, though tall and well-built, for the scars from his childhood accident marred the right side of his face. Mottled, puckered skin stretched from his temple to his jaw, pulling his eyelid into a squint and drawing the corner of his mouth into a perpetual grimace. Adan held a meat-filled pastry, which he ate with obvious relish. At his feet, the ginger tomcat danced in anxious circles, begging for a taste.

Tynan's smile returned, and his brown eyes sparkled. "What's going on here?" He strolled toward them. "Adan, are you torturing my link-mate?"

"Silly question." Adan noisily sucked gravy from his fingers and pretended not to see the cat. "Of course, I'm torturing your link-mate."

[[He won't give me any.]] The cat ran to Tynan and jumped onto his shoulder. [[Make Adan give me some, or I'll die of starvation.]]

Tynan reached up and ran a comforting hand down the cat's sleek back. "You won't die."

Communication with his link-mate was a strange thing, difficult for Tynan to explain. Though always aware of the cat's emotions, he could not read its thoughts. It "spoke" without words: a meow, a flick of the tail, a silent glance. Tynan "heard" them all as speech. Likewise, his link-mate could not read Tynan's thoughts but perfectly understood gestures and inarticulate sounds as well as spoken language. When in physical contact with Tynan, the cat even comprehended the words of other humans.

Plump, succulent morsels of fowl in a savory-smelling gravy peeked from the pastry in Adan's hand. Though sated from a grand feast, Tynan found his mouth watering. "I have to admit," he said casually, "it looks pretty good."

"Delicious," Adan replied with his mouth full. "Some kind of fried hunt-bread stuffed with pheasant."

Now hungry again, Tynan glanced toward a table loaded with breads and pastries. "Where did you get it?"

Adan swallowed. "Last one."

"Oh," Tynan said forlornly.

Adan lifted the pastry to take another bite, then paused and looked at his little brother. "Would you . . . like some?"

"No, no," Tynan said softly. "I don't want to deprive you."

Adan shrugged. "Please yourself." He started to take a bite and stopped again. For a long moment, he gazed at his brother, then he abruptly held out the pastry. "Here. Take it. I'm full."

Tynan blinked in surprise. "Are you sure? I don't want—"

"Yes, I'm sure." Adan forced the pastry into Tynan's hand. "I'm sure I can't stand the two of you staring at me."

"Thank you." Tynan sat cross-legged on the soft grass. "It smells wonderful."

The cat hopped from Tynan's shoulder to his lap. [[Hurry! I'm dying!]]

"You are not," Tynan muttered affectionately. "Calm down, Cat-of-the-Noblest-Whiskers."

An incredulous grin spread over Adan's scarred face. "Cat-of-the-Noblest-Whiskers?" he echoed. He settled near a tree, facing his brother. "Is that his name now?"

"Yes, as of this morning." Tynan pulled a chunk of pheasant from the pastry and offered it to his link-mate.

The cat delicately sniffed the proffered tidbit, then flicked his ears back. [[Yuck. Smells like onions.]]

Tynan shook the meat enticingly under the cat's nose. "You don't mind a little onion."

The cat turned his head, shuddering the fur on his back. [[Onions are stinky.]]

"I'll eat it, then."

[[Please yourself.]] The cat curled into a ball on Tynan's lap. [[I'll take a nap so I don't have to watch.]]

Tynan popped the morsel into his mouth. It tasted of pepper

and marjoram, but not onion. He licked his fingers. "It's good,"
he told his brother, knowing the cat would hear. "Thanks again."

The cat did not look up, but the tip of his tail twitched.
[[Stinky.]]

Adan laughed. "Well, I could hardly let the two of you
starve."

Tynan tilted his head, smiling at his brother. "I didn't see you
leave the feast. Why did you go?"

"Because Tassi, our dear sister-in-law, kept pestering the bard
to sing 'The Death of Sea Cloud' over and over again. I hate that
song."

Uncomfortable with the rancor in Adan's voice, Tynan
dropped his gaze. He had hoped Tassi and Adan would set aside
their differences while visiting Dorlach Tor.

Adan continued, seeming oblivious to his brother's uneasiness. "Also, I couldn't stand another moment in the company of
that smarmy blackguard, Vecco."

Tynan gasped in shock. Vecco was one of Tassi's distant cousins from the Low Marches, newly confirmed in a high rank within
the priesthood of the Joyous Reunion. "But you can't—"

"Every family with the slightest political ambition is filling the
temples with their surplus offspring, priests and priestesses to
carry out covert feuds with the Great Houses."

"Adan—"

"Lord Stane's uncle killed Vecco's father. You think he's going
to forget something like that? Mark my words, that oily villain is
out for revenge."

Tynan forced himself to smile, worried that Adan would work
himself into another of his dark moods. "Please. Can't we talk
about something nice?"

Adan snorted. " 'Nice?' "

"Please?"

Adan folded his arms behind his head and leaned against the
tree trunk. He studied the people around them with an unreadable expression. "Whole clan turned out for this. Good thing the
weather's been fine. The lot from Ewyas Skarrd traveled for five
days, with all those children."

Glad for the change of topic, Tynan bit into the pastry. The buttery crust of fried bread gave way to savory meat and gravy. For a moment, he was too overwhelmed by the flavor to think. He chewed slowly and swallowed. "Saw cousin Badhg. He has a wife and a baby."

"Lucky man." There was still an odd tension in Adan's voice.

Concerned, Tynan studied his oldest brother. The left side of Adan's face evinced a bloodline as pure as snow-water. The high cheekbones, long nose, and strong jaw were characteristic of the clan's heroic ancestors. Highlighted with a rich cast of red, Adan's brown hair fell in a shining cascade to his shoulders. His hazel eyes looked perfectly green in some kinds of light. Tynan could not understand why the girls never seemed interested in Adan, at least not since Culan married Tassi. *Can't be the scars. They're barely noticeable, once you get used to them.* He cleared his throat. "Do you ever—?" He paused and felt his cheeks grow hot.

Adan returned his gaze to Tynan. "Ever what?" he asked mildly.

"Think about—" Tynan shrugged. "You know . . . marriage . . . starting a family . . ."

Adan laughed. "I've been too busy raising my younger brothers. I was your age when Mother and Father died in the fire. Just seventeen years old and suddenly responsible for a burned-out House and four snot-nosed piglets."

"I mean children of your own."

Adan shook his head. "I don't have any sentimental notions about rearing children."

Tynan took another bite of the pastry and mulled Adan's words. There was a song about the five brothers of Sarn Moor: Adan, Culan, Tynan, Fian, and Dod. It was a lament for orphans, composed just after the destruction of the Great House, but it did not account for Adan's indomitable spirit. The eldest of the five brothers had marshaled the folk of Sarn Moor and rebuilt the House. "What about a wife?"

"A what?"

Still curled in a ball, the cat flicked its ears. [[He heard you.]]

Tynan smiled and ran his little finger along the cat's spine. "You heard me."

"I'm not in the habit of wanting what I cannot have." Adan

tilted his head. "Why? Don't tell me you're thinking about marriage."

Tynan shrugged one shoulder. "Very well. I won't."

Groaning, Adan straightened and met his brother's gaze. "Who is she?"

Surprised, Tynan blinked. "No one," he protested. "I mean, I haven't met her yet. I'm just thinking."

"Well," Adan drawled. "Be thinking of a lady with a House of her own, because if you bring her to Sarn Moor, Tassi will rip out her lungs."

Tynan dropped his gaze again. He could not understand why Adan disliked Tassi, why he refused to accept Culan's wife as the new Lady of Sarn Moor. As the wife of the first brother to marry, she deserved the title.

The cat flicked his ears again and raised his head. [[Adan's right. Tassi would.]]

"I'm just thinking," Tynan repeated. "I'm not about to get married tomorrow."

Adan snorted. "Good."

The cat stood up, stretched, and fixed his amber eyes on the pastry in Tynan's hand. [[That smells good. Give me some.]]

Relieved for the distraction, the youth grinned. "It's full of onions. You hate onions."

[[No, I don't.]] He patted Tynan's wrist with one paw. [[A little lower, please. I can't reach.]]

"But you said—"

The cat hooked a claw into the tender flesh between Tynan's thumb and forefinger and pulled the hand down.

"Ouch," Tynan said reproachfully. "That hurts."

[[Don't try to resist, and it won't hurt.]] The cat sniffed the pastry, then delicately extracted a sizable morsel of pheasant with his teeth. [[This will do for a start.]] He released his link-mate's hand and hunkered down on his lap to enjoy the feast. [[Thank you.]]

"You're welcome." Glumly, Tynan gazed at the line of blood welling from the finger webbing. "Why didn't you just gnaw off my thumb?"

[[Not that hungry.]]

Adan stirred. "Of course, there's always Kiarda."

Tynan squinted. He could not understand what Lady Wylfre and Lord Stane's oldest daughter had to do with pastries and cat claws. "Pardon?"

"Kiarda," said Adan patiently, "would be a good wife for you."

Horrified, Tynan gaped at his brother. Cousin Kiarda, skinny as a stick, with a stubborn jaw and two blonde braids, was not his idea of a wife. "I can't marry *her*."

"Why not?" All traces of humor disappeared from Adan's scarred face, and his expression turned calculating. "I thought you were friends."

"We are," Tynan blurted. "But she's just a child."

"Sixteen. Merely a year younger than you." Adan tilted his head. "And the future Lady of Dorlach Tor."

Tynan could understand how the ancient fort's wealth and prestige would lure other men to ask for Kiarda's hand, but he was not interested. It would seem like marrying a sister. "She only inherits when Lady Wylfre dies. Pardon me, but I can't see myself living the next twenty years waiting for the death of a noble and great-hearted woman."

"It was just a thought," Adan said mildly.

"Then why don't you marry Kiarda?"

Adan leaned back against the tree and regarded his brother with a level stare. "Because, at one time, you and Kiarda were betrothed; but the Joyous Reunion changed all that. No more blood feud, war, or arranged marriages."

Tynan found it suddenly hard to breathe. "I never—" He swallowed. "I never knew."

Adan turned his gaze toward the Great House. "It's in the past. But I think Lady Wylfre and Lord Stane would like you for a son-in-law. Your spirit-link makes you a choice prospect."

Thoughts still churning, Tynan tried to follow Adan's words. "But it doesn't work that way. Spirit-links don't run in the blood."

"I'm not suggesting that the Lady and Lord of Dorlach Tor are trying to breed link-mates like hounds. I'm just saying that they covet the political advantages that a spirit-link's longevity creates."

"Political advantages?" Tynan shook his head. "That's just silly."

"Don't be naive. Why else have they tried for the last sixteen years to force a link to occur?" A sly grin lifted the left corner of Adan's mouth. "Kiarda is their only child who wasn't born in a barn."

Appalled, Tynan made a noise of protest.

Adan rose and stretched. "It's true." He regarded his brother fondly. "Your spirit-link, on the other hand, was an accident."

Cat-of-the-Noblest-Whiskers flicked his tail. [[A blessing.]]

Tynan smiled at his link-mate. "A blessing."

"Oh, really?" Adan's expression turned distant. "I'm haunted, at times, by the thought of all those babies who die because no one recognizes their link to the newborn mole beneath the floorboards or the bat in the rafters."

Tynan gazed up at Adan, wondering why his eldest brother seemed determined not to enjoy the festive occasion. "I doubt that happens very often," he replied in a mild tone. "Most midwives are gifted with the Sight, as are the priests who officiate at dedications. Spirit-links are extremely rare, but as I understand it, they're perfectly visible to anyone with the merest talent for magic."

Adan nodded once, curtly. "Good thing spirit-links are limited to creatures who give birth. No fish, fowl, or insects." His hazel eyes glinted with sudden mischief. "Otherwise, you might have linked with a blindworm. A cat is bad enough."

The Cat-of-the-Noblest-Whiskers washed his paws with meticulous care. [[And I might have linked with Adan of Sarn Moor.]] He ruffled his fur. [[Dreadful thought.]]

Tynan chuckled.

Clearly unaware of the cat's retort, Adan also laughed and affectionately mussed his brother's hair. "But I see the kitchen just brought out another basket of that hunt-bread. I'm going to get another. Do you want one?"

"No, thank you."

The cat glanced up, licking his whiskers. [[Yes, please.]]

"On second thought," Tynan amended hastily, "yes, please."

Adan glanced back and forth between the link-mates as if he had heard the cat speak. "Very well, then." He turned and sauntered away.

The cat sat up tall on Tynan's lap and sniffed half-heartedly at the pastry.

"Want some more?"

The Cat-of-the-Noblest-Whiskers turned his head away. [[No, thank you. I'm full.]]

Tynan made a helpless noise. "But you made me tell Adan—"

The cat interrupted. [[Adan likes to take care of us.]] He stood on his hind legs, resting his front paws on his link-mate's shoulder, and pressed his nose into Tynan's ear as if telling a secret. [[Soon, we will need to take care of Adan.]]

Perplexed, Tynan shook his head. "What do you mean?"

[[This is a nice place. We need to arrange it so that Adan can live at Dorlach Tor.]]

"What?" A slight pang of anxiety joined Tynan's confusion, and he twisted his head to meet the cat's gaze. "His home is Sarn Moor. He belongs there."

The cat's eyes went somber. [[Tassi is the Lady of Sarn Moor now, and she doesn't like Adan. She believes he undermines her authority.]]

Tynan shifted uncomfortably. Tassi was proud and ambitious but levelheaded, a perfect match for the fiery-tempered Culan. "She's only the Lady because she married my brother." He could not believe Tassi capable of plotting to break up the family. Fian was nine and Dod only seven. They both still looked up to Adan as a father-figure. *So do I.* Tynan swallowed. "I'll admit there's friction between Tassi and Adan, but that's just because she's not used to him yet. She doesn't understand when he's teasing."

The cat patted Tynan's cheek with a velvety paw. [[I know it's nearly impossible for you to think ill of anyone, but I'm not mistaken about Tassi. My ears are better than yours.]]

Tynan stroked the cat's orange-and-white fur, twining a finger along a darker stripe. "Well, I'm sure Tassi and Adan will become good friends."

[[I won't argue with you,]] the cat replied. [[But remember

what I said about arranging residence at Dorlach Tor. Otherwise, Adan may have to go live in the Old Forest. And we would miss him terribly.]]

Kiarda hesitated in the doorway to the shrine of Hernis and dragged her sleeve across her blue-gray eyes. Hordes of visitors occupied all her usual hiding places, even her bedchamber; and she hoped the Lord of the Hunt would offer her a haven. She needed a safe place to cry.

From the Great House overhead, the roar of feasting kinfolk echoed down the narrow stairwell, as incoherent as the tumult of a waterfall. The underground vault smelled of damp earth, cold stone, and lamp oil. A branch from an apple tree, still bearing green leaves and golden fruit, decorated the curtained doorway's lintel, for the Lord of the Hunt was also Lord of the Harvest.

Kiarda eased aside the heavy curtain and edged into the shrine. A myriad of tiny windows cut just above ground level filled the air with slanting streams of sunlight. Carved to resemble tree trunks, a double row of stone pillars outlined a center aisle, leading from the door to the raised altar. A veil hung over the image of the god on the wall behind the altar since no one any longer worshiped Hernis in his unwed aspect. Silence hung in the air along with the elusive scent of apples.

Finally alone, Kiarda let the scalding tears well up, unable to name what troubled her. A strange grief darkened her thoughts. She did not seem to fit in anywhere, to belong with anyone. Though the heir to a great estate, and surrounded by an adoring clan, Kiarda had never felt more isolated.

A thin shaft of sun fell upon the steps to the altar. Kiarda wandered up the central aisle and sat in the patch of warm light. She wanted to talk to someone, but guests preoccupied her parents and cousins surrounded her younger brother and sister. Kiarda considered only two cousins close friends, but Tynan seemed to be avoiding her and Adan was in one of his moods where he considered everything a joke.

The loneliness magnified within Kiarda, smoldering with a

heat much like that of anger. She bowed her head, blonde braids swinging forward, and rested her hands, palms up, in her lap. Her hands appeared oversized, callused, and strong, a gift from her mother along with a stubborn jaw. In every other respect, she seemed more her father's daughter, sharing even his easygoing kindliness and steady temperament. Kiarda squeezed shut her tear-laden eyes and struggled against sobbing aloud. *What's wrong with me? Why am I acting like this?* She hunched over and crushed her hands into fists. "Why?" The cracked whisper echoed through the shine. "Why?"

A sudden draft brushed Kiarda's damp cheeks. She jerked her head up.

An unfamiliar woman stood in the doorway. "Kiarda?" She spoke with the River People's clipped accent. "What's the matter?"

Kiarda held her breath and remained motionless.

The woman let the curtain fall and paced up the aisle. From her indistinct silhouette, she appeared short and heavyset.

Kiarda swallowed hard to clear her throat. "Go away." Despising the beseeching quality in her tone, she attempted to roughen it. "Leave me alone."

The woman stopped and raised her hand. "Light." All over the shrine, in wall niches and dark corners, clay lamps lit themselves and spread a flickering glow.

Kiarda shot to her feet and stared at the woman in the aisle.

Sandy-brown ringlets escaped from a loose ponytail to frame the young woman's plump face, and she wore a voluminous apron over her long skirt. "I don't suppose you know me." She smiled shyly. "I'm new here."

Kiarda licked her dry lips. Rare magic-users of every type came to Dorlach Tor to study under old Sygil. "I suppose you're right. Please leave me alone."

The stranger did not seem to hear Kiarda's dismissal. "My name is Bevin."

"Go away, Bevin."

"I'm sorry," Bevin replied with soft sincerity, "but I can't." Her eyes were round, gray, and filled with compassion. "I'm a healer, and I sense a pain within you that rises to the sky like a thunderhead."

Fighting another humiliating rush of tears, Kiarda hastily turned away.

A tastefully arranged offering of golden wildflowers, scarlet corn, and green apples adorned the altar, along with dozens of flickering clay lamps. On the wall behind the altar, the veil fluttered to the side, revealing a life-sized and lifelike painted image of the smiling god.

"Oh." Kiarda pressed the back of her hand to her mouth. Depicted as a young man with red hair and beguiling green eyes, Hernis spread his arms in welcome. Used to seeing the god represented as the fatherly, bearded figure of the Joyous Reunion, Kiarda felt blood rise to her face. "Oh . . . my . . . goodness."

Bevin climbed the steps to stand beside Kiarda. "He's beautiful, isn't he?"

Kiarda tore her gaze from Hernis to glare at Bevin. "We're not supposed to see this," she hissed. "He's married."

"It's only a painting." Bevin's expression was somehow both shy and determined. "Besides, I needed to surprise you, and lighting lamps didn't seem to work." She reached into a deep apron pocket, pulled out a folded kerchief, and handed it to Kiarda. "Here. Dry your eyes."

Moving stiffly, Kiarda shook out the square of linen and dabbed at her tears. The warm, soft cloth smelled of fresh bread and herbs.

"I was helping in the cookhouse," Bevin explained, seemingly to reply to Kiarda's unspoken thoughts. She settled on the altar's top step and spread her wide skirts around her. "I love to cook," she continued and patted her stomach. "Trouble is, I also love to eat what I cook."

Ashamed of her earlier surliness, Kiarda shrugged one shoulder. "I'm not much of a cook, but I do all right with a campfire and fresh trout." She sat next to Bevin and gazed at her feet, unable to think of anything more to say.

"I adore fresh trout," Bevin said. "Why were you crying?"

Kiarda's mouth twitched. She decided she liked the healer. "Why did you need to surprise me?"

"To help you stop crying." Bevin spoke matter-of-factly. "It's an old trick."

"It's sneaky."

"Yes."

Kiarda waited, but Bevin remained silent. Smiling slightly, Kiarda looked at her. "Is this another trick? Will it make me answer your question?"

Bevin raised her brows and returned the smile.

Kiarda shrugged again. "I don't know why I was crying," she said. "It scared me." Her smile fading, she gazed up at the shrine's vaulted ceiling and studied the shadows that danced in the lamplight. "I remember feeling a bit sad at first. The bards kept singing 'The Death of Sea Cloud.' And I was tired, I guess, not used to all these people." She narrowed her pale eyes. "But the feeling just got worse, and no one had time to talk to me, and I began to think about how the whole clan came to see Elrin and his link-mate, and I—" She broke off, shaking her head. "Why am I telling these things to you?"

Bevin laughed. "I'm magic."

Kiarda tried to laugh also but found her throat suddenly tight with tears. "I was . . . supposed to be spirit-linked."

"I know," Bevin said.

Kiarda twisted the kerchief in her hands. "I'm jealous of Elrin. I know I shouldn't be, but I can't help it. And it makes me so . . . mad at myself."

"Jealous of the attention Elrin receives? Or jealous of the link?"

Kiarda flinched as the healer identified the source of her pain. "The link." She closed her eyes and forced herself to continue. "I felt so alone, so cut off from everyone—"

"As if you had lost a part of yourself."

"Yes." Kiarda turned to regard the healer. "As if something in me had died."

Bevin's gray eyes were solemn. "Maybe you're sensitive to a certain kind of magic."

Drawing her brows together, Kiarda tilted her head. "What do you mean?"

"Some people can't eat certain foods. My sister turns

splotchy if she so much as touches a strawberry." Bevin gestured to the air around them. "At this time, magic lies thick over Dorlach Tor. Sygil and the others are raising a tremendous amount of power, preparing for the great ceremony involving your baby brother."

As Kiarda understood it, the Pronouncement entailed an assemblage of magic-users who would officially give witness to the existence of Elrin's spirit-link, then make it visible for a few moments to those without the gift of Sight. "And you think this fog of magic affects me the way strawberries affect your sister?" Kiarda shook her head. "I doubt it. I think I'm a spoiled, self-centered brat. And a rotten big sister. Elrin deserves much better."

Bevin's expression remained serious. "Don't be so hard on yourself." She scrutinized Kiarda, as if to take in every detail. "I can see things that most people cannot." She paused a long moment, then added: "In fact, that's why I'm not helping with the Pronouncement. I'm seeing spirit-links that . . . are not there."

Uneasy under the close examination, Kiarda hunched her shoulders and allowed her gaze to wander around the shrine. Plans were to desacralize the holy place and turn it into a storage room. She tried to imagine the shadows filled with stacks of pumpkins and barrels of winter apples. Hernis looked down at her, his grin oddly familiar and mischievous. "You know," Kiarda said, trying for a conversational tone. "He reminds me a little of my brother, Leith. Same red hair and green eyes."

Bevin turned her attention to the painting, her manner still peculiar. "Yes."

Kiarda pulled one of her braids taut and twisted it to catch the lamplight. "I'm getting a touch of red in my hair, too. It's been changing all summer. Father says I'm just imagining it, but—"

"No," Bevin interrupted gently. "I see it quite plainly." Her gray eyes seemed to fill with grave concern. "It isn't your imagination, Kiarda. The magic raised for the Pronouncement is intensifying and hastening a condition you may have possessed for years without noticing. You *are* changing."

Changing. The word filled Kiarda's head like a chant. And, in the warm comfort of the sun's beam, an icy shiver traversed her.

CHAPTER TWO

MADDOCK parried his teacher's sword thrust and dodged left, seeking an opening. Relatively small in stature, his lithe and well-muscled frame hearkened back to the ancient bloodlines of the little wild people who once lived in the High Marches rather than to the tall, fair ancestors of the nobility. His hair slipped from its restraining ribbon and fell over one shoulder: soft, black, and glossy as a raven's wing. He shook it from his face, working the motion into his turn. The duel had reached the point where body and spirit fought as one, and the heavy burdens of his daily life no longer encumbered his mind. A slight smile curled his lips.

Hard and strong as wind-scoured granite, Gaer stood his ground, his lean face impassive, his silver hair blowing unheeded in the wind. Despite years spent living in the wilderness as an outcast, the Swordmaster maintained a timeless quality, an appearance of age without infirmity. He kept his bright eyes on Maddock, the blunt point of his practice sword describing tiny circles in the air.

October wind stirred the branches of the surrounding trees, which hissed and whispered like excited spectators. In daylight, Scratter Wood seemed a serene, lovely place; but it possessed an evil reputation as the abode of the Dark Court. Since no one else came near it, it became a sanctuary for Maddock and Gaer to meet for sword lessons.

The advent of the Divine Peace abolished arranged marriages and blood feuds, along with instruction in the art of war. Gaer had refused to cease his daily sword training, and the powerful priesthood of the Joyous Reunion had insisted that he become outcast. Lord Stane had begged for clemency, arguing that martial skills were an art form, but the priests remained adamant. Maddock remembered the Lady Wylfre weeping as Gaer took his leave.

Every few days, Maddock brought Gaer supplies and stayed to learn. No one at home asked the Horsemaster's son why he went walking alone so often in Scratter Wood. Most believed he consorted with the Other Ones. Offending even the Fair Folk of the Light Court was perilous, and there was no more certain way to gain their ill-will than by meddling in their affairs.

Gaer made a series of airy feints, silently teasing his student for timidity.

Maddock ignored the subtle gibe, sidestepping to avoid a patch of wet leaves. Though he usually found the Swordmaster hard to read, his movements sometimes turned delicate just before a forceful attack. Maddock tightened the two-handed grip on his sword.

Gaer stalked him, graceful and predatory.

Metal clashed. Impact shocked through Maddock's arms, and his hands stung. Only at that moment did he realize Gaer had attacked, and he had parried the blow by instinct. *I did it!*

Maddock's elation was short-lived. The Swordmaster pressed his attack with relentless fury. Maddock's sense of inner balance vanished. To keep his feet under him, he threw his weight forward. The blunt edges of their swords grated as they slid across each other. The hilts locked. Maddock and Gaer stood nose to nose.

"Never allow your opponent to get this close." Gaer lightly punched Maddock in the ribs with his free hand. "That was a dagger. You're dead."

Shoulders sagging, Maddock lowered his sword. "Master, I'm sorry. That was stupid."

"Self-recrimination is wasted energy. You made a mistake. And, again, you're keeping your sword arm too tight." Gaer pulled a kerchief from his belt and patted his damp face. Though he lived in a cave, he still retained the elegant habits of a gentleman. "Let's examine the combat, shall we?"

They resumed their positions from the start of the match and repeated it in slow steps. Gaer kept up a running analysis, praising

Maddock's successes and pointing out errors, his student's and his own. Maddock listened intently, marveling at the Swordmaster's ability to recall the tiniest details. When they reached the point of Maddock's fatal mistake, Gaer demonstrated the correct dodge, explaining it from inception to follow-through. "You see? Now, you shall learn it." He broke position. "Time for a new Dance."

A "Dance" was a set of sword figures, part physical training and part meditation. Some Dances one did alone, some with a partner. Maddock would start slowly, gaining speed with repetition, aiming for precision and beauty. Gaer only taught him another one when he had gained a fresh level of proficiency. "A new Dance? What's it called?" He grinned with anticipation.

" 'The Sun and Moon.' I created it myself." Gaer gazed at his student, his expression turning quizzical. "You seem awfully happy."

Though Maddock knew a grueling workout awaited him, he could not vanquish the smile. "Yes, Master. Very happy."

Gaer's dark eyes filled with obvious pride and affection. "Happy, huh? I'll fix that."

Several hours later, Gaer glanced at the sky. "It's late. That's all for today."

Soaked with sweat, lungs burning, Maddock lowered his practice sword. Though his arms felt like lead, and his right calf throbbed from a self-inflicted blow, he did not want to leave. "I can take a little more, Master." He panted. "I'm not tired yet."

"You'll have to leave soon if you want to reach home by twilight." Gaer gestured at the surrounding trees. The slanting rays of the sun turned their leaves molten gold and scarlet. "This place isn't safe after sunset. Even I don't venture out of my cave at night. The Neighbors are a dangerous lot. I rather suspect they only tolerate my presence because I am evil in the eyes of my fellow mortals."

Maddock shrugged, loath to return to Dorlach Tor and the web of deceit that defined his ordinary life. "I'm not afraid of the Dark—" He broke off with a shudder. The friend of a cousin's in-law had been dragged into a river by a creature of the Dark Court, and the next day they found only his liver and eyeballs floating on the water. Maddock *was* afraid of Those Who Walked the Night. Any sensible man was, but his fear angered and shamed him.

Gaer took the practice sword from his student and strolled to the stump where they had left their gear. "You're twenty summers old, my son." His eyes crinkled. "I should hope you're not afraid of the dark."

A neatly folded square of oily wool lay at the base of the stump. Maddock picked it up and shook off bits of bark and leaf mold. "It's just so hard to go back sometimes. When I'm here with a sword in my hand, I feel like—" He stopped, having said too much.

Gaer took the cloth from Maddock and wrapped up the swords. "Go on."

If Maddock started to describe the tangled strands of inner pain, he would break down and weep like a maiden. "It's nothing."

The Swordmaster's tone turned gentle. "Did you have another fight with your father?"

Throat tight, Maddock nodded.

"About Kiarda?"

"Yes." To prove to himself he could say her name, Maddock repeated, "Kiarda." His childhood playmate and best friend, she belonged to the few clear certainties of his daily life. He recalled the moment he first realized he loved her as a man loves a woman, merely a year ago at the summer horse fair. Delayed by a balky colt, he had rushed to ready Lord Stane's old bay stallion for the grand procession only to find Kiarda already there. Horsehair covered her good clothes, and a light glimmered in her blue-gray eyes as she nimbly braided Blood Rage's mane. Maddock's voice thickened, but he forced himself to continue. "I made the mistake of admitting to my father that I love her still."

"Ah." Gaer leaned the bundled swords against the stump. "I take it he disapproves. Still."

"He said I wasn't good enough. That I'm only the Horsemaster's son. That she and I . . . that—"

Gaer made a sympathetic noise but looked thoughtful. "Kiarda has never given you any sign that she might return your love?"

Nothing beyond sisterly affection. It hurt. "No."

"Then maybe you ought to consider another lass."

Maddock flinched as another face filled his mind: widely-set eyes, an upturned nose, a ready smile. Vonora loved him completely, and she deserved so much better than to be any man's second choice. "Another lass." He cleared his throat but could not bring himself to tell Gaer about the Hunt-Keeper's daughter. *So it comes to this. More evasions and half-truths. Hiding thoughts from my Master.* "Yes."

Gaer peered at him. "That's not all that's troubling you, is it?"

"I don't know. I—" Maddock glanced around the clearing at the massive oak that overshadowed them. A restless breeze tugged at its bronze leaves. "I feel as if I'm being poisoned by all the secrets in my heart."

"Poisoned by. . . ?"

"It's been growing on me, this feeling." Maddock spoke in a rush. "When I was younger, I used to enjoy having a secret. Meeting with you, learning a forbidden skill. I told myself I had a destiny."

"I see." Gaer lifted one brow. "But no more?"

An obscure shame brought heat to Maddock's cheeks. "I just feel sad, divided. There isn't a single straight path in my life. It's all twisted, a lie." He gestured at the shrouded swords. "And for what? A skill I'll never use."

"You think not?" Gaer's tone remained mild, but his words emerged with the broad foreign accent that signaled strong emotion.

The young man deeply regretted his choice of words. "I didn't mean to grieve you," Maddock said softly. "I'm sorry."

Gaer did not seem to hear him, his focus inward, turned upon some painful memory. "The time will come when your life depends upon these lessons."

The wind hushed. Maddock stared at the Swordmaster. "What are you saying?"

Gaer crooked his brows, returning to himself. "How did the

bards put it? 'A dark shadow hovers over mortal-kind. Almighty Hepona has stretched forth her hand.' " Their cloaks lay on the stump. He picked them up and offered Maddock's to him. "Or something like that."

Maddock accepted his cloak and absently folded it into a bundle. "War?" He hugged his cloak to his chest. "But that's impossible. The Joyous Reunion . . . the Divine Peace . . ."

Gaer closed his eyes and pinched the bridge of his nose. "Maddock—" He sighed and looked at his student. "You're old enough to set aside childish stories."

Maddock's lips parted, but no sound came out. He had never questioned the marriage of Hernis and Hepona. It was simply a fact of life, like the sky overhead, Kiarda's smile, the law of Lady Wylfre.

With a showy flourish, Gaer swung his cloak over his shoulders. "Cover up, son. Keep warm, or you'll go stiff." He nodded toward the trail that led to Dorlach Tor. "You need to go, but I'll walk with you for a while. You've told me some of your secrets, now I'll tell you some of mine."

Maddock had been six when the Joyous Reunion occurred. He remembered his father's return from the battle of Wray Valley with Lord Stane, how all the men carried green branches instead of swords as they rode through the gates. He recalled the adults' excited discussions, the feasts and games, his father's promise that he would never again ride away to war.

As they tramped together through the forest, Gaer told Maddock a story of politics, not religion. Before the Joyous Reunion, civil wars had divided the Marchlands. Raiders from the south, the River People, had pillaged and destroyed the forts of the Low Marches. Some of the southerners stayed to farm the fertile river valleys and to raise families. When they heard about a southern king named Vernon amassing an army, they opened negotiations with their former enemies.

Lord Stane had single-handedly unified the warring tribes of the Marchlands and persuaded them to join the River People in combat against invading forces. The victory at Wray Valley had been conclusive, and Lord Stane forced Vernon to swear to a peace agreement whereby the king would defend the Marchlands from other invading countries in exchange for valuable trading privileges.

Gaer continued, "It was at that point that Hepona's priests wondered if the peace treaty represented the prophesied reunion. Not an unreasonable question, but the notion gained immense popularity overnight. Everyone felt weary of bloodshed and horror. A priestess of Hernis had a dream, little children saw visions, and pious speculation changed to fanatical belief."

"But Lord Stane made the treaty. Why does he believe in the Divine Peace?"

"Because he was quite young when he made the treaty. Only twenty-three." Gaer paused, then added with obvious reluctance, "And because Lord Stane is an honest man, and he is confident in his own honesty. This often leads to self-deception."

"But the Peace has lasted. How can you say—"

"It's lasted fourteen years. Not a very long time." Gaer's accent grew thicker, the vowels heavier. "King Vernon died last spring, and his heir is embroiled in a war of succession."

Maddock shrugged. "But, Master, that's in the south. The Marchlands are still—"

Gaer stopped walking and gazed sidelong at his student. "Listen to yourself. Are you saying the gods love only the Riders of the Marchlands? That their Peace is only for those who worship them?"

Maddock stopped as well. "I—" He spread his hands. "I don't know what I'm saying, what I'm thinking. This is . . . unsettling."

"Yes. Well." Gaer's tone softened. "I'll let you think about it on your own. But remember that your lessons with me are not in vain."

Maddock forced himself to smile. "I'll remember."

"Then I'll take my leave of you. Meet me in the clearing in three days." Gaer kissed Maddock's forehead. "Go with the gods, my son."

"And you." Maddock still did not want to leave. "Someday, I hope we may walk all the way to Dorlach Tor together."

"It will be so." Gaer shook his head sadly. "Maybe sooner than you think."

As Maddock followed the trail home, his initial confusion settled into a familiar sense of oppression. Secrets wrapped his entire life, disconnecting him from the others of Dorlach Tor. The truth behind the Divine Peace did not surprise or sadden him; he only felt a weary and somewhat childish desire to evade unpleasant knowledge in the future. The idea that Lord Stane might be deluding himself about the Peace proved the most unsettling revelation of all. If the Lord of Dorlach Tor had allowed the priests to renounce the Swordmaster, rather than challenge them with the truth, then everything became a lie. Perhaps even the gods themselves did not exist and the veil of reality would someday tear like a cobweb, fraying into oblivion, unraveling all their lives.

The sky darkened toward dusk, and Maddock's breath steamed in the increasingly chill air by the time he reached Dorlach Tor. The beginnings of a small village nestled against the fort's outer wall, inhabited by those among the Lady's retainers who wished for private dwellings. Maddock passed through it with his head bowed, striding down its single lane. Light filtered from around the shuttered windows of the cottages, along with the laughter of families sharing the evening meal. They thought they lived in an era of peace, he reflected bitterly, that they were the protected children of the gods. *Lies. All lies.*

A whisper softer than velvet drifted to his ear. "Maddock. . . ."

Maddock paused and raised his head. "Hello?"

A young woman slipped from the shadow of a hedge and beckoned him off the lane. Though dressed in the loose tunic and high boots of a Rider, she wore a shawl draped over her head. Maddock did not immediately recognize her.

"Forgive me," Maddock said, thinking of ghosts and fairies. "But who are you?"

"Who do you think I am?" Vonora whispered indignantly. She cast back the shawl, revealing her huge, green eyes and upturned nose. "Get over here before my grandmother looks out her window and sees us."

Maddock stepped off the lane into the shadows. Vonora's

grandmother, Anra, had been the Lady's Hunt-Keeper, an altogether terrifying old woman. "I'm sorry," he murmured. "I thought perhaps the Queen of the Fair Folk had come to seek me as her champion."

"Don't—" Vonora turned her head away. "Don't talk like that."

Maddock raised and opened his hands. "I was only joking. I didn't—"

"Don't. Not even in jest."

Lashed by remorse, Maddock went silent. *She knows. She found out my heart belongs to Kiarda.*

Vonora toyed with the knotted ends of her shawl and avoided his gaze. "The rumors about you are growing." Her whisper became even softer. "People say you're a changeling, that the real Maddock is being held prisoner beneath a hill."

Maddock released a pent-up breath. *She doesn't know.* Guilt assailed him. *She doesn't know.* He folded his arms and stared up at the stars. "That's just—"

"They say that's why you disappear every few days to walk alone through Scratter Wood. And why you've taken to quarreling with your father, whom you used to love. And why you never smile."

Stung, Maddock looked at her. "I smile."

Vonora lifted her face, her beautiful eyes bright with unshed tears. "No, my love. You don't."

Maddock dropped his gaze to his boots. "I have things on my mind." He wanted suddenly to tell her everything, wishing she could reunite the torn halves of his spirit. "Be patient with me, please. I just need . . ." He shrugged. "I don't know what I need."

"Oh, Maddock," Vonora said, with concern. "I'm so worried about you." Abruptly, she snatched up his hands and clasped them between hers. "Talk to me."

Blood rushed to Maddock's face and beat like a drum. He could not rip his gaze away from their entwined fingers. Unless kinfolk, unmarried men and women did not touch. It was indecent. "Vonora." A hundred thousand thoughts roared through Maddock's mind, snatches of songs coupled with the blissful awareness of the warmth and softness of her hands. He told himself he ought to feel ashamed, but a strange elation seized him. His voice throbbed. "Oh . . . my Vonora . . ."

She gasped and pulled away, as if only just made aware of her actions. She paced a few steps from him, pulling her shawl around her throat and bosom.

Quivering, Maddock blew out his cheeks, unsure of what to say. "Well—"

"Well," Vonora echoed breathlessly. She peeked over her shoulder at him, her tone turning arch. "At least I know you're a man and not a changeling."

Maddock's heart galloped in his chest. His hands still tingled from her touch. He swallowed hard. "I didn't mean to worry you."

Vonora's expression turned earnest. "Then talk to me." She glided close and looked up into his face. "I love you. I'm willing to marry you. As the mother of our future children, don't I deserve your trust?"

Maddock's blood burned at her closeness, but he forced himself to think through the haze of desire. Vonora would become the Hunt-Keeper someday, like her mother and her mother's mother. She was clever, beautiful, and she truly loved him. A great respect for her awoke within him, coupled with a compassion that rivaled the strength of love. "Yes," he whispered. The words seemed to speak themselves. "I trust you, Vonora."

"Then you must break the hold the Others have over you. You must—"

Maddock shook his head, a slight smile tugging at his lips. "Those stories about me are not true."

"Then why do you walk alone in Scratter Wood?"

Maddock studied Vonora's anxious face, liking the concern he saw. "If I tell you the truth, dearling, I will literally place my life in your hands." He tilted his head. "And also, you might not love me anymore."

Vonora straightened her back and glared, looking very much like old Anra. "There is nothing you can say that will kill my love for you." She folded her arms. "So. Tell me. Why do you go to the woods? Do you meet a woman out there?"

"No. An outcast." Maddock listened to his own words in surprise. He had not planned to break his secret. It was so easy, as easy as walking. "I bring him supplies."

Vonora's breath caught, and understanding flashed in her emerald gaze. "The old Swordmaster?"

Maddock nodded. It was forbidden to speak Gaer's name within sight of Dorlach Tor's walls.

"I remember him." Vonora's expression gentled. "He was like a grandfather to me." She hesitated, seeming to search for words. "How is he?"

The heavy burden Maddock had carried alone for years slid from his back. At her words, something healed within him, as if she had turned his guilty secret into something noble. He would never love her as he did Kiarda, but he felt grateful to Vonora. She would always be a staunch friend. "He's good." Maddock allowed himself to smile. "Although he misses everyone."

Vonora's gaze went distant. "I miss him, too. The next time you see him, tell him—"

"Hey!" A man's furious shout issued from the deeper shadows near the hedge. "Get away from my sister!"

Startled, Maddock sprang between Vonora and the unknown threat, reaching for his sword. Only when his fist closed on empty air did he remember he was unarmed.

Vonora's twin brother, Damas, strode into the moonlight, his usually placid features twisted with rage. "Didn't you hear me?"

Bewildered, Maddock lowered his hands. "It's only me."

Damas' voice shook. "I know who you are. But I never guessed, until now, just what you are."

An icy sense of disaster invaded Maddock. *He heard everything.*

Vonora rushed around Maddock and faced her brother, arms still folded. "Keep your voice down!" she hissed. "What's the matter with you? Do you want the whole village—"

Damas did not seem to hear. He kept his burning gaze fixed on Maddock. "You!" He pointed accusingly. "You fiend! You . . . you . . . scratter-wight!"

Vonora yanked his hand down. "Shut your mouth, Damas! You're speaking to my future husband!"

"I'm speaking to a minion of the Dark Court! A sly, lying

wretch who hates his own father, who traffics with a blasphemous warmonger, who—"

Maddock stood motionless, frozen by the knowledge that he had betrayed Gaer.

Vonora seized her brother's shoulders and shook him. "Quiet!" she whispered harshly. "Be quiet, Damas! Have you gone mad?"

Damas finally turned his gaze to her, and the anger drained from his face. "Vonora. Don't you see?" His tone grew pleading. "He doesn't love you. He's only using you. He'll never—"

Maddock's cheeks burned with shame. "Damas." His voice wobbled. "I thought we were friends."

"So did I." Damas' eyes filled with tears, and he dragged his sleeve across his face. "So did I. But I heard you say it. You meet with an outcast, that thrice-cursed Swordmaster."

Maddock's thoughts tumbled helplessly through his head. He wanted to explain that he had not chosen to make his life a tangle of deceit. They based their entire existence on a lie. The Divine Peace was a fabrication, and war threatened to toss the Marchlands into chaos. "Damas—"

"What does he teach you out there in the woods?" Damas demanded. "How to wield a sword? How to kill?"

Maddock drew a breath to deny it but choked on the words. He remembered the wholeness he felt with a sword in his hand, the purity of spirit, the swift precision of body and mind. "You don't know what you're talking about," he whispered tightly.

Vonora glanced at Maddock uncertainly. "Supplies. You take supplies. Tell him."

Damas sniffed and wiped his eyes again. "No. Don't tell me. I can't stomach anymore." He put his arm around his twin's waist and glared at Maddock. "But I warn you. Whatever you're involved in, leave Vonora out of it."

Vonora twisted away. "Damas, you can't tell me—"

"I care . . ." Maddock started. "I care deeply about your sister."

Damas studied Maddock. "Liar! If you loved her, you wouldn't drag her down with you."

Vonora punched her brother in the arm. "Idiot! And if you loved me—"

Distant hoofbeats thudded through the night.

Maddock lifted his head to listen, making out a single horse clipping along at a fast pace. His blood chilled. The Light Court sometimes rode just after dusk, but always as a cavalcade. Things of evil traveled alone, things that carried away babies and young women.

A man cried out from the village, a wordless, urgent warning. Shutters and doors banged shut. Lamps dimmed.

Maddock spun toward Vonora. "Inside! Quick!"

She reached toward him. "You come, too!"

Damas grabbed her hands and dragged her toward their cottage. "Come on! Hurry!"

Maddock motioned for her to flee, thinking only of her safety. He shouted harshly. "Go!"

Vonora's lips parted in shock, as if he had struck her.

"Please!" Maddock waved to her brother. "Damas, get her away from here!"

Damas tossed Maddock a dark glare but forced his still-protesting sister through a gap in the hedge.

The alarm bell of Dorlach Tor shattered the air. The unseen horse broke into a smooth canter.

Maddock stood still, arms hanging limp. He knew he ought to run, but something bade him stay. A childhood memory blazed through him: the clang of a hammer against an old iron cauldron, a snowy courtyard, a thrashing horse, and Gaer's lean arm hefting him from danger.

The hoofbeats clattered up the lane, moving toward the fort. Maddock sank back into the shadows near the hedge.

The horse was white, like the stallion in his memory, the rider tall with long, dark hair. In the clear moonlight, Maddock's experienced eye picked out the steed's impeccable training, details of the glittering tack, and the rider's obvious skill. He recognized them then. *Lord Adan and Dream Cloud.*

They flew past. The stallion snorted at Maddock's presence but did not shy or break his gait. Lord Adan's gaze seemed fixed upon the fort ahead, his scarred face unusually grim.

Maddock listened to the hoofbeats continue through the darkened village and wondered what brought Lord Adan all the way from Sarn Moor. The silken gauze of reality rippled in a strange wind, marred by a multitude of tiny rips. Gaer's words echoed within him. *Almighty Hepona has stretched forth her hand.*

Maddock shivered.

CHAPTER THREE

K IARDA leaned against Blood Rage's shoulder, drawing solace from the old stallion's familiar presence. A hush lay over the stable as it settled for the evening. Phos-lamps hung from the ceiling beams, glowing without flame or heat. Horses in the surrounding stalls drowsed in the dim, green-gold light. The two stable hands on duty for the night spoke in low murmurs from a tack room near the far wall, trading liniment recipes.

Fatigued from a day-long battle against loneliness and a sense of disconnection, Kiarda stroked the stallion's lean neck. She missed her friend, Bevin, who was off visiting her family before the winter snows made travel dangerous. Kiarda needed someone to talk to about the changes she felt stirring within her, but her attempt to confide in her younger sister earlier that day had descended into a shallow conversation about hair. Worst of all, in the back of her mind lurked a suspicion that she had suffered another memory lapse. In spite of careful thought, the recollection of her hours following the midday meal eluded her entirely.

Once used to store battle gear for horses, a chamber across the aisle from Blood Rage's stall currently served as a temporary bedroom for the Lord and Lady. Comfortable furniture filled its snug confines. The scents of baby and rose-scented lamp oil wafted from its open door, mingling with the smells of hay and dust. The fire in its modest hearth sent shadows of Kiarda's gathered family flickering across the floor. With a strange combination of reluctance and longing, she raised her head from the stallion's shoulder and gazed through the bedroom's open door.

Stane sprawled in his chair, the baby asleep in the crook of his left arm. Her father had shaved off his mustache at the time of Elrin's birth, and Kiarda was still unaccustomed to seeing him looking so young. In front of Stane stood a small table with a chess game in progress. Kiarda's twelve-year-old brother, Leith, sat at the opposite side of the table, perched on a heap of pillows, scowling in concentration at the board. Her sister, Ladayla, age fourteen, knelt in front of the hearth, combing out the damp strands of her golden hair. Wylfre crouched on the floor amidst her hunting gear, sorting through it, preparing for the upcoming season. Cousin Adan sat cross-legged beside her, telling a story about Tynan's link-mate and how the tomcat boasted he could chase a dog up a tree.

Elrin's link-mate slept. The colt lay on his side in the middle of the floor, his long legs sticking straight out, his belly fluttering with every breath. The colt's mother, Snow Drop, dozed in her spot by the hearth, hip-shot, her chin resting contentedly on the back of a cushioned chair.

A strange ache formed in Kiarda's throat, and she returned her attention to her father's elderly stallion. Blood Rage had his nose tucked into a bucket of warm sweet-mash, no longer actually eating it but playing, sucking it through his teeth and letting it slobber out of his mouth. Kiarda kissed his shoulder. "You big baby," she murmured. "Big, sweet baby."

The stable door clattered open. Maddock strode in, windswept, his eyes full of the wild night. He saw her and froze.

As always, Kiarda's knees went weak and her hands trembled. As always, she fought to conceal her feelings. He was the most beautiful man in Dorlach Tor, as spirited and graceful as a purebred horse, but lately given to unpredictable moods. She did not believe the rumors, since they had grown up together; but Kiarda no longer understood him.

Maddock touched his forehead in courtesy to her rank. "My lady."

Kiarda nodded stiffly. Until just a year ago, he'd called her 'Yarda. The new formality made her feel even more distant from her own identity. "Maddock."

He gestured toward a stall near the end of the aisle. "By your leave, I thought I'd look in on the Dreamer—" He cleared his throat. "Your pardon, Dream Cloud. See that he's settled."

There was no need for the Horsemaster's son to take the trouble, but Maddock had helped Adan train the stallion and obviously still felt some proprietary affection. "That would be nice," Kiarda replied. It was a polite phrase, one used upon hired servants; and she hated that it passed her lips, hated that her old playmate kept acting so horridly proper. She continued with effort, trying to recapture their former ease of conversation. "In fact, it might be best that you pay your respects, or the Dreamer may not forgive you."

For a rigid moment Maddock did not respond. Then, his face softened. "Yes, my lady." He did not quite smile, but his tone gained warmth. "He's always been a stickler for courtesy." He touched his forehead again and headed toward Dream Cloud.

Kiarda's knees shook so badly she could barely stand. She leaned over the stall partition to watch Maddock walk away, admiring his muscular grace.

Blood Rage lifted his nose from the bucket and lipped at Kiarda's braid, slobbering sweet-mash over her hair and shoulder.

"Hey!" Surprised more than upset, Kiarda backed out of easy range, trying to wipe the mess away with her hands.

Blood Rage snorted and shook his head vigorously. Flecks of drool and mash flew everywhere.

Laughing in spite of herself, Kiarda flung her arms up and twisted her face away.

The stallion stopped and peered at her, ears up, a merry light in his eyes.

Kiarda shook her finger at him, still laughing. "You think that's funny, don't you?"

Blood Rage snorted again.

With a rush of fondness, Kiarda wiped the remaining sweet-mash from his graying muzzle with the cuff of her sleeve. "You think you're so funny," she cooed. "Yes, you do."

Maddock reappeared, his face creased with the beginning of concern. "What in the name of—?"

"It's all right," Kiarda said, forgetting her earlier nervousness. "Just another of his little pranks."

Maddock's dark eyes slitted, and he crushed his lips together. "Mm." Tack cloths hung on a nearby peg. He found a relatively clean one and offered it to her. "My lady," he said in a strangled tone, "you have a blob of . . . something . . . about to slide into your ear."

Kiarda took the cloth but lifted her chin. "Maybe I like it there."

A sudden shadow fell over them as Adan sauntered out of the bedroom. "Ah, yes." He nodded approvingly, a wide grin spreading over his ruined visage. "Very becoming."

Kiarda carefully dabbed at her hair with the cloth. She found a lot more sweet-mash than she expected. "Eeew, it's all over!"

"I'm certain it will start a new fashion," Adan said in an utterly sincere voice. "Soon, all young ladies will use horse slobber as a hair dressing."

It felt like old times again. Kiarda glanced at Maddock. "At least it's not Sygil's cough elixir." A mare had once spit a whole dose of the thick, green substance in his face. "I hear that stuff tastes worse than it smells."

Maddock chuckled. "True. But I haven't caught a cough since then."

Blood Rage stretched his neck over the stall's gate and nuzzled Adan. "Oh-ho, you old monster! So I'm next, am I?" He stroked the stallion's velvety nose and looked at Maddock. "I rode the Dreamer in. Have you seen him?"

The Horsemaster's son nodded. "He's asleep. Curled up in the straw like a big cat."

"He's tuckered out, poor lad." Adan kept his attention on Blood Rage. "I was in a hurry to reach Dorlach Tor before dark."

Maddock's brows crooked, and his grin faltered. "Is everything all right?"

Adan's smile turned careful. "Oh, yes. Fine. Thank you for asking."

The sense of free camaraderie evaporated. Kiarda stood still, clutching the cloth in her hand.

Adan shifted, as if chagrined at destroying the mood. "And how are things with you, Maddock? Is your father well?"

"Yes, my lord." Maddock swallowed. "Thank you."

A long, uncomfortable silence ensued. Kiarda gazed imploringly at her cousin. *Say something.*

Adan seemed to grope for words. "And you? Find a nice girl, yet?"

Maddock flicked his gaze to Kiarda, then back to Adan. "Yes, my lord. Actually, I have. Vonora, the Hunt-Keeper's daughter. Perhaps you remember her?"

In a stinging instant, Kiarda felt her heart freeze, then shatter.

Adan's lopsided grin returned. He seemed unaware that the world had come to an end. "Of course, I remember Vonora. When we were both quite small, she pushed me into a water trough, and I came up covered with slime and snails." He clasped Maddock's shoulder. "This is happy news. Have the two of you discussed marriage?"

Abruptly, Maddock turned red to the roots of his hair. "Yes, my lord," he stammered. "But it isn't—we haven't—"

Scalding tears filled Kiarda's eyes. She turned and stumbled to the rear of the stall.

"Well, best of luck," Adan said warmly. "I'm sure it's destiny."

"Thank you, my lord." Another long silence followed. "I should be going. Father will worry. With your leave, my lady?"

Kiarda swallowed and forced herself to speak. "Good night, Maddock."

"My lady," Maddock said formally. "My lord."

The stable door opened and closed again. In the ensuing silence, Kiarda heard her family laughing. Evidently Leith had scored a major tactical advantage over their father in the game of chess.

Adan spoke tentatively, "Kiarda?"

She tried to answer but could not.

"Hey." Adan let himself into the stall and approached Kiarda. "Don't cry. It's for the best. Really."

Kiarda hastily wiped the tears from her cheeks and moved to put Blood Rage between them. "I'm not crying." She folded her arms and faced him defiantly. "And I don't know what you're talking about."

Adan put his hands on his hips and smiled at her over the stallion's glossy rump. "I'm ugly, not blind." He dropped his voice to a whisper. "You're in love with the Horsemaster's son."

Kiarda glared at him.

"So," Adan continued, still whispering. "What are you going to do now that he's found someone else? Make his life a living hell?"

Kiarda flung the dirty tack cloth at him. "No!"

Adan plucked the cloth out of the air near his face. "No?" he repeated good-naturedly. "Why not?"

Kiarda wished she had something else to throw. "Why are you being so awful?"

Adan's smile turned wan. "To make you think. It's high time you did." He stroked the stallion's neck. "Take your lesson from my unfortunate brother, Culan, and the Lady Tassi. She's from an old family, but unlanded, and so is naturally disinterested in maintaining the traditions of an ancient and honorable House. Culan did not marry within his class, and the folk of Sarn Moor are suffering for it."

Kiarda did not know what he meant. It was unlike Adan to insult and bully her. She wanted to dismiss his words and walk away, but something in his voice held her. For the first time, she noticed lines of fatigue around his eyes, caused by more than a long ride. He looked thinner, worn, oddly desperate. "What is it? What's the matter?"

Adan shrugged and turned his gaze away. "A few days ago, Lady Tassi installed her whole family at Sarn Moor, forcing our folk out of the House to find what shelter they could."

Kiarda stared at him. Such things were not done. The retainers of Sarn Moor had served, parent to child, for generations. They had their own rights and entitlements. "But she can't—"

"Oh, yes, she can. She has." Adan paused and seemed to consider whether or not to go on. "And it's getting worse. For example, one of Lady Tassi's uncles took a fancy to our Hunt-Keeper's horn, which has been passed down from mother to daughter since anyone can remember. It's a beautiful instrument with a clear, ringing tone. You've heard it."

Feeling sick, Kiarda nodded. "Lady Tassi stole the Hunt-Keeper's horn?"

"Yes. And gave it to her uncle." Adan sighed shakily and continued in a colorless voice, as if reciting ancient history. "So I stole it back and hid it for safekeeping, along with a number of other treasures. This morning, Lady Tassi found me in the library, reading hero stories to Fian and Dod. She went berserk, screamed, threw things. My little brothers started to cry. People came running. She stood in the midst of the wreckage, tears rolling down her cheeks, and blamed me for everything. And everyone believed her. Even Fian and Dod. You should have seen them run to her."

Kiarda felt her heart break again. "They're just little boys. It must have scared them to see her cry."

"I know," Adan said heavily. "But it hurts."

Blood Rage shook his head and stamped, impatient for more attention. Kiarda stroked his shoulder. "Is that why you rode all alone to Dorlach Tor?"

Adan raised his brows, pulling his right eye into a tight squint. "Actually, I came to see if Lady Wylfre would consider buying the Dreamer."

"What?"

"He's the only thing of value I own, and I need the money to build cottages for the folk of Sarn Moor. Lady Tassi won't, so someone has to. Winter's coming on."

Kiarda gazed at him helplessly, not knowing what to say.

"So," Adan said with forced brightness. "Let this be a lesson to you. Don't marry outside your class. It only leads to tragedy."

Kiarda shook her head. "Don't change the—"

"Not that the two of you could marry, even if Maddock returned your love. Your lady mother would certainly not approve, nor would your father."

"Adan—"

"And the folk of Dorlach Tor? Well, they would think poor Maddock was getting above himself, and they would make things very uncomfortable for him." Adan kept his eyes on Blood Rage, running his hand along the stallion in broad sweeps, as if grooming him. "In fact, they may already be jealous of him, suspicious of your childhood friendship. You saw how he was acting tonight."

"That's not . . ." Kiarda paused, thinking of the rumors and how some people in the village shunned the Horsemaster's son. Adan's words suddenly made a lot of sense. "I just wanted . . ."

She sighed, feeling the remains of her world turn bleak and gray. "I guess I just wanted something to stay the same. Everything seems to be changing." A deep chill clutched her. *Changing.* She huddled close to Blood Rage for warmth.

Adan continued stroking the stallion, smiling sadly. "Ah, yes. Everything is changing."

"I'm turning into something." Aghast, Kiarda froze, mouth hanging open, unable to believe she had blurted her anguish after her sister's blithe dismissal.

Adan's smile faded. "Pardon me?"

Kiarda backed away a step. "Nothing."

"No. Tell me." Adan studied Kiarda. "What do you mean?"

"I'm changing." Kiarda lowered her head, pressing her cheek against Blood Rage's soft side. "I mean, I'm changing into something else. I can feel it inside. And lately I've been blacking out and finding myself in strange places." She shifted her face and peered at Adan. "Yesterday, I was brushing my hair in my room. Next thing I knew, I woke up on top of the hen coop."

Adan's brows shot up. "On the roof? How did you get there?"

Kiarda gestured helplessly. "I can't remember."

Adan's forehead wrinkled with concern, drawing the scarred half of his face into crimped angles. "What do your parents say about it?"

Kiarda drew a breath to speak, but in a sudden noisy rush Leith, Ladayla, and their father emerged from the temporary bedroom. Her brother made a dash for Adan, letting himself into the stall. "Guess what," he said. "I won the match!"

Adan tore his gaze from Kiarda. "Quite an accomplishment." He spoke with determined enthusiasm. "Good job!"

Stane smiled warmly at his eldest daughter. "Time for bed, dear heart. Go and say good night to your mother and Elrin, then I'll walk you all back to the House."

Somewhat relieved by the interruption, Kiarda grinned back at her father and slipped through the gate. As she made her way to the bedroom, she heard Leith resume his chatter about the chess game.

Wylfre sat beside the hearth with Elrin to her breast. Firelight touched the curve of her cheek and the baby's head with a golden glow. In the corner, Elrin's link-mate also nursed, his little tail whisking back and forth. Kiarda approached softly. "Mother?"

Wylfre lifted her head, her expression remote and dreaming. Kiarda knelt beside her chair and gazed up at her. "Mother, I've been talking to Adan. He told me what Lady Tassi has done, how she's turned the folk out of the House."

Wylfre narrowed her eyes and nodded pensively. "Dark days are ahead for Sarn Moor. Tassi is unfit for the Ladyship."

"Can't you do anything about it?"

"Perhaps." Wylfre sighed. "Though it will take some time, and Tassi is unlikely to listen to instruction."

Kiarda kept her voice steady, with difficulty. "But Adan is going to sell the Dreamer. You can't let him go through with it."

Her mother gently brushed stray strands of hair from Kiarda's forehead. "If I buy the Dreamer, Adan will have the money to purchase building materials."

Tears sprang to Kiarda's eyes. "But he loves that horse. Couldn't you just give Adan the money?"

"But if the Dreamer is my property, then he is beyond Tassi's reach. Yes?"

Kiarda had not thought of that. "I suppose," she said in a small voice.

"And then, since Dorlach Tor has no immediate use for the stallion, I'll board him out to Adan, paying for his upkeep. That will give Adan a steady income to use for the succor of his folk." Wylfre gave her daughter an impish grin. "And if our arrangement annoys Tassi, so much the better."

Kiarda's heart leaped with a joy as intense as pain. She scrambled to her feet, clasped her mother's shoulders, and kissed her. "Oh, thank you! Thank you so much."

"Anything to make you happy, sweeting." Wylfre chuckled. "You will wash your hair before you retire, won't you?"

Kiarda touched her sticky braid. "Oh. I forgot." She flicked clinging bits of sweet-mash into the fire. "Yes, I suppose I'd better." She bent and kissed Elrin's head. He grunted like a piglet in response. "Good night, Elrin," she whispered. She kissed her mother again. "Good night, Mother."

"Good night."

Feeling light inside, buoyant and whole, Kiarda strode out into the stables.

Ladayla stood with her back to Kiarda, clutching her damp, golden curls. "It's turning red!" She spoke in a tone of comic hysteria. "My hair is turning red! I'm changing into something!"

Adan looked distressed, her father wore a bemused expression, and Leith was openly snickering.

Kiarda's smile faltered. She froze, staring at them.

As if sensing her sister's presence, Ladayla whirled. "Oh!" Color rose in her cheeks. "I was just—"

For a long moment, Kiarda felt only numbness. Then, realization struck like a kick in her gut. Ladayla had betrayed her confidence, holding her deepest fears up to ridicule. Leith was joining in the mockery, and her father was permitting it to happen.

Reeling, Kiarda looked at Adan, unable to find words.

Misery dulled Adan's eyes. "I'm sorry," he said. "I told them. I was worried."

Stane put his hands on his hips and tilted his head. "Kiarda, you're overreacting again." His voice was calm, with just a hint of reproof. "Ladayla was merely teasing."

Kiarda's hands and feet tingled. She tried to moisten her dry lips, struggled to draw breath. She wanted to answer her father but could not remember how to speak. *Changing. Changing.*

Ladayla giggled, nervously biting her thumb knuckle. "You're not mad, are you?"

Emptied of thought or emotion. Kiarda wordlessly strode to the stable door. Leith burst into more laughter. She shoved at the latch, pushed the door open, and walked out into the night.

A rush of wind tugged at Kiarda's braid, carrying with it the scents of earth, dung, and fading leaves. Clouds scudded across the sky, top-lit by the ghostly moon. Longing for solitude, Kiarda slipped into the shadows beneath the trees lining the paddock's fence line. Her family came out of the stable. Her father called her name. She heard everything clearly, but the sounds made less sense than the wind whispering through the dying autumn grass.

Kiarda traveled along the back ways of Dorlach Tor, behind the silent smithy, through the woodyard full of the furtive skitter of mice. Fear and resentment melted away, replaced by a deep restlessness, a primal need to reclaim a part of herself.

A fox called from the apple orchard. Kiarda froze in mid-step, with one foot poised in the air. The thin, birdlike cry came again. It spoke to her of hunger and loneliness, of freedom and the hunt. Survival depended upon speed, cunning, and the savage blessing of Hernis, Lord of the Wild. Life was a full belly and a warm den, death the ultimate fate.

Kiarda ached to answer the fox's call. It promised release from an uncertain future, an end to confusion and the pain caused by love.

"Kiarda!" A man's voice rang through the night air. She lifted her head, listening, suddenly aware that a lot of people were calling for her and had been for some time. With an inner surge of surprise, she remembered her own identity. *Kiarda. That's me.*

The man spoke from behind her. "My lady?"

Kiarda turned slowly, thinking she knew his voice.

Maddock stepped into the starshine, the wind whipping his hair like black flame. His eyes, equally dark, seemed enormous. " 'Yarda?"

Kiarda did not know what to say. *I've always loved you.*

For a long moment, Maddock simply gazed at her. Then, he seemed to come to himself and raised his voice to shout to the others. "Over here! I've found her!"

❧

Hours later, scolded, hugged, fed, bathed, and sent to bed, Kiarda lay awake, staring into the darkness. Though she recalled only a brief walk, her family told her she had wandered past midnight. Scratches she could not explain covered her arms and hands, and her legs ached with exhaustion. She clutched fistfuls of blanket, wanting to talk to Bevin. The healer would listen to and believe her when her own parents would not.

The House lay silent, the only sound the autumn wind stirring the trees outside. Kiarda rolled onto her side and tried to think quieting thoughts. She remembered what her mother planned to do for Adan and the folk of Sarn Moor, concentrating on that happiness. *Dear, kind Adan.*

Kiarda slowly sat up in bed. Adan had believed her. He had spoken to her as an adult, without condescension. She wondered if he was asleep after all the excitement. *Maybe he'd like someone to talk to.*

Kiarda chewed the inside of her lip, undecided. It would be an obscene act to seek him out in the guest chamber, and it might cause him trouble. Tradition ruled that a young man could not touch a young woman, except to save her life. Kiarda could touch no males but her father and brothers until she married. Adan was a third cousin, not a close kinship; and for her to visit him in the night would compromise both of them.

Maddock returned to Kiarda's thoughts. Proud, high-tempered, full of unexpected moods, he had always been a part of her life, like the looming presence of Dorlach Tor itself. Her love for him ran like a golden thread through her childhood. She did not want to believe she had lost him to another. She looked to the future, to a time when she ruled as Lady. Parents dead, brother and sister married and gone, she would live alone through the passing years, harboring her secret grief, watching Maddock's and Vonora's children grow.

Kiarda drew up her legs and wrapped her arms around them. *Alone.* The concept brought an unexpected pleasure.

A fox called outside Kiarda's window.

Kiarda held her breath, listening. The animal's thin wailing seemed to hold words for her. Self-knowledge came only with solitude. Avoiding the company of others meant sparing herself vexation and pain. Loneliness fostered happiness.

With a sigh, Kiarda lay back down on her bed. She did not need to talk to anyone, she realized; it felt so good to be all alone. Some small corner of her mind protested the thought, urging her to flee her room, wake up her maids, and light all the lamps.

Kiarda slipped her hands behind her head, closed her eyes, and listened to the voice of the fox.

Cold air on Kiarda's bare skin awakened her. She lay on a smooth and unyielding surface, not her bed. Gasping, she jerked her head up. For a heart-stopping moment she did not recognize her surroundings. Then, the nightmarish shadows and strangely angled walls resolved themselves into the safe confines of her bedroom. She lay on the floor near the window, naked.

Chilled to the bone, muscles cramping, Kiarda sat. *It happened again.* Grasping the wall for balance, she climbed to her feet. The bed seemed undisturbed, but her gown hung over the edge beneath the blankets, twisted into a loose rope. In two long strides, she reached the bed and yanked her gown free. Strong scent wafted from the linen folds. She lifted it to her nose, sniffing gingerly. It smelled dark and earthy, with overtones of urine and wet fur. *Fox musk.*

Kiarda stood still, trying to understand. The night air seeped into her spirit, inducing a cold she knew she would never shake. *Changing.* The word once again filled her mind like a chant. *Changing.*

CHAPTER FOUR

BROTHER Honesty sat crossed-legged in the open doorway of his tent, his portable writing desk balanced on his lap. Overgrown from the long sea voyage, mouse-brown wisps of hair fell around his mild visage, making him appear younger than his thirty-two years. He absently tucked his hair behind his ears, and the enormous diamond on his ring sparkled in a dazzling array of colors. The ring symbolized the eternal nature of his mission; he was a priest of the One Light, consecrated to the task of making all men and women heirs to its undying glory. His only ornament, the ring, clashed with his unadorned white robe, patched, thread-bare, and fraying at the cuffs and the hem around his ankles. His sandals were fashioned of coarse rope. Earthly clothing held no importance for Brother Honesty, the love of the One Light his true raiment.

A burning candle in a simple clay holder perched on the ground by his right leg. He repositioned it to lessen the danger of smothering it with his sleeve, and picked up his pen.

The slanting rays of the late autumn sun cast a glow over the camp, tinting the hundreds of canvas tents pink and gold. Off-duty soldiers cleaned their gear or napped. The wholesome aroma of bread wafted from the mess kitchen, and Brother Honesty's stomach rumbled. He would eat after the soldiers received their rations, he reminded himself. He needed to write while the daylight lasted.

Brother Honesty glanced down at his journal, a scroll of fine-grained, supple leather. Its top roll contained his observations of the long journey by sea; its bottom roll had yet to be filled. He lifted his pen, held its nib in the candle flame, and waited for the tip to turn a smoldering orange. The nib's special alloy would hold the heat long enough for him to write several sentences:

"Hunter's Month. Day Fifteen." The pen squeaked as Brother Honesty burned words into the leather. "Our third day in the new world. I can still scarcely take it in. The camp is well-established now, and the troops are in fine spirits. Even the threat of a fast-approaching winter cannot daunt them, so glad are they to be free of the confinement of shipboard life. Reportedly, Commander Swift is confident that we can complete the task of building permanent winter barracks before the snow flies."

Brother Honesty paused to reheat his pen, his soft blue eyes turning round and thoughtful. Though the officers and troops treated him with courtesy, he knew they regarded him as so much unnecessary baggage. Never before had a priest traveled with the advance army of an invasion force. In spite of their misgivings, Brother Honesty trusted the workings of the Light, confident it would soon reveal its plan for him. He need only prepare himself to follow where it led.

"The Marchlands, as they are named by the primitive savages who dwell here, are a vast and largely unpopulated region. To the north lie the desolate mountains of the arctic wastes. To the south, more mountains fence the region from its barbarous neighbors. My greatest concern is . . ." His pen chilled. Brother Honesty sighed, wishing for the hundred thousandth time that some clever person would develop a magical pen capable of writing without pause. His thoughts always ran more quickly than the glowing nib could burn them into leather.

A shadow fell across Brother Honesty's scroll, and he glanced up. As if summoned by his thoughts of magic, a Hooded Mage bent over him, robed, masked, and cowled in impenetrable black. Magic set apart the Hooded Order of Magicians and kept their lives concealed. Three traveled with the army: Skull, Claw, and Wraith. The mightiest of all those who wielded magic, they commanded destructive forces capable of the instantaneous annihilation of a small city.

The Hooded Mage appeared to hover above the ground. Brother Honesty shivered but reminded himself that, beneath the hood, dwelled another heir to the Light. "Good afternoon, my child," he said in a friendly tone. "What do you require of me?"

The dark figure bowed and beckoned politely. The Hooded Order lived under a code of silence and secrecy, forbidden to show their faces or speak aloud to outsiders.

Brother Honesty clutched his pen in both hands. "You want me to come with you?"

It bowed again. Embroidered black on black, a cloth badge on its shoulder depicted a stylized human skull.

Brother Honesty stared at it. Then, realizing his rudeness, he hastily rose, snuffed the candle, and bundled his journal and writing desk into his tent. "Is this a matter of exhortation or cleansing?" His voice shook, and he tried to steady it. "Shall I bring the Ewer or the Staff of—?"

Skull raised its hand in a soothing gesture. Its obvious attempt to allay his uneasiness contrasted strangely with its intimidating appearance. It graciously indicated the banner-decked tent of Commander Swift, which dominated the center of the encampment.

Brother Honesty blinked. "Commander Swift wishes to see me?"

Skull nodded deeply, motioning for Brother Honesty to follow, and glided off in the direction of the tent. The Mage seemed to drift along like smoke, its long robe brushing the ground.

Caught off guard, Brother Honesty hurried after Skull. He had no idea what prompted the commander to send for him, for he had never spoken to the army's leader and had only glimpsed him once from a great distance.

As the white-robed priest and the black-robed Mage passed, soldiers glanced up, then quickly averted their eyes. Brother Honesty raised his hand in calm benediction as he walked, diamond ring glinting like a splinter of the One Light. He understood the fear he saw in the soldiers' faces and knew his own humble person did not inspire it. A Hooded Mage conducted the vast energies of magic the way a metal rod played host to the erratic power of lightning. When employed in battle, the magic often overflowed from its wielder and sought another vessel. If it happened to fall upon an unprepared human, it caused an agonizing death. No matter that dying in such a manner guaranteed exalted status in the Realm of Light, no soldier liked or trusted a Hooded Mage.

For the first time, the priest imagined living his life as the object of others' fear and the sense of helplessness, isolation, and anger that might foster. Skull, Claw, and Wraith had only one another for solace and companionship. An odd, but heartfelt, compassion stole over Brother Honesty. He must find a way to extend his ministry to the powerful, dangerous strangers who dwelled among them.

Abruptly, Skull paused. It turned and regarded the priest for a long, silent moment.

Brother Honesty read no emotion from the shrouded figure. "Yes, my child?"

Skull bowed its head, tucked its gloved hands into its sleeves, and walked on.

Far from his initial nervousness, Brother Honesty's concern for the threesome took deep root. As he followed Skull, he soundlessly offered up a prayer for courage and guidance: *Light of the ages, most holy and unutterably good, I humbly beseech you to make me your vessel so that all souls may remember themselves heirs to your eternal triumph.*

Clusters of high-ranking officers muttered in grim conference outside the commander's tent. All wore resplendent uniforms: tabards emblazoned with heraldic devices, jewel-encrusted belts, and shining boots. Though they subtly shifted away from Skull, none spared a glance for the priest in his patched robe.

Guards armed with pikes stood at the tent's doorway, their postures alert and expressions grim. They gazed through the priest as if he did not exist. Several harried aides-de-camp filed from the tent, loaded with scrolls and folding stools, obviously too busy to trouble with questions.

Brother Honesty bit his bottom lip. No one had time for him, it seemed. He looked at Skull. The Hooded Mage seemed to hover in the air beside him like a fragment of starless night, head still bowed, hands still tucked out of sight.

Another young man with a bundle of scrolls under one arm emerged from the commander's tent. Fresh-faced, with keen gray eyes, he wore an unornamented tabard of Imperial green; a ribbon of the same color tied back his white-blond hair. He sauntered past the guards, who snapped to attention, then caught sight of the priest and Hooded Mage. He stopped in his tracks.

Uncertainly, Brother Honesty stepped forward. "Good afternoon, my child."

The youth studied him for a moment, then broke into a radiant smile. "Brother Honesty?" He extended his free hand. "It's an honor to meet you. I'm Commander Swift."

The priest abruptly realized he had addressed the Supreme Commander of the Imperial Legions and a Lord Prince of the Holy Court as "my child." Mortified, he took the young man's proffered hand. "Th-the honor," he stammered, "is all mine."

"I was about to send a message to you, requesting an audience." Commander Swift flicked his gaze to the Hooded Mage. "Evidently, it has already been delivered. Thank you, Skull."

It bowed.

Brother Honesty cleared his throat. "I'm at your disposal, Commander."

The young man's smile widened. "You're most kind to come on such short notice." He nodded toward his tent. "Let's talk inside, shall we?"

Brother Honesty turned to take leave of Skull. "My child—"

The Hooded Mage floated gracefully to the ground. It lowered its veiled head over its folded hands as if to receive a blessing.

Commander Swift inhaled sharply. The gathered officers broke into startled whispers.

No less surprised, Brother Honesty nevertheless extended his hands over the Hooded Mage's head. "May the Light shine upon you . . . and from within you," he murmured. "So that all shall be heirs to its glory."

Skull silently arose, bowed to the priest, and glided away. Feeling humble and grateful, as if he had received the blessing instead of bestowed it, Brother Honesty watched the dark form until it disappeared among the tents.

Commander Swift spoke with a new measure of respect. "You appear to exercise a certain influence over the Hooded Order."

The priest drew a trembling breath. He could not, in good conscience, claim any such thing; but he did not wish to contradict the commander. "Even the darkest shadows cast by the Light are holy."

The officers muttered, nodding approval. The commander turned to one of them, a tall man with lines of humor around his eyes, and passed the scrolls he carried. "Please take care of these for me, would you, Valor?" Then he gestured to the doorway of his tent, and the guards raised their pikes. "Brother Honesty, if you please?"

Suddenly feeling shy, the priest ducked through the canvas doorway. He expected to find the air perfumed and warmed by braziers, a real bed with feather pillows, and fine carpets on the floor. Instead, he discovered accommodations as comfortless as the most common soldier's. A bedroll sat in one corner of the tent; beside it, a tin plate and cup perched on a battered wooden trunk. The only luxuries appeared to be a sizable desk overhung by a good oil lamp; but mountains of scrolls, lists, and maps covered the desk's surface.

"I need your advice." Commander Swift strolled to the desk and spread a large leather map over all the paperwork. "One of our spies brought disturbing news last night. A significant bit of information eluded our earlier reconnaissance, and it jeopardizes the success of our entire campaign."

Brother Honesty shifted closer. He saw a diagram of the Marchlands, the rivers, mountains, and forests neatly labeled. Cross within a circle symbols that represented towns lay scattered over the surface. "I had no idea this region supported so many settlements."

"They're quite small, mostly clans residing in crumbling ancestral forts." Commander Swift pointed out several markers stained with crimson. "These, however, are the problems."

Brother Honesty peered at the label on one. "Dorlach Tor?"

Commander Swift spoke in a calm, measured tone. "Each settlement indicated in red is defiled by the Abomination."

Aghast, Brother Honesty stared at the commander. The worst of all evils, the Abomination infested human flesh, chaining human souls to the base instincts of animals. "Are you certain? It's been over three hundred years since—"

"Oh, yes. The natives make no attempt to hide the Abomination. They view it as some form of blessing."

The priest's stomach roiled. According to scripture, the Abomination tainted the lives of all it touched, and there was only one way to deal with it. "Then—" His voice wobbled. "Then they must all be put to the sword."

Commander Swift paced away from the desk, then turned and folded his arms. "I really don't want to do that."

Brother Honesty pressed his fingertips to his eyes and fought for self-control. "Everyone. Every man, woman, and child. Every animal." He swallowed. "It's the only way to prevent the Abomination from spreading."

"The only way? I was hoping you could suggest another." Commander Swift approached the priest. "Emperor Justice, may he reign forever, sent us here to bring these poor savages under his wise governance. Our task is to subdue the population, then bestow the blessings of civilization, beginning with proper sanitation. These horse people, these Marchlanders, are to become members of the Empire. They are to help stem the conquest of the southern armies. They can't do that if we reduce the entire population to carrion." He clasped the priest's shoulder. "My troops are loyal, but they are good men. To order a massacre of civilians would invite revolt."

Brother Honesty shook his head, seeking the necessary words. "But the Abomination spreads. If you kill one manifestation, the demon merely leaps to another victim. Even then, it's already polluted the souls of every living thing near it. The troops—all of us—are in grave danger of losing our immortal souls to evil."

Commander Swift leaned against his desk and folded his arms, his gray eyes narrowing in thought. "What if the tainted people were cleansed? Can't the Light purify all things?"

The priest drew a breath, then paused. The commander's astute question revealed a deep faith. "Yes," he replied slowly, a new idea forming in his mind. "The One Light burns away all evil." He looked down at the map, counting the number of stained settlements. *Fourteen. Not many.* "Perhaps you're right, Commander Swift. There may be another way."

"I'm listening."

Trying to curb his rising hope, Brother Honesty clasped his hands over his heart. "If we sanctified the boundaries of a settlement and cleansed all who dwelled within before destroying the Abomination—" He paused, wishing someone wiser than he were on hand. "Then, perhaps, the demon would have nowhere to go. It would perish utterly." He added apologetically, "But I may be wrong. We'd have to test it."

"For the moment, let's assume you're correct." Commander Swift bent over the map. "As the first leg of our campaign, we send out the Hooded Order with a small, mobile strike force. They will move swiftly from one large settlement to the next, destroying the native magic-wielders. If you ride with them, Brother Honesty, you can systematically cleanse the Abomination from the Marchlands." He traced a probable route with his index finger, his gray eyes lighting with excitement. "This, in itself, may prove enough to subdue the population. Our spies tell us the Marchlanders are a superstitious people who believe themselves living in an era of peace. They'll be reluctant to fight, at first, and that may gain us the time we need."

Brother Honesty nodded. He had also read the reports on the Marchlanders' primitive beliefs in order to better prepare himself to teach them the ways of the Light. "They possess another superstition which may work to our advantage, Commander. They are convinced that the land around them serves as the dwelling place of mysterious and powerful spirits. They fear these beings and call them the 'Fair Ones' or the 'Neighbors.' "

"Yes, I recall that." Commander Swift crooked his brows. "Demons?"

The priest shook his head. "It's a common belief among uncivilized peoples, probably a dim memory of ancestor worship or veneration of the dead. But the Marchlanders maintain that these spirits take human form and ride from place to place in majestic cavalcades."

"Yes, I remember—" The commander's face opened with surprise. "A perfect disguise for our strike force if it's spotted."

He grinned, suddenly exuberant as a boy. "Brother Honesty, I've got use for that cunning mind of yours." He offered his hand. "Congratulations. I'm promoting you to honorary field officer. From now on, you'll report to all meetings and planning sessions."

"But I–I'm just—" Brother Honesty gestured at his patched robe. "I'm only a priest. Your officers won't like—"

Commander Swift chuckled. "They have no choice. Neither do you." He pulled the Imperial green ribbon from his hair and tied it around the priest's right arm. "You're stuck with my company. Let's go find something to eat. I'm starved."

⚘

A mean, searching night wind blew through the pine grove. It penetrated Brother Honesty's threadbare robe as he knelt in prayer on the ground and pierced his heart with a deep chill. Usually, the priest grew oblivious to his surroundings, or the passage of time, when involved in his devotions, but this vigil among the pines felt different. He was afraid. *The Abomination. Can it truly be vanquished by a simple cleansing?* No answers came from the One Light, but his fears whispered to him that he had made a woeful mistake. The Abomination could not be contained. It would consume them all, and the fault would lie upon him. *I wanted to appear wise before Commander Swift. My vanity may become the ruin of us.*

A man spoke behind him. "Come, come, Brother." His tone was kindly, amused. "You're far too hard on yourself."

Startled, the priest raised his head. "Who?" A warm cover fell over his head and shoulders. He fumbled to push it back, and his fingers encountered the oily softness of sheepskin. "What?"

A woman laughed. "Oops. Sorry about that."

Brother Honesty peeked from beneath the sheepskin. Two men and a woman settled opposite him on the ground. One of the men leaned over an oil lamp, his long hair swinging forward to hide his face. The others unpacked food and drink from a large basket. None looked familiar. All three wore black robes, which gave the impression of disembodied heads and hands floating in the night. "Hello?"

The woman flashed her teeth at him, eyes sparkling. "Hello, Brother." She appeared to be in her forties, and her hair spilled in black ringlets over her forehead. She tugged flirtatiously at the Imperial green ribbon around his sleeve. "Promoted?"

Brother Honesty stared at her. The army had no women. "It's honorary."

She studied him with the same intensity. "You must have told Commander Swift exactly what he wanted to hear."

The lanky man helping with the basket nudged her with his elbow. "Claw, be nice." He pressed a cup into the priest's hand and filled it with something that smelled like mulled cider. "Please forgive her, Brother. She's a cynic."

Brother Honesty tore his gaze from the steaming cup. "You're—?" His mouth dried. "You—?"

The man with the lamp gave a small crow of triumph. "Got it!" The lamp's wick ignited and spread a golden light over the huddled group. The man raised his face, and his hair fell back, revealing a thin nose and large expressive eyes. "Little things are more difficult," he explained. His voice carried great warmth, and the priest recognized him as the initial speaker. "I could set every tree in this forest ablaze more easily than light this lamp. A matter of focus, I suppose."

Claw snorted derisively. "Focus. Why not just use a tinderbox like the rest of us?" She unwrapped a loaf of bread, ripped off a hunk, and passed the loaf to the lanky man. "Here, Wraith. You're a growing boy."

Brother Honesty's hands trembled, and he set down his cup before he spilled it. He looked at the man with the lamp. *Skull?*

"That's me." He cut a slice of cheese from a wedge and offered it to the priest. "It's quite sharp. I like to take a bite first, then a sip of cider. They taste good together, almost like spiced apple tart and cream."

Brother Honesty gazed at him in growing bewilderment. "Do you read minds?"

Skull pursed his lips and pressed the cheese into the priest's hand. "Not all minds. Not all the time. It's just that you shout your thoughts."

The priest looked at the other Magicians, wondering if they possessed the same talent.

"No," Skull replied. "Just me."

Claw drew her brows down, speaking through a mouthful of bread. "Would you two stop it? It's annoying to hear only half of the conversation."

Brother Honesty ducked his head in apology. "I'm sorry, my child."

Long-legged Wraith shifted uneasily, nudging the woman again. "Don't talk like that to a priest. It isn't respectful."

"My child, I—"

"You're not eating." Skull leaned forward. "Don't you like cheese?"

The priest tried to find words. "I—"

Skull interrupted in a reassuring tone. "I promise you, there's nothing magic about the food. We brought our own supplies for the campaign."

Brother Honesty looked from the steaming cup of cider to the slice of cheese in his hand. "I—" The situation suddenly struck him as funny. He laughed. "I just never expected a midnight picnic with Magicians of the Hooded Order."

"We never expected it either," Claw said dryly. "We don't often do this sort of thing." Her expression turned mischievous. "I must admit it's fun."

Brother Honesty took a polite sip of cider and a nibble of cheese. It did taste good. "I thought you were forbidden to show your faces or to speak with anyone outside your Order."

"We are." Skull cut slices from the wedge for the others. "But we know you won't tell anyone else."

Wraith nodded and gestured to the air around them. "I've enclosed us within a bubble of secrecy. It's a lesser version of the spell we cast when walking among the uninitiated, to make us float in silence. No one else can see or hear us."

"Really?" Wide-eyed, Brother Honesty gazed around. "Where is it?"

Claw accepted a piece of cheese and folded another hunk of bread around it. "Don't be stupid. You can't see it. You think it glows in the dark or something?"

Wraith spoke in a scandalized tone. "Claw! Stop being so—"

Skull sighed. "Both of you, stop bickering." He looked at the priest. "Now, perhaps, you understand the wisdom of the rule of silence."

"Please speak freely," Brother Honesty urged. "If anyone ought to keep quiet, it's me."

The three Magicians exchanged unreadable glances. Skull cleared his throat. "We know you're troubled, good Brother; and we know why. We came to tell you that you're worried over nothing." He paused, seeming to search for words. Around them, the wind silently swayed through the pines, robbed of its chill. "We're not priests or experts in holy rites. We know nothing of the Light, but we do understand the deep workings of magic. We know that the thing you call the Abomination is not as powerful as you think. The plan you gave Commander Swift will prove more than adequate to deal with the problem."

Tamping back hope, Brother Honesty began to tremble again. "But the Abomination . . . I've studied the scriptures. It's a manifestation of demonic evil."

Skull shook his head. "No. Linking a human soul to that of an animal is merely a quirky bit of magic. Revolting, to be sure, and no civilized people would tolerate it; but it's hardly the threat you believe."

Brother Honesty clutched his cup of warm cider and pondered how to explain the subtlety of evil, how it first convinced its victims it did not exist.

Skull raised a forestalling hand. "I don't want to argue theology with you. I'm quite certain I'd lose. I don't know anything about the Light. I don't know anything about evil. I know only magic."

"But what is magic if not another manifestation of the Light?" The priest found himself gesturing earnestly with his piece of cheese. "Knowing magic is the same as knowing the Light."

Claw broke in, "Knowing magic is the same as not knowing magic." She seized a pine cone from the ground near her knee and lifted it. Her expression turned solemn; and she spoke in a formal tone, as if quoting a sacred text. "This is a pine cone."

Skull took it from her and also held it aloft. "This is not a pine cone."

Wraith intoned: "You are both incorrect."

The three looked expectantly at the priest.

Brother Honesty shook his head. "I'm sorry. I don't understand."

Claw made an exasperated noise. "Of course, you don't! If you did, you'd be a Hooded Mage."

Wraith shifted and seemed ready to protest.

Claw whipped toward Wraith. "And if you gouge me with your elbow again, I'll break your arm!"

Skull threw his colleagues a warning glare, then turned his attention to the priest. "Believe what you will of the Abomination, just rest your mind as to the danger involved. Your clemency toward these savage Marchlanders will not result in the defilement of all living souls."

Brother Honesty regarded him sadly. "I pray you're right, my child."

Skull picked up the loaf of bread, broke off a piece, and handed it to the priest. "If you can't trust us, then trust in the Light."

Touched and humbled, Brother Honesty accepted the morsel of bread. "I choose to trust both the Light and the Light within you." Some might find his words shocking, to speak of Hooded Magicians as vessels for indwelling holiness; but he had been praying for guidance when they arrived. He had grown accustomed to unusual answers to his prayers. "The Light within all of you." The priest gazed earnestly at Wraith, who grinned, then at Claw, who glanced away, blinking. "You are all three heirs to its great goodness and love, whether you know it or not."

Claw muttered, "You almost make me believe it."

Wraith gave her a baffled stare. "You don't believe in the Light?"

"No."

"Neither do I." Skull smiled at the priest, his large eyes filled with affection. "But I do believe in human goodness, and I see great goodness in you."

Brother Honesty awoke. The first hint of dawn turned the walls of his tent a pale pink, and his breath steamed in the frosty air. He remembered his midnight picnic in the pine grove with the Hooded Magicians. *Strange dream. Felt so real.* His pallet felt snug and warm, with a thick black sheepskin thrown over his two threadbare blankets. *Sheepskin. Just like the dream.* Sighing in deep contentment, he rolled over.

A small bundle wrapped in leather lay beside Brother Honesty's pillow. Shaking off sleep, he propped himself on his elbow and gazed at the strange parcel, wondering about its origin and content. Carefully, he unfolded the leather. A pen fell out, its barrel carved from obsidian and its nib fashioned from clear crystal. On the inside of the wrapper someone had burned a brief note:

Honesty—
Gave pen a little thought. Came up with something. Hope you like. Stays hot a very long time. Just remember to quench in cup of water when done. Otherwise, might burn down tent!
—Claw

Blue eyes growing wide, Brother Honesty sat and clutched the pen. Rare and magical, it was a gift fit for the Emperor Justice himself. Admiring its fluid beauty, he lifted it to catch the dawn's light filtering into his tent. The crystal nib snatched up the pale pink glow and flung it away in bright spangles. The priest laughed in simple pleasure, and his own words returned to him. *Even the darkest shadows cast by the Light are holy.*

A calm assurance filled Brother Honesty. His fears of the night before were groundless, he realized. Working with Commander Swift and the Hooded Order, he would help them rid the Marchlands of the Abomination and cleanse the horse-people of evil. Pure, holy, unutterably good, the Light would triumph. The demon would die.

CHAPTER FIVE

M ADDOCK awakened before dawn. For a long moment, he
lay motionless and listened to the keening song of the January wind. He could not recall a winter of such bitter and relentless cold, or a season of such personal darkness. Every passing
day brought new torment, fresh burdens he had to bear while
maintaining a pretense of happiness. His heart felt like a mass
of sores; each emotion, each thought, brought a new measure of
pain.

Maddock's father slumbered beside him in the bed they
shared, snuggled up under blankets and straw. The frigid weather
stiffened the Horsemaster's joints and aggravated old war
wounds. Some of Dorlach Tor's similarly afflicted folk stayed inside all day, keeping busy with light handwork. Maddock wished
his father would do the same but knew better than to suggest it.
Cadder always insisted upon doing his morning chores, pursuing
them as relentlessly as Gaer did his daily sword practice.

Unbidden, Gaer's welfare came to mind. Maddock imagined
the Swordmaster's body frozen in a tangle of tree roots, his limbs
contorted, his white hair clotted with ice. Horror struck Maddock like a physical blow. He jerked fully awake and clenched his
blankets, heart racing. *Stop it,* he ordered himself. *Just stop.* He
had not seen Gaer in two months, knew there was no way to
contact him. *Two fathers. One in the woods. One at home.* Maddock slipped out of bed. *Take care of the one at home.*

Chilly air bit at Maddock's nose and fingers. Inhaling in a soft
hiss, he quietly moved to the small hearth. The coals slept under
a thick cover of white ash. He stirred them, fed them kindling,
and watched until the flames took hold. He hoped he might warm
the room somewhat before his father got out of bed.

As the fire grew stronger, golden light flickered over the Horsemaster's quarters. Barely twelve feet wide in any direction, the room adjoined the stables, the bed its only real furniture. Sections of tree trunk, borrowed from the woodlot, served as a table and two stools. Cadder and Maddock owned a few simple eating utensils, a dented iron cauldron for the hearth, a washbasin and ewer, and a covered chamber pot which they kept near the curtained doorway. Harnesses in various degrees of disrepair dangled from the ceiling beams, and Maddock's late mother's hunting bow hung on the wall over the bed.

Shivering, the young man went to the chamber pot and relieved himself. When he moved to the ewer, he found a layer of ice over the water. He pounded it with a knuckle to break it, poured a little of the frigid water into the basin, and washed his hands.

Cadder stirred in bed. "Been thinking about that roan filly," he said drowsily.

Maddock's heart sank. Evidently, his father intended to work out in the bitter cold that day. Busying himself so he would not have to look up, he dumped his dirty water into the chamber pot and poured fresh for his face. "Yes, Father?"

"Need to start her on the short poles."

The young man splashed the icy water on his face, breathing in gasps, and considered Cadder's words. An acquisition from the autumn horse fair, the filly possessed the finest conformation points of the old blood: swift as a hawk, graceful as a deer, spirited as the east wind. *Mean as a weasel.* Maddock kept his tone casual. "Thought you planned to go over the feed accounts with the Lady."

The Horsemaster yawned. "Not until next week."

Face still dripping, Maddock carried the basin and ewer to the hearth, placing them near the fire to warm and holding his cold fingers near the flames. He did not say what he really thought; it would only lead to a futile argument. "Why the short poles?" he asked. The first set of lessons for teaching a horse to jump, it entailed walking her over poles arranged on the ground like rungs on a ladder. The roan filly had leaped every fence in Dorlach Tor, even vaulted her stall partition. "She already knows how to jump. It's the only thing that daughter of the Dark Court enjoys."

Cadder chuckled. "Don't talk that way about your sister."

Maddock made a noise of facetious protest. They had long shared this private joke, an affectionate dig at the Lord and Lady. "She's not my sister!" He poured water into the small cauldron, added a measure of barley, and set the porridge in the flames to cook.

"Son, what are you up to?"

Maddock did not want his father doing the morning chores without warm food in his belly, and the day meal at the Great House was hours away. "Making breakfast. I'm hungry." He glanced over his shoulder toward the bed. "Want some?"

Cadder grunted. "Hungry. Seems you're always hungry. Maybe you've got some growth coming on."

Maddock chuckled. "Maybe." He needed to talk to Vonora about living arrangements for his father but dreaded the discussion. He wanted Cadder to stay with them, and he feared she would not understand. His impending marriage brought a fresh stab of pain from his wounded heart. Hastily, he returned his thoughts to the previous conversation. "Tell me about the poles. Are you thinking our darling lass will kick them into kindling? Save toil for the fellows in the woodlot?"

The Horsemaster sat up in bed, pushing back the straw and blankets. "When we bought her from Ewyas Skarrd, they said her rider had died. Remember?"

Maddock nodded. "The cheating blackguards. 'Poor Spring Lark, pining for her mistress, won't let anyone else near her.' The liars knew that filly was trouble."

"I'm not so sure." Cadder ran a hand through his rumpled white hair, worsening its disarray. He was a large-boned man of massive strength, but his weathered face bore the stamp of his gentle spirit and boundless patience. "I'm guessing our lass suffered an accident, maybe out hunting, and took a bad fall. She got up, but her mistress didn't." He shook his head sadly. "A smart horse won't forget something like that, son. In her own mixed-up way, that filly blames herself for her rider's death. That's why she won't let anyone mount."

Not allowing himself to look at the bow over the bed, Maddock wondered how much of his father's interest in the filly stemmed from his grief over the hunting accident that left him a widower. *Gods! All the things we cannot say to those we love.* "So you'll start her all over again with baby lessons on jumping, since that's what she loves to do. Build up her confidence, comfort her, and teach her to want to cooperate."

"That's right. No more attempts to mount. Nothing but kind words, the lunge line, and easy jumping lessons." Cadder eased out of bed with painful care. "By midsummer, we'll have her so tame a newborn kitten could ride her."

Maddock stirred the porridge and furtively watched his father walk to the chamber pot, back and shoulders held stiffly. The young man averted his face, lest the pity in his eyes betray him, and cleared his throat. "Wind's blowing hard today. Damp. I can feel it in my elbow, from that clip old Harebell gave me last summer."

Cadder grunted. "Little sore myself."

Maddock never recalled his father admitting pain before. He watched the porridge bubble. "Do you suppose we might work the filly in the arena? It's a bit dark, I know, but it would be out of the wind."

Mostly utilized to store extra hay and feed, the arena had once served as the temple of the unwed Hepona. Dug below ground level, roofed over with heavy thatch, and lined with heaps of bundled straw, the building would be warm and dry.

Cadder lumbered to the hearth and picked up the ewer. "I suppose we might."

Maddock thought he detected a trace of laughter in his father's voice, and wondered if his motives had become that transparent. "I'm only thinking of the filly," he lied.

"Your sister?"

Maddock raised his chin. "My aunt."

After the morning chores, Maddock, Cadder, and the stable hands headed to the Great House for the day meal. A crowd filled the main hall, since the Lady had summoned everyone in from the village for the duration of the bitter weather. Some sat at the trestle tables lining the walls; others stood chatting in small groups. Despite the cold, a festive air reigned and laughter echoed along the stone ceiling.

Tousled by the wind, but pink-cheeked and bright-eyed, Maddock shouldered his way through the mob of grooms to reach a basket of fresh bread.

"Hey, there, Horsemaster's son!" one of the men called in a good-natured tone. "How many days till you wed?"

Pain lanced Maddock's heart. Feigning a single-minded interest in the bread, he snatched up a small loaf. "How many days?" He and Vonora would not exchange vows until March. He squinted, as if mentally calculating. "Three."

Another fellow clapped him on the shoulder. "More like fifty."

Maddock shrugged broadly. "Can't I dream?"

It was just what the other men wanted to hear. They whooped with laughter. Forcing himself to smile, Maddock ducked away.

The Lady's family sat together at the head table, all except for Kiarda's brother, Leith. Shoulders straight, eyes alight with pride, he stood behind his mother's chair holding a tall pole hung with the shimmering gold-and-burgundy banner of Dorlach Tor.

Weaving through the press, Maddock found his father by one of the side tables. "Why isn't Master Leith sitting down?"

"Old tradition," Cadder answered around a mouthful of bread. He swallowed and continued in a tone of approval. "The eldest son becomes Standard Bearer when he's thirteen, and today is Master Leith's thirteenth birthday."

"Oh."

"Our Lady Wylfre does things properly," he continued. "Why, I remember when—"

Four of Cadder's cronies strolled up just then, and the Horsemaster broke off to greet them. Their talk quickly turned to past winters, old traditions, and departed friends. Lost in conversation, Cadder wandered away with them to sit closer to the great hearth.

Finding himself suddenly alone, Maddock sat at the side table and studied Kiarda. She sat beside her mother, her narrow face unusually pale. He wondered if she felt unwell or sad. Once, he could simply have asked her. *What's wrong, 'Yarda?*

The Lady and her family carried the high blood, descendants of gods and heroes, keepers of ceremony and custom. The poor son of a Horsemaster, a mere liege man, had no right to love the Lady's heir; but love her he did and always would. He could not deny it to himself. *If only you knew, 'Yarda, how much it hurts. I miss you so.*

With a sudden, deep shock, Maddock realized Kiarda was looking back at him, staring into his eyes. Imagining she found his open regard offensive, he jerked his gaze away and touched his forehead in silent apology. A lump formed in his throat, and he had to swallow.

The next moment, Vonora settled opposite him at the table, eclipsing his view of Kiarda. "Good morning, my love."

Heart still stinging, Maddock turned his attention to his future wife. "Morning." He softened his expression, but his voice held a husky note. "Did you sleep warmly last night?"

Vonora's green eyes sparkled, evidently mistaking his tone for desire. "Very warmly, indeed," she purred. "I dreamed of you."

So sweet. Deserves better. "Really?" Maddock dragged his mind away from Kiarda and concentrated on his betrothed, focusing on the drift of musky scent from her hair, the luscious curve of her lips. "What a coincidence," he lied. "I dreamed of you."

Vonora's voice turned arch. "Well? Tell me."

"Can't." He floated his gaze to the ceiling, feigning coyness. " 'Tisn't something for a maiden's ears."

Any sort of teasing used to drive Kiarda wild. He recalled the abrupt flare of mingled playfulness and temper in her pale eyes, the way she jerked her chin up, the steely tone of her usual retort: "Do you want me to kick you to death?"

Vonora merely giggled.

Maddock's heart constricted.

"Then I'll tell you what I dreamed," she murmured.

Maddock managed to smile. He did not love her in the same way she loved him, but he would never allow her to discover that.

He owed her an eternal debt of gratitude for the return of his self-respect, for somewhat easing the pain of daily life. "Yes," he said softly. It felt like a lesson with Gaer: how to continue fighting in spite of a wound. "Tell me your dreams, my love. I hope some day to make them all come true."

Maddock paced out the distance between the twelve poles on the dirt floor, a lowly task more fit for a stable hand than the Horsemaster's son; but he had volunteered. The warm, dark confines of the arena curved around him, perfumed by last summer's clover. Phos-lamps glowed from brackets along the walls, casting a green-gold light over the arena's rough-beamed interior. Bundles of hay and bags of grain took up much of the space, leaving only the central area of the floor clear. Opposite the door, a life-sized statue of the unwed Hepona stood enshrouded in old horse blankets. The cruel winds seemed unable to penetrate the structure; and, for the first time in a week, Maddock felt comfortable enough to remove his cloak.

Maddock reveled in the moments of privacy as well. The intense loneliness of the great hall full of people had nearly overwhelmed him. He missed his walk to and from Scratter Wood, with its opportunity for contemplation. *I miss Gaer.* An abrupt pang of sorrow brought tears to his eyes, which he hastily blinked back. He wished he knew if his mentor were alive or dead.

Maddock's gaze fell upon the covered figure of the goddess. He remembered worshiping her as a child, with Gaer officiating as chief priest. He recalled nicking his finger for the blood offering and the Swordmaster's voice raised in prayer. *Almighty Hepona, I am yours. I dare expect nothing from you but death. Use me as you will.*

A sudden urge to invoke her, to plea for her intercession came upon Maddock. Without thinking, he left the poles lying on the floor and went to the statue.

Dust, straw, and bird droppings covered the blankets. Carefully, Maddock peeled away the shroud. Portrayed as a young woman with golden hair and blue eyes, Hepona gazed out over her former temple. She held a sword in her left hand, her expression cold and pitiless. Maddock swallowed. A deity of dread power, the unwed goddess little resembled her image at the Reunion: a motherly figure with a comforting smile. It had been a mistake to imagine approaching her for intercession. *As well ask the wind for mercy.*

Bundles of oiled wool lay at the statue's feet. Thinking of Gaer's practice irons, Maddock unrolled one and discovered it contained several swords. Phos-light sparkled along richly worked hilts, twinkling in the occasional jewel. Lips parted in wonder, the young man crouched, unmoving. One of the swords possessed no ornament but its own graceful lines. Hands trembling, he freed it from the wraps and raised it. Dim light played along its length, marking the subtle weave of the damasked blade. He rose, testing its balance. *Perfect.*

An excitement more appropriate to the marriage bed raced through Maddock. He executed a simple thrust and parry maneuver, and the weapon sliced the air like a swallow's wing. "Beautiful," he whispered.

Maddock found a clear space on the dirt floor and performed an elementary series of warm-up Dances. The sword seemed a living extension of his body, directly connected to his will, linked to his spirit. For the first time in months, Maddock felt whole again, free from hampering doubt. He worked into more advanced Dances, using the short poles for added complexity. He turned, feinted, and leaped. Every movement flowed seamlessly into the next. His breath came easily. A slight smile curved his lips. He wished Gaer could see him.

Outside, the wind screamed.

Maddock froze. *Gaer.* The grief grew so intense that, for several heartbeats, it banished all thought. A veil of tears covered his vision; his shoulders locked. He fought to retain a manly composure, but a sob tore his throat. Dropping the sword, he pressed his face into his hands. *Oh, Master.* He thought the helplessness and sorrow would kill him. *I'm sorry.*

A small noise, like the scuff of a boot heel, came from behind him. Maddock whirled.

Heavily cloaked and disheveled by the wind, Lord Stane

leaned against a pile of bagged oats. His voice was calm. "That's no way to treat a fine weapon."

Maddock dashed the tears from his eyes and touched his forehead. "My lord, I—" He cleared his throat. "I didn't hear you come in."

"You were busy." Though Stane's tone betrayed no anger, his blue eyes glinted. He stalked toward the young man. In the golden-green light, he seemed as shadowy and mysterious as one of the Fair Folk: shining hair, rich clothing, an aura of danger. "So the rumors are true."

"My lord?"

"Don't play stupid with me. I saw you." Stane indicated the sword with the toe of his boot. "Pick that up."

"Yes, my lord." Shoulders trembling, Maddock obeyed. He held the hilt loosely between both hands, trying not to display too much confidence with the weapon, and wondered how to explain. "My lord, I—"

"Quiet." Though spoken without heat, the word snapped like a whip.

The Horsemaster's son flinched.

Stane moved to the statue of Hepona, studying the heaps of blankets, the pillaged cache of swords. "I heard the stories, of course, but I didn't want to believe them." He turned to the young man. "What shall I do with you?"

"My lord?"

Stane gestured at the sword in Maddock's hands. "Blasphemy."

Outside, the wind keened. Ice glazing his heart, Maddock stood motionless, remembering the exaltation he felt while performing the Dances, wondering how something so holy could be called profane.

Stane regarded Maddock sidelong, seemed to gauge his reaction, and nodded slightly. "Yes, you'd better think about it. I have a sworn duty to inform the priests. They may declare you outcast." He sighed and turned toward the statue of Hepona. "This is going to kill your father."

"My father," Maddock breathed. He closed his eyes against a sudden image: Cadder as a broken old man with no one to care for him. *My father.* He saw the Swordmaster lying dead in the snow, silver hair whipped by the wind. The cold in his heart deepened, and he opened his eyes. "You'll sell me to the priests? As you did Gaer?"

Stane turned slowly and spoke in a tone of tightly reined fury. "How dare you speak that name in my presence."

In a single instant, all Maddock's careful control shattered, all respect, love, and loyalty swept away by a flood of pain too long concealed. "Why?" he demanded. "Does his name remind you of your lies? The Holy Peace? The Divine Reunion? Those are your blasphemies!"

"Impudent whelp!" Stane raised his hand as if to deliver a backhanded slap.

Without thought, Maddock jerked into a defensive posture, sword ready.

Stane's eyes widened. A peculiar expression stole over his face, part respect, part scorn, overlaid with an air of speculation. "So. You think you can take me, do you?"

Maddock warily backed away, not trusting himself to speak.

Keeping his bright gaze on the Horsemaster's son, Stane bent and picked up a sword. "I asked you a question, lad." He unfastened his cloak with his free hand and let it slide to the dirty floor. With blinding speed, he performed an immaculate series of movements. His blade sang as it cut the air. "Think you can take me?"

Maddock's skin prickled, but something warned him to show no fear. "I have a good Master."

"The best." Stane laughed mirthlessly and shifted into a crouch. "I had the same Master." Without warning, he cut for Maddock's head.

Stunned by the sudden attack, Maddock backstepped more by instinct than intent. The blade sliced the air where he had stood with deadly speed. Terror ground through him, sweat springing from every pore. He raised his sword in time to catch Stane's next lightning attack. Impact hammered through his fists, nearly driving the hilt from his fingers. He retreated another step, holding his gaze on his opponent's hands, as Gaer had taught him.

Stane made a crisp motion with his free hand, as if directing

Maddock to attack. Even as he tensed to obey, Stane bore in again. Maddock sprang aside, parrying, and this time he managed a return strike. A thought rushed into his head with the action. *If I harm the Lord of Dorlach Tor, my life is over.* Panic turned the offense into an awkward thrust. Yet, Maddock realized as he barely blocked another charge, if he did not defend, he would be just as dead.

Twice more, Stane's sword jabbed for him and Maddock dodged, giving ground. The tears he had suppressed returned to his eyes, hopeless and hot. Trapped in an unwinnable situation, he blocked, parried, and evaded, without thought to attack. Exhaustion pressed his movements, and he worried for his strategy. Eventually, he would have to attack or forfeit his life. Honor warred desperately with the instinct for survival. As Stane's blade swept toward him for what seemed like the hundredth time, he wove his blade around it, then surged for the opening.

Sidestepping the attack, sword locked with Maddock's, Stane hurled himself at the Horsemaster's son. Before Maddock could think to move, Stane crashed against him. The young man staggered backward, heel slamming down on a pole Stane had surely seen. It rolled beneath Maddock's foot, pitching him backward. He tumbled, balance wholly lost. Stane's fist, weighted by his hilt, slammed Maddock's mouth as he fell.

Pain exploded through Maddock's face then, an instant later, through the back of his head. His hand crashed against the floor, and his sword skittered into the shadows of the bundled hay. Shaken by the blow, panting for air, he sprawled on the dirt floor, tensed for Stane's final blow. Blood trickled down his chin, and his tongue found the split in his lip. When the death strike did not come, he peered blearily up at his lord, who knelt at his side. Stane no longer held a weapon either.

The Lord of Dorlach Tor reached down. Gently, he wiped away the young man's blood, then displayed the crimson smears on his fingers. "See that?" he asked calmly.

Maddock nodded dizzily.

"That's what war is all about." Stane's kindly tone lacked its earlier anger. "Your blood, your opponents' blood, the blood of horses, and the blood of people you love. It is sheer butchery, bearing no resemblance to those pretty Dances Gaer teaches. Think long and carefully, lad, before you give yourself to the warrior's way. Do you understand me?"

Maddock found himself trembling. "Yes, my lord."

"Good." Stane's expression softened. He offered his hand. "Let me help you up. I'm sure that floor is cold."

Maddock gripped the hand in both of his. "Thank you, my lord." He allowed himself to be hauled to his feet.

Stane released his hold with an encouraging smile and patted the young man's shoulder. "Not bad, actually," he murmured in an undertone, barely loud enough for Maddock to hear. "But you keep your elbow too tight."

The young man touched his forehead. "Yes, my lord." Then he raised his eyes and saw his father standing by the door.

Cadder's face seemed colorless, locked in an expression of grief.

Maddock felt as if his heart stopped. He wished the Horsemaster would shout, strike him, call him names; he could bear anything better than the knowledge that he had caused his father pain.

Cadder's mouth twitched, as if attempting to frame words.

"Father—" Maddock found his own voice thick with tears.

The Horsemaster spoke in a whisper. "Son—" Sorrow deepened the lines of his careworn face. "Why?"

"I—" Maddock did not know what to say.

"You raised a sword against your liege."

Retrieving his cloak from the floor, Stane cleared his throat. "My fault, actually. I forced the fight."

Cadder turned his reproachful gaze to the lord. "And now?" he asked softly. "Will I lose my son?"

Stane tilted his head. "I must confess this event to the priests, but I doubt they'll outcast Maddock." His blue eyes flashed. "If they do, they'll have to toss me out, too. And I'm jolly well not going anywhere."

Maddock's lips parted as the sudden realization hit home; the fight had been a ploy. *He saved me!*

The Horsemaster sank to his knees and kissed the hem of Stane's cloak. "My most gracious lord."

"Oh, Cadder," Stane said affectionately. "Get up off the floor. It's dirty." He raised the other man and briskly brushed the straw from his clothes. "And stop looking so sad. No real harm done, eh?"

A new respect for his lord took root in Maddock, strengthened by an unfamiliar awareness of Stane as simply another man. He remembered what Gaer said about Stane; confidence in his own honesty made him prone to self-deception. Maddock wondered if that remained true, if Stane lived with a burden of compromises greater than the one he himself bore. Moving stiffly, he approached the lord and presented a deep bow. "My life is yours. I will gladly endure any punishment you deem just."

"You've already been punished." Stane's tone was firm. "The priests undoubtedly will find something appropriate for me. Fasting, most likely, interspersed with long prayers and lots of incense. Dashed dull."

Cadder turned to his son, still looking shaken. "How—?" He stumbled over the words. "How did you learn to handle a sword?"

"I—" Maddock wiped blood from his mouth and chin with the back of his hand, the cut on his lip and a headache the worst of his injuries.

"He's been taking lessons," Stane interrupted.

Cadder glanced in confusion from his son to Stane. "Lessons?"

Stane nodded. "With a certain outcast who lives in Scratter Wood." He raised his brows. "But the lessons will stop. Won't they, Maddock?"

Horror raced through the young man. *No!*

"Yes," Cadder answered. "Of course, my lord." He gently laid his hands on Maddock's shoulders. "Swear you'll never touch a sword again."

Utterly trapped, Maddock dropped his head. His black hair fell over his eyes, shielding them. "Never again." The enormity of the lie scalded his spirit, bathed him in shame, and caused his voice to come out in a strangled whisper. "I swear it."

Cadder embraced him, his voice thick with tears. "Good lad."

Maddock glanced over his father's shoulder toward the statue of Hepona. The thought seemed to come from outside, that he had been a coward long enough. In spite of the killing temperature, he needed to go to Scratter Wood, to see if Gaer still lived. It was time.

Merciless, stern, powerful, the goddess seemed to meet the young man's gaze. She offered no solace or certainty, only strength. The Lady of All Battles, she reigned over not only the bloody conflicts fought with swords, but also the endless turmoil in every man's spirit.

Maddock would not forswear the sword, though it meant betraying his liege lord's trust, breaking his father's heart, and losing the only home he had ever known. Forsaking everyone and everything he loved, he would give himself to the warrior's way. *Almighty Hepona, I am yours.*

The wind stopped as the afternoon faded into early evening, but the cold remained. Kiarda lay in bed beneath every blanket and cloak she possessed. Frost thickly covered the hinges on the shuttered windows, and the bright tapestries on the wall swayed in the continuous draft which crept along the floor. It would be warmer in her parents' bedchamber, she knew, snuggled up with Leith and Ladayla in the extra bed; but she could not bear to see her father. He had submitted to another flogging from the priests.

Kiarda should not know that secret, but she could always tell when it happened. Though both the Lord and Lady took care to behave as usual, her father's gaze seemed glassy and distracted and her mother seethed with suppressed fury. Vecco of Egas Cairn, whose clan recalled a long history of blood feud against her father's family, had gained supremacy within the priesthood of the Joyous Reunion by a series of complex political maneuvers. Even if Dorlach Tor could endure the economic hardships of openly defying the priesthood, they could not risk alienating the other Great Houses by such a tactic. Vecco and his cohorts took full advantage of the situation, repeatedly accusing Dorlach Tor's folk of heresy or blasphemy. Kiarda's father always took the punishment for his people. It was an act of pride, and a message to Vecco that Lord Stane knew his true motives. Kiarda bit her lips. *Whose punishment did he take this time?* It nearly hurt her too much to contemplate. *Mine?*

A random gust of wind wailed. Kiarda rolled onto her side and tried to think about something else, something pleasant. Bevin would sense her unhappiness and would come to offer comfort; she did not want to impel her friend to leave a warm bed in the cookhouse. *Nice things: Leith is Standard Bearer, Elrin got a new tooth, Ladayla braided my hair this morning.*

From outside came another thin, ululating cry. Kiarda abruptly realized it was not the wind she heard, but a fox. Acting on wild impulse, she scrambled from bed and dashed to the window. Her breath steamed as she shot back the bolts on the shutters and flung them open. Snow from the window ledge fell onto the floor, and a deadly chill invaded the room. Gasping from the cold, she leaned out the window, listening.

The fox called again from the direction of the orchard. Kiarda looked toward the trees, believing she understood. Only passion, only the heat of mating could defy winter's domination. In a life filled with death, the few pleasures must be embraced. [[*Fire burns my loins,*]] sang the dog fox. [[*Come to me, come to me, my willing vixen.*]]

Kiarda hoisted herself onto the window ledge and swung her feet out. In the next instant, aghast, she stopped herself. "What am I doing?" She stared down at the sloping rooftop five feet below, still fighting a strong urge to jump. Her vision blurred and darkened. "Gods help me . . ."

⁂

The vixen shook herself free of the encumbering fabric, leaped through the window, streaked across the roof, and jumped to the ground. Frightened and disoriented, she paused in the shadow of a stone fence and lifted her nose. She sifted through the scents of humans, dogs, and woodsmoke, seeking traces of her own kind.

The entrancing song of the male resonated through the still

air, pulsing with desire. She pricked her large ears toward the call and hesitantly yapped in reply.

The summons turned insistent, a quavering howl of longing. It awakened a strange hunger within her. White fur blending smoothly with the snow, the vixen glided away to meet the male. It was time.

CHAPTER SIX

M ADDOCK leaned against the rough bole of an oak to rest. Though a sudden thaw tempered the winter chill, the warm air made the drifted snow heavy. After several hours of sloughing his way through the woods, the young man worried that his breath came too slowly to match his laboring heart. Birdsong filled Scratter Wood, and the bare trees seemed to bask in the golden sunlight. Water sparkled on melting ice or fell in a musical patter from overhanging branches. A stream chattered nearby, its voice at last free of winter's grip.

Slowly, Maddock straightened and looked around. Everything seemed different covered with snow. Angles were softened, the trees and the contours of the land sculpted in white. He thought he followed the trail to the practice clearing, but a wraithlike concern flitted through his mind. He might be lost. "At least it's warm," he muttered.

The ground rose to the right, where the trail ought to be. Gathering his strength and resolve, Maddock resumed his awkward journey. As he battled his way through the snow, he reflected again on the unspoiled loveliness of Scratter Wood. It struck him as odd that the Dark Court did not hold sway over a swamp or abandoned mine but chose instead to dwell among towering oak trees. *Perhaps even evil things appreciate beauty.* It made sense. He was evil, according to the laws of the Joyous Reunion; and he cherished Scratter Wood as a second home.

Maddock imagined the Queen of the Dark Court appearing in front of him. Raven-haired, cloaked in shadows, she would beckon to him and he would follow her down hidden ways to the center of a hill. Together, they would enter a great hall lit by colored torches and join a feasting throng. The tables held steam-

ing platters of roasted venison and boar, running with juices, sea-
soned with marjoram; frosted goblets of wine; and trenchers of
crusty bread filled with butter-fried mushrooms. The ringing
chords of a brass-strung harp mingled with the laughter of those
who dined.

Maddock saw a childhood friend, Threv, who had drowned in
the river; old Fawley, who used to keep watch at night; and his
own mother, a small woman dressed in hunting leathers. Heart
beating in his throat, he rushed toward her smiling embrace. "I
knew you weren't dead," he said through rising tears. "I just
knew it."

His mother wrapped her arms around him and laid her head
on his shoulder. "My little boy," she whispered. "A grown man."

Lost in trembling, bittersweet joy, Maddock closed his
eyes. Her hair softly brushed his cheek, and he felt her heart
beat against his ribs in a birdlike flutter. He never wanted to release her.

A familiar voice cut through the music and laughter. "Maddock!"

The young man opened his eyes and turned.

Gaer stood beside a great hearth of fieldstone. The Swordmaster's elegant features were rigid with alarm, and he raised his
left hand in the horned sign of Hernis, a ward against evil en-
chantment. "Maddock!" He spoke as if awakening a sleeper.
"Maddock!"

Gasping, the young man found himself jerked back to the
sunny morning and the tinkle of falling ice. Gaer's voice seemed
to hang in the air.

"Master?" Maddock spun, wildly searching for his beloved
mentor. He saw only the trunks of trees, rabbit tracks in the
snow, and leafless whips of undergrowth. He was alone in the
woods. His voice sank to a whisper. "Master?"

Maddock's heart raced, and he also made the sign of Hernis.
It had seemed so real: the aroma of venison, his mother's embrace. He might have stood there for a hundred years and a day,
caught in the Dark Court's snare, if not for the Swordmaster's
warning. Maddock licked his dry lips, trying to think. He could
not allow fear to turn him from his purpose. He needed to find

Gaer, to know whether his master was alive or dead. He had sworn by Hepona. Clenching his jaw, he trudged one step forward.

An inhuman cry split the air.

Maddock's blood turned to ice. His joints unknit, and he fell to his knees in the snow. *Dark Court!*

The wail echoed through the sunlit wood, stark, filled with unutterable grief.

Each blow of Maddock's heart shook him to the core. He swayed, and his vision darkened. He was going to faint, he knew it, like a maiden at the sight of a rat. Anger for his own weakness filtered through his terror. "Almighty Hepona," he hissed.

The cry came again, drawn out, anguished. "Hau . . . ah!"

Over the thunder of his own heart, Maddock strained to listen. A creature of the Dark Court would not sound so sad.

"Hau-au. . . ." The wail faded into a doglike whine.

Maddock abruptly recognized the cry. *A fox.* The chill in his blood melted with the heat of shame. He clambered to his feet, trembling. "Idiot!" He straightened his clothing and smoothed back his hair. "Cowardly fool!"

The fox called again, desperate, sorrowing.

Maddock started off toward the sound. Perhaps it was hurt. He knew only a little doctoring, mostly for horses, but he could not ignore the poor creature. Wading hip-deep through snow, he followed its cries to a clearing.

Sunlight filtered through the trees in long bars. Sparrows chirped in the leafless undergrowth, rejoicing in the unseasonable warmth. In the middle of the clearing, a naked young woman lay facedown in the melting snow, her pale hair fanned across her back. A fox, white in its winter pelt, stood by her head like a faithful dog. It pawed her shoulder, whimpering, then threw up its muzzle and howled its grief.

Maddock stood rooted, lips parted in wonder. His gaze traveled from the sweep of the woman's hair down the graceful curve of her back to her shapely bottom and long legs. His blood reared like a stallion, and heated fantasies crowded his mind, even as he realized he ought to avert his eyes, ought to help her.

Galvanized by his own shame, Maddock pulled off his cloak

and held it up, blocking his view of everything but her head. "Hey," he called softly, trudging toward her. "Lady? Can you hear me?" Careful not to glimpse her nakedness again, he draped his cloak over her. "Lady?"

The fox's ears pressed flat against its skull. It retreated a few steps, then returned to the woman's side. It nuzzled her ear, whining, then turned its eyes to the young man, as if pleading for his help.

"It's all right, my lad," Maddock murmured gently. "I won't harm her."

Her back rose and fell with deep, untroubled breaths. She seemed merely to sleep, though she lay in thawing snow.

Hand trembling with several strong and conflicting emotions, Maddock brushed the hair from her face, trying not to notice how it flowed like silk through his fingers. Her features looked serene, dreaming. It took him a moment to recognize her. *Kiarda!*

Maddock flung himself backward, as if burned. He had done the unforgivable. He had touched the future Lady of Dorlach Tor. He staggered to his feet and pressed his hands against his hot face. "Gods, gods, gods!"

The fox pawed Kiarda's shoulder, then curled into the curve of her neck and laid its head against her cheek. Maddock stared at it, struck by its devotion. No wild animal would behave like that, and he wondered if she had somehow secretly kept the fox as a pet. Its tracks marked the snow all around her.

Scalp prickling, Maddock studied the clearing. Aside from his own churned path, the fox tracks were the only prints in the snow. He saw no trace of Kiarda's trail, and several horrid scenarios involving the Dark Court harried his mind. He recalled his recent waking dream and Gaer's voice dragging him back to reality.

The Swordmaster's training, and Maddock's own strong will, reclaimed his spirit. He clenched his jaw and shook the hair from his eyes. Right or wrong, he could not leave Kiarda lying in the snow. He knelt beside her again. " 'Yarda? Wake up. It's me." He cautiously felt her over for injuries, trying to ignore how warm and soft she felt beneath the cloak. He found no obvious wounds. " 'Yarda?"

The fox watched Maddock but did not move, seeming to sense that he meant to help.

"Don't worry, little laddie," Maddock said gently. "I'll take good care of her." Moving with a new sense of purpose, he wrapped her up in his cloak and used his belt to tie it into place.

The fox backed away a few steps, still watching, large ears quivering at the slightest sound.

" 'Yarda? This is Maddock." He did not know whether or not she could hear him, but he spoke in case she could. "Don't be afraid. I'm taking you home." He picked her up, relieved when his cloak did not fall open to reveal anything. Loose-jointed and warm in his arms, Kiarda proved heavier than her slender figure suggested. Maddock gazed at her face. Childhood playmate, friend, and future Lady, she was his world. Love mingled his physical desire with tender protectiveness, until he could no longer tell the two emotions apart. He knew he ought to be ashamed of himself, yet he would rather die than stop loving her.

Maddock turned toward Dorlach Tor and began to retrace his path. The fox pattered along beside him, its feet making soft, crisp sounds in the snow. "Don't be afraid, 'Yarda," he repeated as he walked. "Don't be afraid. I won't let anyone hurt you."

Not even me.

The sun slanted from the opposite direction by the time Maddock arrived at Dorlach Tor. His concern for Kiarda had deepened with every step; she remained unconscious and he feared for her life. Maddock's worry had prevented him from stopping for rest, pushing him onward long after exhaustion racked his body. He scarcely realized when he reached his goal and stood in the main hallway. His lungs burned, and he gasped for air as he tried to answer the questions flung at him.

The women took Kiarda from Maddock and carried her away. Soaked and muddy, he crouched on the flagstones of the Great Hall.

Lord Stane bent to look him in the eye. "Well? I'm waiting."

"In the woods," Maddock panted. "I found her in the woods.

Carried—" His dry throat constricted, and he coughed. "Carried her . . . no other way . . . sorry. . . ."

The folk of Dorlach Tor gathered around the two men in a tight circle, silent and listening. Maddock's memories stirred: a crowded courtyard, a dying stallion, Gaer's face in the torchlight.

Someone brought a cup of water. Stane took it and gave it to Maddock with his own hand. "You carried Kiarda all the way from Scratter Wood? How did she get there?"

"Don't know." Maddock emptied the cup in three eager gulps. "I think maybe . . . the Other Ones. . . ." He clamped his eyes shut, trying to speak clearly. "I'm not sure. I think I saw them. They had my mother. And old Fawley. And Threv—" He broke off, shaking his head. He sounded like a madman. "Lady Kiarda was lying in the snow. And there was a fox." He opened his eyes and looked at Stane. "A white fox."

The Lord of Dorlach Tor blanched. "A fox," he whispered. "No."

The gathered folk broke into fearful muttering. "A sign . . . the Dark Court."

Maddock glanced around. "I think it followed me all the way to the village."

"And you." Stane gripped the young man's chin roughly. "What were you doing in Scratter Wood?" His blue eyes narrowed dangerously. "Visiting the outcast?"

"Yes, my lord. But—" Maddock raised a placating hand. "Only to see if he still lived. I was worried."

The anger melted from Stane's face, and he released Maddock's chin. "And did you find him?"

"I'm not sure." Maddock tried to sort through the morning's events, but none seemed real. Even his discovery of Kiarda felt dreamlike. "I think he called my name, but—" Maddock could not bring himself to finish, did not want to believe Gaer among the dead in the halls of the Dark Court. "I'm not sure. It was all so confusing."

A plump, young woman stepped from the crowd and timidly curtsied to Stane. She wore full skirts in the style of the River

People, rather than trousers; and flour covered her wide apron. Maddock recognized her as one of old Sygil's students.

Stane raised his brows. "Yes, lass?"

"My lord." She curtsied again, her round face turning bright red. "If you please, my name is Bevin. I'm gifted with the Sight, and I can see that Maddock is telling the truth."

The crowd stirred and broke into a new round of murmurs. "Saved her life . . . the Horsemaster's son. . . ."

Stane smiled at her. "Thank you, Bevin."

Bevin curtsied a third time, then pressed her floured apron to her face and fled through the throng.

The Lord of Dorlach Tor stood up and offered Maddock his hand. "Get up, son."

Heart stinging with both pride and the memory of their duel, Maddock accepted the offered hand and allowed Stane to pull him to his feet. "My gracious lord."

"Forgive me, please," Stane said unsteadily. "I doubted you when I should have thanked you."

Maddock's throat tightened with a rush of tangled emotions. "I live but to serve, my lord."

Stane placed his hands on Maddock's shoulders. "You're too modest, my faithful liege man. I shall not forget your loyalty."

Remembering how his blood had burned at the sight of Kiarda's naked body, Maddock dropped his eyes in shame. "My lord."

Stane surveyed the gathered folk, raising his voice to carry through the hall. "Saddle my stallion. Call the hounds and bring my bow. I've a mind to go hunting in Scratter Wood." His blue eyes gleamed with rising fury. "And woe to the evil wight who snatched my daughter from her bed."

Maddock's head snapped up. "My lord, I crave a boon!" He fell to his knees. "Let me ride with you!"

"And me!" shouted another man. "And me!" cried a third. The crowd dissolved into roars, as men and women pressed forward to kneel before their lord.

Stane swept his arm in a wide gesture of command, as if summoning his folk to battle. "To horse!"

The hunting party set off through the gates of Dorlach Tor at a brisk pace. Stane rode at the fore, the Hunt-Keeper on his left and Maddock on his right.

Though Maddock's head felt like a lead weight, his stomach gnawed at its own lining, and his thoughts were tangled by exhaustion, he could not help falling under the spell of his lord's anger. Consumed with the idea of vengeance against the Dark Court, he ignored his body's demands for food and rest. At the back of his mind lurked the notion of redemption. He would cleanse himself of the horrible crime of desiring Kiarda and of abandoning his sworn quest for Gaer.

The riders quickly found the point where the fox's tracks diverged from Maddock's. It had apparently stopped at the edge of the village, paced a bit, then returned to Scratter Wood. Stane nodded with grim satisfaction. "I've heard stories about this. The creature of darkness is trapped in animal shape until sundown."

The hunters rode through the sloppy snow and mud as fast as the horses could bear. Stane's face seemed lit from within. His golden hair streamed against the flawless blue sky. Again, to Maddock's eyes, he appeared inhuman, like one of the Fair Folk, magical and dangerous. Following Maddock's trail, they entered Scratter Wood single file. Byrta, the Hunt-Keeper, led the way, leaning low in her saddle to scan the snowy ground for tracks. When they reached the clearing, she dismounted and studied the area for a long while in silence.

"Well?" Stane said finally.

Byrta looked up at her lord from a crouch, her lean brown face creased with astonishment. "It's as young Maddock claimed. There're no tracks but those of foxes." She inclined her head toward an irregular depression, the deeper portions frozen to ice. "And there's where she lay in the snow, with not a sign of how she got here."

Maddock knit his dark brows in confusion. "Foxes?" he repeated. "I saw only one."

Byrta pointed at something in the snow, evidently obvious to her. "Two different tracks, maybe male and female. Hard to tell with all the melting."

Stane's eyes narrowed. "Doesn't matter. Where do the tracks come from? I want their lair."

Grunting, Byrta jabbed a mittened hand toward the heart of Scratter Wood. "That direction."

Stane dismounted, and all of his companions did as well. He indicated several members of the party with brisk jerks of his hand. "Keep the horses," he ordered the reluctant riders he had selected. "And stay alert. If we don't return by nightfall, carry the news back to the Lady."

The remainder of the hunting party, including Maddock, clambered over slippery rocks and pressed through knotted undergrowth, their progress slow and toilsome. Gradually, dusk settled over the gaps in the foliage, and Maddock's bleary vision registered only a smear of endless gray. Evening wind rolled between them, chilling where it touched.

Byrta suddenly cried out, "My lord!"

Blinking rapidly, Maddock peered over Stane's shoulder. A hill rose up in front of them, perfectly shaped and covered with thorn. "Bend your bows," Stane commanded. "Spread out. Let nothing escape." He reached into the pouch on his belt and pulled out a tinderbox. "I should have done this years ago."

Maddock took position with the others, standing beside Vonora. The hunting bow felt unfamiliar in his hand, and he found himself wishing he held a sword instead.

Stane kindled a torch. Clutching it high above his head, he approached the hill with firm, deliberate steps. Shadows fled before its brightness. "Foul creatures of evil." His voice turned awful with barely contained rage. "Never again will you cause the innocent to suffer. I, Stane, son of Stane, Lord of Dorlach Tor and servant to Lady Wylfre, judge you guilty of the foulest of crimes. And I shall carry out your doom." He thrust the torch into the thorns. The flames caught greedily on the dry vines and spread, sizzling against melting collections of snow.

A hare bolted from the burning hill.

Face pale, Vonora shot the hare cleanly through the heart. It collapsed, hind legs tumbling over fore, churning up narrow gouts of snow.

"Well done!" Stane ran to where the carcass lay, picked it up by the piercing arrow, and flung it into the fire. "Burn!" he shouted. "Burn!"

The flames blazed, orange prancing through red, throwing coils of smoke into the air. The hunters stood, watching, until the last of the thorns crumbled to ash and Maddock's exhausted eyes turned the hill to another gray blur. The minuscule effort of shifting his vision seemed too great to bother.

The sun was sinking toward early winter night when Stane finally said, "Let's go, my friends." He trudged to Maddock and laid a fatherly hand on his shoulder. "Before our folk with the horses decide to make us walk to Dorlach Tor."

Lady Wylfre awaited the hunting party in the Great Hall. She sat in her chair upon the dais, with young Leith holding the standard and all the priests and healers ranged about her in formal assembly. The tables leaned, folded up, against the walls and all the people from the village and the House formed an aisle leading to the dais.

Cheeks scarlet from cold, hair and clothing acrid with smoke, Maddock walked through the crowd with the rest of the hunting party. The grim expressions he observed on every face awakened a caution that supplanted fatigue. Every eye dodged his, and he could not locate his father in the hall.

Apparently oblivious, Stane mounted the dais steps with an easy grace and knelt before the Lady. Wylfre stood to greet him and raised him with her hand. Then, she leaned to whisper in his ear.

Stane's smile vanished, and he glanced at Maddock. A fire hotter than the one in Scratter Wood sparked in his pale eyes. His fingers winched to bloodless fists.

Unconsciously, Maddock backstepped, seized by sudden understanding. He had seen Kiarda unclad, and they meant to punish him. He recalled how he had wickedly lusted for her. *Deserve a whipping.* Maddock held his shoulders straight and schooled his features to composure, as if facing an enemy with a sword. He would not argue against the Lady's judgment but would suffer like a man.

Stane and Wylfre continued their whispered conference for a few moments, the Lord's hands opening and clenching. Tensed like an overdrawn bowstring, he stormed from the hall by a side door accompanied by an edgy crowd of priestesses and healers. The Lady resumed her chair, her expression revealing nothing. "Maddock, come forward," she ordered evenly. "The rest of you stand aside and attend."

Maddock's heart sank, but he took three steps toward the dais and waited. Behind him, the others from the hunting party shuffled into the crowd.

Wylfre nodded toward the remaining healers, and three of them gathered beside her chair. Old Sygil took the left-hand position, shriveled and bent like a twig, her expression bright and fierce. The second, a pasty-faced male newcomer named Glist, chewed nervously on a hangnail. Bevin stepped to Wylfre's right, her gentle eyes pink and puffy from weeping.

"Maddock," Wylfre said. "Tell me why you went to Scratter Wood."

The young man blinked in surprise. It was not the question he had expected. "To find Master—" He stopped himself from speaking Gaer's name. "To find the outcast Swordmaster, my lady. I was—still am—concerned for his well-being."

Sygil grunted. "Truth."

Glist nodded in anxious agreement.

Bevin stared reproachfully at the Horsemaster's son and pressed her thumb knuckle against her bottom lip.

Frowning slightly, Wylfre seemed to notice the healer's hesitation. "Yes, child?" she said mildly. "Speak up."

Bevin swallowed and turned her gaze to the lady. "The truth," the healer said reluctantly. "But he's hiding something."

A hissing whisper spread through the gathered folk.

Maddock's heart beat faster. Clearly, the healer somehow sensed that he meant to continue his sword training. He would have to guard his tongue.

"Silence," Wylfre called, and an abrupt hush fell over the hall. "Hiding something," she repeated thoughtfully. "Hiding many things, I shouldn't wonder." She leaned back in her chair and regarded the young man in front of her. "When you found Kiarda in the woods, did you touch her?"

Heat rose to Maddock's face. "Not—not indecently," he stammered. "Not beyond what was necessary to cover her up and bring her here." Stung by guilt, he remembered the rush of desire he felt holding her in his arms. "I wouldn't—I—"

Wylfre interrupted, "Your father has confessed everything. He told me you have lusted after Kiarda for years."

"No!" Maddock blurted. "It wasn't like that! I didn't—"

"Cadder said the two of you argued over the matter constantly. That you refused to listen to—"

"No, no, no!" Horror robbed Maddock of any sense of courtesy. "That's crazy! I would never—"

Wylfre's tone remained calm and impersonal. "Yesterday, my Lord Stane caught you in an act of blasphemy and beat you for it. And so, last night, in retaliation, you lured my daughter to the black heart of the Scratter Wood—"

"No!"

"—and ravished her!"

"No!" Maddock's voice broke with the force of his denial. He glared at the healers. "Tell her!"

Glist shifted and licked his lips. "He seems to be telling the truth, but—" He broke off and looked at Sygil.

"Oh, yes," the old healer said sourly. "But not all the truth."

Bevin slowly shook her head. "Until now, I have never seen the shadows of deceit covering a person so thickly." She turned her earnest gaze to Wylfre. "My lady, it's as if he wears a cloak spun of lies."

Vonora pushed her way through the crowd, her enormous eyes filled with tears. "Maddock! Tell me it's not so!"

The sight of her grief was nearly too much for Maddock. He swallowed painfully. "Vonora, I love you. I would never—"

"A lie!" Sygil jabbed her bony finger accusingly. "A bald-faced lie!"

"Seize him," Wylfre commanded.

With a roar, the assembly in the hall swept toward Maddock in two converging waves. He tried to protest, tried to reason with them, but their shouts drowned out his words. Hands crushed into his flesh, hot and violent. *Kiarda violated.* The realization sapped what little strength fatigue and shock had left him. *The healers could tell.* Belatedly, he attempted to struggle as the crowd spread-eagled him above their heads. Their fingers gouged bruises into his arms and legs. "I didn't do it!" As before, his words were lost in the hubbub. His own thoughts mocked him. *Who did?*

"Get him out of my sight," Wylfre said in quiet contempt. "And out of my House. Lock him up in one of the sheds. We'll hang him at sunrise tomorrow."

⟡

Maddock woke up cold and alone. He lay on his belly, hands tied behind his back, clothing stiff with his own blood. He attempted to raise his head. Pain knifed through his skull. He stifled a gasp, letting his face sink to the dirty ground.

The citizens of Dorlach Tor had dragged him from the hall and beat him. Maddock recalled only isolated fragments, dark and red with pain: features twisted with hatred, childhood friends pinning him down while others kicked him, Vonora spitting in his face. He withdrew from the memories with the ease of long practice, disconnecting them from the agony in his head and battered ribs, from the cut of the ropes into his wrists.

Carefully, Maddock opened his eyes. The arena curved around him. Rough timbers, hay, and bags of grain were stacked halfway up the walls, all illuminated by phos-lamps. The statue of Hepona was gone. He suffered a new sense of despair, certain that even the goddess hated him.

Outside the door, several young men spoke conspiratorially, their whispers punctuated by bursts of unpleasant laughter. ". . . or how about a red-hot poker?" one suggested. "We could stick it you-know-where."

"That's right," another said, giggling. "Then he'll know how it feels to be violated."

Maddock's blood ran cold. Obviously, they planned to torture him, and that realization struck through his brain like a steel wedge. He could not defend himself, and no one would try to stop them. Frantically, he sought a way to cut his bonds. A swift visual sweep of the room brought nothing but slivers of pain shooting through his head and limbs. He looked again, squinting against the aches that pounded every part of him. Nothing. Dizziness crushed his head back to the floor. As Maddock's eyes glided closed in despair, he noticed something metallic glinting dully beneath a heap of hay. He whipped his lids open, staring, then gradually recognized the sword he had used in his duel with Stane. He recalled how his lord had kicked it away after disarming him. "Almighty Hepona," he whispered.

The guards outside broke into another round of snickering.

Gagging from pain, Maddock clumsily rolled onto his side and drew his bound hands over his legs. A white-hot ball of fire seemed to explode inside his skull. His vision wavered, and unconsciousness threatened. He paused, panting, and forced himself to concentrate.

The arena stopped spinning. Moving as quietly as possible, Maddock scrabbled to the sword's hiding place and pulled it free of the hay.

"No, wait." The voice belonged to Vonora's twin brother, Damas. "I've got a better idea. Let's do what the River People do to their unruly stallions. Let's make a gelding of him."

Breath whistling in his throat, Maddock clasped the hilt between his feet and slid his bonds along the gleaming blade. It sliced the thick rope like a single strand of horsehair.

The lock shot back, and the door rattled open. Damas and three stable lads swaggered into the arena. "Wake up, lover boy," Damas sneered. "We've got a little fun—"

Maddock rolled to his feet and held the sword in a defensive posture.

The four young men froze, gaping.

"That's right, don't make a sound." Maddock forced speech through swollen lips. "Just move over there." He nodded his head toward a pile of feed bags, immediately wishing he had not made the gesture. Then, all the hopeless anguish of the last few hours sparked into rage. "I'd like to say I don't want to hurt you, but that would be a lie."

Damas snorted in disgust. "Everything you say is a lie."

Warily, Maddock circled them, heading for the door. "Not everything. Try to stop me, and I'll kill you. I mean it."

Damas broke for Maddock without warning. "Get him!"

Reacting with lightning-like instinct, Maddock slashed. The blade opened Damas' throat, choking off his scream. Blood sprayed Maddock's face. Damas toppled backward into the others.

Maddock did not wait. He sprinted through the door, slammed it shut, and slid the bolt securely home.

"Oh, gods!" one of the stable-boys shouted from inside. "He's dead!"

Still clutching his sword, Maddock ran. Night air chilled through him, numbing the pain. His legs moved more from desperate habit than intent. The road seemed to scroll beneath his feet, and cottages whisked by like shapeless shadows. No one stirred or offered challenge as he slipped through the open gates of Dorlach Tor and fled through open fields. Moonlight reflected from the remaining snow, brightening the ground in patches.

Feeling nothing, thinking nothing, Maddock ran on. Trees and rocks familiar to him since childhood disappeared into the darkness. Pain became as abstract as wind. His mind grasped only the need to keep moving, to run without rest; and, trained for endurance, his body obeyed.

Gradually, the east turned lavender and pink with approaching dawn. Exhaustion finally caught Maddock. Heart pounding, every part throbbing, sweat dripping down his face, he sank into the muddy snow. The cold wet refreshed him. He lay still, allowing his breath to return, his heart to slow.

He was not safe, he knew. Would never be safe again.

Maddock glanced behind him. The rising sun cast its pastel light over the granite face of the tor and the walls around the Great House. Abruptly, a rising mist obscured them. Maddock drew his hand across his eyes and found them wet with tears. With distant surprise, he stared at his damp fingers. He could not remember when he had started to weep. And then, thinking back over his life, he could not recall a time when he had not wept, deep within his spirit.

The sun climbed higher. Maddock sighed and stood, staggering a little with pain and fatigue. His mind groped for a simple concept in a world that seemed senseless and utterly changed. He found it in his hand: his sword was dirty. He had to clean it before he went any farther.

Maddock lifted a corner of a tunic soaked with melted snow and scrubbed at Damas' blood. As the blade came clean, an engraved inscription appeared in scrolling letters. He held the weapon to the dawn light and spelled out the word: *Gaer*. It was his master's sword.

Sorrow ached through Maddock, as intense as the pain of his wounds. He clasped the hilt to his heart and bowed his head, fighting back more tears. "No," he said thickly. "I won't cry. Never again."

Somewhere in the distance, a hound belled.

Maddock spun toward Dorlach Tor and raised his sword in defiance. "Do you hear me?" he shouted. "Never again!"

As if emphasizing the words, collected sunlight reflected, in glimmers, from the blade. Thrusting the sword through his belt, Maddock limped southward.

CHAPTER SEVEN

BROTHER Honesty knelt within the meager shelter provided by a coppice of beech trees, his breath steaming in the chill air. The growing light of day against his closed eyelids tugged his mind away from prayer. Feeling refreshed, as if from a night of undisturbed slumber, he sighed and opened his eyes.

Dawn painted the sky pink and gold. Only traces of the recent snow remained, but frost glittered on the stalks of dead grass. Small birds hopped through the undergrowth of thorns, silent but for the occasional whir of wings. Two miles away, on rising ground, the stronghold of Dorlach Tor emerged from the fading darkness.

The cold nipped at Brother Honesty's fingers. He folded his hands under his arms for warmth and stared at the abode of the Abomination. Crowning a large hill, the two concentric walls of Dorlach Tor encircled an enormous outcropping of granite. All night long, he had kept vigil as the power of the Light cleansed the stronghold. It merely remained for the Hooded Order to sever the demon-link and remove its terrible menace from humankind forever.

Brother Honesty's original doubts had vanished, calmed by the repeated assurances of the Magicians; and a deep certainty of success filled his mind. He only regretted that they would have no contact with the inhabitants. He longed to meet them, to proclaim their freedom from the evil that had plagued them, but Commander Swift insisted upon secrecy. For the invasion to go as planned, they had to remove all internal resistance first, best accomplished if the Marchlanders remained unaware of the army's presence. Traveling with a flying squadron only thirty men strong, Skull, Claw, and Wraith would not only destroy the demon-link but also neutralize the powers of all magic-wielders. By midsummer, the Marchlands would harbor no magic.

The morning sun touched the distant stronghold, turning its walls to rings of gold. It seemed timeless, indomitable, nothing like the "crumbling ancestral forts" of earlier description. Brother Honesty was glad their current mission relied upon the power of the Light, rather than the power of the sword, for he doubted whether their entire army could conquer Dorlach Tor.

"No," said Skull from behind him. "Probably not."

Brother Honesty turned without agitation to greet the Hooded Mage, now accustomed to having his unspoken thoughts answered. "Good morning, my child."

Dregs of the spell of silence still clung to Skull's black garments, visible as faintly glowing distortions in the air. The Mage shook them off and pulled back his hood. "Good morning, Brother." His narrow face seemed more pale than usual; his large, expressive eyes filled with a strange light. "Everything ready for me?"

"Yes." Brother Honesty glanced around, expecting to see Claw and Wraith emerge from the beech trees. "Where are the others?"

"Back at camp."

"At camp? What are they doing there?"

Skull's gaze turned to Dorlach Tor and gained the intensity of a stalking panther. "Doing?" he repeated absently. "Eating breakfast, I suppose."

"But—"

The Mage blinked and seemed to come back to himself. He looked at Brother Honesty and smiled. "You remember where the camp is, don't you? Just a quarter of a mile south."

The priest had no intention of returning to camp until the Abomination was destroyed. "Yes, but—"

"Commander Swift told them to keep a few bannocks warm for you." Skull patted his friend on the shoulder. "You look as if you could use a good meal. Wish I'd brought your breakfast with me. And your blanket."

Brother Honesty had also gotten used to the Magicians' habit of interrupting. It came, he supposed, from limited social contact. "Why aren't Claw and Wraith here?"

Skull's dark brows rose in surprise. "Do you think all three of us need to be involved? We drew straws. I won." He settled on the frosty ground beside the priest. "I don't need help, really. This is quite an easy little mission."

Brother Honesty's soft blue eyes grew round with sudden apprehension. "At our last staff meeting, I heard they have about a dozen magic-wielders living within those walls. This may not be as easy as you assume."

"Different sort of magic." A drop of moisture formed on the end of Skull's nose, and he sniffed. "Oh, drat. I think my cold's coming back."

"But at the meeting, Field Officer Trust said—"

Skull waved his gloved hand, cutting off the priest. "He's not a Mage. He doesn't know." His nose dripped again, and he gingerly dabbed at it with his sleeve. "If I practiced the same magic as the Marchlanders, I could cure this persistent affliction."

"The ability to heal is a gift of the One Light," Brother Honesty reminded.

Skull looked at him sidelong, smiling fondly. "You believe everything is a gift. I wish I lived in your world."

"And I wish," the priest countered in a placid tone, "that I lived in yours. Or at least understood it better. Claw told me that knowing magic is the same as not knowing magic, but somehow the reverse is untrue."

Skull laughed, nodding. "Magic is like—" He broke off and gestured helplessly. "Magic."

"Thank you," Brother Honesty teased. "Now I understand."

"Magic is like . . ." Skull tried again. ". . . a fountain."

"Of water?"

"Close enough for an analogy, I suppose. Yes, of water." Skull's voice faded out, and he cleared his throat. "Imagine an ornate fountain, like the one on the front lawn of the Imperial Palace. Within its marble basin, five jets of water stream toward the sky. Can you picture it?"

"Easily." Certain he did not fully understand, Brother Honesty scratched the back of his head. "And that's what magic's like?"

"Sort of. Except the water never falls. It goes up forever." Skull sniffled and wiped his nose again. "This is the magic wielded by Marchlanders. It's small and useful, capable of delicate functions like healing a sick child or seeing the truth behind someone's words."

Brother Honesty remembered his first meeting with Skull and the trouble the Mage had lighting a lamp. "A matter of focus."

"Exactly." Skull's tone grew thoughtful as he searched for words. "Imagine the fountain again. Set in its center, within the ring of five streams, a single, heavy cascade of water thunders downward. That's the power I wield, a magic of force and mass destruction." The Hooded Mage turned his attention to Dorlach Tor and narrowed his eyes. "In fact, the only difficulty I foresee in this mission is to keep the greater resonances channeled and controlled. Otherwise, I could kill every living thing within those walls with less effort than it takes to lace my boots."

Appalled, Brother Honesty stared at him.

Obviously picking up the priest's unspoken thoughts, Skull turned to him, looking wounded. "But you knew that."

"Yes, but I—" Brother Honesty laid an apologetic hand on the other man's shoulder. "I'm sorry, my child. I'm simply unaccustomed to hearing you speak of it so casually."

Skull's gaze slid away, and he shrugged. "Talking about it is nothing, good Brother. Just wait until you actually see me strike."

"I'm sorry," the priest repeated. "I didn't mean to hurt your feelings."

"I know."

"It's just that I—" Brother Honesty broke off with a sigh. "I guess I'd rather wield those five little magics."

Skull's gentle smile returned. "I don't doubt that. But just remember, it takes power to fight power. Destruction is not always a bad thing." He nodded toward the distant stronghold. "Come high noon, the magic-wielders who dwell within those walls shall be stripped of their powers, and that spirit-link you all find so fearsome, that so-called Abomination, shall be severed.

Dorlach Tor will fall to us in silence and secrecy." Skull raised his brows. "And most of the inhabitants won't feel a thing."

$$\sim\!\!\mathcal{L}\!\!\sim$$

Eyes closed, Kiarda sat by an open window and drank in the scent of clean, cold February wind. It seemed to speak to her of a wild and uncomplicated way of life, easing the turmoil in her heart and the heavy malaise of her body. In the day room behind her, her three personal maids murmured softly, heads together over their needlework. They had given up trying to draw her into conversation. She suspected that they feared her, that they somehow sensed her strangeness, but she could not think of the words to reassure them. Even in the best of times, she never had much to say to them. At the moment, she simply wished they would leave her alone.

Someone tapped at the door. Kiarda's lips thinned at the thought of facing yet another inept attempt at consolation. "Rina," she said, without turning from the window. "Please see who it is."

The maid's voice was scarcely audible. "Yes, my lady."

Kiarda listened as Rina crossed the room. Cousins arrived daily at Dorlach Tor to share the family's tragedy. She sorted through a mental list of probable visitors, weighing whether or not she could endure their company. *Maybe it's Adan. That would be nice. He never stays very long.*

"My lady," Rina said. "It's the healer, Bevin."

A painful hope awoke within Kiarda, and she raised her head. "Bevin?" She turned to look at the maid. Noting the girl's pale face, she tried to make herself smile. "Thank you, Rina. Please show her in." Her voice shook. She hastily twisted toward the window in case she began to weep.

The door opened. Kiarda heard footsteps and the rustle of long skirts, smelled kitchen spices. Bevin's tone was warm with true compassion. "Kiarda?"

Kiarda felt the knot in her throat dissolve. "I'm glad you're here, Bevin." She raised her voice slightly. "The rest of you are dismissed." She waited through the maids' demure farewells and did not turn from the window.

Bevin moved to stand behind her. "Such pain," she murmured, placing gentle hands on Kiarda's shoulders. "Talk to me."

"I'm late."

"Pardon?"

Kiarda turned to look up at her friend. For days she had lived alone with the bitter knowledge, scarcely permitting herself to think about it. "My time. I'm late."

Bevin's perplexed expression vanished. "Do you mean your monthly time? Are you sure?"

Kiarda nodded. Having it spoken aloud made it seem manageable, more like a real problem with a solution than a living nightmare. "Ladayla and I are always together, but her time has come and gone. I haven't started yet."

Bevin knelt beside Kiarda's chair, and her gray eyes gained an unsettling intensity. "Time." She repeated absently, "time." Fixedly she stared at Kiarda's midsection for a few moments. Abruptly, all the color drained from her round face. "Oh, gods."

"I'm pregnant." Kiarda marveled at how calmly she spoke. "I knew it."

Bevin struggled for words, her eyes filling with tears. "Yes," she said finally. "I'm sorry."

Abruptly, blind panic fell upon Kiarda. Acting on an irrational impulse to flee, she launched herself from her chair and across the room. The wall stopped her headlong rush. She pressed the palms of her hands against the cold granite and bowed her head. "So. That's one more thing he stole from me. Bad enough he took my love and trust, my virginity, and all prospects of a decent marriage. Bad enough he stole my past, tainting every memory of my happiest moments with his presence. But now there's this. Now he has destroyed my future."

"Kiarda—"

Grief for all she had lost mingled with Kiarda's fear. "This should be a happy time, discovering that I'm going to have a baby. I should be married. My husband and I should be declaring a feast day. We should be holding horse races and torch dances. We should—" Her voice wavered. She paused to battle for self-control. "I know I'm not the only one to suffer at his hands. He betrayed poor Vonora and murdered her brother. He lied to his father, to all the folk of Dorlach Tor. He used us and despised us, and then escaped his punishment. But I—" She settled her forehead against the wall. "I don't understand why I have to bear the burden of his evil. Why are the gods doing this to me? Have I done something wrong?"

"No." The healer's voice went hoarse with tears.

The granite's hardness seemed to filter into Kiarda's spirit, and her anguish relented as a new thought occurred to her. "Help me, Bevin. Cure me of this disease."

"Cure you—?"

Kiarda turned and glared at the healer. "You must know how. You have more magic than anyone else, even Sygil. Destroy this evil thing growing inside me!"

Bevin's mouth opened in obvious horror. "No. I can't. It wouldn't be right. Kiarda—"

The refusal struck like a physical blow, and Kiarda pressed her back to the wall. "But it would be right for me to suffer? Is that what you're saying?"

"No!" Emphatically, Bevin shook her head, brown curls flying with the force of the motion. "I can't use my magic to destroy or kill. It doesn't work that way. If I—"

Heart pounding, Kiarda cut her off. "Then use your herbcraft! There has to be something that can end a pregnancy."

Bevin held up her hands and walked toward Kiarda slowly, as if approaching a frightened and dangerous animal. "Every deed, every choice I make, has a direct effect on the source of my magic." Her tone was calm, earnest. "If I willfully destroyed life, then my powers as a healer might diminish. There isn't—"

Choked by a rising tide of anger and despair, Kiarda gestured sharply for silence. "You—" Her voice threatened to fail her, but she forced herself to continue. "You'll let my entire life fall to pieces just so you won't risk a bit of your own precious magic? I thought you were my friend."

"I am!" Tears filled Bevin's eyes and trickled down her nose. "Oh, Kiarda, I would do anything to help you. But killing your unborn children is not the answer."

Between one heartbeat and the next, time seemed to stop. *Children?* Rage and desperation evaporated in the looming shadow of complete disaster. "I'm carrying more than one?"

Bevin wiped the tears from her face and sniffed. "I'm not sure, but I think it's twins."

"I see." Kiarda waited for emotion to return and sweep her away, but she felt empty. She recalled her past discussion with cousin Adan, his advice to seek love and companionship only from members of her own social class. His words, once so reprehensible, now made perfect sense. She could no longer consider Bevin a friend. "And just when did you intend to reveal this fact to me?"

"I wasn't—I didn't mean—" The healer gazed at Kiarda imploringly. "I may be wrong."

"No," Kiarda said in an even tone. "Your Sight is the strongest. I'm confident you're correct." Holding her back straight, she swept past Bevin and resumed her chair by the window. Folding her hands in her lap, she looked the other woman directly in the eyes. "I understand that you intended no disrespect, so I shall not have you reprimanded. However, I must insist that you keep our conversation here confidential. I wish to inform my lady mother of my condition in my own time."

Bevin's face turned pale, her red nose the only spot of color. "Kiarda, I—"

Kiarda raised her chin. "And in the future, you shall address me by my title. Do you understand?"

Bevin's voice emerged with a dry whisper. "Yes . . . my lady."

"Good." Kiarda gave the healer a slight, formal smile. "Thank you. You are dismissed."

For a moment, Bevin stood motionless and staring. Then she lowered her gaze and spread her skirts in a curtsy. "Yes, my lady."

Kiarda turned to look out the window, gazing at the blue sky and frosty roof tiles. She heard Bevin walk to the door, pause, then open the door and leave.

The room went silent. In spite of a sorrowful and uncertain future, Kiarda felt strangely at peace. She closed her eyes. Solitude, long wished for, enwrapped her like her mother's embrace. She needed nothing, relied upon no one. *So good to be alone.*

Queasy from a fierce headache, Tynan tried to eat the piece of
bread in his hand but could not bring himself to open his mouth.
The texture of the crust seemed repulsive and dry, like old tree
bark; he wondered why everyone else at the table seemed to
enjoy it. He had never felt ill a day in his life, thanks to the magic
of the spirit-link, and worry only intensified his nausea. Adding
to his distress, his link-mate lay limp and miserable across his lap.
[[Sick,]] the tomcat said in the strange language they shared. [[So
sick.]]

Tynan dropped the bread onto his plate and ran his hand over
the cat's sleek back. "I know." He mouthed the words, not needing to speak aloud. "I wish I could make you better."

Tynan and his family sat together at one of the extra tables
near Lady Wylfre's dais. Tassi presided at the head, with Fian and
Dod on either side. Culan, her husband, sat beside Fian; and
Tynan sat across from him. Tassi's aunts and uncles filled the next
four seats.

Adan stood at the end of the table, a linen towel draped over
his left arm and a pitcher of wine in his right hand. An unfortunate misunderstanding the day before, culminating with Tassi
slapping a serving maid, prompted the eldest brother of Sarn
Moor to insist upon taking a servant's role. It was an act of nobility, but Tynan knew Tassi perceived it as a subtle attack upon her
Ladyship.

Kinfolk filled the Great Hall of Dorlach Tor, as if celebrating
a feast; but the faces of those gathered around the tables were
grim and the discussion centered on Kiarda's rape and the plans
to hunt down her attacker. A recent report indicated that Maddock still haunted the region.

"It was the sword training," Tassi declared. She took a delicate sip from her wine goblet, rings and bracelets flashing in the
firelight. A young woman with dull gold hair and pale brown eyes,
she wore a velvet cloak of bright green over her festively embroidered tunic and trousers. She looked lovely, but the garb was
more appropriate for a wedding than a family tragedy. Tynan
wondered why she had not worn something more somber.

"Learning how to fight is what made him violent. It's obvious. Any man who knows how to handle a sword can't be trusted."

Embarrassment added heat to Tynan's already feverish cheeks, and he lowered his gaze to the cat. All around them sat men who had grown up in the warrior's way before the Divine Peace had made warfare a sacrilege: most notably Lord Stane. Tassi intended no insult, Tynan felt certain, but he wished her voice did not carry so clearly. He risked a glance at Adan and found his eldest brother glowering at Tassi. *No. Don't argue with her,* Tynan begged with his eyes. *Not here. Not now.*

"I mean," Tassi continued loudly, "the whole thing was their own fault. If they had simply done away with that horrible old blasphemer, instead of allowing him to live as an outcast, then none of this would have happened." She paused and added in a sweet tone, "Don't you agree, Tynan?"

Temples throbbing, Tynan jerked his attention to Tassi. The strict courtesy of the Marchlands forbade him to criticize her opinions, though she espoused unvarnished murder. "My lady," he answered politely, "I would never dream of disagreeing with you."

"So diplomatic." Tassi took another sip from her goblet, regarding him over the rim with a strangely provocative glance.

Obviously bored with the adult conversation, seven-year-old Dod wiggled in his seat and made a face at Fian. Tynan tapped the boy on the shoulder to remind him to behave.

"But I'm curious," Tassi said, smiling indulgently. "Tell me what you really think. Speak to me as openly as—" She flicked her bejeweled fingers toward the end of the table. "—as dear Adan does."

Put on the spot, Tynan struggled to find words while the world seemed to spin around him. "My lady, I—" He pressed his fingertips to his temples. "I have no real thoughts on the matter. I just don't understand how Lady Wylfre's kindness and leniency could be repaid with such evil. Why the gods allowed it, I mean."

"Ah," Tassi said wisely. She narrowed her eyes, considering his words. "You believe the gods are punishing Lady Wylfre for some past sin."

Aghast, Tynan shook his head, though the movement incited the pain. "No, no! That's not what I—"

"Then Lord Stane must have performed some heretical misdeed in his youth. Wouldn't surprise me. He's from the Low Marches, you know."

A burning bubble of nausea climbed up Tynan's throat. He swallowed it back with difficulty. "My lady, I—"

Dod flicked a piece of gristle at Fian.

Tynan tapped his shoulder again, with a little more force. "Doddy-lad, stop it!"

Tassi gave the boy a look of gentle remonstrance. "I know it's hard to just sit and listen, Dod, but we don't want to do anything to vex Adan, do we? Because if he gets mad, he shouts and makes me cry. You don't want him to make me cry again, do you?"

Dod's expression grew anxious, and he answered in a muffled whisper. "No, Tassi."

On Tynan's lap, the tomcat quivered. The young man slipped a hand under his link-mate's head and hefted it. The cat's watering eyes lay half open, revealing only the dense white of third eyelid. His breath rattled, labored. "Cat-of-the-Lightning-Swift-Paws?"

[[Dying. . . .]]

Tynan raised his stricken gaze to Tassi. "My lady, may I be excused from the table?" He gathered the limp, furry body to his heart and started to stand even before she answered. "My link-mate is terribly ill."

Tassi's eyes flashed, and she inhaled sharply through her teeth in a little hiss that usually signaled a brawl with Adan.

"I'm sorry, my lady." Tynan did not know what he had done to make her angry. "Please?"

The heat remained in Tassi's eyes, but she gave a brittle laugh and gestured for Tynan to go. "By all means. Get the beast away from me before he sicks-up on my new boots."

Tynan tried to step backward over the bench, lost his balance, and began to tumble. Suddenly, steady hands gripped his arms. Startled, his hold desperately tight around the cat, he flung a glance over his shoulder and discovered Adan. "Oh," Tynan said breathlessly. "Thank you."

"Careful." Adan helped Tynan over the bench, then threw a supportive arm around his waist. "You need a healer, by the look of it. Come on."

Together, the brothers walked from the Great Hall into a side corridor. The noise and heat gave way to cool darkness. For a moment, Tynan felt a touch of relief, then he shivered violently. Agony lanced through his skull, and he leaned against his eldest brother. He lost track of the cat's sides heaving against his chest. "Can't—" He clenched his jaw and squeezed his eyes shut. "Can't stand it."

"Come with me," Adan repeated gently. "We don't have far to go."

Clutching his link-mate, Tynan allowed Adan to lead him down the corridor. Every step jarred an increasing level of anguish through him, and he found himself wishing he would die, desiring only relief from the pain.

After a seeming eternity, Adan paused. Tynan heard a door creak open. Warmth rushed over him, along with the scent of herbs. "Step up over the threshold," Adan murmured. "Don't trip."

Tynan obeyed, carrying his link-mate into the room. The pain slackened.

Tynan's shoulders sagged in relief. "Oh." He opened his eyes. "Gods be praised."

Phos-lamps filled the room with a green-gold glow. Shelves laden with bottles, jars, and books lined the walls to the ceiling beams. The aromas of cinnamon and cloves mingled with the medicinal smells of camphor and vinegar.

Cat-of-the-Lightning-Swift-Paws mewed like a tiny kitten and also opened his eyes. [[I feel better. Are we dead?]]

Tynan bent his head and kissed his link-mate between the ears.

Standing at a large worktable in the center of the room, a plump young woman looked up from a mortar and pestle. She studied Tynan for a moment, and her brows lifted in an anxious expression.

Tynan thought he recognized her as one of the kitchen staff. "Hello, maidy. Are you a healer?"

Ignoring Tynan's question, the young woman desperately waved her hand at Adan. "Shut the door! Hurry!"

"Of course," Adan said. "Sorry."

Tynan heard the door swing shut behind him. The pain vanished altogether.

[[Wonderful,]] the cat said. He climbed onto Tynan's shoulders and sniffed the air. [[I like it here. Let's never leave.]]

The young woman bustled from behind the table to peer up at Tynan. "Are you all right?"

Tynan smiled down at her, then noticed her red, puffy eyes. "Are you all right?" he asked with concern. "Why were you weeping? Has someone hurt you?"

Seeming startled, she ducked her head. "No, my lord, I just—" She paused and swallowed hard. "I just had a quarrel with a friend." She looked from him to Adan, then abruptly recognized his brother. She curtsied, spreading her wide skirts. "Lord Adan, forgive me. I didn't—" Her gaze drifted back to Tynan, and her voice faded away.

"I'm fine," Tynan assured her. "Truly."

"You were dying," she said.

Only faintly surprised by her words, Tynan nodded. "Well, it certainly felt like it."

Adan's scarred face went blank with shock. "What?"

The cat stuck his nose in his link-mate's ear. [[I know her. Her name is Bevin, and she's a healer. Tell her about our bad headache.]]

Tynan tried to twist away from the tickling whiskers. "In a moment."

"Pardon?" Bevin said.

The cat leaped from Tynan's shoulder onto the worktable. Purring, he strolled to the mortar and stuck his whole head inside. [[This smells awful. Must be magical.]]

Tynan tried to sidle courteously around the healer to reach his link-mate, but she did not yield ground. "Cat, get your nose out of there."

Bevin peered at Tynan intently. "You were in terrible pain when you walked in, and your life energies were waning."

"We had headaches," Tynan said but kept his eyes on his link-mate, who continued his close inspection of the mortar's contents. "Cat, stop it!"

"It's only a mixture of valerian and stevia, my lord," Bevin said. "It won't harm him."

"Nonetheless, he knows better," Tynan said. "Did you hear me, cat?"

The cat lifted his head and glared at Tynan. Bits of brown powder clung to his nose and whiskers. [[My name is not 'cat.']]

Tynan put his hands on his hips. "Cat-of-the-Lightning-Swift-Paws, leave that stuff alone."

Tynan's link-mate sat, curling his tail around his toes. [[That isn't my name either.]]

The young man sighed. "You've changed it again?"

The cat narrowed his amber eyes and assumed a mysterious air. [[I am Cat-of-All-Magical-Knowledge.]]

Tynan smiled. "Well, Cat-of-All-Magical-Knowledge, you have valerian all over your magical nose."

[[I knew that,]] the cat answered with dignity. Then he turned his back on them and began to wash his face.

"I apologize for my brother," Adan said. "He tends to become submersed in the doings of his link-mate."

Flushing, Tynan returned his attention to the healer. "I'm sorry, Bevin. It's just that it feels so good to—" He shrugged, finishing lamely, "—feel good."

Bevin nodded and smiled weakly.

Adan's expression went grim. "What happened? Were they poisoned?"

"Poisoned?" Tynan echoed in disbelief. "Who would—?"

Bevin shook her head. "I don't think so, my lord. It looked like . . ." She wrung her plump hands. "This sounds crazy, but it looked as if they were under attack, as if some great power attempted to sever their link. I've never seen anything like it."

Tynan glanced back and forth between his brother and the healer, unable to fathom their discussion. "But who would want to attack me?"

Bevin looked at Tynan, the anxiety obvious in her wide, gray eyes. "I don't know," she said in a small voice. "But whoever they are, they're using forbidden magic."

The cat looked over his shoulder. [[The Dark Court.]]

"The Dark Court?" Tynan repeatedly incredulously. "Why would they want to—"

"For the love of—!" Adan gestured impatiently. "Because they're evil. And because Lord Stane burned their thorn tree and desecrated their hill in retaliation for Kiarda's abduction."

Bevin cautiously approached the door and laid her hands on it. "This room is heavily shielded, since some forms of magic can affect the potency of herbs or cause their properties to become unstable. When you closed the door, Lord Adan, you literally saved the lives of Lord Tynan and his link-mate."

"Only because you told me to." Adan's voice seemed strangely raw, his scarred face tight with some suppressed emotion. "You saved my brother's life, Bevin. *You* did."

The cat jumped from the table to Tynan's shoulder. [[But we can't stay in here,]] he said. [[We have to warn Lady Wylfre and Lord Stane.]]

Tynan's pulse picked up speed, and he started toward the door. "That's right," he said, before he recalled the others could not hear the cat. "If Dorlach Tor is under siege from the Dark Court, then we have to notify the Lady. Hundreds of lives may be at stake."

Adan whirled on Tynan, hazel eyes blazing. "You're not going anywhere, little brother. You stay here, where you're safe." He strode to the door and grasped its latch handle. "I'll try to be quick, but brace yourselves."

Tynan walked to the worktable and gripped its edge. "Ready."

Adan opened the door.

A hot blade sliced through Tynan's skull. He fell to his knees, choking back a cry. The door slammed shut, and once again the pain vanished.

Bevin rushed to his side. "Lord Tynan—!"

Afraid Bevin might actually touch him, Tynan held up his hand. "I'm all right."

Clinging to his shoulders like a burr, Cat-of-All-Magical-Knowledge stuck his nose in Tynan's ear. [[I'm all right, too.]]

Bevin hovered uncertainly. "Maybe you should sit, my lord. Shall I bring a stool?"

Shaken, Tynan held the worktable and pulled himself to his feet. "No, thank you." He made himself smile at her. "Please don't go to any bother for me."

Bevin returned his smile, dropping her gaze, and spread her skirts in a curtsy.

Only at that moment did Tynan realize he was alone in a room with a young woman, a highly improper situation. He moved to put more of the table between them. "Is Adan—?" The thought became nearly too much to bear. "Is he in danger, do you think?"

"I don't know, my lord," Bevin answered in a troubled tone. "But I don't believe so. You and your link-mate were the only ones affected when he opened the door."

"That's true." Forced at last to the realization that someone wished him harm, Tynan swallowed hard. "Are you gifted with Sight, Bevin? Can you see what's happening in the rest of the House?"

[[No,]] said the cat. [[Not in here.]]

The healer shook her head regretfully. "I'm sorry, my lord. I can't do any magic in this room as long as the door is closed."

[[Told you so. I'm Cat-of-All-Magical-Knowledge.]]

"I understand." Tynan reached up to his shoulder and stroked his link-mate. "We're not in a very defensible position. If this were a game of chess, we'd be at a distinct disadvantage."

Bevin nodded absently and returned to the door. A strange tone entered her voice. "Lord Adan is quite a man of action, isn't he?"

Disconcerted by the question, Tynan raised his brows. "Yes, I suppose he is." He had never considered his brother in such a light. "He likes taking care of people. He should have been a woman."

The healer glanced back at Tynan. "I beg your pardon, my lord?"

"Then he could have been Lady of Sarn Moor when our mother died." The muscles at the nape of Tynan's neck tightened painfully. "But since no one would marry him, the land passed to Lady Tassi when she married our brother, Culan."

Two uneven pink spots appeared on Bevin's round cheeks. "No one would marry him?"

"No. Because of the—" Tynan gestured at his face. "It's so sad."

[[Hold me.]] Cat-of-All-Magical-Knowledge climbed from Tynan's shoulders and into his link-mate's waiting arms. [[I'm starting to feel awful again.]]

Tynan's temples throbbed. "Me, too."

Bevin regarded him quizzically. "My lord?"

The phos-lamps abruptly seemed too bright, and Tynan closed his eyes. A rope of fire encircled his head just above the brows, burning hotter with every heartbeat. "Hurts."

"But the—" Bevin broke off with a gasp. "No!"

Painting with pain, Tynan squinted toward her.

The healer raised both hands, palm up, and stood in front of the door. "It's coming through! I can't hold it!"

"What is it?"

"Dark magic!"

The door's oaken panels steamed. The phos-lamps sputtered, and their light changed from golden-green to deep red. Nightmarish shadows loomed across the walls. On the surrounding shelves, jars of herbal remedies exploded, hurling pottery shards through the air.

Bevin whirled and ran to Tynan. Before he could stop her, she snatched up his free hand.

"What—?" Tynan's torment eased, becoming merely a sense of pressure. "What are you doing?"

"I can shield you, my lord. But only as long as we touch." A jar on the worktable shattered. Bevin pulled Tynan toward the door. "We've got to get out of here."

"But I thought—"

"Hurry, my lord! This room is no longer sealed against magic. You're not safe."

In spite of the danger, Tynan found himself uncomfortably aware of Bevin's hand in his. He hurried along at her side, shards crunching beneath his feet. "But where will we go?" He slipped in a smear of spilled liquid.

Bevin supported Tynan's balance. "To find Sygil and the others." She shoved open the door. "We need to combine our strength."

Cat-of-All-Magical-Knowledge staggered desperately to his link-mate's shoulder. [[Stop asking so many questions. Just run!]]

Hand in hand, they raced down the hall, Tynan matching his pace to Bevin's shorter strides.

A servant carrying a tray stopped and stared as they pelted by, his wrinkled face stamped with disapproval. "My young lord—!"

"Dark Court!" Tynan shouted over his shoulder, praying the fellow would understand. "Tell everyone! Run to the temple!"

The hall ended in a narrow wooden door. Bevin did not slow her pace but made an abrupt gesture of command. Seemingly by itself, the door flew open with a crash. Still hand in hand, Tynan and Bevin sprinted outside, the cat's claws gouging his shoulder.

Sheltered from the wind by high walls, the courtyard felt comfortably warm. Sunlight poured from overhead, melting the frost-packed earth and filling the air with the springlike scent of mud. A knot of worried-looking people gathered beneath a leafless oak tree. From their midst, a baby cried, keening a single sustained note over and over again.

Dread darkened Tynan's heart. *Oh, no.*

As they ran to the gathering, he saw Lady Wylfre sitting on the ground with Elrin on her lap. The spirit-linked foal lay beside them, long legs outstretched, flanks heaving. Lord Stane bent over Wylfre, his hands over her shoulders. Old Sygil and several other healers crouched in front of Elrin, their fingertips lightly resting upon the baby's forehead.

On the edge of the crowd, Adan turned and saw them. "What in the name of all—?"

Tynan started to answer, but Bevin dragged him forward so suddenly the cat scrabbled wildly for balance. She snatched up Elrin's little hand.

The baby's cries stopped. Snuffling, he regarded Bevin with an expression of somber trust. He glanced back at his mother, as if for reassurance, then pointed at Bevin with his free hand and jabbered.

Tynan nodded. He knew exactly what Elrin felt.

Everyone stared at the young healer, frozen with surprise.

Settling onto the ground between Wylfre and Tynan, Bevin jerked her head toward the foal. "Quick! Pull him closer. His link-mate or I need to touch him in order to protect him."

Moving before anyone else, Adan bent and lifted the foal's front quarters. "Where do you want him?"

"Touching me," Bevin repeated with a hint of impatience.

Adan shifted the foal around and settled its head on Bevin's lap, obviously using the greatest care not to touch her himself. For a moment, the animal gave no reaction. Then it sighed deeply and its breathing normalized.

Sygil grunted and rose from her crouch, rubbing her back. "Too old for this."

"Wait!" Bevin protested. "What are you doing? We need to share our magics."

"Don't have any," Sygil replied sourly. "Whatever is attacking us, it took everything away. I'm drained. We all are. Except you."

Bevin gazed around the assembly, her gray eyes wide and terrified. "But I—" She swallowed. "I'm not strong enough."

Feeling oddly protective of the healer, Tynan sat in the mud beside her and gripped her hand in both of his. "I know you're doing your best."

Cat-of-All-Magical-Knowledge slid down Tynan's chest to his lap, too shaken to concern himself with dignity.

Lady Wylfre leaned forward. "Bevin, what is it? What's attacking us?"

"I don't know, my lady. I've never—" Bevin broke off suddenly, choking. "Oh, gods! It found me!"

A peculiar sensation seized Tynan, as if thousands of ants swarmed over his skin. The cat moaned in his lap. The rope of fire once again twisted around his temples. "Fight it, Bevin!"

"I can't! It's too—!"

A clap of thunder tore the air. Tynan jerked his gaze to the sky. Directly overhead, black clouds spread like smoke from an invisible fire. More thunder rolled over them.

Sygil raised her voice. "Use all five magics!"

"I am!" Bevin said frantically.

"Then use the sixth!"

Bevin closed her eyes and shook her head tightly. "Forbidden!"

"Do it!"

Sweat and tears mingled on Bevin's face, and she clutched Tynan's hand like a drowning woman.

Something sizzled inside Tynan's head, just behind his eyes. Searing pain shot through his skull. He gagged.

Abruptly, a nightmarish image filled his mind. Five trees rose from the ground in a ring, so close their trunks touched. They grew with incredible speed, their pale bark racing by his sight as they climbed upward. In the center, a single enormous tree grew downward, its circumference so great it touched all five of the outer trees. Friction arose where the dark and light bark rubbed each other, and a band of flame spread around the ring.

[[The five magics and the sixth forbidden magic.]] The cat's voice echoed through Tynan's inner self. [[She can't win. We're going to die.]]

The blaze burned hotter and brighter, consuming the outer trees and the inner tree.

Tynan felt as if the fire engulfed his body, eating away his bone marrow, drying his blood, charring his teeth. He tried to renounce awareness to escape the torment, to will himself to die.

Adan cried out, his words echoing as if he stood at the end of a long tunnel. "Tynan, hang on! Hang on!"

His brother's voice impaled Tynan to his identity, restraining his spirit from deserting his agonized body. Thunder shook the ground beneath him, then everything stilled.

Tynan lay motionless in the mud. He waited for the pain to return, for the thunder to start again, for the walls of Dorlach Tor to collapse upon him. Nothing happened. From the cold water soaking into his clothes to the warm weight of the cat against his chest, every sensation felt like a sublime gift of the gods. Cautiously, he opened his eyes.

The bare branches of the oak tree intersected the bright sky. The black clouds were gone.

Cat-of-All-Magical-Knowledge reared up, planted himself on his link-mate's collarbone, and peered into his face. [[Some of them died.]]

Tynan had to cough before he could speak. "What?" He slowly sat up. "What do you—?"

Everyone else lay on the ground, too. Some bled from the mouth; some stared with sightless eyes. Adan lay beside him, curled in a tight ball of pain.

Tynan felt as if his heart stopped. Fingers shaking, he brushed aside the red-brown locks. "Adan?" His voice emerged in a squeaking whisper. "Adan? Can you hear me?"

His brother's scarred face contorted for a moment, then his brow smoothed. "I'm all right. Jus' . . ." He sucked in a hissing lungful of air. "Let me . . . catch breath . . ."

"Of course." Tynan blinked back sudden tears. "There's no hurry."

Around him, the survivors stirred. Someone began to weep. Others vomited. The foal whinnied furiously, tottered on its long legs, then collapsed. It bleated with an agony beyond pain. Lord Stane lifted himself on one elbow and reached for Lady Wylfre. She rolled her head and groaned.

Bevin sat up awkwardly. Blood flowed freely from her nose, and both eyes were puffy and starting to darken. "Dear gods."

Tynan remembered the bizarre image of the trees and the ring of fire, trying to connect it with all the suffering he saw. "What happened?"

"He—" Bevin pressed her hands to her forehead and swayed. "I saw him—"

"Who?"

"He—tried—" Bevin moaned and pitched sideways.

Tynan caught the healer and held her upright, discarding the strict traditions of the Marchlands. The situation demanded it. "What are you talking about? Who did you see?"

Lord Stane spoke, his voice unusually tremulous. "Elrin?"

Tynan glanced over. The Lord of Dorlach Tor sat cross-legged in the mud, clutching the limp form of his youngest son in his arms. Blood trailed from the baby's mouth and ears. Horrified, Tynan jerked his gaze to the foal. It stood on legs no longer shaky, staring at the infant with an all too human expression in its dark eyes. Suddenly, it bolted, anguished whinny trumpeting eerily over the silence.

A sense of loss worse than any physical pain pierced Tynan's heart. *Oh, gods, no. Not little Elrin.*

"Stop him!" someone shouted.

Stunned men and women staggered to their feet, though only two had the presence of mind to dive for the colt.

"No!" Tynan heard himself shout, hugging his link-mate with all the tenderness that the Lord of Dorlach Tor displayed for his lifeless infant. He alone truly understood what had to happen next. Had the attack taken the cat's life, he could have done nothing else. Only the method would have differed. "No."

The first man missed the foal cleanly, tumbling through brittle grasses. The second sprang into the foal's path, but it swerved on legs that seemed too slender to hold it. Its hooves left skid tracks in the frost, but its speed scarcely diminished. It struck the wall with a sickening impact, then flopped to the ground, neck twisted, utterly still.

Lord Stane bowed his head, and his golden hair fell forward to veil his face.

Oblivious, Bevin muttered into Tynan's shoulder: "Saw him." She unsteadily waved her hand toward the east. "Saw him . . . beech trees. . . ."

Tynan turned his attention to one he could help, sorrow giving way to righteous anger. Releasing the cat, he lifted Bevin's chin. "Who?" he demanded. "Who did this? Was it the Dark Court?"

Bevin replied with obvious effort. "He . . . wrapped in cloak . . . black cloak . . . hidden. . . ." She abruptly sagged against him, her jaw hanging slack.

Stane raised his head. Though tears streamed down his cheeks, his blue eyes smoldered with rage. "Hidden in a cloak?" he repeated thickly. "It's that devil! That blasphemous liar, Maddock!"

Tynan's heart pounded loud in his ears as he considered the power of the sixth magic. "Then he must be aligned with the Dark Court!"

Stane drew Elrin's body closer to him, the tenderness of his hands belied by the ferocity of his words. "I'll kill him! By Almighty Hepona, I'll rip the beating heart from his chest!"

Frantic with worry, Brother Honesty knelt beside Skull, steadying the Mage's head while he vomited. *All my fault. The demon was too much for him.*

"No." Skull shook his head, then retched violently, bringing up a thread of clear slime. "Link destroyed. But I—" He gagged again, his slender shoulders heaving. "I was so stupid."

Though his hands were wet and trembling, Brother Honesty tried to calm his anxiety for his friend. He did not want to burden the Mage with his unspoken thoughts. "What happened, my child? Why are you ill?"

Skull brushed the hair from his eyes and sat back on his heels, recovering his composure. "Things didn't go as planned." He wiped spittle from his chin and turned to gaze at Dorlach Tor. "They know an outside force acted upon them."

Brother Honesty's gut clenched, but he kept his voice steady. "Did you destroy the demon-link?"

Skull sighed but did not turn to look at Brother Honesty. "My innocent friend, I wish you would release your belief in demons. In all truth, such things do not exist, only people who behave as demons." He added softly, "Like me."

"But you destroyed—?"

"I nearly destroyed everyone!" Skull's tone turned unusually sharp. "Besides a dozen or so petty magic-wielders, the most powerful Mage ever born lives within those walls. She's only sixteen, barely more than a child, and untrained in the use of real magic. But she put up such a fierce resistance that I—" He broke off and shook his head. "I regained control, of course, but I'm afraid a few of them were killed in the struggle."

The priest's breath caught in his throat. "But no one was supposed to—"

"I know. But it's a matter of focus, remember?" Skull ruefully ran a hand through his fine, black hair. "Commander Swift is going to let the archers use me for target practice."

Fighting for inner balance, Brother Honesty pressed his fingertips to his eyebrows and tried to mentally outline his report to the commander. "How many died?"

"Not many. Fifteen or twenty. The rest are feeling rather sick at the moment, as am I."

Brother Honesty released a sigh of relief. The deaths were regrettable, but it could have been worse. "Did you neutralize the magic-wielders?"

"All but the Mage."

"And you're sure about the demon?"

Skull nodded emphatically. "Positive." He tilted his head and added, "But it was strange. A second link seemed to blink in and out of existence, and at times I picked up a faint echo of a third."

Brother Honesty laid his hand on Skull's shoulder. "That would be the demon spreading its influence. Now do you understand my worry of it contaminating us all?"

"Not really. At a guess, I'd say they found some way of shielding the links. But I'll leave the spiritual stuff to you." Skull rose unsteadily. "Perhaps we should start back to camp. They know someone attacked them from the outside and once they recover, they'll probably come hunting."

Still concerned for his friend, the priest also stood and offered the support of his arm. "How did they find out?"

"She saw me. Bevin. The Mage." Skull shook his head. "She touched me with her mind, and I couldn't stop her. I've never experienced such power. She wields all five of the lesser magics, unprecedented in itself; and she also carries an untapped potential for mastering the sixth." He shook his head again. "Incredible. Absolutely incredible. And she's just a girl."

A different kind of anxiety seized the priest, but he made himself keep thinking. "She touched your mind?" He led Skull toward the camp, guiding him around rough ground. "So she knows about the invasion?"

"No." Skull shivered. "She knows about me. My essence, as it were. All the evil and darkness. The sick and violent urges."

"Hush," Brother Honesty scolded gently. He did not like how frail the Mage's shoulders felt beneath his arm or how he tottered like an old man. "You've battled and vanquished a demon. Evil doesn't work against evil."

"If you say so."

"Well, I do." Brother Honesty's thoughts ran ahead of their

present situation, and he mentally prepared his recommendations for the commander. Likely, the superstitious Marchlanders would blame the attack on spirits. Perhaps Claw and Wraith could prepare some harrowing illusions to drive that perception home.

Skull smiled weakly. "They'd enjoy that."

Brother Honesty paused to lift a thorny branch from their path. "I'm afraid I'll have to inform Commander Swift that you've broken your rule of silence with me. I don't know how else to explain—"

"Leave that to me. I have ways of communicating with the commander. Sometimes, I even use 'harrowing illusions.' " Skull laughed, but it sounded forced. "Or maybe you're right, good Brother. Maybe the rule of silence has outworn its usefulness. No doubt, the three of us could benefit from wider social contact." He stopped and looked at the priest. "I'm sorry I interrupt you so much. I'll try to stop."

Compassion wrung Brother Honesty's heart. "Don't worry about it." He resumed leading the Mage toward camp, skirting a clump of brambles. "Nothing I say is that important."

"You're much too—" Skull stopped again and drew a deep breath. "Amazing!"

"My child?"

"I've just noticed." Skull inhaled again, as if savoring the air. "My cold is gone! Bevin healed me!" He turned a troubled gaze to the priest, and his voice grew thin. "Why? She knew I was attacking her. Why would she heal me?"

Surprised and oddly touched, Brother Honesty did not know how to answer. "I suppose," he said finally, "it's what I would do, if I had any magic."

The Mage stared at Brother Honesty for a long moment. "Yes," he said thickly. "I believe you would." His gaze traveled from the priest to the sun-drenched beech wood around them. "So that's what you mean, when you say we're all heirs of the One Light? And when—" Skull's voice shook, and he paused to swallow. "When you call me your child, you're speaking as the Light itself?"

"Yes, my child," Brother Honesty whispered. It was a basic point of doctrine, but he knew that sometimes revelation hinged upon the simplest thing. "I am a vessel for the Light, its servant, and your brother."

Skull sighed but continued to look away. "I don't understand. I just don't understand."

"Come, now." Gently, the priest tugged on his friend's arm. They were both tired and had practical matters to consider. "Let's go back to camp."

Skull nodded and pulled his hood up to cover his face. "Yes, I'm hungry."

The two men continued through the trees, avoiding patches of thorny undergrowth. As he walked, Brother Honesty found his thoughts did not extend toward camp but to Dorlach Tor. He reflected upon those who died, mourning that he would never know them, praying for the grief of their loved ones. He also wondered about the young woman who had nearly defeated Skull: Bevin, the most powerful Mage ever born it seemed, a precious creature who possessed the ability to wield all six magics. And, perhaps, a vessel of the One Light.

"Stop," Skull ordered, his voice cracking with emotion. "Since I can't strip away her talent, she's a danger to the mission."

Brother Honesty spread his hands. "But she—"

"No!" The Hooded Mage swung his arm violently. "This is war! She has to die! I have to—" He paused, as if choked by the words. "I have to kill her."

Shocked to his soul, Brother Honesty froze, staring at his friend.

Skull pressed his gloved hands to his veiled face, and his shoulders heaved with silent tears.

CHAPTER EIGHT

⚓

THE last edge of sun tipped over the horizon, trailing a color-
ful wake of sky that seemed to shimmer in the snapping chill.
Hands sunk deeply into his pockets, Maddock braved the quiet
edges of Dorlach Tor, despairing of ever overhearing news of his
father. He could still picture Cadder's face when the elder had
found liege and son locked in their illicit duel: the proud cheeks
withered into shocked anguish, the dark eyes haunted, the mouth
framing a horrified oval. The Horsemaster had not attended the
gathering where Lady Wylfre pronounced his son's condemna-
tion, but Maddock's imagination placed him there, his body
slumped and his face collapsed in the terrible aftermath of betrayal.

I didn't do it. Maddock rehearsed the obvious, as if merely
thinking the words could transport them to his father's ears. *I
didn't do anything wrong.* Memory returned to damn him: the
rush of hot excitement at the sight of Kiarda lying naked in the
snow, the velvet touch of skin and hair as he checked her for
injuries. He deserved punishment for the sin of his desire, but he
had not ravished Kiarda. The very thought set his stomach roiling,
and only the emptiness of his gut rescued him from sickness. *Kiarda, you know I wouldn't hurt you. Why didn't you tell them?
Why didn't you defend me?*

In the past, the thought had brought a rush of innocent, self-
pitying anger. But, after days of living in the woodlands, Maddock's initial rage had burned to ash, leaving him distraught and
weary. He could not find any sign of Gaer, and his oath to Hepona
seemed like childish folly. He tried to tell himself that, as an outcast and an outlaw, he no longer needed a gentle heart or a sense

of loyalty, just his wits, his sword, and a will to live. But he still grieved for all he had lost.

The darkness that followed the sinking array of sunset transformed the familiar village into hostile shadows. Oddly, Maddock found the sight more comforting, and not only because the lack of light would hide him from friends turned into deadly enemies. The blackness that blurred the world to shapeless traces of its former glory fit better with Maddock's current mood and reality. *I love you, Father. If only I could see you one last time.* Maddock lowered his head. Nothing would ever—could ever—be the same.

A remnant of snow at Maddock's feet became lit with an eerie blue fire. Startled, he stumbled backward, blinking rapidly. The flames remained, and he noticed other patches ablaze, filling the woods with a pale light that put the subtle reflections of moon to shame. *Dark Court!* A chill stabbed through Maddock, like cold fingers reaching for his bones. He glanced upward. Iridescent snakes twined through the treetops, spreading batlike wings amid the branches.

Terror seized Maddock, and he bolted toward the road. Branches scratched his face, clawing at his clothing. Only an abrupt sidestep saved him from colliding with a broad oak that he recognized a moment later. It stood in its accustomed place, branches swaying in a cuttingly cold wind, winged snakes cavorting amid its waving limbs. It had not jumped into his way as he first assumed; rather, he had nearly run into it in a blind panic that ill-suited a warrior. He froze in place, summoning courage with a will battered but not yet wholly crushed. Entering Dorlach Tor meant sure suicide. He would rather die fighting the Dark Court, slashing them to bloody corpses to avenge Kiarda's honor.

On the road to which his mad flight had nearly taken him, Maddock saw movement. He ducked behind the tree as a headless man raced toward him, hands outstretched and groping. For a moment, Maddock stood rooted in horrified bewilderment. Then the boldness trained into him by Gaer took over. He sprang to meet the demon, sword flashing from its sheath and blood spurred by the fires of desperate valor. He cut for the creature as it charged him. The blade cleaved air. The headless man did not stop, rapidly closing the distance between them. Maddock, too, held his ground, sword hovering in a low stop-thrust, anticipating the slam of impact.

But the creature rolled over Maddock like a cold fog. He whirled to find it running along the same track, seeming to take no notice of the surprised young man who stared from creature to blade in confusion. The demon showed no evidence of injury. Maddock's sword reflected the ghostly blue light that afflicted snow and forest, without a spot of blood to mar the steel. Fog condensed along its length.

The hair at the nape of Maddock's neck prickled. The headless man whirled, running back toward him. This time, Maddock crouched, the point of his sword thrust toward the approaching creature. Again, it charged him, faceless and unreadable. Once more, the Horsemaster's son braced himself for a collision, and the creature of the Dark Court flowed over and through him like icy wind. It raced up the pathway, disappearing beyond a bend.

Maddock rose, gaze sweeping the area. Snakes still writhed through the treetops surrounding the old fort. The patches of remaining snow continued to burn cerulean. Scattered twigs humped onto the narrowest of their appendages, creeping toward Dorlach Tor like spiders.

"No!" Maddock assaulted the branches, hacking with broad strokes. This time, his sword met something barely of substance. Chips flew, yet the twigs seemed undamaged. They crawled over the leaf-strewn forest floor like a ceaseless, insect army. Maddock hammered at them until his arm grew tired and the futility of his attack passed well beyond the obvious. Again, he stood, ignored by the Dark Court's minions yet hounded by their very presence. Driven near to madness by need and helpless frustration, he sprinted along the borders of Dorlach Tor, howling challenges at every creature that crossed his path.

Shaggy monsters with eyes of fire shambled in the pastures. Headless men as terrifying as the one he had challenged galloped through the lanes. Wolves charged between outlying cottages, teeth bared and tongues dripping black saliva. Granite boulders opened hidden mouths to groan and wail. Maddock challenged every member of the Dark Court he encountered, his desire for vengeance flaring into reckless need; but the evil wights continued to ignore him, swelling over him like morning fog and as frigid as new melt.

Finally, exhausted and trembling, Maddock collapsed at the base of a hollow tree and tumbled into fretful sleep.

A cloud of ravens swept the afternoon sky, calling to each other in the secret language of their kind. Maddock lay curled within the tangled roots of a deadfall. The cold locked his muscles, sapping his will and strength. Shivering, he raised his head, disregarding the strands of dark hair that fell across his eyes, and scrutinized the birds with clear suspicion. He was not sure they were what they seemed to be.

For the past several nights, Maddock had witnessed the Dark Court's dread power, as helpless to affect them subsequently as he had been the first night of their appearance. Everything had changed. The world was ending; the gods were dead. Nothing was as it appeared.

Hundreds strong, the ravens continued to sail overhead. The young man watched them fly, his gaze black and unwavering. When they did not transform into coils of smoke or rag-clad banshees, Maddock finally believed they were not denizens of the hollow hills but simply wild creatures. In spite of the pain in his stiff neck and shoulders, he raised himself on one elbow to see the birds more clearly. He admired their freedom, beauty, and jeering defiance of earthbound limitations. A peculiar longing awakened within him to become one of their noisy throng.

The ravens flew northeast, winging toward Dorlach Tor. Maddock's throat tightened as his yearning to join them intensified. He wished for the power to change his shape, and he imagined how it would feel to soar upward on black pinions, to hail the flock as brothers and sisters, to belong again.

Maddock's arm trembled with the strain of propping himself up. Sighing, he sank down once more into his nest of dead leaves and rotten bark. He avoided thinking about the future, though he knew he needed to leave Lady Wylfre's land soon. If he stayed much longer, the hunting parties that rode out every other day would eventually catch him.

As if in response to Maddock's thoughts, a horn sounded in the distance, its tone pure and silvery against the raucous cries of the ravens. He stiffened. He had not covered his trail when he returned from Dorlach Tor, more concerned with the doings of the Dark Court. If he stayed where he was, the hounds would lead the hunters straight to his hiding place. *Almighty Hepona!*

Maddock's heart picked up speed as he wormed his way through the protective snarl of tree roots, glad Byrta the Hunt-Keeper was such a stickler for tradition. The horn always provided an advance warning. He would be miles away by the time the hounds picked up his scent.

With soundless grace, Maddock ran through the trees until he came to a small but rapid river called the Coney. Free of ice, its gray waters surged southward, seeking the moors. Maddock jogged along its bank. He remembered a place, just beyond a small clearing surrounded by beech trees, where a willow hung over the water. If he waded into the Coney shortly before that point, his hunters would have to stop to debate whether he took to the trees or kept to the river. By then, he would have already doubled back behind them.

Maddock galloped beside the river, matching his stride to its hurtling flow; the roaring music of its movement seemed pitched and paced to goad him to greater speed. Shortly, he plunged in, water slopping against his boots and frigid droplets stinging his face like hail. For several steps he fought the raging current until he reached the willow. Grasping a thick branch, he swung from the river, hopped along the trunk, and sprang free. He dashed between the beeches. A man shouted. Maddock's heart leaped, and he skidded to a halt, scrabbling for his sword.

Carefully camouflaged with branches, a semicircle of tents faced a fire ring filled with glowing coals. Strangely dressed men looked up from packing their gear and sharpening their swords.

A flash of movement at the edge of Maddock's vision sent him whirling. Among several others, a fair-haired man lunged with a sword.

Lord Stane! Blood pounding in his ears, Maddock dodged and drew. Steel swished by his ear, a near-miss that sparked terror and rage at once. This time, he would not pull his strikes. *This time . . .* Maddock cut for the blond's throat, jarred from his thoughts by realization. He did not cross swords with the Lord of Dorlach Tor; the man was a stranger.

The blond's sword jerked up. Maddock's pinged against it, immediately redirected. The riposte slashed toward Maddock's leg. A sidestep rescued him, his return offense spoiled by another understanding. Other men than the one he fought had brandished weapons and were seeking openings.

Maddock parried another of the blond's attacks, turning the maneuver into a reckless, flailing spin. The men at his back jerked into awkward retreat. As he realigned, he found the blond's sword speeding toward his head. Maddock threw up his blade instinctively. Steel screeched across steel. Tipped toward the flat, the blond's sword hammered a bruise across Maddock's temple. His consciousness spun, but desperation kept him on his feet. He even managed a wild thrust that the other evaded with an agile backstep.

The circle of warriors tightened. Maddock sensed more at his back, knew he had do something swift and urgent. He noticed a branch just behind the stranger's foot, and memory of his last battle assailed him. *That's what war is all about.* The words came to Maddock in Stane's voice. *It is sheer butchery, bearing no resemblance to those pretty Dances Gaer teaches.* Maddock hurled himself at the stranger.

Clearly surprised by the maneuver, the blond raised his sword for a stop-thrust, too late. Maddock crashed against his chest, the impact aching through Maddock's own shoulder. He felt the other barely give ground and worried for his dedication to the same trick with which Stane had felled him in Hepona's shrine. Then, the blond stumbled, footing lost to the unstable branch. Maddock curled his left arm around the man's slender waist, his right guiding his sword to the now-bared throat. He crushed the off-balanced blond against him like a shield.

"Back away!" Maddock snarled, hoping the others would worry enough for the life of one of their own to obey. His heart pounded so hard it felt as if it might slam through his ribs. Agony throbbed in his head. He hid stark terror behind a mask of feigned boldness. "Back away, or I'll slaughter him." For the first time since his escape, Maddock relived the feel of Damas' flesh parting beneath his blade. The impression seemed suddenly stamped onto his fingers, and his mind painted patterns of blood back onto his blade. *Not now.* The more he tried to force the phantasms away, the heavier they imprinted his conscience.

The men in front of Maddock stepped down, to his relief. Clutching his hostage tighter, he cast a wary glance around him. The others stood in tense knots, swords drawn, though they did not attack. Maddock tried not to contemplate the situation. They had time and numbers on their side. In the end, he could only lose, but, for now, he apparently held the upper hand. And he would keep it as long as possible.

A motion to Maddock's right sent him spinning, dragging the blond with his movement. A man stiffened, a step nearer than his companions. His unfamiliar face set determinedly, and pale eyes locked on Maddock's sword arm. "Back!" Maddock shouted, fighting to keep his voice from cracking. As bad as his life had become, he was not ready to die. "Put down your arms." He deliberately winched his hold tighter, gouging the flat of his sword against his prisoner's neck until the blond loosed a stoic noise of pain.

The soldiers glanced edgily from one another to the blond. No one moved.

Maddock swallowed hard. Their disobedience fairly forced him to carry through with his threat; yet if he killed the man in his arms he lost any leverage he once had.

"Wait," a man called in the tongue of the Marchlands. Without loosening his grip on his prisoner, Maddock glanced in the direction of the voice.

Dressed in a threadbare white robe with a green ribbon tied around one sleeve, the man approached slowly. "Wait. Please." He spread his empty hands, a contrastingly large diamond on one finger fracturing sunlight into rainbows. "I am unarmed."

Sweat poured down Maddock's face, and he spoke through gritted teeth. "That's close enough."

The man compliantly stopped. "Please, my child, don't act in haste. Let us discuss this matter." He had a thick foreign accent with broad vowels. "My name is Honesty. I am a priest, a servant of the One Light."

Maddock's self-protective rage faltered at the sound of Honesty's accent. It matched Gaer's exactly. He swallowed but could not reply.

The priest's eyes were the softest blue, his visage guileless and sweet-tempered. "This is a terrible misunderstanding. We truly intend you no harm."

The words made no sense. "Then why was I attacked?"

Honesty cleared his throat, as if embarrassed to bring up a delicate matter. "Why did you slip past our guards and invade our camp?"

"What guards? I didn't see any guards."

Abruptly, Maddock's prisoner spoke. "They did not see you either." Like the priest, he had an accent. And though he stood with a blade to his throat, his tone evinced nothing but friendly admiration. "You must move like a cat."

Maddock found himself absurdly warmed by the praise but remembered to maintain his grip. "And you," he said, returning the compliment with heavy-handed irony, "must have the courage of an eagle. Aren't you afraid I'll get tired of all this chatter and slit your throat?"

His prisoner laughed softly. "I am only afraid of dying a coward."

It was as if Gaer himself had spoken. Maddock's heart twisted. "Who are you people?"

"We are the saviors of the Marchlands," answered the priest.

Maddock scowled. "That isn't—"

A hound belled in the distance, followed by the wild notes of a hunting horn.

Maddock inhaled through his teeth.

"Friends of yours?" his prisoner asked lightly.

"Shut up!" Maddock ordered, quiet a necessity for thought. His wits seemed agonizingly sluggish.

"Let us make a trade," the prisoner continued in the same tone, "as a proof of good faith. You release me, and we shall release you. Yes?"

Torn by indecision, Maddock listened to the approaching thunder of hoofbeats. If the strangers did not kill him, then the riders from Dorlach Tor would.

As if reading his mind, the prisoner spoke again. "Perhaps another trade is in order? Are the hunters after you?"

"Shut up!"

"Your choice. Shall we trade with you or with them?"

The baying hounds grew louder, as did the sound of galloping horses. The surrounding men stirred restively, again hefting their swords.

Anguished, Maddock thought of his father, of Kiarda, and of the familiar stables of Dorlach Tor. Then he recalled the accusations of Lady Wylfre and the cruel hatred in Damas' face. *Can't go back.*

"Decide now."

"With *me.*" Cautiously, Maddock eased the blade from his prisoner's throat and stepped back.

The man turned and for the first time, Maddock got a good look at him. He had an open, agreeable expression tempered by shrewd gray eyes, laugh lines around his mouth, and a firm chin with just a hint of stubbornness. "With *you*, then." He extended his hand. "My name is Swift."

Warily, Maddock clasped his hand. "Maddock."

Abruptly, the hounds broke into the clearing. When they spotted Maddock, they broke off baying and ran to greet him, wagging their tails and snorting. That they still loved him, even though no one else did, proved nearly too much for the young man. He fondled their soft ears and caressed their sleek heads. "Down," he commanded in a thick voice. "Sit."

Still unseen, the hunters entered the beech grove, forcibly slowed by the undergrowth. Horses grunted in protest and tack jingled as riders urged their mounts forward.

Swift issued a series of orders in a language Maddock did not recognize, and his men hid themselves among the beeches surrounding the clearing. Only then Maddock realized he had battled the force's very commander. *Thank you, Almighty Hepona, for making him blond.* Had Maddock not mistaken Swift for Stane, he might have chosen a different opponent. A lesser hostage may not have won him the same concessions.

Twelve folk from Dorlach Tor rode from the trees, a mix of men and women, all carrying bows. The leader perched on a wild-eyed roan filly, and a horn dangled from the saddle. With a start, Maddock recognized the horse as the one his father was attempting to retrain. The poor creature wore a cruel "spike" bit in her mouth. Lather covered her flanks, and bloody foam dripped from her extended tongue.

Maddock inhaled in a hiss and jerked his gaze to the filly's rider. *Damas!*

The leader glared back at Maddock, green eyes burning with hatred.

Damas? Scalp prickling, Maddock stood motionless. *Impossible! I killed him!*

The roan squealed and hopped sideways. Cursing, its rider raised the bow and sighted down the arrow. Only at that moment did Maddock realize he faced Vonora, not her twin brother. She had cut her glorious auburn locks, and her face had grown lean and hard. A different sort of horror seized Maddock then, all the worse for mingling with grief and a strange pity. She had cut her hair, he realized, because he had loved it. *Oh, Vonora.*

The other riders fanned out around her and also bent their bows. Swift stepped in front of Maddock, shielding him. "Put up your weapons. This man is my friend and under my protection."

Vonora's emerald eyes flashed. "He is no man! And he is no one's friend!"

Maddock stood rooted, staring at the familiar faces. Most of the men worked in the stables; he had toiled with them every day. Vonora still looked beautiful, even with her cropped hair. He knew they hated him and meant to kill him, but he could not stop his heart's long habit of affection and loyalty. His inner battle suddenly seemed funny. Maddock began to laugh, then a sob tore from his throat. "Hello," he said, speaking the simple and ridiculous truth. "I'm glad to see you."

Vonora's brows drew down, but she kept her attention on Swift. "I'm warning you, stranger, stand aside. I have no quarrel with you, but I'll not let you interfere with justice. You're protecting a lying blackguard who murdered my brother and my mother, ravished my lady's daughter, and slaughtered seventeen innocent people—including my lady's infant son."

"No!" Maddock blurted. "I'm not—!" Then all her words sank in. *Seventeen people? Her mother? Little Lord Elrin?* "What—?" His voice cracked. "What are you talking about?"

Disregarding all the archers with a courage that seemed like folly, Swift turned around and gripped Maddock's shoulders. He looked the young man squarely in the eyes. "Did you commit any of those crimes?"

"No!" Maddock repeated. "But no one will believe me!"

Swift lifted his chin. "I believe you." He faced Vonora again. "You heard that."

"He's lying! He killed Damas! There were witnesses!"

"That was self-defense!" Maddock shouted hoarsely. "Do you know what they were going to do to me?" He pointed at one of the stablehands. "You were there, Ghan. Tell us what you planned to do. 'Gelding a stallion,' wasn't it?"

Ghan's square face twisted with scorn. "No worse than you deserved!"

"Enough!" Vonora called. She glared at Swift. "If you don't stand aside, stranger, you'll die with him."

Swift did not move but spoke a single word in his own tongue.

Three hooded figures in black robes glided from beneath the beech trees. Seeming to hover several inches from the ground, they drifted over the dead grass in absolute silence.

Maddock felt his hair lift. His breathing became uneven. *Dark Court!*

A low rumble shook the ground. Maddock gasped and spread his arms for balance. The tremors grew more intense, and the surrounding trees creaked and swayed. Screaming, the horses bucked, their riders fighting an impossible battle for control. The earth seemed to fall away from beneath Maddock's feet. He pitched to his knees. The horses danced frantically, shrieking in terror. Many tumbled, and each one threw its rider. Though Ghan had slid more than fallen from his saddle, he lay still, eyes glazed in death yet also wide with terror. A tree crushed in two.

Another died beneath her mount's trampling hooves, her body smashed into the dirt, her lips drooling blood.

Swift spoke again. The quaking stopped. His men broke from hiding and rushed into the clearing.

Arrows lay scattered, stomped into snow-wet ground. The remaining hunters staggered to their feet, abandoning their bows for boot knives, corn shears, and wood axes, all except Vonora. Clutching her bow, eyes blazing with frenzied hatred, she commanded her followers forward when retreat was clearly the only wise recourse. *Unarmed, untrained townsfolk against an army.* Maddock clung to his hilt so firmly the knurling gouged patterns into his fingers. Unable to assist, Maddock watched in horror as brave women and stablemen fell to swords like wheat beneath scythes. Within moments, only Vonora remained alive, shrieking commands to followers beyond hearing. Only the wild, unpredictable arcs of a bow wielded like a whip kept the swordsmen at bay, her heated stare always on Maddock.

For a moment, their eyes met. Maddock read madness there and a hostility he would have believed the sole domain of the Dark Court. A splash of scarlet caught the corner of his vision, and the anger he had vented on the nightmare creatures that haunted the woods after dark flared back to vigorous life. If not for Vonora, the hunting party could have left in peace. The blood of friends would not be soaking a clearing in the Old Forest. A bonfire seemed to scorch Maddock's veins. He watched, helpless, as the woman he would have married, who would have borne his children, to whom he would have dedicated his life and his honor, his everything, died beneath the swords of strangers. Her folly had claimed her. And eleven others as well.

Maddock howled. Black rage usurped vision. As if disembodied, he charged the corpse, blind to Swift's men scampering from his path to stand by in shocked silence. He knew only the urge to plunge his blade deep inside Vonora, to hammer anguish and rage home and home again until nothing remained to mark her passing. He wanted to destroy the happy memories that had turned so impossibly grim. He wanted to blot the whole from his memory, from reality itself. He needed to erase her very presence from the universe. And, perhaps, his own.

A hard hand gripped Maddock's wrist. Jerked from inner torment, he twisted to see who held him. It was one of the soldiers, an older man with a balding pate and crooked nose. Astonishment, disgust, and pity stamped the fellow's weathered features.

Heart still pounding with need, Maddock studied the other man's face in rising confusion.

The soldier spoke earnestly in his own language. Only then Maddock realized he stood with his sword raised. He glanced down at Vonora's body, remembering his welling hatred and the things he had wanted to do.

The soldier carefully lowered Maddock's sword arm. He spoke a single word repeatedly, as if soothing a frightened horse.

He thinks I'm insane. A deep shudder worked its way through Maddock's frame, and he let both arms hang limp. *Maybe he's right.*

The fellow released his hold and gave Maddock a fatherly pat on the shoulder. Speaking slowly and distinctly, he gazed at the younger man and pointed at Vonora's body.

Maddock needed no translator. *She's already dead.*

Honesty approached and asked something, spreading his hands.

The soldier burst into a stream of talk, gesturing at Maddock. Honesty nodded, looking solemn.

"What did he say?" Maddock asked.

The priest's quiet voice took the sting from his words. "He says it is a sick thing to take such revenge against a fallen opponent. Sad enough our need for secrecy forced us to kill unarmed enemies. A soldier must learn to conquer hatred, to fight with a pure heart, and to honor his foe."

Secrecy? The single word explained much, but Maddock was in no mind to contemplate. Nearly choking on his own shame, he said, "Yes, I know. Tell him he's right. It's just that—" He had to swallow. "She used to love me. She was my betrothed."

Honesty blinked in obvious surprise but relayed his words to the other man.

The soldier's brows shot up. "Ah?" Then he spoke a single word, patted Maddock's shoulder once more, and walked away, shaking his head.

"He says he understands."

Maddock's eyes burned. "Well, I don't." He gazed down at Vonora. The Hunt-Keeper's daughter lay sprawled in the grass, shards of the broken bow around her. Blood soaked the vest of her hunting leathers, but her green eyes lay closed and her limbs relaxed. He could imagine her merely asleep. "She and I . . . we . . ." Tears threatened. Maddock clenched his jaw. "I never wanted to hurt her. I must be going mad." Stane's words came to him again: *That's what war is all about. Your blood, your opponent's blood, the blood of horses, and the blood of people you love. . . .*

"Don't blame yourself, my child." Honesty's tone was warm. "The human soul is a great mystery. There is hatred in love and love in hatred. Everything carries within itself its own opposite."

"But—"

Honesty raised his hand. "Let me finish," he insisted gently. "We are what we are. But within us—" he pressed his fists to his heart, "—we are what we are not."

Maddock's swelling grief and self-loathing abated slightly. He could not recall hearing anyone speak in this manner before, certainly not a priest.

Tilting his head, Honesty smiled at him. "Do you understand me, my child?"

"I'm not sure. A little, I think." Maddock studied the other man, again noting the simplicity of his garb, the kindness in his eyes. He remembered the ever-changing flow of fat, self-satisfied clerics who passed through Dorlach Tor and how quick they were to judge and punish. "What god do you serve?"

"The One Light."

Maddock tried to connect the strange deity with the priest's philosophy. "And is there darkness within the Light?"

Honesty's expression turned pensive. "A few days ago, I would have answered 'no.' " He looked away from the young man, and appeared to gaze over the carnage. Dorlach Tor's dead still lay as they had fallen. The shivering horses gathered in a cluster at the clearing's edge, too frightened to let anyone close and too well-trained to flee. Backs humped and tails tucked, the hounds slunk between the bodies, sniffing death wounds. Vonora's favorite, a bitch named Honeycake, pawed her mistress' shoulder and whimpered.

The priest sighed and shook his head. "Darkness within the Light? I don't know. Perhaps."

Swift's troops wasted little time with the battle's aftermath. After the soldiers cleaned their swords and attended their own minor wounds, some stripped the dead of weapons and jewelry. They laid the bodies in a neat row, covering faces and straightening contorted limbs, then heaped each individual's personal belongings in a modest pile at his or her feet. Watching the soldier's respectful treatment of former enemies brought the flush of fresh shame to Maddock's face.

Some of the men began to break camp, while the rest collected the animals. They tethered the hounds next to an uprooted beech and provided a leather pail of clean water. They caught most of the hysterical horses and picketed them upwind of the bodies. Maddock watched the animals, sharing their fear and sorrow. Worry for them mercifully dragged his thoughts from the human carnage, at least for a little while. Swift's men would keep the horses, he felt certain, to add to their own supply. The dogs were a whole other matter. If loosed, they would return to Dorlach Tor, perhaps to lead another hunting party against him. Maddock could not bear the thought of killing them, yet he could never care for so many nor contain them when he needed to hide. Somehow, he would have to convince the commander of their usefulness to his army.

Soon, only the roan filly evaded capture. Trailing her reins, she charged around the clearing, wheeling from pursuit, rolling her eyes until they showed white. One of the soldiers made the foolhardy mistake of trying to approach her from the rear. With a tidy kick of her near hind hoof, the filly sent him sprawling.

"Wait!" Maddock called. He motioned to the other men attempting to catch her, miming for them to back away. Red-faced and out of breath, they obeyed, gesturing for him to try.

Maddock took a few careful steps toward the filly to get her attention, speaking in a low, cheerful voice. "Hello, lass. Remember me? I'm your brother."

The roan tossed her head, shaking bloody foam from her lips. Pity wrung the young man's heart. "Poor thing. Poor thing. That bit hurts you, doesn't it?" He eased closer. The Children of Hepona were wiser than other horses, and Cadder always maintained that they understood the sense of simple phrases. He slowly extended his hand. "Let me help you. I can make the hurt stop."

Ears flat, the filly lowered her head and scooped her neck like a striking goose.

"Steady, now, my darling lass. None of your tricks."

Maddock continued to hold out his hand. "Father taught you better than that."

Blood welling at the corners of her mouth, the filly tongued the bit, then tossed her pretty head in obvious pain.

Maddock closed the gap between them and laid his hand on a shoulder sticky with dirt and sweat. "That's a good lass." With a quick, gliding motion he pulled the bridle off. It fell to the ground, its spiked bit red with blood. "There we go."

The filly stood utterly still for a moment, head lowered. Then she groaned, spread her jaws, and stuck out her tongue. It resembled a piece of raw venison.

Cadder would never permit anyone to abuse one of his horses. Maddock's eyes stung. *He's dead.* Understanding surged through him, too painful to contemplate. Memory of Stane's words in Hepona's temple added terror to his grief: "This is going to kill your father." *Father's dead, and it's my fault. They put him to death because of me.* Tears spilled from Maddock's eyes, blurring his vision and leaving tracks in the dust on his cheeks. "Poor lass. My poor wee sister." He stroked her filthy shoulder, wondering how much time had passed since anyone showed her the least kindness, how long since his father last touched her. "We're quite a pair, aren't we? Both of us orphans."

Nickering curiously, the filly twisted her long neck and sniffed Maddock's face.

Through all the pain in his heart, the Horsemaster's son felt a slender and tremulous joy. *She knows me.* He stood still, letting her puff warm breath on his tears, and recalled what a nuisance she had been in the stables. A beautiful horse but as rampant and prickly as a wild rose bush. *Everything holds its own opposite. Roses have thorns, and thorns have roses.* "Come, lass," he said thickly. "Time for you to rest."

The filly permitted Maddock to lead her to the picket line, though she rolled her eyes and squealed if any of the soldiers drew near. Maddock stripped off her saddle, all the while murmuring gentle nonsense, and gave her a hasty rubdown with the saddle blanket. The other horses drew close, nosing her over and snorting in greeting. When he judged them all reasonably calm, Maddock turned away.

Swift's troops had completed striking camp and stood in a loose ring around the slain. All eyes were on Maddock.

Maddock froze, wondering if he had the strength for another fight.

Raising his hands in peace, Swift approached Maddock. "It is our custom to salute our fallen opponents with a Dance. We are going to perform 'Circle Around the Moon.' Do you know it?"

Unable to speak, the young man nodded. Gaer had taught him the long, stately form, which emphasized the swordsman's strength and balance.

Swift's brows arched up to disappear beneath his white-blond bangs, but he did not offer comment upon Maddock's knowledge. "Would you like to participate?"

An indefinable emotion seized Maddock. It felt like a combination of pride and gratitude, and it spread over his pain-filled spirit like a balm. He nodded again.

The commander's face opened in a surprisingly gentle smile. "Come, then." He laid his arm along Maddock's shoulder, as if he were a longtime comrade, and led him to the ring of waiting soldiers. "You stand by me."

Taking the position indicated, Maddock glanced around the assembled men, finding every face solemn and intent. Reluctantly, he looked at the dead of Dorlach Tor. They lay in a formal row, shrouded in their own cloaks. At the feet of each body lay a sad little pile of personal belongings.

Maddock swallowed hard. He had known these people all his

life, knew their dreams and what made them laugh, knew the stories behind their bracelets and gilt hunting knives. But he did not belong to them anymore. *They want me dead. They killed my father.*

High overhead, a raven called.

Commander Swift assumed a fighting stance, his knees flexed and weight balanced. "Ready!"

In unison with every other man, Maddock snapped into the same stance. In the next instant, he realized he had understood the order, spoken in the special language reserved for sword training.

Swift drew his sword. "Present!"

Matching his movement with the men around him, Maddock also drew his sword. Clasping the hilt in both hands, he held the blade at a slanting angle, poised for the Dance.

A flock of ravens flew over the clearing and filled the air with their clamor.

"Commence!"

With slow, liquid grace, Maddock swept his blade down and to the right. He watched the soldiers opposite him in the ring, careful to mirror their moves. As always when he performed a Dance, Maddock forgot himself. Anguish of the spirit and exhaustion of the body ceased to exist. Every precise feint, every shift of balance brought a sense of inner unity. But this time, he also felt at one with a group. Twisting, thrusting, turning in a dreamlike rhythm, he let himself merge with the strangers around him.

When the Dance drew to its dignified close, Maddock held the final position, unwilling to lose the feeling of belonging. The soldiers dispersed, talking softly amongst themselves.

A warm hand fell on Maddock's shoulder. "Put up your sword." Swift's tone was not without sympathy, but it clearly conveyed an order. "Time for us to ride."

A shadow fell over Maddock's heart. *It's the end.* He watched the men go to the picket lines and saddle their horses. Then he looked at the commander, seeking words to describe the magnitude of what he felt. They were going to ride away and leave him. He wished they would instead plunge a sword through his vitals, wrap him in his own cloak, and lay his body with Vonora and the others. He drew breath to try to find the words that might rescue the hounds.

His brow creasing, Swift studied Maddock. "Did you understand me?"

Swallowing, Maddock nodded. "I just—"

Swift's forehead smoothed. "Are you too tired to sit a horse? Would you rather go in the baggage cart?"

"You mean—?" Maddock's heart beat so hard he could scarcely breathe. "You're taking me with you?"

"You are free to come or go as you choose, but I hope you come." Commander Swift gave Maddock a charming smile. "You're my friend and under my protection. Remember?"

Heart stinging with gratitude, Maddock blinked against a rush of tears. "Thank you."

"You're welcome. Now, put up your sword."

Hastily, Maddock obeyed. "Sorry."

The commander's smile widened. "Choose: horse or cart?"

"Horse."

Swift pointed toward the captured mounts from Dorlach Tor which his men had begun untying to lead. "They're all fine beasts. Which one do you want for your own?"

Maddock's lips parted in shock. "My own?" He heard his voice emerge as a reedy squeak, and he cleared his throat. "You mean, to keep?"

Swift laughed, obviously pleased by the young man's startled reaction. "Of course. But hurry, we need to leave soon."

Maddock looked at the horses. They stood in a tight, defensive herd with their heads up and their ears flicking at every sound. He knew them all, had trained several of them personally, but even as he considered the best qualities of each, his heart spoke for him. "The roan filly."

"The wild one who kicked poor Friendship?" Swift peered at him. "Are you sure?"

"Yes," Maddock said, though he was not.

Swift whistled in admiration. "If you can handle that she-wolf, you're a better man than I." He clapped Maddock on the back. "Don't take too long to saddle her. We must be far away before the Hooded Magicians call down the fire that will consume our fallen foes." He favored Maddock with another smile, then strode toward his men, giving a string of orders in his own tongue.

Croaking to each other in a language just as strange, the circling ravens swooped from the sky to settle on the surrounding beeches.

Heart skipping, Maddock drew a deep breath and approached the horses. It occurred to him that he may have made the most stupid decision of his life. He could not afford to seem incompetent in front of Commander Swift. "Little Sister," he called softly. "Come here."

The filly tossed her head and snorted, then nervously stepped away from the other horses.

"That's a good lass," Maddock said in an encouraging tone. "Come to your brother. Come."

She squealed, took a little hop sideways, then charged him.

Maddock stood his ground.

The filly swerved just before reaching him, then pranced in a circle to face him.

The Horsemaster's son was not sure whether to cheer or curse. *At least they didn't break her spirit.* "You think you're clever, don't you?" He cupped her delicate chin in his hand and studied the torn corners of her mouth. "Too sore for a bridle."

She snorted and swished her tail.

"I won't tack you up again," he said, "but you have to be a good lass. Understand? No tricks, or the two of us will be in trouble."

The filly stretched out her nose and nuzzled his cheek. "All right, then." With practiced grace, Maddock swung to her side, grabbed a fistful of mane, and vaulted onto her back. The filly stood as still as a statue. "Good lass!" It felt wonderful to sit horseback again. Maddock squeezed his knees, signaling her to walk, and the horse obeyed. "That's my good Little Sister."

Maddock's scabbard flopped awkwardly, and he fumbled to adjust it. He suddenly realized he had never worn a sword while riding. Gaer had never trained him in mounted warfare.

Worried about appearing inept, Maddock glanced toward the commander.

Swift sat upon his heavy and undistinguished mount, staring at Maddock with a peculiar expression. "Are you speaking to your horse?"

Surprised by the ridiculous question, Maddock nevertheless answered respectfully. "Yes, I am."

A mutter traveled down the column of soldiers, and some of them regarded him with sudden suspicion.

Swift's brow furrowed. "And does the horse . . . understand you?"

A strange anxiety seized Maddock, and he wondered if he had done something offensive. Shifting his weight, he signaled the filly to stop. "A little. Mostly she responds to the tone of my voice. It soothes her."

Granted a wide berth by the soldiers, the three hooded figures hovered together beside an uprooted tree. Swift looked at them and asked a question in his own language. The tallest made a violently negative gesture. Swift's brow cleared, and he smiled at the young man. "It is not our custom to speak to animals beyond giving them commands."

Maddock licked his dry lips, thinking fast. "In the Marchlands, we also train our horses to respond to verbal commands. That's why we talk to them, so they learn to listen and to obey only the voice of their rider."

"Interesting." Swift beckoned. "Come ride beside me, so that we may talk. I want to hear more about the ways of the Marchlands."

And I want to learn about you, too. Maddock drew up beside the commander, realizing he had never gotten an answer as to their identity. But first, he began his plea for the dogs.

⚜

Clean, fed, and slightly drunk on sweet wine, Maddock lay on his bedroll near the fire, curled beneath the warm bulk of a borrowed sheepskin. His muscles ached from the grueling day-long ride, but his spirit floated in a golden haze of contentment. He had lost his old family but gained a new one.

Around him, the soldiers sorted gear and sharpened swords,

speaking softly in their strange language. Maddock listened, feeling as if he understood. They spoke of past battles, close calls, sweethearts and wives. They were his brothers. He belonged with them.

For the first time in days, Maddock's mind relaxed easily toward sleep. A hound snuggled up beside him to share his warmth. Smiling drowsily, he closed his eyes and burrowed deeper beneath the sheepskin.

CHAPTER NINE

B EVIN paused beside a ribbon-seller's stall. Nearby, a courting couple laughed, playfully arguing over a choice between a length of scarlet satin or green embroidered velvet. Forbidden to touch before marriage, the youth and maid each held the end of a horse hobble already decorated with scores of bright ribbons.

With a pang of jealous regret, Bevin walked on, lifting her skirts above the mud. She had been looking forward to the spring horse fair, traditionally a time for young men and women to meet. But, after a morning spent walking alone among strangers, her anticipation was fading. None of the boys spared her a glance, though she had spent hours on her hair and wore her goldstone earrings. *What did I expect? Why should today be different than any other day?*

The aroma of buttery pastries and melting cheese drifted from a nearby booth. Suddenly hungry in spite of a generous breakfast, Bevin glanced toward its source. Guilt assailed her, and her hands folded over the soft bulges at her middle. She knew her craving stemmed from sadness and a desire for comfort, but she could not resist. *Just one.*

A soft weight landed on Bevin's right shoulder, accompanied by a trilling purr. Startled, she jerked her head and stared into the amber eyes of an orange tabby. "Well, hello!"

The cat dragged his nose across Bevin's cheek, leaving a wet smear, and increased the volume of his purr.

Bevin then recognized the creature as Lord Tynan's link-mate. "Cat-of-All-Magical-Knowledge, what are you doing wandering alone at the fair?" She studied the milling throng, searching for anyone wearing the colors of Sarn Moor. "Aren't you afraid you'll get trod upon?"

The cat slipped from Bevin's right shoulder to her left, gliding behind her head, and curled his striped tail under her nose.

Bevin laughed. "Thank you so much. That's all I need: a mustache."

A man spoke from her left side, screened from her sight by the cat. "I agree. Quite attractive."

Bevin turned.

Lord Adan stood grinning down at her, the scarred half of his face pulled into a roguish squint. "But not every maiden can carry the look off with such charm."

Bevin's pulse fluttered, but she spread her skirts in a flowery curtsy and replied in a bantering tone. "My lord is most gracious."

Adan responded with a deep bow. "Merely overcome by your elegance. However did you find a cat whose eyes so exactly matched your earrings?"

Bevin felt her face turn hot even as she smiled. Though she found Lord Adan unnervingly handsome, his manner inspired confidence. "Say rather, my lord, that he found me."

Adan's hazel eyes sparkled. "Lucky cat."

Bevin's heart skipped, and she had to look away. Adan was known for his kindness to underlings. She knew that was all his flirtation meant, but she could not help reveling in the attention. Groping for conversation, she gazed at the blue sky and budding trees. "A fine day, is it not, my lord?"

Adan's voice was warm. "It is now."

Still purring, the cat rubbed his cheek against Bevin's ear. She reached up to stroke the creature's silky back. "I imagine Lord Tynan is anxiously seeking his link-mate."

Adan laughed. "True. Shall we find my brother and set his mind at rest?"

Though Bevin believed Adan was merely being polite, she wanted more than anything to spend time in his company. She risked a glance at him. "It seems, my lord, a worthy errand of mercy."

"Quite worthy." Adan assumed a facetiously grave expression. "And extremely merciful. We are both just—" He gestured as if at a loss for words. "—a blessing."

Bevin laughed, shaking her head. *Sweet.*

Adan gestured toward the far end of the fairgrounds. "I last saw him by the horse pens, braiding ribbons into Dream Cloud's tail." He strolled leisurely in that direction. "The Dreamer hates fussy stuff. I wonder whom we'll rescue from the other?"

Feeling both self-conscious and happy, Bevin walked beside Adan. The cat rode balanced upon her shoulder, sniffing the air and looking pleased with himself. Bevin had not seen Tynan for several months, not since the day the Dark Court took its revenge upon Dorlach Tor. "How is your brother, my lord? Does he suffer from nightmares?"

"At times. As do I." Adan's expression turned gentle as he gazed down at her. "Do you?"

"Sometimes," Bevin admitted. "Most of the folk from Dorlach Tor have troubled sleep. I've developed an herbal tea of mint and heartsease that seems to help a little. I'll give you some, my lord, if you like."

"I'd be grateful. Thank you." Adan paused, then added. "I've heard you lost your magic. I'm sorry."

Bevin's stomach turned cold. In truth, her magic remained intact. She dared not use it, however, or the evil force that had attacked the other healers would return to strip away her powers. Living under a falsehood remained her only protection. "It's been difficult, my lord." She made herself smile. "Fortunately, I still know a bit of herb-craft."

"You're a brave lass, Bevin." Adan looked at the sky and took a deep breath. "Ah, spring air! I thought the winter would never end."

Feeling like a deceitful wretch, Bevin bit her bottom lip and nodded.

"Forgive me," Adan said quietly. "I was a fool to bring it up."

"Oh, my lord." Bevin's voice shook. "I—"

"Look!" Adan interrupted with forced brightness. He pointed at a stall just ahead that sold a variety of baked goods. "Sweet-twists! I'm starved. Will you share one with me?"

Surprised by the offer, Bevin stared at Adan. The double rings of bread symbolized a courtship hobble, meant for couples to share. "But, my lord, it isn't—" She swallowed hard. "Won't people talk?"

Adan's smile faded, and he rubbed the mottled skin on his right temple. "I suppose they might."

Horrified that she had hurt him, Bevin hastened to add, "I mean, my lord, that you're of noble blood. And I'm a nobody."

Adan made a noise of outrage. "A what? Who called you that?"

"I mean, I'm not a lady."

"You saved my brother's life! You're a lady as far as I'm concerned."

Feeling as if she were drowning, Bevin gazed into Adan's hazel eyes and could not look away. He owed her this courtesy for rescuing Tynan. Once he fulfilled his obligation, he would surely find himself a slender and noble woman. Until then, Bevin intended to enjoy his company. "My lord is too kind."

For a long moment, Adan stood motionless. Suddenly, he grinned. "It's just that I've always wondered how sweet-twists taste. With all those walnuts and cinnamon, they must be delectable, don't you think?"

"Absolutely, my lord." Bevin forced herself to remember that Adan only intended to put her at ease. "And it would be unlucky if you ate one by yourself."

"Terribly unlucky," Adan answered in an earnest tone. "I beg of you, save me from an inauspicious act."

Bevin nearly wept at his kindness. *Gods help me. I think I love him.* "Of course, my lord."

They walked together to the bakery stall where a pink-cheeked old woman in a white kerchief presided over trays of breads and cakes.

Cat-of-All-Magical-Knowledge sniffed the air again and emitted a prolonged wail.

Bevin laughed and reached up to stroke the tabby. "Don't worry. We'll share with you."

Adan cast an appraising glance over the sweet-twists. "They all look good." He spoke as if assessing fine jewelry. "Which one should we take?"

Bevin pretended to consider the tray of walnut-encrusted pastries, then pointed to one at random. "That one. It seems to have a touch more cinnamon than the rest."

Adan nodded judiciously. "Ah, yes. Quite right." He fished a small coin from the money pouch on his belt and laid it on the plank counter.

The old woman grinned toothlessly. "Good day, my lord. Good day."

Adan nodded courteously, picked up the selected sweet-twist by one end, and turned to Bevin. "I've never actually done this before. As I understand it, we're to each take a ring and pull the thing apart." He tilted his head. "Which seems backward to me as a symbolic act of unity. But I suppose it would be hard to eat if we left it whole and nibbled our way toward the center."

Again, Bevin's face turned hot as a vivid fantasy of doing just that flashed through her mind. "Then people really would talk, my lord."

Adan also blushed, obviously mortified. "Sorry, I need to learn when to shut up."

"No offense taken, my lord." Bevin took her end of the sweet-twist. "Maybe we should make a wish."

"A wish?"

Bevin shrugged shyly. "It's a silly southern custom. When two friends share a single loaf, they make a wish."

Adan smiled. "I don't think it sounds silly. Let's do it."

Bevin dropped her gaze to the sweet-twist. *I wish I were a beautiful lady, so he would love me.* "Ready, my lord?"

"Not yet. My wish is very complicated." Adan paused a long moment. "There! All done."

They pulled the pastry apart, then stood gazing at each other. A strange tension hung between them, and Bevin's heart labored to keep pace with her rapid breath.

The cat tapped Bevin's cheek with a plushy paw. "Me-Yow!"

The moment fled.

Adan chuckled. "Persistent little beast." He took a bite of his pastry, chewed and swallowed with gusto. "Oh. Good."

Bevin pinched off a piece of her sweet-twist and offered it to the cat. "Here, Cat-of-All-Magical-Knowledge."

The tabby sniffed the morsel, then turned his face away and shuddered the fur on his back.

Bevin laughed. "Then I'll eat it. See?" She popped the bite

into her mouth. It tasted sweeter than she expected, with over-tones of cardamom and clove cutting through the cinnamon. "Quite tasty. Thank you, my lord."

Adan was chewing again, and he gestured helplessly. "Mmm." Then, too courteous to speak with food in his mouth, he pre-sented her with another deep bow. "Mm-mmm-mm."

They resumed their stroll through the fair. Torn between an-guish and elation, Bevin ate her sweet-twist in silence.

A little girl carrying a basket ran up to them. She looked no more than five or six years old, her clothing faded and much-mended. She regarded Adan with wide, terrified eyes and prof-fered her basket. "Buy a hobble, my lord?"

Adan blinked at the child in obvious surprise and confusion, then knelt to her level. "Buy a hobble," he repeated in a friendly voice. "How clever of you to see we needed one." He shot Bevin an apologetic glance.

Smiling, the healer shrugged and peered into a basket filled with knotted bits of rope and scrap leather festooned with pine-cones, bedraggled chicken feathers, and uneven strips of gaudy rags. "I like the way they're decorated."

"Me, too," Adan said enthusiastically. He grinned at the little girl. "Did you make these all by yourself?"

The child nodded, curls bouncing. Then she sighed and rolled her eyes. "Well . . . my brother helped."

A gentle light formed in Adan's eyes. "Did he? Good for him." He reached for his money pouch. "I have a brother, also. Four brothers, in fact, but only one needs a hobble." He dropped several coppers into her basket, enough money to purchase a dozen loaves of bread, and gingerly lifted two hobbles from the tangle. "So I'll buy one for me and one for him. Do we have an honest trade, my good woman?"

The little girl giggled, evidently tickled to be addressed as an adult, and dropped an awkward curtsy. "Thank you, my lord." Then she darted off into the crowd, shrieking: "Mama! Mama! Look what I got!"

Adan straightened and raised the hobbles. "They have a cer-tain . . . innocence. A refreshing lack of pretense." He hung one on his belt. With a guarded look, he extended the other toward Bevin. "It would be a shame to let it go to waste."

Bevin felt as if she walked in a dream. Her knees quaked, and her heart seemed to hammer in her throat. She told herself it meant nothing, that Adan simply did not want to disappoint a small child; yet she savored the only chance she might ever have to share a hobble. "Yes, my lord. A shame." Scarcely daring to believe her own boldness, she took hold of the other loop. "Perhaps others will admire her handiwork and seek her out."

Adan beamed at Bevin. "I've always believed in promoting the arts."

From around the corner of a leather goods tent, Tynan came running, his brows drawn down in a rare expression of vexation.

Bevin waved with her free hand and called to him. "My Lord Tynan!"

Tynan's head snapped toward her. His gaze fell upon his link-mate, and his face cleared. "Bevin! Well-met!"

"Well," Adan said in an undertone. "Looks like the Dreamer didn't break too many of his bones."

Tynan ran up to them. He appeared a bit taller and broader than the last time Bevin had seen him, but he still possessed a boyish air.

Tynan bowed to Bevin, nodded to Adan, then glared at the cat. "Where have you been?"

The ginger tom shifted his weight on Bevin's shoulder and howled.

Tynan made a noise of exasperated disbelief. "I did not! You did!"

The cat jumped from Bevin's shoulder to Tynan's, then struck his nose in his link-mate's ear.

Tynan folded his arms. "I love you, too, but I'm still angry. I looked everywhere for you. I even—" He broke off and glanced at his brother with a sudden smile. "I have to tell you. I ran into Uncle Yos, and he said Krilla and Denn are expecting a baby!"

Adan chuckled. "Wonderful news!" He glanced at Bevin and explained: "A cousin and her husband on our mother's side."

Bevin smiled. "How nice!"

Tynan suddenly looked woeful. "Everyone's getting married

except me. Everyone's having children, and—" He glanced at Adan and Bevin's hobble. His mouth fell open. "What—?"

Adan shook his head. "It's a long story, but it boils down to this: a wee lass dressed in rags was selling them." He lifted the second hobble from his belt and handed it to his brother. "Here. For you."

Tynan held the tangled mess of knotted rags and rope at arm's length and stared at it.

Bevin pressed the back of her hand to her lips to hide her amusement.

Adan inclined his head, a strange expression tightening his scarred features. "Speaking of cousins, have you paid your respects to Kiarda?"

Tynan tore his eyes from the hobble and looked at Bevin. "Is she here? In her condition?"

Bevin's heart sank. Kiarda had not spoken to her since that terrrible day in February. "She's here, my lord, but I—" She swallowed hard. "She seems to be staying near Dorlach Tor's camp. Not venturing out."

Adan's voice held an unusual edge. "It must be painful for her to be the subject of so much gossip. And she has no champion, no man to stand between her and all those curious eyes."

Tynan nodded, seeming troubled. "I wasn't—I didn't—" He sighed and rubbed the back of his head. "How is she, Bevin?"

"I don't know, my lord." Bevin licked her dry lips. "My Lady Kiarda won't talk to me, and I—" Kiarda's pregnancy was not yet showing but, after five months and with twins, it should have been. Without her magic, Bevin could not evaluate the trouble. "I'm so worried."

Adan kept his gaze on his younger brother. "Maybe I should talk to her."

"No, no." Tynan lifted his head and looked toward the edge of the fairgrounds and Dorlach Tor's camp. "She needs someone her own age. I'll talk to her." He nodded a hasty farewell and strode away. His link-mate, perched upon his shoulder, looked back at them with a self-satisfied expression.

Some of Bevin's inner pain eased. She hoped Tynan could help Kiarda. "That's such a relief."

"Isn't it, though?" Adan grinned down at her, and a feverish brightness burned in his eyes. "I think I'm going to get my wish."

⌖

Tynan paused in the doorway to the horse tent and tried to force his eyes to adjust to the gloom. "Kiarda?"

The straw-strewn tent sheltered only a single white mare who lifted her head and nickered at Tynan. Kiarda stood with her back to the door and her face pressed against the mare's shoulder. "Whoever you are," she said in a choked whisper, "go away."

Tynan froze. His link-mate swished his tail. [[She's crying. Go talk to her.]]

Tynan wanted to run, suddenly realizing his total inadequacy. He wiped his sweating hands on his tunic and edged forward. "Kiarda, it's me. Tynan."

"Go away, Tynan."

Sick at heart, he turned to leave. The cat lashed his tail. [[Oh, dog turds,]] he swore. [[I'll do it myself.]] He leaped from Tynan's shoulder, streaked across the tent, and jumped on the mare's back. Purring loudly, he marched up to Kiarda's bowed head and nuzzled it. [[Pet me,]] he demanded. [[Pet me. Now! It will make you happy.]]

Kiarda sniffed and raised her head. Her voice contained both tears and laughter. "Hello, my lad. What's your name today?"

Still ready to flee, Tynan trod softly toward his cousin. "I'm sorry. He can be a pest, sometimes. Like his link-mate."

Kiarda gathered the cat into her arms and turned.

A flood of emotions poured over Tynan, and he could not move. Kiarda was no longer a skinny little girl with braids. Her hair fell in a shining red-blonde mass to her waist, her blue-gray eyes grown enormous, her figure full and womanly. Always feeling what his link-mate did, Tynan found himself in Kiarda's arms, cradled against her bosom. His blood pounded through him. "Beautiful!"

Kiarda glanced at Tynan. "Pardon?"

Tynan had not meant to speak aloud. "Beautiful . . . mare."

He gestured toward the horse, knowing he sounded like an idiot. "Is she yours?"

"Yes. A birthday present from my mother." Kiarda stroked the cat.

Tynan reeled with inward pleasure. He tried to think of a way to get his link-mate from Kiarda, fearing it would embarrass her if he told the truth. "I didn't mean to bother you. We'll go if you want to be alone."

"No." Kiarda shrugged and gave Tynan a sad smile. "I'm sorry I snapped at you. I've just been thinking about . . . everything. Everyone who died, who should be here now."

Tynan nodded. Not only had Dorlach Tor suffered loss on the first attack, but a hunting party that rode off to capture Maddock had disappeared without a trace. "I've heard the news."

Kiarda sighed. "Have you heard about Cadder?"

"What happened?" Tynan discovered himself drifting closer, and he made himself stop. "Did he die, too?"

Kiarda dropped her gaze to the cat in her arms. "He left in the night. I didn't see him go, but he talked to Father. Cadder said he wanted to find . . ." She paused, unable to speak Maddock's name. " . . . him. Wanted to ask him why."

Tynan did not know what to say. "The fair won't be the same without Cadder."

"No," Kiarda said unsteadily. She ran her hand down the cat's back. "Nothing is the same."

Caught by desire and desperation, Tynan heard the words spill from his lips. "I would do anything to make you happy."

Kiarda lifted her face, an alarmed expression forming, then her gaze focused on something just below his belt. "What is that?"

Tynan suffered a moment of panic before he remembered Adan's gift. He lifted it off his belt. "What? This?"

Kiarda's eyes crinkled with an abrupt and dazzling smile. "Is that supposed to be a hobble?"

Tynan's spirit soared at her change of mood. "Believe it or not, yes. Some little ragamuffin was peddling these, and Adan couldn't resist buying. You know what a soft heart he has."

"Runs in the family." Kiarda drew close and touched the dangling bits of rope and leather. "What are—? Oh. Pinecones. That's actually rather pretty. All the girls at the fair will be fighting each other to hold the other end of this."

Tynan ruefully shook his head. "Girls don't seem to like me. They always say they're interested in the spirit-link, but then they resent the attention I give my link-mate. Sometimes I despair of ever finding someone to love."

Kiarda cuddled the cat under her chin, as if seeking comfort. "Your chances are better than mine. No man would ever want me now."

Shocked, Tynan stared at Kiarda. "Don't be silly. There are plenty of men who—"

Kiarda's eyes hardened, and she set her jaw stubbornly. "Who?"

Tynan remembered that expression from childhood games and knew he had to speak carefully. "Almost any man with a half measure of good sense."

"Oh, really?" Kiarda replied. "Would you marry a woman who carried another man's children?"

"Yes!"

Kiarda blinked, and she took a step backward. "I believe you actually mean that."

Tynan did not understand her evident astonishment. "I do. If I—" He shrugged. "If I loved her, then I would love her children too."

Kiarda bowed her head. Her hair swung forward to veil her face. "What of the half of their blood that should have been yours?"

Tynan spread his hands, searching for words. "I don't know, I—" He sorted through his thoughts, trying to be honest, trying to imagine how it would feel. "I guess it might involve some pain for me, but that's—that's just the way things are. Blood doesn't matter. That's where the love comes in."

Kiarda stood motionless.

The cat mewed, peering through the curtain of strawberry blonde hair. [[She's crying again. Say something!]]

Aghast that he had caused her further grief, Tynan struggled not to weep himself. "I'm sorry you're suffering. I can't even

begin to understand what you're going through. But, Kiarda—"
His voice cracked, and he paused to swallow. "You have a chance
to redeem the horror of it all. You're going to have a baby."

"Twins."

A sudden shaft of joy pierced Tynan's heart. He pictured the
children, a boy and a girl, skipping through the Great Hall of
Dorlach Tor, the air ringing with their laughter. They would have
Maddock's dark hair and eyes, but Kiarda's spirit. "Twins," he
echoed. "Won't it be fun to teach them to ride? Or to count
cherry stones?"

"No." Kiarda turned her back to Tynan and spoke in a low,
wooden tone. "I'm sending them away, after they're born, to a
village in the Low Marches."

Tynan's happiness evaporated. "Sending them away? But
why?"

"It's for the best."

Tynan felt as if the ground had opened at his feet. He pressed
his free hand to his forehead. "But it's not their fault!"

Kiarda sighed through her teeth. "I hate them."

"But—" Nausea roiled through Tynan's gut. "But they're not
accomplices to your suffering. They're victims, too!"

Kiarda turned and glared at him. "Victims?"

Sorrow threatened to choke Tynan again, but the words
spilled out of him in a rapid spate of desperation. "What a fine
victory for the Dark Court, to turn a mother against her innocent
unborn. If you couldn't raise them, if you didn't have the wherewithal, then finding a better home would be a true act of compassion and caring. But don't let evil spirits deceive you into
relinquishing them without first loving them."

Tears filled Kiarda's eyes and painted glistening trails down
her cheeks. "Love them? How can I love them?"

The sight of Kiarda weeping proved nearly too much for
Tynan. "How can you not?" He clutched the hobble against his
heart. For reasons he could not comprehend, he wanted those
children. "I have no claim upon them but the weakest ties of
kinship, and I love them!"

Sobs wracked Kiarda, and her mouth contorted in a grimace
of pain.

Tynan wanted to draw her close, to dry her tears, to hold her as she held his spirit. He clenched his fists to prevent himself from moving.

The cat gave a thin, worried cry and stretched his paw up to her face. [[Don't be sad.]] Gently, he patted her cheek, brushing away the teardrops with a touch of velvet. [[Everything will be all right. You'll see. We'll take care of you.]]

A trace of laughter mingled with Kiarda's sobs. "Oh, my poor little lad, am I scaring you?"

"No," Tynan said softly. "He just can't bear to see you sad. Neither can I."

"Don't mind me." Kiarda sniffed and struggled for control. "My moods swing back and forth like this. The healers say it's the pregnancy."

Relieved to return to a practical level, Tynan nodded. He had always listened eagerly to women discuss matters of childbirth, and he remembered hearing about emotional storms. "Maybe you should eat. That old man who sells the sweet buns has pitched his tent not too far from here. Come with me." He added in a tempting tone: "I'll buy you one with raisins."

Kiarda shook her head, smiling tremulously. "I can't go out there. I look awful."

Tynan grinned. "Awfully beautiful."

Kiarda shook her head again, but without conviction. "When did you turn into such a flirt?"

"Maybe you inspire me." *Oh, gods! Why did I say that?* "Or maybe I'm trying to make you laugh."

Kiarda sniffled again and wiped her sleeve across her face. "Just what I need, a man who'll make me laugh."

Tynan's heart began to pound, but he forced himself to speak casually. "Well, until you find him, maybe I can be a substitute."

Kiarda studied Tynan a long moment, an unfamiliar light dawning in her eyes. She pointed at the hobble he still held against his heart. "In that case, perhaps I could help you carry that thing."

Tynan felt the blood rise to his cheeks. "This?" he squeaked, fumbling with the hobble. "You want—?"

Kiarda lifted the cat to her shoulder and approached Tynan

slowly. "Only so you don't run off before you buy me a sweet bun."

Tynan stood rooted in a fear that was also ecstasy. Coherent thought fled. "Sweet—?"

Carefully, Kiarda pulled one of the hobble's loops free and wrapped her fingers around it. "Something to hang onto," she murmured. "It feels good."

Tynan found it hard to catch his breath. "Feels good."

Kiarda adjusted the hobble's decorations, straightening and smoothing the strips of rag. "And I'll think about what you said. You may be right about the twins. Keeping them, I mean."

"Kiarda, I—" Tynan shook with joy and suppressed desire. *I want to kiss you.* "I'm so happy."

Kiarda smiled. "Really?"

Tynan nodded, then had trouble making himself stop. He grasped the other end of the hobble.

Kiarda looked at Tynan sidelong, that new sparkle still in her eyes. She gave the hobble a slight, playful twitch. "Come on . . . cousin."

Tynan walked with her out of the tent's gloom into the warm spring day.

CHAPTER TEN

T HE clear, lucent tones of the watchtower bell awakened Kiarda from a fitful night. She rolled over in bed, wondering who had come to call so soon after the horse fair. A warm wind blew through her room's open windows, carrying the scent of horses, smoke, and early roses. Midmorning sunlight spilled across the bedside table, illuminating an enameled cup of valerian tea. She wrinkled her nose at the memory of its thin, brown contents. Sygil had brewed the stuff, and it smelled as fetid as a dead mouse. The old healer did not believe in coddling her patients. In contrast, when Bevin made valerian tea, she always mixed in a sweetener like stevia or anise.

Thoughts of the gentle healer brought tears to Kiarda's eyes. Whenever chance brought the two in contact, Bevin displayed the shy courtesy Kiarda had demanded of her. Gone were the days of sitting on the pasture gate, sharing confidences or comparing the relative merits of Dorlach Tor's men in furtive giggles. A part of Kiarda desperately sought the solitude her moodiness brought her, the part that shied from hounds she used to love and made her secretly glad they had lost most of the dogs with the hunt party, the part that found a perverse pleasure in her blackouts. But a deeper portion of Kiarda clung to memories of their friendship. She wished things could have turned out differently, wondered if she could fix the parts of her life that seemed irrevocably broken.

Gingerly, Kiarda sat, tensed for the burning sensation that had spread through her gut with every movement last evening and through the night. To her surprise, she felt much better. Her stomach ache had disappeared, replaced by a sharp appetite. She luxuriated in this unfamiliar sense of well-being, glad she could forego Sygil's tea, and wondered what the kitchen had prepared for the day meal.

A knock sounded on Kiarda's door.

Kiarda smoothed the hair from her face. "Come."

One of her maids, the timid Rina, peeked in. "My lady, how are you feeling?"

"Quite well, thank you." Kiarda smiled at the girl. "I'm ready to get up and get dressed."

Rina brightened. "Lis and Darda are just down the hall in the sunroom. Shall I fetch them, my lady?"

"That would be nice, Rina. Thank you."

Rina curtsied and swept away on her errand, leaving the door slightly ajar.

Carried through the open window, men's shouts and laughter rang out in the courtyard. Kiarda held her breath to listen. She heard her father call a joyous welcome. Horses whinnied and received trumpeting answers from the direction of the stables.

Curiosity seized Kiarda but before she could rise, the light sound of slippered feet pattered toward her door.

The three maids rushed into the room, their eyes bright and cheeks flushed. "My lady," Rina said breathlessly. "Lord Tynan and his retinue just rode through the gate!"

Caught up in their excitement, Kiarda pressed her hands to her lips. The surprise visit could mean only one thing: In accordance with the most ancient traditions of the noble houses, Tynan had come to plead for her hand. "Dear immortal gods," she gasped. "Just like in the songs!"

Her maids squealed and clapped in unabashed happiness. "Oh, my lady," Darda said. "It's so romantic!"

Kiarda's heart beat faster. It *was* romantic. And for Tynan to make such an extravagant and public display meant that he saw her still as a pure maiden, that he was unashamed of her pregnancy. "Oh, gods." Emotions tangled within her. She turned in a circle, helplessly trying to think. At the horse fair, she had managed to forget the loneliness that defined her everyday life for a while. The sweet companionship of Tynan and his link-mate had eased her worries for the future. He was in love with her, he said, but Kiarda suspected he was actually in love with the idea of marriage and a family. *Still, I could do worse than marry Tynan.*

Worse came to her thoughts in an instant. Kiarda clutched the coverlet. She cared deeply for Tynan, but she did not feel the excited, almost desperate, desire she once knew in Maddock's presence. *Maddock.* Sucking in a tight breath, she braced for the rush of bitter rage that used to paralyze her every time she thought of the Horsemaster's son, but it did not come. She released air slowly through her teeth, savoring the dulling of sensation that time and logic had finally granted. Instead, she sought solace in the differences in her feelings toward the two young men. Her heart had steered her toward a vicious murderer leagued with the Dark Court. Her brain could only do better.

Tynan was a handsome man, Kiarda reflected, well-bred, lively, and a good listener. She could barely imagine sharing her bed with him, yet there was much more to life than romance. As future Lady of Dorlach Tor, she needed a Lord who would serve as her helpmate and ally, who would uphold her judgments and defer to her decisions. Tynan would fit perfectly into that role. He knew the workings and traditions of a Great House, he possessed the ability to bring out the best in people, and he would make a superb father. Kiarda closed her eyes. There was also the matter of Tynan's spirit-link. It prevented illness and extended the normal life span. Barring accidents, he would live long enough to see their daughter's daughter rule as Lady.

Oblivious, the maids remained beaming in place, waiting for Kiarda to speak.

"Oh, gods," Kiarda repeated, suddenly realizing how disheveled she must appear after a night of restless tossing. Matters of clothing and ornament had never concerned her in the past. "I look awful. What shall I do? What shall I wear?"

All talking at once, fluttering like doves, Kiarda's maids burst into motion. Rina brushed and plaited her hair while Darda and Lis laid out all her best gowns and jewelry. They seemed genuinely pleased for her, and Kiarda found herself touched by their efforts. *They're tired of feeling sad. We all are.*

It occurred to Kiarda that the Ladyship was more than governing her people, more than keeping them clothed and fed. She needed to be their best hope, their living pride, their lucky star. After a dismal winter of horror and death, the folk of Dorlach Tor needed a reason to rejoice. *I can give them that. Me and Tynan and Cat-Who-Brings-Happiness.*

After a quarter of an hour spent in a frantic rush of preparation, Kiarda hurried up the corridor that led to the great hall, the maids flittering in her wake. In the excitement, her stomachache had returned, but she could not stop smiling. *Tynan's here.*

A soft roar of voices poured out to meet Kiarda before she entered, signaling a gathering of the folk of Dorlach Tor. Nervously, Kiarda paused just outside the door and turned to her maids. "How do I look?"

Eyes bright, Darda smoothed Kiarda's hair from her face. "My lady, you look beautiful."

Kiarda's heart beat rapidly. "I'm so scared!" She laughed breathlessly. "Isn't that silly? Scared in my own hall?"

Lis patted her shoulder encouragingly and whispered, "With all due respect, my lady, I'll wager you're no more frightened than Lord Tynan."

Kiarda nodded, laying her hand over her heart. "Poor Tynan. Everyone staring. I'd better go rescue him." Before she could think about it too much, she drew a deep breath and strode through the doors.

Dressed in leather work clothes, Lady Wylfre and Lord Stane stood on the dais, smiling. Tynan stood between them. Dust from the long ride coated his hair and face, but when his eyes met Kiarda's, he seemed to glow with an inner light.

Kiarda caught her breath and lengthened her stride toward the dais. All around her, the people of Dorlach Tor watched. She saw the love and pride in their collective gazes, how much hope they had for her future. With every step closer to Tynan, Kiarda felt as if she moved toward the acceptance of some great destiny.

Kiarda reached the dais and took her place at her mother's right hand.

Wylfre kissed Kiarda's cheek and murmured, "You look lovely."

Trying to control the thunder of her heart, Kiarda ducked her head. "Thank you. There wasn't much time." She surreptitiously peeked around her mother's shoulder to find Tynan doing the same thing.

Wylfre laughed, drawing everyone's attention to the exchange. "Am I in the way?"

The gathered people broke into good-natured chuckles.

Wylfre looked back and forth between Kiarda and Tynan. "Never let it be said that I stood in the way of true love." She crossed behind Tynan to Stane's side and slipped her arm around his waist. She smiled at the two young people. "There. No obstacles."

Kiarda felt warmth rise to her cheeks. Her mother had just given her blessing.

Tynan seemed to have trouble breathing. His brown eyes sparkled with unabashed happiness. Beyond him, at the foot of the dais, Kiarda saw Adan standing with the other men in the retinue. His lopsided grin lacked its usual irony, and his expression appeared hopeful. Tynan's link-mate lay draped across his shoulders. The cat's yellow eyes followed every movement on the dais.

Tynan cleared his throat. "My Lady Kiarda. I—"

A commotion at a small side door near the dais interrupted Tynan. Leith spoke in a carrying whisper, "Hush! He's already started."

Everyone turned to look. Breathless, disheveled, red-faced, Ladayla and Leith stood by the door.

Stane beckoned them to approach, then nodded to Tynan. "We're all here now."

Tynan swallowed and wiped his hands on his dusty tunic. "I—" He paused and gazed at Kiarda for a moment in silence. "I love you, my lady, though I am unworthy. Allow me only to serve you, and I am content."

"And I love you." The time-worn words slipped out easily, but Kiarda suddenly wondered what they meant.

On the floor of the Great Hall, the people of Dorlach Tor watched with wide-eyed attention. Young and old stood together, grinning and tearful, all of them believing they witnessed the first stanza of a love ballad.

Kiarda could not destroy their fragile hope. She groped for the traditional reply, the one they expected. The one Tynan expected. "I accept your service, but only if you swear it for a lifetime . . . as my wedded husband."

Tynan's voice shook. "I so swear."

An exuberant cheer swelled up from the crowd. Tears streaming down her face, Ladayla rushed forward to kiss and embrace her sister. Wylfre also swept to Kiarda's side. "Wonderful," her mother whispered in her ear. "Just wonderful!"

Oh, no. Cold filled Kiarda. *What have I done?* In just four months, after the birth of the babies, she and Tynan would marry.

✦

That night, Adan lay awake, staring up at the shadowy blur of ceiling beams. *Strange bed, strange room, strange mood.* He ought to feel elated. Tynan's match with Kiarda was a plan long laid, an advantage to everyone involved. Adan would stay with Tynan at Dorlach Tor, and this too should have made him happy. For the first time in his life he was free of burdens and responsibilities. *Why do I feel as if I've died?*

Outside, a rooster crowed. Adan shifted his gaze to the window. No light showed around the edges of the shutters. He rolled from bed, padded to the window, and opened it to rooftops, treetops, and sky. Clouds obscured the stars, and the air felt heavy with the threat of an early summer storm. A smoldering ribbon of red light defined the eastern horizon. "Rain today," he muttered to himself. He could not go out riding. "Damn."

The rooster crowed again, and a horse whinnied in the stables. In spite of the previous day's mad celebration, Adan would surely find someone stirring. There was always work to do at a Great House. Thinking that haying horses would prove more useful than moping in his room, he turned from the window.

Adan washed and dressed in rugged work clothes. Moving softly, he slipped out the door. On the anteroom floor, serving men lay snoring on pallets, sleeping off the wine. Adan smiled.

He did not begrudge them their rest. They were hard-working lads, not normally given to excess; and they had felt truly happy for Tynan and Kiarda. He saw no need to wake them.

Encountering only busy servants, Adan made his way through the house to the main hall. Men were straightening chairs, strewing fresh rushes, and scrubbing the tables with sand. A gingery man with a steward's chain around his neck and a fistful of keys at his belt approached Adan. "Good morning, my lord. How may I be of service?"

"Good morning." Adan did not recognize the fellow, and he supposed the old steward had died. "Please don't worry about me. I'm just reacquainting myself with the house. There've been a few changes."

"Yes, my lord." The steward touched his forehead politely. "If my lord is hungry, I could send to the kitchen. The new bread should be ready."

Adan could just imagine himself eating breakfast alone in the main hall while nervous servants neglected their normal duties to wait upon him. "No. But thank you. I'm just passing through." He nodded a courteous farewell.

After walking aimlessly for a few moments, Adan recalled that he meant to visit the stables. Looking for a way outside, he opened the nearest door. A tidy herb garden lay under a gloomy morning sky. Bevin knelt beside a flourishing patch of catmint, a basket heaped with leaves and flowers on the ground beside her. A breeze tugged at her sandy brown curls. Obviously preoccupied, she smoothed the hair from her face as she studied the catmint, her gray eyes full of unusual intensity.

Adan cleared his throat.

Bevin looked up and smiled. "My Lord Adan!"

The unfeigned welcome in her voice made Adan quiver. "Hello, Bevin. I didn't mean to interrupt."

Bevin stood and spread her wide skirts in a curtsy. Adan loved the way she moved, dipping like a plump little hen about to settle on a nest. "I hope you slept well, my lord."

Not a wink. "Very well, thank you." Adan groped for more. "And you?"

Bevin turned pink. "Yes, my lord. Thank you."

Adan stepped from the doorway into the garden. "I didn't see you last night at the party."

"I was in the kitchen, my lord." Bevin picked up her basket of herbs. "Helping with the food."

Adan suffered a touch of indignation. "But surely they have staff to do that sort of thing."

Bevin ducked her head, her smile turning mischievous. "But, my lord, I am staff."

Adan blinked. "Oh. Yes. Sorry." He grinned ruefully. "It's just that I will always see you as a lady."

Bevin laughed deep in her throat. "A kitchen lady?"

"Why not?" Adan drew a breath of heavy, storm-laden air. When he released it, he felt as if he discharged every care and burden. *I'm free.* The joy that had evaded him through the night arrived with unexpected and surprising ease. "Now I know why the food was so extraordinary last night."

Bevin curtsied again with a coquettish swish of her skirts. "My lord is too kind."

Adan could not look away from her. "I'm not joking. I think I ate a whole basket of that fried hunt-bread. And those crispy things stuffed with cheese and sausage. Were they your recipe?"

Bevin's eyes sparkled. "Yes, my lord. I call them 'piglets.' "

"Well, they certainly made a piglet of me. I couldn't stop eating."

A sudden gust of wind swept through the garden. It smelled strongly of cold rain.

Bevin looked at the sky. "My lord, I think we should go in—"

Lightning branched through the dark clouds overhead, followed immediately by a crackle of thunder.

Bevin gathered her basket close and started for a gate in the garden wall. "My lord!"

Rain poured from the sky. Instantly soaked to the skin, Adan ran ahead of her and opened the gate. "My lady!"

Shouting with laughter, they raced through the salad garden. Adan took the basket for Bevin, and she hiked up her skirts as she ran. The unexpected sight of her pretty little feet and ankles enticed Adan, as if he glimpsed something forbidden. Everything suddenly seemed lusciously sensual: the garden's green fragrance, the kiss of raindrops on his lips, the awareness of his own body's strength.

They rushed up the flagstone path to the kitchen. Laughing, breathless, they stood in the shelter of the doorway and watched rain cover the garden like a gray curtain.

Water dripped from Adan's auburn hair and trickled down his face. Panting, heart pounding, he gazed down at Bevin. He wanted the moment to stretch to eternity. He would always stand by her, always share her storms. Before he could think to stop himself, he started to blurt out his love. "Bevin, I—"

From the kitchen an elderly woman spoke over him. "My Lord Adan!"

Recognizing the voice from his childhood, Adan turned.

White-haired and round as a dumpling, old Yasly the cook waddled toward them. "My lord, you're drenched!"

Adan looked down at himself. Muddy water puddled on the immaculate tile floor around his boots. "Sorry."

Yasly did not seem to hear him. "And Bevin-child!" She clicked her tongue in worried vexation. "Both of you, step in here at once. Why, the very idea!"

Every cook in the kitchen descended upon them. Orphaned as a youth and unaccustomed to any kind of solicitous attention from women, Adan suddenly found himself in the possession of a dozen grandmothers. They scolded and fussed over him, gave him dry towels for his hair, chased him to a warm corner by the bake oven, installed him on a tall stool, and commanded him to stay out of the way.

Trying to look meekly obedient, Adan finger-combed his damp locks and watched them prepare the day meal. He understood why Bevin did not mind working in the kitchen. The enormous room was airy, bright, and spotlessly clean. The cooks all seemed to be close friends. They bustled around the tables in their white aprons and kerchiefs, chattering about the cooling racks of fresh bread or the kettle of bubbling oatmeal.

Bevin appeared to be their favorite. At times the older women spoke to her either as if she were a toddler or as if she were Hepona incarnate. Yasly ordered her to sit by the fire on the other side of the kitchen, evidently thinking it proper to separate her from Adan, and told her to sort through a bowl of dried beans.

Adan did not mind that he could not speak to Bevin. He felt content to simply look at her from across the room. The happiness that had seized him in the garden had not faded but continued to grow.

Yasly swept up to Adan. She carried a tray that held a goblet of steaming liquid, a small loaf of bread, and a few 'piglets.' "Here you are, my lord. A spot of mulled cider to drive away the chill."

Adan did not dare refuse. He lifted the tray from her hands. "Thank you, Yasly. I'm sorry to be such trouble."

"No trouble at all, my lord." Yasly whisked away, returning to her regular duties.

Adan balanced the tray on his knees and carefully tasted the hot cider. Cinnamon and clove mingled with a darker flavor. Thoughtfully, he rolled the drink around on his tongue, trying to identify the unfamiliar ingredient. *Pennyroyal? Sickle wort?* He glanced toward Bevin.

She watched him with an obviously anxious expression.

Suddenly understanding that the cider recipe was hers, Adan grinned and raised his goblet in a solitary toast. *To my secret love.* The thought stole the joy that had carried him through the morning, and the cider filled him like a hot dose of reality. Memory assailed him, of the last time he had felt this way about a woman, shortly before his parents' deaths. A cool breeze had softened the summer heat, and love had driven him to leap two pasture fences and roll like a child down a grassy slope. He had always enjoyed secretly staring at Gwynneth, his then-betrothed, a slight and agile young woman with a cascade of golden hair. That day, he had studied her beauty from a row of cultured evergreens, reveling in the music of her voice.

Adan still recalled Gwynneth's words to her sister verbatim, though five years had passed since their speaking. ". . . has a good heart. Adan won't mistreat me." She had sighed deeply then. "I can endure a lifetime of his ugly face to become the Lady of Sarn Moor." Adan lowered his head, remembering how those words had devastated him. He had collapsed to the dirt and lain there sobbing, long after Gwynneth and her sister had left to go inside.

The pain had passed, along with his love for Gwynneth, but understanding remained. At first a relief, Culan's marriage had rescued Adan from women who pretended to love him to gain the Ladyship of Sarn Moor. *If only my brother hadn't chosen Tassi.* That no woman had shown an interest in Adan since the wedding demonstrated the truth that Tynan and others so vehemently denied.

As Adan drained the goblet, Bevin's face brightened.

Warmed by her sweetness, Adan set the empty cup aside, glad Yasly had stopped him from humiliating himself in the entryway. He must never tell Bevin how he felt about her. It would not be fair to her; she might believe she could not refuse a nobleman's advances. And, in any case, she deserved a more comely man. *I could find a good husband for Bevin.* The bare thought stung, but he clung to it. *I owe her that much for Tynan's life.*

The gods had decreed Adan's existence would be filled with loss, that he would always give what he most loved into the keeping of others. His parents were with the gods. Tassi had taken Sarn Moor and three of his brothers. Lady Wylfre owned Dream Cloud. The Dark Court possessed his childhood friend, Maddock. Kiarda claimed Tynan. That he would lose Bevin to another man seemed inevitable. *But not yet. Not this summer.* Adan picked up a piglet and devoured it with exaggerated enthusiasm, for Bevin's benefit. *I want a single season of happiness.*

❧

Whistling, Tynan strode across Dorlach Tor's dewy courtyard, relishing a rare moment of joy in the month since he had asked for Kiarda's hand. He loved the early morning rides, mounting up with the sky still pink to tour the boundaries of the estate. Though potentially dangerous, considering the disappearance of a hunting party the winter before, Tynan still found the long rides a relief. Once on horseback, away from the Great House, he savored his freedom from Kiarda's stormy, unpredictable moods and Adan's lecturing. The young women of Dorlach Tor treated him as the most desirable man ever born, staring at him when he turned his back and lowering their eyes coquettishly if he so much as glanced in their direction. They attended his every utterance. Their pretty smiles formed pleasant opposition to the pointed glares of his beloved and her dour, capricious demands for solitude.

A ball of warm fur nestled inside Tynan's tunic, the cat broke into a rumbling purr. [[I'm happy.]]

Tynan smiled. "Me, too."

The riding party gathered at the gate, led by the new Hunt-Keeper, Gaina, the youngest daughter of a landed Lady in the Low Marches. Rumors claimed Gaina's mother had sent her away to prevent her from usurping the rightful heir's place. Smart and aggressive, she wore her black hair short, feathered from starkly contrasting blue eyes and fine features. Other young women dressed in hunting leathers spoke softly together or tested their bows. The green-gold light of phos-lamps glinted in their hair and on the jeweled knives in their belts. Excited hounds snuffled and pranced around the horse's legs.

The cat squirmed and stuck his head out the tunic's neck. [[Our brother Adan brought us eggs.]]

Tynan stopped in his tracks. "What?"

The cat nosed his link-mate's chin. [[Our brother Adan. He's standing by the oak just inside the gate.]]

Tynan jerked his gaze to the tree.

Wearing an annoying grin, Adan stepped from the shadowed side of the trunk. "Good morning." He scrutinized the hard-cooked egg in his hand and picked off more of the shell. "Promises to be a beautiful day."

An obscure sense of guilt warmed Tynan's ears, though he knew he had done nothing wrong. "Good morning." He kept his tone casual. "What are you eating? A little pre-breakfast breakfast?"

"Oh, yes. Care to join me?"

The cat scrambled onto Tynan's shoulder. [[Egg! Egg! I must eat an egg, or I'll die!]]

Adan chuckled. "I don't need a translator for that. Come here, my little fur-bearing brother."

The cat jumped from his perch, streaked across the wet grass, and sprang onto Adan's shoulder. [[Give it to me!]]

Adan held the peeled egg up within the cat's reach. "Calm down. It's not going anywhere." He looked at Tynan with a peculiar intensity. "And speaking of not going anywhere . . ."

Tynan shifted uneasily. "I'm beating the bounds."

"For what? Trouble?"

Trying to disguise a sudden flash of impatience, Tynan looked at the brightening sky. "I really have no idea what you're talking about."

The cat bit at the egg, gobbling it down while growling and purring at the same time. [[Good egg. Mine. Good.]]

"Here." Adan tossed an egg to Tynan. "Bevin also made one for you."

Tynan caught it. "Thanks. But I have to go. The others are waiting."

"I'll just bet they are." Adan nodded toward the gate. "Are you the only man in the party?"

"What's that supposed to mean?"

"Tynan—"

"I'm not doing anything inappropriate." *There's nothing sinful about enjoying the view.*

"To be blunt, yes, you are." Adan approached and lowered his voice. "You're avoiding your responsibilities."

"You're a fine one to talk," Tynan whispered back heatedly. "We've been here for nearly a month, and all you do is hang around the kitchen and mooch food."

Adan's grin widened. "But I am not the future Lord of Dorlach Tor. If I start garnering duties, power, and influence, a lot of folk will see it as usurping your place."

That was true. Caught in a surge of frustration, Tynan punched the egg in his hand, cracking the shell. "My place, as you call it, is by Kiarda's side."

"Really? Then why aren't you there?"

Tynan's shoulders sagged. He looked at the bits of broken egg in his palm, remembering the fire in Kiarda's pale eyes whenever she ordered away his link-mate and him. He tossed the mess from his hand. "Because nothing I do makes her happy."

"Happy?" Adan echoed in a mystified tone. "Why in the

name of Holy Hepona should she be happy? Think about what she's going through! She's pregnant with—"

"I know!"

"And you still expect her to be happy?" Adan tilted his head. "Well, that would make it nice for you, wouldn't it?"

"Adan—"

"But she's sad, and in pain, and angry about the terrible choices she has to face." Adan's voice remained low and reasonable. "And you're punishing her for it, as if she possesses no right to be human."

"I am not!"

"Then why are you spending all your time in the company of unmarried women?"

Tynan spoke through clenched teeth. "I thought I was supposed to give Kiarda time alone when she demanded it."

Adan grimaced gently. "You know what I think? You believe that women exist only to admire you. And if Kiarda refuses to watch you with shining eyes while you play the rescuing hero over and over again, then you'll find another audience."

"What—?" A knot formed in Tynan's throat. Dozens of cruel retorts crowded his mind, but he answered from simple hurt. "Why are you saying these things?"

"Because I love you, you little idiot. And I love Kiarda. I want the two of you to have a good life together."

Tynan swallowed. "Then you have to stop trying to—trying to—" He gestured helplessly. "Just stop acting like a jealous big brother. And start acting like a friend."

Adan's lips parted, and his scarred face went blank.

Tynan could not draw a breath, could scarcely think beyond the knowledge that he had said the unforgivable.

In the next instant, Adan's expression softened. "Very well." He sounded strangely pleased. "I'll do that. If you stop acting like my self-absorbed little brother and become my friend."

Tynan paced a few steps, wounded inwardly and fighting to conceal his pain. His own words still burned his tongue. *Why did I have to say jealous? It's not his fault the ladies don't find him attractive.*

The young women in the riding party stood at the gate, holding their horses and watching the exchange with wide eyes.

Tynan waved at them, forcing himself to smile. "Sorry," he called. "Just a minute." He turned toward Adan. "I've got to go," he muttered. "They're waiting for me."

"Have fun."

Tynan beckoned to his link-mate. "Come on, cat."

The cat looked up from the egg and licked his whiskers in satisfaction. [[Where are we going?]] He jumped from Adan's shoulder and gingerly picked his way through the dew-drenched grass. [[It's time to take a bath and sleep.]]

"Not now." Tynan picked the cat up and cradled him against his chest. "We're going riding."

Adan spoke in a conversational tone. "Maybe Lady Kiarda would like to go with you. It's going to be a beautiful day. She might enjoy the fresh air."

Tynan's shoulders tensed, but he retained his smile, fully aware of Adan's intention. "No, I've already sent a servant to speak to her maids. Kiarda isn't feeling well this morning."

Adan's expression turned somber. "I'm sorry to hear that." He started toward the Great House, squeezing Tynan's arm as he passed. "I'd better look in on her. She may need a . . . friend."

Watching his brother saunter up the path. Tynan spoke to his link-mate. "He's at it again."

[[At what?]]

"Trying to make me feel guilty." Tynan spun and walked toward the riding party. "It's not my fault Kiarda's sick."

The cat looked at him anxiously. [[Don't we want her to get better?]]

"Of course," Tynan murmured. "But seeing us hovering over her will only make her cranky."

[[I don't hover. I lay on her pillow and purr.]]

"You stick your stinky tail in her face."

[[My tail is not stinky.]]

Tynan paused in the gateway.

Gaina gave him a radiant smile. "Good morning, my Lord Tynan."

Tynan nodded. "Good morn—"

The cat jumped onto his link-mate's shoulder and waved his tail under the young man's nose. [[Smell that. It smells wonderful. Better than fish heads. Better than catmint.]]

All the young women in the hunting party broke into a round of giggles. Irritation rising, Tynan brushed aside his link-mate's tail. "Cat, I don't want to smell your furry old—"

[[My name is not "cat,"]] the creature replied with dignity. [[My name is Cat-of-the-Most-Fragrant-Tail.]]

Gaina raised her bow, obviously struggling to smother her laughter. "All mount."

Tynan bent his head to murmur in the cat's ear. "Time to climb back inside my tunic."

A groom led Tynan's stallion forward.

[[No,]] Cat-of-the-Most-Fragrant-Tail protested. He planted his claws in the young man's shoulder. [[I want to go see Kiarda.]]

Flinching, Tynan smiled his thanks to the groom and took Storm Cloud's bridle. He pitched his voice only for his link-mate's ears. "If Kiarda wants us, she'll send for us."

[[How can she send for us? We'll be out riding.]]

Tynan sighed in exasperation and prepared to mount. Unbidden, Adan's words returned to him. *She may need a friend.* Tynan froze.

The Hunt-Keeper urged her mare over to him. "My lord?" Her eyes matched the sky, and black wisps of hair curled around daintily symmetrical features. "Is anything wrong?"

"Me." *A friend.* The words echoed through Tynan like a song's refrain, and the tender beauty of the woman in front of him only worsened his discomfort. *She may need a friend.* He ran his hand through his hair. "I'm wrong."

Gaina crooked her brows. "My lord?"

Handing Storm Cloud back to the groom, Tynan dismounted. "I'm sorry. I can't beat the bounds with you today." He looked toward the Great House with stalwart resignation. "I just remembered that I promised to do something for a friend."

CHAPTER ELEVEN

DRESSED in sturdy canvas work clothes, carrying a small bouquet of daisies and catmint blossoms, Tynan followed his link-mate over the threshold of Kiarda's bedroom, treading softly.

Kiarda lay propped up on pillows. Her face seemed unusually pale. Her eyelids looked shiny and sore, as if from recent weeping. Lady Wylfre sat in a chair by the bed, and Adan sat cross-legged on the floor. All three gazed silently at Tynan.

He cleared his throat, brandishing the flowers. "I—"

Cat-of-the-Most-Fragrant-Tail trotted across the floor, chattering like a squirrel. [[Don't worry. I'm here now. Everything will be all right.]] He jumped onto the bed and butted Kiarda's chin with his forehead. [[Kiss-kiss.]]

Kiarda smiled feebly and raised a shaking hand to stroke him. "Hello, my lad. I'm glad to see you, too." She looked at Tynan. Her voice sank to a whisper. "And you."

Impaled by shame, Tynan found himself unable to move.

Adan scrambled from the floor. "With your consent, Kiarda, I'll ask a maid to fetch a vase of water for the flowers."

Kiarda nodded slightly. "Yes. Thank you."

Adan sauntered toward the door. As he passed Tynan, he grinned and pressed his knuckles to his brother's cheek in a gentle parody of a cuff.

Tynan returned the grin, swallowing hard against a rising knot in his throat. "Thanks."

The cat curled up by Kiarda's side and broke into a rumbling purr.

Her green eyes softening, Lady Wylfre gestured at the bouquet. "An interesting choice."

189

Tynan licked dry lips. "Thank you, my lady. Cat-of-the-Most—" He broke off, his ears turning hot. "My link-mate insisted. He said daisies are Kiarda's favorite, but we also needed flowers with a lovely fragrance." Tynan paused and added in a note of apology, "He thinks catmint smells good."

Kiarda made a soft sound deep in her throat. "Please tell him they're beautiful."

Tynan looked at the cat. "Kiarda says the flowers are beautiful."

[[I know.]] The cat twitched the tip of his tail. [[Tell her my name. My true name: Cat-of-the-Most-Fragrant-Tail. The name I shall answer to for the rest of our lives.]]

Tynan shifted his gaze to Kiarda. "He says they're not as beautiful as you."

Kiarda smiled weakly and closed her eyes. "Sweet."

Lady Wylfre glanced back and forth between the two young people and stood up. "I have a few matters to attend to." She bent and kissed her daughter's brow. "I'll be back in a short while. Perhaps Tynan will sit with you until then?"

Though quailing inwardly, Tynan hastened to reply, "An honor and a privilege, my lady." He braced himself, expecting Kiarda to protest, but she only nodded, still smiling.

Lady Wylfre swept from the room, leaving the door wide open. Two of Kiarda's maids sat just outside, needlework in their hands. A lopsided grin on his scarred face, Adan leaned over the girls, asking silly questions, obviously trying to make them laugh.

Tynan shifted uneasily, wishing his brother would return to the bedchamber and help him talk to Kiarda. He did not know what to say.

Kiarda murmured, "Being unwell has certain advantages. I get to spend time alone with the most handsome man in Dorlach Tor, aside from my father."

Tynan tried to smile, but he felt like a heap of rubbish. "Kiarda, I—" He sighed. "I'm sorry I haven't been more attentive."

"I haven't exactly let you." Kiarda opened her eyes again. "I'm sorry I've been so moody."

Tynan recalled what Adan had said, how he expected Kiarda to be constantly happy. "Don't apologize. You have a lot on your mind. It's just—" He gestured loosely with the bouquet. "I can't stand to see you suffering. I don't know what to do."

"What to do?" Kiarda's faint smile turned mischievous, and she rolled her head on the pillow toward the chair her mother had vacated. "Start by sitting down."

At her movement, the cat repositioned, finding a new hollow to snuggle against, still purring.

Tynan obeyed, again noticing Kiarda's pallid skin and how sore her eyes looked. "I wish I could make you feel better."

"I know," Kiarda said. "But it's not your fault I'm ill." She studied the ceiling. All traces of humor vanished from her expression. "I need to tell you while we're alone. I think, maybe, something's wrong. With the twins, I mean."

"Wrong?"

Kiarda nodded. "Sygil says I worry too much, that lots of women have trouble with their first pregnancy. But I—" She swallowed. "I don't know."

The pain in Kiarda's voice was unbearable. Tynan blinked against the threat of tears, glad she could not see him. "Do you think you'll . . . lose . . . the babies?"

"I don't know," Kiarda repeated in a whisper. "Sygil says it may mean nothing. But I think . . . at sunrise . . . I think I felt . . ." She paused, then finished in a wooden tone, "There was blood."

Shock made it hard to think, to fully grasp her meaning. *Sunrise*. As he was preparing to ride. Tynan bowed his head. *Oh, gods*.

"It isn't fair," Kiarda continued unsteadily. "When I first learned I was pregnant, I would have done anything to be rid of them. But now that I want them, now that I love them, they may be taken away."

"Kiarda—" Tynan battled back rising grief and guilt. He would not burden her further with his own feelings. "I don't know what to say."

"Don't worry." Kiarda finally looked at Tynan and presented a forced smile. "Maybe I'm wrong. Maybe Sygil's right, and I'm just a hysterical mother-to-be."

Tynan recognized that sort of courage. He had seen his eldest brother employ it every day of his life. But it suddenly occurred to him that some things needed to get dragged into the light, not covered with a smile. He would not let her dismiss his own failure; he would accept the blame she was too brave to place. "I should have been here for you."

"Tynan—"

He could not prevent his anguish from surfacing. "How can I serve as a good husband when I can't even be a good friend?"

"What are you talking about?"

"Loyalty. And the strength to stay by your side, even when—" Tynan stopped, not wanting to shift the focus to his emotions and needs. He pressed his hand to his forehead. "I love you, Kiarda. I will always love you, whatever happens."

Kiarda turned her face toward the wall.

"How soon—?" Tynan could not think of a gentle way to phrase his question. "When will you know for sure . . . about the twins?"

Kiarda sounded suddenly weary, "I'll talk to Sygil later today. Maybe she—"

Someone knocked on the open door. Tynan glanced in that direction and discovered his brother standing in the threshold holding a white ceramic vase. "Hello, Adan."

Kiarda rolled her head on the pillow to look, without disturbing Tynan's link-mate. "Come in, please."

With an air of comic pomp, Adan carried the vase to her bedside and dropped to one knee to present it. "The water for your bouquet, my lady."

Tynan suddenly remembered the flowers in his hand. Uncertainly, he stuffed the stems into the vase, worried he might spill the water.

"Very good," Adan said approvingly. He shifted a stalk of catmint and coaxed one of the daisies to stand taller. The tiny rearrangement turned a fistful of weeds into a harmonious blend of white, green, and gold.

Tynan raised his brows in surprise. "Looks nice."

Adan grinned. "How could they not? You gathered them with love."

"Yes," Kiarda belatedly agreed. "They're beautiful."

Tilting his head, Adan regarded her with obvious affection and concern. "How are you feeling?"

"Tired." Kiarda smiled weakly. "And a little as if I'm braced for a storm."

"I don't doubt it." Adan set the vase on the bedside table. "But remember, my lady, that storms pass quickly."

Kiarda sighed. "I'll try."

Looking at Kiarda's pale face and listless eyes, Tynan suddenly shuddered. He remembered the storm that had struck the day the Dark Court attacked Dorlach Tor. True to Adan's words, it had passed quickly. But not everyone had survived.

The next few hours did pass quickly, a return to the easy companionship of their childhood, only with a firmer base. It seemed to Tynan as if they had both endured a rigorous test and became more worthy of each other for passing.

Kiarda drifted into a gentle doze just before Lady Wylfre returned, and Tynan did not have the heart to wake her as he took his leave. His link-mate remained curled by her side. [[I'll take care of her,]] he said, slowly blinking his eyes. [[I am Cat-of-Watchfulness.]]

Tynan nodded. He would feel what his link-mate felt. If Kiarda wanted him back, he would know. Bowing to Lady Wylfre, he left the bedchamber.

Feeling whole and sound for the first time in a month, Tynan headed for the training paddock. *Best to make myself useful.*

Tynan dismounted from a fractious two-year-old colt and handed the reins to a groom. Dust hung thick in the air between the high walls of the training paddock. The whitewashed boards of the fence seemed to capture the mild radiance of the July sunshine and intensify it to the heat of a blacksmith's forge.

Grit coated Tynan's hair and lashes, filled his nose, and soiled his tongue. Sweat ran in rivulets down the sides of his face, his bare chest, and back. Bone weary, though it was not yet midday, the young man strode to the gate. It felt good to work hard. He had forgotten the pleasure of testing his strength, though all he wanted at the moment was a cold, clear drink from the water jar.

Another man fell into pace beside Tynan, boots scuffing in the powdery dirt. Tynan glanced at him and discovered the Lord of Dorlach Tor, also stripped to the waist and covered with dust.

"Lord Stane," the young man blurted. "Forgive me. I didn't see you."

"Not your fault." Stane grinned, teeth flashing white. His arms and torso bore the evidence of old battle wounds. "I'm disguised as a groom."

Stane's smile, dry humor, even his tone of voice reminded Tynan of Kiarda. He thought of his betrothed lying in bed, struggling against her pain, and the brave face she presented. "My lord, I'm surprised you trouble yourself with this menial work, training green colts."

"But I like it. Don't you?" Stane wiped his mouth with the back of a dirty hand, then spit the dust from his lips. "Makes me too tired to think. Too tired to worry."

Nodding, Tynan opened the gate and held it for the older man. He wondered, however, if worry actually caused his exhaustion. "Yes, my lord, I like it. It falls within the scope of my few skills."

Stane passed through the gate and sauntered toward the water jar. Beneath the clinging dust on his back lay the pale scars of past floggings. "Where's your link-mate?"

Tynan closed the gate behind them, pretending not to see the lash-marks. Everyone knew the Lord of Dorlach Tor accepted punishment from the priests on behalf of others, paying for the misdeeds of his people. No one spoke of it openly. "With Kiarda, my lord."

Stane paused and cast a sharp, approving glance over his shoulder. "So you have the ability to be in two places at the same time."

Tynan shrugged. "It is a useful gift, my lord. I can feel what my link-mate feels. If Kiarda becomes distressed, I'll know."

Stane lifted the water jar's lid, drew a dipperful, and handed it to the young man. "Drink." His tone permitted no courteous demurral.

Tynan accepted the dipper and drank the cool water in three large swallows. "Thank you, my lord."

Taking the dipper back, Stane studied Tynan. "I know how hard all this is for you."

"My lord?"

"Starting your life over at another House. Walking the line between loyalty and self-respect. Learning to stay in love with a strong-willed woman." Stane took a long drink of water, then returned the dipper to the jar. "No real power, just a set of half-realized responsibilities." He tilted his head, gazing at his future son-in-law. "At least I didn't have an older brother to contend with. Adan's pretty tough on you, isn't he?"

Tynan looked at his boots, remembering how Adan had saved him from a terrible mistake. "He has to be, my lord."

"Maybe. But he's never been in your situation. I have." Stane briefly clasped the young man's shoulder in a fatherly fashion. "And I think you're doing quite well."

Choking on shame, Tynan shook his head. "Thank you, my lord, but I don't deserve your praise."

"Mmm." Stane sounded both thoughtful and amused. "So you're feeling unworthy? Incompetent? Strained to the limit of your abilities?"

It was exactly what he felt. Tynan raised his eyes. "Yes, my lord."

"Good."

"My lord?"

Stane's pale eyes crinkled with a sudden smile. "Adan is a shrewd man with an uncommon amount of insight into the human spirit. I'm not advising you to ignore your brother. Just trust yourself sometimes to find your own way, even if you're worried about making mistakes." He paused and lowered his voice. "I heard about this morning."

"I almost went riding alone with a dozen unmarried women."

"Those women are part of the generation you will help Kiarda to govern. Perhaps you were forging a bond with your people."

"Perhaps I'm part tomcat."

Stane laughed. "Are you telling me you seriously intended to behave improperly with a dozen maidens?"

Tynan sighed but forced himself to answer honestly. "No. Actually, I wasn't thinking about them at all." He looked at Stane, seized by a sudden uneasiness. "I just wanted a little space to breathe, a bit of freedom."

"Freedom?" The humor died in Stane's eyes. "Forget that. You'll never be free."

"I can't—" Tynan's sense of distress magnified. "I wasn't—" He clasped his fingers to his temples, abruptly recognizing the source of his agitation. His link-mate was wildly anxious. "Kiarda!"

Tynan broke into a flat run toward the Great House. He distantly realized that people stared at him as he sprinted past, that the sound of running feet behind him meant Stane followed. As Tynan burst into the inner courtyard, he saw a servant hurtling down the path toward him, face a mask of grief. "My Lord Tynan!" he panted. "Your lady—"

Tynan darted past the man without answering and flung himself through the door. He ran past gaping servants, up the main stairs, and down the hall to Kiarda's room.

A crowd had already gathered. Tynan saw Leith and Ladayla, their cheeks pinched and tear-stained. Kiarda's maids huddled in a corner. Tynan headed for the door but found his way blocked by a smiling priest with a bald head and beady eyes.

The priest spoke in a tone of satisfaction. "You can't go in there."

Behind the closed door, Kiarda cried out.

The hot and unfamiliar hand of rage closed around Tynan's heart. He shouldered the priest aside and opened the door. "Beat me for it later."

The priest began to protest, but Tynan shut the door in his face.

Kiarda lay in bed, panting and tossing her head in pain. Sweat and tears spangled her cheeks and forehead, darkening the red-gold tendrils of hair that clung to her skin. Old Sygil and two other healers hovered over her, muttering tensely. Lady Wylfre stood by the window, arms folded, expression tight.

Cat-of-Watchfulness jumped from the bedside table and raced to his link-mate. [[Poor Kiarda. Poor Kiarda.]] He sprang into the young man's arms. [[I tried to help, but I couldn't make her better.]]

Tynan pressed his nose between the cat's ears. "I know," he whispered. "It's not your fault."

Wylfre moved to put herself between Tynan and Kiarda. "You should not be here." Her voice carried no trace of emotion. "She's in travail."

It was too soon. The babies could not survive. Tynan's mouth went dry. "Please, my lady, let me stay."

Wylfre's gaze traveled over him in cool assessment.

Tynan suddenly remembered he was half-naked and covered with dirt. "I came straight from the training paddock. I have to be with Kiarda."

Wylfre regarded him narrowly. "It isn't permitted."

"My lady. I beg you." Tynan sought an argument she might understand. "Those are my children. I wasn't there when they were conceived, so I want to be present when they're born." Tynan blinked against encroaching tears. The twins would die soon, if not already dead. "Don't you see? This may be my only time with them."

Wylfre's face did not soften. "Safer for you if you go."

Desperation raised the pitch in Tynan's voice. "But, my lady, if you were in Kiarda's place, wouldn't you want Lord Stane by your side?"

Wylfre drew a breath to answer, but at that moment Kiarda shrieked.

Tynan's knees threatened to buckle. He pressed his back to the door for support.

Wylfre turned away from him, seeming to forget his existence, and strode to the bed.

"Mother," Kiarda said, panting. "Mother, I can't."

Wylfre murmured something, lost in a stream of snappish commands from Sygil: "Hold that! Get out of my light! Get rid of these!"

Someone threw the blankets from Kiarda, baring her straining legs and the blood-soaked sheets.

Tynan hastily averted his eyes and crossed to the window. He turned his back to the bed, wondering if he had made a mistake by insisting on staying.

Cat-of-Watchfulness curled beneath Tynan's chin. [[Poor Kiarda.]]

The young man stroked his link-mate, unable to offer other comfort. It was somehow worse to listen to Kiarda's breathless cries without seeing her. The air filled with the whispered oaths of Sygil and the stink of blood and pain. Time stretched, measured only by the beating of Tynan's heart and the agony in Kiarda's voice.

Abrupt silence fell over the room. Then, Kiarda moaned.

"There," Sygil said, her voice rusty. "That's it."

Wylfre spoke quietly. "Stillborn?"

"Yes. Praise the gods."

Tynan bowed his head. He waited for the tears to come, for the grief to rise up and swallow him, but his thoughts remained strangely clear. *Kiarda. Oh, Kiarda, I'm sorry.*

The old healer continued to speak, "Cover her up. Let her rest before you try to bathe her."

Tynan listened as someone fussed with the blankets, then chanced a glance over his shoulder. Once again, only Kiarda's head was visible, her face nearly as white as the linen.

Thinking only of Kiarda and what she had suffered, Tynan knelt beside the bed. He did not speak, not wishing to trouble her with his presence. The cat seemed limp in his hands, boneless with sorrow.

Her lined face filled with loathing, Sygil laid something covered with a cloth into a basket. "Better ask the priests what to do." She set the basket on the floor, as if reluctant to touch it. "They'll know the best way to dispose of these things."

The cat quivered and raised his head, sniffing. [[What's that smell?]] He slipped out of his link-mate's hands and trotted to the basket. [[I smell foxes!]]

"Foxes?" Tynan repeated softly. He glanced up at Sygil and found her staring at him in consternation. With feline speed, the young man lunged for the basket and tossed back the concealing cloth. Two small bodies, no bigger than his hand, lay among the folds. Wet, lifeless, covered with gray fur, there seemed little human about them. Their limbs looked distorted, jointed at wrong angles. They had snouts, pointed ears, and tails.

Cat-of-Watchfulness gazed up at Tynan somberly. [[Foxes.]]

Ladayla's bedchamber held more light than Kiarda's, expressed more innocence and femininity. Dolls and painted wooden horses, toys that Ladayla cherished too much to relinquish, perched on top of a storage chest, vying for the eye with the embroidered vests and scores of ribbons that hung from pegs on the wall.

Seated on a cushioned stool, Kiarda brushed the hair from her eyes and stared at her younger sister. "They're saying what?"

Ladayla sighed. "Stop squirming. It's hard enough to braid your hair without you—"

"Just answer my question." Kiarda stood up and put her hands on her hips. "What are folk saying?"

Ladayla flounced away a few steps, the comb still in her hand. "You don't have to get mad."

The two young women glared at one other.

After a long moment, Kiarda took a deep breath and forced herself to speak calmly. "I'm sorry. I'm not mad. I'm only surprised. You're the first person who's told me any of this." Trying to salve her sister's wounded feelings, she added, "I count on your honesty, you know that."

Ladayla shrugged one shoulder, but the tension left her delicate features. "Well. I thought you ought to know." She returned to Kiarda and gestured to the stool. "Sit down. You look silly with your hair only half done."

Letting go of her own impatience, Kiarda sank onto the stool, bowed her head, and let her sister comb the hair down over her eyes again. "Who had a dream?"

"One of the healers. I forget his name." Ladayla reparted Kiarda's hair. "The nervous one who's always biting his nails."

"I know who you mean." The fellow had been personally devastated when he lost his magic and, though he displayed little aptitude for healing, Wylfre did not have the heart to turn him away from Dorlach Tor. "Glist."

"Yes. Him." Ladayla divided a lock of Kiarda's hair into several strands. "He said Hernis came to him in a dream wearing the shape of a fox."

Glad her hair curtained her expression, Kiarda permitted herself a tight frown. *Maybe he dreamed about Maddock, not Hernis.* "Does Mother know about it?"

"Everyone knows about it. The priests are in a blistering rage."

"The priests—?" Kiarda broke off in thought. The clerics of the Joyous Reunion rode in and out of Dorlach Tor on a monthly basis, never permitted to stay longer lest they develop more loyalty to the fort than their own order. The newest rotation, led by a small dark-eyed man named Kag, seemed an unusually cruel and judgmental lot. Kiarda remembered overhearing Adan suggest that the real priests lay dead in a ditch along the road, and that a gang of cutthroats in holy robes now served the temple. "Why in blazes are the priests angry?"

"Because folk are saying—" Ladayla fell silent and began to weave together strands of hair.

"Go on."

"I just—" Ladayla sighed. "I just don't want to upset you."

Kiarda reached behind her and gently patted her sister's leg. After a week of weeping, bed rest, and people tiptoeing around her person and her feelings, she appreciated Ladayla's brutal honesty. "Thank you, but I'd rather know. And I'd rather hear it from you than from some sneering priest."

"Well . . ." Ladayla still seemed reluctant. "There's lots of different stories floating around. But most of our folk are saying that you were especially chosen."

"Chosen?"

"To be the earthly vessel for the children of the gods."

Kiarda jerked her head up. "What?"

"Maybe I wasn't supposed to tell you. If Mother hasn't said anything—"

"Children of the gods?" Kiarda wanted to laugh, then she wanted to cry. She remembered the furry bodies, the misshapen limbs of the Dark Court's spawn. Agony flared anew at the loss of the normal twins that had existed only in her imagination. She battered down tears, knowing their presence would silence her sister, and forced out, "If they were children of the gods, why were they stillborn?"

"I don't know. People aren't making any sense."

Kiarda lowered her head again, thoughts clotted by desperate loss. She needed to discuss the rumors with her mother and father. Someone ought to talk to Tynan, as well. He might not know how to comport himself in the midst of the storm of conjecture, though Adan would shield him as much as possible. No doubt, Kag and the resident priests would turn the situation against the Lord of Dorlach Tor. *As if we haven't suffered enough.* "Not making any sense," she repeated. "None of it makes sense. I suppose they're just trying to salvage something positive from the nightmare."

Ladayla abruptly hugged Kiarda from behind, poking her shoulder with the comb. "I wish it hadn't happened. I keep praying that we'll all wake up to find it was only a bad dream."

Touched, Kiarda leaned her head against her sister's. "Me, too."

Ladayla straightened, sniffing. "It just seems like everything is changing. I want to put out my hands and stop it, somehow. Hold onto everything good so it doesn't disappear."

"I know. But you can't. None of us can." Kiarda shivered. *Changing.*

CHAPTER TWELVE

FEELING as if she were about to step off the edge of a cliff,
Kiarda slipped through the gate of the kitchen garden. Tidy
rows of vegetables and herbs blazed green against the dark loam,
bees and butterflies flitting among them. At a respectful distance,
Tynan's assigned steward, Oric, leaned against the far wall, casually whetting his knife. He spotted Kiarda, touched his forehead,
and returned to his task.

With his link-mate on his shoulder, Tynan crouched in front
of an enormous spiderweb that stretched between two bean
bushes. Half a dozen small children, the offspring of servants,
crowded around the future lord. "You see?" Tynan said. "See
how hard she works to keep her web repaired? It isn't nice to tear
it just for fun." He pointed at the black-and-yellow spider. "She
has a special task, an appointment from Hepona, to catch the flies
that torment our horses. Do you understand?"

The children nodded, wide-eyed and solemn with wonder.

The ginger tomcat leaped from his perch and ran across the
garden's grassy border to Kiarda, calling her name in his own fashion, "Ee-ar! Ee-ar-rr-ra!"

Warmed by the cat's greeting, Kiarda bent to fondle his silky
head. "Good morning, my lad."

Purring, the cat butted his forehead against Kiarda's hand. He
circled her ankles, leaning into the turn, twining his tail around
her. "Ee-ar!"

Tynan stood, smiling, his brown eyes alight. "Kiarda! My
lady!"

The children fled, scampering like frightened rabbits through
a gate at the bottom of the garden.

Tynan whirled to see the last disappear, then returned his attention to Kiarda. "They're shy."

Kiarda made herself smile. "They didn't used to be. Maybe they've been hearing scary stories."

Tynan dropped his gaze, obviously discomfited.

Oddly ashamed of herself, Kiarda shrugged. "I don't mind, really. In a few days, they'll forget all about it." She gestured to the cat, seeking to change the subject. "He's getting good at saying my name."

"Yes." Tynan's expression lightened. "Speaking of names, guess what he wants to be called now."

"Not Cat-of-Watchfulness?"

Tynan laughed. "Not anymore. He's now Cat-Who-Eats-Crickets."

"Oh, dear." Kiarda smiled down at the cat, who beamed up at her. "At least it's not Cat-of-the-Most-Fragrant-Tail."

"At least."

Kiarda groped for more to say, wanting the gentle conversation to continue, craving a respite from the unhappiness that had consumed her life for months. She glanced around the garden. Out of earshot, Oric paid elaborate attention to the edge of his knife. "It seems we're almost alone."

Tynan's eyes grew warmer, and he spoke in a soft imitation of Adan's bantering tone. "It's almost shocking, isn't it? Almost scandalous." He sauntered toward Kiarda and stopped at arm's length. "And now I'm almost close enough to almost kiss you."

Kiarda found her cheeks turning hot, but she laughed. "I keep forgetting what an accomplished flirt you are."

"My lady is too gracious."

Cat-Who-Eats-Crickets circled Kiarda's ankles again, purring smoothly.

Kiarda shook her finger at the cat. "You're a flirt, too!"

"Perhaps," Tynan said, "the solution would be to move up the wedding date. After all, it's no sin for married people to be alone together."

"Wedding?" Unable to account for her sudden uneasiness, Kiarda stared at him. "You mean—?"

Tynan tilted his head. "Why wait until autumn?"

Words failed Kiarda.

Tynan regarded her with sudden anxiety. "What's the matter? Did I say something wrong?"

"No." Kiarda's voice emerged in a harsh croak, and she had to swallow before she could continue. "I just—I—" She spread her hands, unsure of her own feelings. "You simply caught me off guard."

"How?"

Helplessly, Kiarda shook her head. "I don't know. I guess I'm just surprised you still want to marry me."

"Of course I do!"

Kiarda gazed at Tynan, tormented and bolstered by the pain in his voice. "I wouldn't blame you if you didn't. I know how much you wanted children." *I know that's why you requested my hand.*

Tynan half turned away, his lips stretched tight. He hesitated too long for reassurance, and his response lacked conviction. "There's no saying we won't have children."

"Perhaps," Kiarda said softly. "But the healers aren't sure if I can conceive again. There may have been . . . damage."

Tynan closed his eyes. "Or you may be fine."

"Don't—" Kiarda paused to choose her words carefully. "Don't gloss over what may be an unpleasant reality. You want children."

Tynan stood motionless for a moment, then he loosely swung his arm, as if throwing something away. "I want you."

The gesture haunted Kiarda. Standing full in the sun of late July, a whisper of cold breathed at the nape of her neck. She said unsteadily, "Are you telling me you're willing to risk your most cherished dream to marry me?"

"Kiarda—"

"I won't let you do it."

Tynan turned to look at her, his face blank with shock. "What?" He swallowed. "Kiarda, what are you saying?"

Kiarda raised her hands, fingers flexed, trying to frame the enormity of what she felt.

Tynan's voice was barely audible, "Are you calling off the wedding?"

"No," Kiarda said, then realized the lie. "Yes." That also felt untrue. "I don't know."

Cat-Who-Eats-Crickets loosed a yowl of distress and leaped onto his link-mate's shoulder.

Tynan blurted, "Don't you love us anymore?"

An unexpected anger seized Kiarda. "Of course I love you!"

"Then why—?"

"Because I love you too much to let you throw your life away on me!" Kiarda looked away from Tynan's anguished expression. Still slouched against the far wall, Oric continued to sharpen his knife, giving no sign he heard her outburst. The garden lay green around them in the sunshine, the vegetables growing in perfect rows, bordered by a fence, deceptive in its tacit assertion of human control and order. *Everything is changing.* "Can't you see it? The cloud of doom hovering over me?"

"No." Tynan ran his hand through his hair in a rare gesture of exasperation. "And let me remind you: I've seen a cloud of doom before, when the Dark Court tried to kill me. So I know what one looks like."

Kiarda folded her arms. "I'm serious."

Tynan pretended to study the air above her head. "I do see a cloud of some sort. Perhaps a cloud of stubbornness?"

"Very funny."

"I can be stubborn, too." Tynan's voice gentled. "Don't call off the wedding, Kiarda. I want to marry you." He held up a forestalling hand. "And the fact that I want children is not an obstacle. You want them, too, I know. I would have been thrilled to raise twins I didn't sire. I obviously have no problem with adopting."

Kiarda closed her eyes, barraged by emotion. The loss of the twins still pained too much to consider more children now.

"I'm sorry I mentioned moving the wedding closer. Stupid of me, trying to rush after everything you've endured." Tynan pursed his lips. "Please forgive me when I act as if you have no feelings of your own. It's just that I'm used to knowing how my link-mate feels. And you, Kiarda, you're my mate, but there's no link. Do you have any idea how hard this is for me? To love someone as intensely as I love you, without knowing—without feeling—that connection to my spirit?"

A new understanding washed over Kiarda, swamping her inner distress. Shoulders sagging, she opened her eyes to look at the young man and the cat. Childhood friends, kinfolk, they suddenly assumed a new shape in her mind as magical creatures, rare and mysterious as the Fair Ones of the Light Court.

Evidently mistaking Kiarda's silence for something else, Tynan extended his hands in entreaty. "Please. At least don't publicly announce that the wedding's off. Think about it first. Please?"

Kiarda licked her dry lips. "Do you expect me to change my mind?" She might. Given time to meditate upon the bleak future, she could lose her nerve and once again agree to hold Tynan hostage to her loneliness. "I'm only thinking of you."

"Well, don't." Tynan raised his chin, a shadow of temper invading his voice. "Think of Adan. If you call off the wedding, it will just kill him."

Tynan spoke truth. Kiarda clenched her fists. "Unfair."

Tynan pretended not to hear. "Think of your people. They're yearning for your happiness."

"Stop it!"

"Then think of yourself. You need me."

Kiarda glared at Tynan, wanting to deny it. "Maybe."

Eyes bright, cheeks dimpling with a suppressed grin, Tynan tilted his head. Cat-Who-Eats-Crickets began to purr.

Historically, the men of Sarn Moor were a difficult breed: high-mettled in love, subtle in thought, deadly in battle. Tynan, Kiarda belatedly realized, possessed those qualities as well, though his sweet nature kept them reined. She abruptly understood why all the young women of Dorlach Tor spoke of her betrothed in breathless whispers. He was beautiful and, aside from her father, the most perfect man she had ever known. A trickle of the deep, questionless love she had once felt for Maddock surfaced, dragging months of hatred like flotsam. *Why can't I feel like that with Tynan?* Kiarda bit her tongue, the answer obvious. *Because my heart is foolish, my head so much smarter.*

Tynan's expression grew warmer and more hopeful. "My lady?"

Kiarda could not bear to hurt Tynan again. She did not wish to raise false hopes, but now did not seem a good time to make such a bold decision permanent. "I'll think about it."

Tynan and the cat on his shoulder exchanged triumphant glances.

Kiarda would have a quiet word with her mother and father about the marriage. They could advise her. If necessary, they could help her break it off gently, perhaps even arrange a more suitable match for Tynan. *No reason to cause more pain.* "In the meantime, will you walk with me? I think we need to show folk they're in no danger of being blasted to cinders for merely looking at me. I am *not* the gods' Chosen One. I'm just Kiarda."

She forced herself to add, "I haven't changed."

❧

The priests' lash sang through the air, tearing another line of agony across Stane's back. Driven to his knees, he grunted against clamped lips, biting back rage and the explosive curses burning his tongue. For a moment, his senses swam, and he feared he might pass out. He forced himself to breathe deeply, to focus on keeping his weight evenly balanced, to use even the pain to clear his head. He had learned these lessons early in life, strategies that enabled him to keep fighting in the heat of battle even when wounded. He grounded his senses on the realization that the next fall of the whip would be the last.

The room was secluded, an underground chamber of the temple devoted to what the priests liked to call "purification." Rivers of incense flowed through the still air, blurring and spreading the light of hundreds of candles burning in racks along the walls. Larger-than-life statues of Hernis and Hepona sat upon carved thrones on a raised dais, their painted stares empty of human compassion.

Another thong whistled and landed, desperately stinging. Stane coughed out a wordless noise, again wrestling with unconsciousness. The pain was supposed to free his mind for remorse and shame. The rite demanded that he think only of begging the gods' forgiveness, but regret eluded him. He felt fiercely glad to have prevented the priests from taking their intended victim. Poor Glist was too frail to endure a flogging. *Damned if I let a liegeman die for simply having a nightmare.*

"Done." The priest's leader, Kag, sounded suspiciously disappointed.

Drenched with sweat, scarlet welling from the gashes on his back, Stane staggered to his feet and pushed blond hair from his eyes. Memories erupted in erratic flashes, the most significant events in his life condensed to bright pinpoints: his younger brother's death in battle, his own wedding, the births of his children. He had relived all of those moments repeatedly, especially in the aftermath of beatings. Yet, this time, the thrashing had seemed more brutal than in the past, and it brought up long-buried details with the same hot discomfort as the bile in his throat. Sickened now as then, he saw the mother fox's red-furred body, sticky with blood and viscera. The kit's squeal echoed through his head, in duet with baby Kiarda's cries. *Gods!* Denial had allowed Stane to forget minutiae, to uncouple Kiarda's plight from the fox's mauling, from his own mercy-slaying of her kit. *I angered the gods at Kiarda's birth. I killed at a time I should have been celebrating new life. I caused all of her problems.*

The four officiating priests walked toward Stane, moving with ceremonial slowness. Two held censers. The others carried whips still wet with Stane's blood. They stopped directly in front of him.

Stane schooled his features to an impassive expression. Ironically, the beating *had* triggered remorse, just not for the sin the priests had intended.

Kag took the whips from his assistant and extended the handles of both toward Stane.

Repulsed, Stane lowered his gaze and kissed the handles. Not all priests demanded this extra submission from the petitioner, only the worst, the ones who actually enjoyed what they did.

Kag handed the whips to his assistant, who bowed and withdrew along with the priests who carried the censers.

Keeping his head bowed humbly, Stane peered through the curtain of his own hair and watched them go.

Kag waited until the door closed, then beamed at the Lord of Dorlach Tor. "My superiors are correct. You have great stamina."

Stane's mouth twitched, but he did not trust himself to answer. He realized how he must look to the priest: stripped to the waist, back flayed, sweaty belly heaving with every breath. *Reduced to an animal.*

Kag's smile widened. "Or perhaps it is not stamina so much as strong will, a prideful stubbornness. Am I to think the purification has failed? That our blessed Lord and Lady would wish us to try again?"

Stane hid his revulsion with difficulty. *Greasy bastard wants me to cower.* "Chasten the body," he said hoarsely, "and the spirit will follow."

"Ah, so they say. But you do not look chastened to me."

Stane's back blazed with pain. Each lash mark felt as if it simmered and smoked, and his conscience ached as well. "A second . . . purification?" It was hard to control his breath enough to speak. "Is that . . . new doctrine?"

Kag licked his thick lips, suddenly seeming nervous. "I did not say that."

"No?" Stane swallowed against the sudden dryness in his throat, knowing he walked a fine line. Though the priesthood wielded the authority to punish both nobles and common folk for moral crimes, it exerted an even tighter control over its own members. Heretical priests were burned at the stake. Stane wondered if he might use their own power against them. "I thought you said . . . that the holy rite of purification . . . failed. That the gods wished—"

Kag's voice cracked. "I did not say that!"

"Ah." Inwardly gloating, Stane raised his hands and let them fall, unable to move his shoulders in a real shrug. "I must have been . . . mistaken."

Kag's breath hissed through his nose. His heavy-jowled face grew red with anger. "You are mistaken."

"Sorry." Stane pulled his mouth into a tight smile. "Am I free to go?" He did not wait for an answer but turned and walked stiffly to the door. He put his hand on the latch, and glanced over his shoulder at the priest. "My lady is waiting for me."

"Very mistaken." Kag spoke in a tone of unvarnished threat. "Let's hope I hear no more blasphemy from your people, since you insist upon taking the rite of purification for them. I doubt, my lord, that you would survive."

Stane paused to consider the priest's words. "I do what I must."

"And when you are gone?" Kag rubbed his plump hands together. "Who will take the purification then? Your lady? Your lovely daughter, perhaps?"

For a long moment, Stane stood motionless, entertaining a mental image of Kag disemboweled and screaming his way to a slow, bleeding death. "I'm not gone yet."

"No," Kag purred, "not yet."

For a priest to stand in the Lord and Lady's own temple and casually confess a plot against Dorlach Tor shocked Stane to the core of his being. Wylfre had long desired to take more drastic action against the priesthood, and it seemed now that Stane should have listened to her. In any case, there would be no forestalling the Dark Flame once he passed along the word. Stane forced himself to smile. "Gods be with you."

Stane lay in bed, bathed, tended, and drugged until the pain finally became tolerable. Wylfre reclined beside him, running cool fingers through his hair. He did not want to open his eyes, to see the worry and anger in her beautiful face. "We alone?"

Her voice was gentle. "Yes."

"The children—?"

Wylfre anticipated his question. "I've spoken to Oric and the others. They'll see to it the children are accompanied by their attendants at all times and never left alone with any of the priests."

Stane grunted softly and relaxed more deeply. She must have given the orders while Sygil treated his back. "Kag . . . dangerous."

"I know." Wylfre drew the tip of her little finger down his cheek. "I'm going to arrange for him to have an accident."

"Good." Stane immediately regretted saying it. It was not good; it was simply necessary. The priesthood that he had helped to shape had turned into a force more destructive than the Dark Court. He sighed. "My fault."

Wylfre kissed his forehead. "No."

"Wasn't supposed to be . . . this way." Stane's speech was slurred, but he knew she would understand. "Joyous Reunion. Peace. No more war."

Wylfre pressed tender fingers against his lips. "Hush. You did what you thought best."

Stane kissed Wylfre's fingers. He should have foreseen the trouble years ago, when the priests began to gather power, gaining control of the main trade routes. He had helped them, believing a strong priesthood could prevent the outbreak of more fighting. "Been lying to myself." *About a lot of things.* He considered telling Wylfre about Kiarda and the foxes, but gathering words for the story seemed too difficult at the moment. *Besides, Kiarda has the right to hear it first. To decide whether or not to forgive me, and to choose who else learns the details.*

Wylfre smoothed the hair from Stane's face. "Try to rest, my love."

Stane felt strangely outside himself. His body hovered between pleasure and pain, his mind between confusion and clarity. From the Low Marches came rumors of war in the southern countries. If true, it would prove the Joyous Reunion had not occurred. Everything would unravel; chaos would again descend. Yet, if the priesthood gained enough power, it could hold together the fabric of the Marchlands. Peace would prevail. "What price?" he murmured. "What price for everlasting peace?"

Stane felt Wylfre shift closer. Her breath warmed his cheek, and he caught the scent of her hair. "Hush," she whispered, then kissed the tight spot between his eyebrows. "Go to sleep."

Stane recognized a command when he heard it, even when delivered lovingly. The time had come to yield to the inevitable. He smiled without opening his eyes. "Yes, my lady."

Rain fell in a steady torrent from a slate-gray afternoon sky. From the stable door, Kiarda watched a small lake forming in one of the training paddocks. The air smelled fresh, thick with the clean scents of horses, hay, and water.

Leith, Ladayla, Adan, Tynan, and Cat-Who-Bites-Priests gathered in the little room that had once served as the Lord and Lady's bedchamber. After three days of insisting the young men and women remain constantly attended, Wylfre had at last relented and permitted some freedom from servants on the condition that they promised to stay together. Kiarda supposed she could leave the crowded room for a few moments. The rest chatted merely a wall away, and the door stood ajar. A few stable hands worked at the other end of the aisle of stalls, oiling tack and talking about the upcoming summer horse fair in Sarn Moor, quite properly ignoring her. It felt almost like being alone.

In his commodious stall by the door, her father's elderly stallion swished his tail and nickered.

Smiling fondly, Kiarda looked at the horse. "And what do you want?"

Blood Rage stood with his ears up, peering at Kiarda hopefully, and snorted.

Kiarda left the doorway and crossed to the gate of his stall. "You want my attention?" she murmured, reaching to stroke his dark muzzle. "Is that what you want, you big baby?"

Blood Rage pushed his velvety nose into her hands.

Petting him, Kiarda tried to imagine the stallion in his prime. He had carried her father to war, fought for him like an extra set of arms, and saved his life more than once. Like her father, the horse also bore the scars of old battle wounds, but Blood Rage had never been touched by a whip.

Bitterness infused Kiarda's tranquil mood. According to the priests of the Joyous Reunion, war had become a thing of the past. She wondered, then, why the priesthood administered violence in the name of discipline and seemed to have declared a secret war against her family.

Blood Rage pulled his head from Kiarda's grasp and lifted his nose, snuffling the air. Someone approached the stables, sloughing through the muddy puddles. The stallion let loose with a pealing whinny of welcome.

Kiarda spun.

Stane appeared in the doorway. He pushed back the hood of his cloak, scattering raindrops over his face.

"Father." Kiarda went to Stane and dried his cheeks with the cuff of her tunic, speaking in much the same tone she used with the horse. "You shouldn't be out in this weather."

Stane laid a gentle hand on Kiarda's cheek. "Dear heart, you sound just like your mother."

Kiarda found herself smiling in spite of her worry. "Well, you shouldn't."

"House is too full of priests." Stane sauntered to Blood Rage and ran his hand down the stallion's nose. "Hello, old friend. I've missed you."

Blood Rage lowered his eyelids in pleasure and snorted softly.

A burst of laughter came from the converted bedchamber, along with Adan's strenuous protests. He had evidently lost at a game of forfeits and was commanded to stand on his head.

"Kiarda." Stane did not look at his daughter but continued to stroke the stallion. "Why are you out here alone?"

"Not completely alone." Kiarda shrugged one shoulder. "And I doubt any of the priests would come out here in the pouring rain."

"I'm not—" Stane shook his head. "I'm not scolding about your safety. I'm talking about this habit of solitude. It worries me."

"Well, don't worry." Kiarda leaned against the gate. "I'm fine."

"Are you?" Stane's voice held a strange note Kiarda did not know how to interpret.

"I will be. Once all these bizarre rumors settle."

"And if they don't?"

Kiarda bit her bottom lip. "I'm sorry. I don't understand."

Stane glanced around and lowered his voice. "Dear heart, there's something I need to tell you. Something I should have told you a long time ago."

Kiarda shifted uneasily. "What?"

Her father regarded her for a long moment, his eyes full of pain. "I think . . . I think it's all my fault . . . what you're going through. The day you were born, I think I . . . put you under a curse."

Kiarda shook her head. "No, you can't—"

"I killed a fox."

Kiarda's breath caught in her throat.

"It was just a kit. An untimely birth. The hounds had killed its mother, and I thought the most merciful thing—"

"A fox." Kiarda swallowed hard. It suddenly all made sense: the changes she felt within, the fox who had followed from Scratter Wood, her disfigured children. "A fox."

Stane sighed shakily, expression pained. "I suspected a curse when your hair began to turn color, but I didn't want to believe it. I didn't want to believe that I'd done anything to hurt my little girl." He touched the curls that spilled over her shoulder and blinked back tears. "My precious daughter."

Kiarda could not bear her father's sorrow. She threw her arms around him in a frantic embrace. "It wasn't your fault. How could you know?"

"Can you ever forgive me?"

"There's nothing to forgive," Kiarda said fiercely. "You did what you thought right." *A curse. I'm cursed.* She wondered who had bestowed the curse. Whether the Light Court or the Dark, it did not matter. The gods had maliciously allowed it to occur. "The Other Ones are at fault."

Stane drew back and clasped Kiarda's face between his two hands. "I wouldn't blame you if you hated me for it. If I could take it from you onto me—"

Kiarda laid her hands over his, knowing he spoke truth. He would willingly accept her lot, just as he took the beatings due his people. "Father, don't."

Stane smiled sadly, kissed Kiarda's forehead, and released her. "Thank you."

An unfamiliar sense of relief flooded Kiarda's spirit. "And I thank you." She glanced around the stables, feeling as if she had been absent for a long time, as if she had become the old Kiarda again. "The worst was not knowing."

Evidently weary of being ignored, Blood Rage nudged Stane's shoulder and grunted. Stroking the stallion, the Lord of Dorlach Tor regarded Kiarda thoughtfully. "Not knowing," he repeated. "Perhaps secrets are what lie at the heart of the curse. Perhaps the only way to break the curse is to tell the secrets. And try to make amends."

Make amends. The words struck a deep chord. Kiarda nodded. No more half-truths and evasions, no more proud denials of what she really felt, no more blaming the innocent. *Make amends. So many mistakes. Where do I start?*

⚜

The rain faded toward evening, and the clouds rolled away. Stars burned clear in the cool summer sky. Kiarda sat at the window of her room, gazing out at the shadowed shapes of trees and rooftops.

There came a knock at her door, followed by a familiar voice. "My lady? It's Bevin."

Kiarda turned from the window and rose. "Come in. Please."

The door opened a crack, and the healer peeked inside anxiously, sandy ringlets escaping from the bunching at the back of her head. "You sent for me, my lady?"

Kiarda crossed the room and drew the other young woman in by the hand. "Yes. Please come in. I need to talk to you."

Bevin shyly edged into the room and curtsied. "My lady."

Guilt lashed Kiarda. She shut the door and indicated the window seat. "Please sit down."

Bevin's round face betrayed nothing but confusion and worry; but she obeyed, settling nervously.

Steeling herself, Kiarda sat beside her. "Bevin, I owe you an apology. And it's long past due."

Bevin twined her hands in her apron. "My lady?"

"Don't—" Tears threatened. Kiarda fought them back. "You don't have to address me by my title anymore."

Bevin's soft voice was barely audible. "I don't understand."

Kiarda drew a deep breath, then let it out. "Bevin, I'm sorry. I shouldn't have asked you to slay my unborn children, and I was wrong to be angry at your refusal. I don't expect you to forgive me, but I hope—"

"Of course, I forgive you." Bevin's mild manner evaporated in the heat of indignation. "In fact, I forgave you as soon as it happened."

"But—"

"Just what kind of friend do you think I am?" Bevin demanded. "I knew you were in pain. Do you think I'd abandon you merely because you got angry with me?"

One tear escaped and trickled down Kiarda's nose. "Maybe you should have."

Bevin spread her hands. "It's not in my nature."

"I'm glad." Kiarda dragged her sleeve across her face and sniffed. "Because I've missed you, Bevin."

"I've missed you too . . . Kiarda."

They clasped hands, laughing and weeping.

Kiarda finally pulled herself together and brushed the hair from her eyes. "This is wonderful. Every time I apologize, I feel the curse lift a little more."

Bevin's gray eyes widened. "Curse?"

Kiarda nodded, then related everything her father had told her that afternoon.

With a considering expression, Bevin rose and paced across the room. "He killed a newborn fox. That explains why—" She turned toward Kiarda. "You're not under a curse. You're linked."

"What?"

"I sensed it from the first day we met. When I found you in Hernis' old temple. Remember? I told you I couldn't take part in Elrin's Pronouncement because I was seeing links that weren't there. I saw one in you, but it looked strange, twisted and looped in upon itself. I thought it was my imagination."

"Me?" Kiarda's mind raced, trying to fathom the full sense of the healer's words. "Linked?"

"Remember?" Bevin's voice rose in excitement. "You said you felt as if something inside you had died. That you were changing—"

Kiarda jumped to her feet as the events of the past year abruptly fell into place. "The fox kit was my link-mate! And when it died, it somehow stayed connected to my spirit. Became a part of me."

Bevin clutched her friend's shoulders. "That's why your hair turns reddish in summer and paler in winter. Why you crave solitude. Why you—"

"Why I sometimes change into a fox," Kiarda interrupted.

Bevin's lips parted, but she seemed unable to find words.

Kiarda nodded slowly, the conviction growing. She recalled the episodes of forgetfulness, awaking in strange places. "At first, only my spirit changed. Then my body changed, too. One night last fall, I woke up naked on the floor—" She pointed to a spot near the window. "—there. The whole room reeked of fox, and my nightgown hung beneath the blankets like—" A new realization hit. Kiarda broke off and pressed her hands over her mouth. *Maddock!*

"What?" Bevin asked anxiously. "Kiarda, what is it?"

"Last winter. The Dark Court didn't carry me off. I wasn't ravished. I'd gone to Scratter Woods on my own, in fox shape." Kiarda gazed helplessly at her friend. "That's why they found only fox tracks around me in the snow. And why the dog fox followed all the way to Dorlach Tor. He was my . . . husband!"

Bevin's hands tightened on Kiarda's shoulders. "And that's why the babies were malformed. They were half fox. They couldn't grow properly."

Kiarda could scarcely comprehend it all. Maddock had not raped her. He was still guilty of blasphemy and crimes committed as an ally of the Dark Court, but she wondered if the false accusations had driven him to those acts of hatred. If so, then everyone at Dorlach Tor shared a part of the blame. Kiarda closed her eyes, breathing hard. The tragic past upended, shattered, and rebuilt itself in a new shape. Though a victim of evil, she was not cursed, not tainted by the Dark Court. Instead, strange magic had warped her, so much of her grief caused by a misunderstanding.

Kiarda tried not to dwell on the realization that she had lost a bond as deep and special as Tynan's with his cat. She had heard the tales of Elrin's link-mate, how the foal had galloped past those who tried to help, consumed by a fierce and terrible sorrow. Grief and bitterness had tainted Kiarda's life long enough. The time had come to let go, to allow truth to heal what months had not. Her father had been right, though for the wrong reasons. Ultimately, secrets had worsened the situation, and revealing them could begin to heal her soul. And others.

Bevin's voice filled with concern. "Kiarda? Are you all right?"

"I am now." Kiarda smiled and opened her eyes, no longer a creature of pity or horror. She had a peculiar destiny before her, but it could turn out bright. Everyone knew foxes possessed the ability to make safe passage over treacherous ground. One way or another, she would find her path.

CHAPTER THIRTEEN

THOUGH shaded by the massive shadow of the tor, the walled courtyard grew warm as midday approached. Sighing sleepily, Bevin cast a glance over the remains of the meal on the blanket spread upon the grass. Only a heap of bones marked the former existence of two roasted chickens. Nothing remained of the cheese but its rind, and not a crumb of the fried hunt-bread survived.

Bevin's companions also seemed drowsy and replete. Tynan lay on his back on the grass, his link-mate curled up on his chest. Both appeared asleep. Kiarda, dreamy-eyed, reclined against a propped up elbow. Adan slowly worked his way through an enormous bowl of walnuts, cracking the shells with his strong fingers, then laying the bounty on the blanket so Bevin could pick out and eat the nut meat.

Excused from kitchen duties for an afternoon, Bevin felt liberated. They had planned the picnic lunch for the benefit of the betrothed pair, Kiarda and Tynan. Bevin and Adan were present as chaperones. Though Bevin had grown up under the more relaxed traditions of her people, she had become accustomed to the Marchlanders' strict courtship practices. The four of them there together, without servants or onlookers, smacked deliciously of scandal.

With a warmth climbing to her cheeks that had nothing to do with the summer sun, Bevin peeked at Adan. His aristocratic features betrayed no sign of strain as he broke the walnut shells. His expression seemed bored and slightly contemptuous, as it always did when his thoughts lay elsewhere. Bevin wondered if it were this intimidating demeanor, rather than the scars, which other women found so dismaying.

Suddenly, Adan met Bevin's gaze, and his mouth crooked in a lopsided smile. "What?"

For an instant, words failed Bevin. "My lord," she finally managed to get out. "Aren't you going to eat any walnuts?"

Adan's brows shot up in feigned astonishment. "Merciful gods! You mean to tell me these things are edible?"

Certain her cheeks had turned pink, Bevin giggled.

Kiarda roused. "Uh-oh, Bevin. Now you've done it. We've kept that a secret for years."

Adan spoke in an enthusiastic tone. "I'm going to try one." He picked up a nutshell and pretended to gnaw on it like a squirrel. "Not bad, but a little dry."

Smiling, and surprised by her own boldness, Bevin selected three succulent walnut halves from the hoard on her lap. "Hold out your hand, my lord."

Wrist limp and fingers drooping, Adan extended it languidly, as if offering the back of it to kiss.

Kiarda snorted. "My lord cousin, you are a loon."

Bevin's smile grew so wide it hurt. Adan was sweet to tease her as he would a younger sister. "Palm up," she instructed patiently.

"Oh." Adan obediently flipped his hand to revel a palm heavily callused and ingrained with dirt. More than the shade of his hazel eyes or the auburn cast of his hair, his hands marked him as a scion of the old blood. The nobility of the Marchlands worked with horses and worked hard, both lord and lady. Among her own people, Bevin reflected, the wealthy spent their time vying with each other in fashionable clothing and games of chance.

With an odd sense that she performed some intimate and forbidden act, Bevin dropped the walnuts into Adan's hand.

Eyes sparkling, Adan closed his fingers over the nuts as if they were jewels and pressed his fist to his heart. "Thank you."

Bevin found it hard to breathe. She wondered if she might faint.

Kiarda yawned and reached for some of the cracked walnuts on the blanket. "Loon."

Cat-Who-Bites-Priests woke up with a startled squeak.

Tynan opened his eyes, jerking his head up. "What?"

Kiarda yawned again. "Nothing," she said. "You dozed off."

Tynan relaxed and rubbed his face. His shining hair fanned out on the grass. "I did?" he murmured. "Sorry."

Adan regarded his brother down the length of his nose. "You snore. Both of you."

Still sitting on his link-mate's chest, the tomcat presented Adan with a resentful glare.

Adan grinned. "I know you understood that." He spoke as if he heard the animal's thoughts. "You ought to change your name to Cat-Who-Snores-Like-Thunder."

The cat looked away and flicked his tail.

Tynan's usually sweet-tempered face lit up with a mischievous grin. "How about Cat-Who-Ignores-Brothers?"

Adan gave a facetious gasp of pain. "No! Not that! Claw me, chew me, but please—I beg of you—don't ignore me!"

Kiarda shifted her attention to Bevin. "Both of them. Loons."

Bevin shrugged shyly. "I think they're funny."

Cat-Who-Bites-Priests hopped off his perch and padded across the blanket to Kiarda. "Ee-ar-rra!"

"No, not you," the future Lady of Dorlach Tor crooned. "You're not a loon. You're my good lad."

Purring loudly, the cat butted his forehead against Kiarda's chin.

Adan glanced pointedly from Cat-Who-Bites-Priests to his brother. "Was that a kiss I just witnessed?" He turned to Bevin. "Should we summon the priests? Force poor old Kag to hobble out here on his broken ankle?"

Kiarda shook her head. "Don't say that. Not even in jest."

Confused, Bevin looked at Kiarda. "What's this? He broke his ankle?"

Kiarda's expression turned sour. "We tried to keep it quiet, but I'll wager you're the only one who hasn't heard. Some of our folk found Kag lying at the bottom of the back stairs. He'd fallen and broken his ankle."

"Oh, dear." Bevin bit her bottom lip. The back stairs led to the suite of servants' quarters where the unmarried young women lived. "What was he doing there?"

Kiarda made a disgusted noise. "He wouldn't say, but I doubt it was a holy rite."

Bevin's stomach went cold. These sorts of things were not supposed to happen in the Marchlands.

Tynan sat up slowly, a severe expression on his handsome face. "I knew he broke his ankle. I hadn't heard the details."

Adan narrowed his eyes. "Me either."

Kiarda continued in a wooden tone. "As I said, we're trying to keep the stories from spreading. The poor lasses who sleep above the back stairs are terrified they'll get called to the temple for purification. Fortunately, Kag doesn't seem to recall the incident. He was roaring drunk when the steward and his men found him."

Tynan's scowl darkened. "Sounds like some of the stable lads and I should stand guard on the back stairs."

"No," his older brother said calmly. "That would only give Kag reason to make accusations. Besides, Lady Wylfre is more than capable of protecting her own." He paused. "Pity that he broke his ankle." *And not his neck*, Adan's tone seemed to imply.

Bevin wrung her hands, not wholly sure it had been an accident. Everyone knew Lady Wylfre made a dire opponent when angered. "Could we please change the subject? We were having such a pleasant time."

"Yes," Kiarda agreed. "Let's talk about . . . cats." She stroked the sleek back of Cat-Who-Bites-Priests. "And spirit-links."

Tynan scooped a half-dozen walnuts from the bowl. He still appeared upset, breathing hard and frowning, as he methodically cracked nuts with his fingers. "What about spirit-links?"

Bevin turned to look at Kiarda. The future Lady of Dorlach Tor had made no secret of the discovery of the phantom link within herself. Everyone knew and eagerly discussed the revelation.

Kiarda tilted her head. "Do you ever wonder what it would be like to be your own link-mate? To be a cat?"

"I don't have to wonder," Tynan said. "I am a cat."

"I mean literally."

"So do I." Tynan crushed a walnut more thoroughly than necessary. "One spirit in two bodies."

Kiarda glanced at Bevin. "And I'm two spirits in one body."

Tynan pulverized another walnut. "Just who does Kag think he is?" he said abruptly. "Is this what the world is coming to? Men taking advantage of young women?"

Adan warned, "Tynan—"

His younger brother did not seem to hear. "It makes me sick! First, Kiarda was attacked by—"

Kiarda threw a walnut shell at Tynan. "No one!"

Tynan gaped at her.

"No one," Kiarda repeated. "I'm a shape-shifter, remember? I was in fox form."

"Oh. Yes." Tynan swallowed. "So the Horsemaster's son was innocent of that."

Bevin flinched, blurting, "And maybe innocent of the rest, as well."

The others stared at Bevin.

The healer dropped her gaze to her lap. "The attack the day we lost little Lord Elrin. I was never positive he was behind it."

Tynan cleared his throat. "But you said you saw a man in a cloak."

Bevin felt the heat of shame rise to her cheeks. "I know. But the man I saw wielded the forbidden magic. The Horsemaster's son possessed no magic at all."

Tynan still sounded certain. "But the Dark Court gave him the power. Remember the hunting party he destroyed?"

Bevin nodded, knowing she could never persuade Tynan to change his mind. "Perhaps."

"Well," Adan said in a soothing tone. "In all events, we know he studied swordcraft. That alone makes him outcast."

Bevin risked a glance at Kiarda. Her friend sat utterly still, her face pale, her expression rigid.

Tynan smashed another walnut. Bits of the shell dusted his tunic. "And he killed Damas. My man Oric says it was self-defense, but I—"

Kiarda jerked her gaze to her betrothed. "Self-defense?"

Tynan nodded. "Damas and his friends were going to—"

Adan interrupted firmly. "Stop. That's not a fit topic for mixed company."

Kiarda suddenly stood. "Stay seated," she ordered, forestalling their respectful attempts to rise. "I'm going—" She sighed and ran her hands through her fox-red hair. "Excuse me, I need to . . . to go . . . think." She strode off through the gate.

Tynan turned to the others, looking worried. "Do you think I should go after her?"

Adan snorted. "No."

Bevin sadly surveyed the picnic. "I wish I hadn't mentioned the Horsemaster's son. I ruined everything."

Adan's expression turned dour. "I think we all had an equal hand in that. It's as if we don't know how to be happy anymore, as if misery were a strong wine that we cannot refuse."

Tynan started to rise. "I'd better go talk to her."

Adan lifted his brows. "And leave me here alone with Bevin? The priests will skin me!"

Looking sulky, Tynan settled again.

Adan gave Bevin a secret smile, both fond and triumphant. Then, he slowly ate the walnuts she had given to him.

❧

As the afternoon sank into dusk, Bevin made her way from the kitchen to Kiarda's rooms. She found the maids talking softly and laying out clothes for the next day.

Bevin hovered uncertainly in the doorway. "I'm sorry. I expected to find Lady Kiarda."

The maids exchanged amused glances. The tall one said, "We haven't seen her all day. We thought she was with you." Rina added, "Maybe she's at the paddock watching Lord Tynan train horses."

Bevin's pulse gathered speed, but she nodded. "Thank you."

With a rising anxiety she could not place, Bevin hurried to the stable yards. It was unfamiliar territory to her, full of the smells of mud, hay, and manure. She picked her way through the maze of fences, watching her feet, averting her eyes from the figures of sweaty and bare-chested men.

A man abruptly blocked Bevin's path. "Hey, maidy." A tall, broad-shouldered fellow with filthy clothes, he spoke with the unpolished accent of the common folk. "You shouldn't be out here in those little slippers. You'll get them muddy, or a horse will step on your toes."

"I—" A bit frightened, Bevin swallowed. Then, something in the groom's voice made her look at his face. Hazel eyes gleamed from a thick mask of dust. He gave her a lopsided smile. Bevin stared. "Adan?" Realizing her discourtesy, she spread her skirts. "Your pardon, Lord Adan."

"Perhaps you were right the first time," Adan said. "I may give up my title to live the life of a—"

"Kiarda's missing." Bevin spoke without intention. "Her maids haven't seen her all day."

Adan's smile faded. "That's not good. All afternoon, everyone in her family has asked about her whereabouts. I told them she was with you."

Bevin's disquiet deepened to certainty. "She's run away."

"In fox shape?"

Bevin twisted her fingers together. "I don't know, my lord. Maybe."

Adan frowned in a moment of thought. "At least it's not the mating season." He cast a sharp glance around the stable yard. "Let's see if her horse is gone." He motioned for Bevin to walk beside him. "This way. Watch your step."

Bevin quickened her pace to keep up. "Thank you," she said, panting a little, "for taking me seriously."

"We both know Kiarda."

Bevin did not have the breath to keep talking, trying to match Adan's long stride. When they reached the stable, he led her to an empty stall.

"Snow Bell's gone. Wait here. I'm going to check the tack room." Adan jogged down the aisle of stalls and disappeared around a corner.

Fighting to stay calm, Bevin pressed her back against a wall. Horses peered at her over the gates of their stalls. She loved horses, though they unnerved her and she did not enjoy riding. The Children of Hepona, as the Marchlanders called their special breed, seemed even more intimidating than other steeds. The beasts who gazed from their stalls seemed to know she did not feel at ease, and they regarded her with varying degrees of pity or amusement.

The stable door opened, and Tynan sauntered in with his link-mate balanced on his shoulder. "Bevin. What are you doing here? Going riding?"

Bevin drew breath to answer, but Adan reappeared, carrying a saddle and bridle.

Tynan glanced back and forth between the two. "What's going on?"

Adan looked around for listeners, then spoke in a low tone. "Kiarda's ridden off on her own. Without telling anyone."

Tynan blinked. "Why would she do that?"

Bevin thought she knew. "To find the Horsemaster's son and make amends. That's all she's done the past three days, apologize to people she thinks she's wronged."

Tynan shook his head. "But she wouldn't just leave without—"

Adan looked pained. "You're forgetting your family history. On receiving news of my accident, Lady Wylfre attempted to ride from Dorlach Tor to Sarn Moor eight months pregnant. Kiarda is her mother's daughter."

"But—"

"Stop wasting time. Saddle up. Kiarda is probably heading for the Ash Pit, where that hunting party disappeared. If we hurry, we can catch her and bring her back before dark, and the priests will never find out about it."

Tynan folded his arms. "You're not—"

Cat-Who-Bites-Priests stuck his nose into his link-mate's ear. "Mow!"

Sighing, Tynan headed for the tack room.

Heart racing, Bevin turned to Adan. It was her fault Kiarda had left. She had some atoning of her own to do. "You have to take me with you."

Adan smiled sadly. "No, my kitchen lady."

Desperation lent the healer courage, and she offered the first argument that came to mind. "You have to. If she changes into a fox, she'll wake up undressed. And what will you do then?"

For a long moment, Adan stood motionless, gazing at Bevin.

"All right," he said softly. "I suppose it won't hurt anything. But you'll have to keep up. We'll be riding fast."

Bevin lifted her head and tried to convey a confidence she did not feel. "I will." Her hands shook at the prospect of a breakneck chase across the countryside, and she folded them in her apron so Adan would not notice. "After all," she added, "we'll be coming right back."

☙

Brother Honesty stepped from the commander's tent and drew a breath of sweet evening air. *Wonderful.* The entire camp lay beneath the shelter of a single massive pine with a trunk so thick two dozen men could not spread their arms around it. The enormous branches drooped to the ground from twenty feet overhead, sheltering them from a cold wind blowing down from the snow-capped mountains. Fragrant needles carpeted the ground and spiced the air.

As the mobile strike force continued to move south to meet the main force, they discovered the land grew richer. Wide, placid rivers fed lush tracts of farmland. Mountains contained veins of gold and iron. Endless forests teemed with game and offered a wealth of useful timber. The Marchlands were generous and beautiful, and Brother Honesty praised the Light for leading him there.

Commander Swift strolled from his tent and rested his hand on the priest's shoulder. "Smell that air! I wish I could put some in a box to present as a gift to Emperor Justice, may he reign forever."

Brother Honesty smiled at the younger man, thinking of his magical pen. "Speak to the Hooded Order. They may know a way."

"They may, indeed," the commander answered absently. His gray eyes raked the camp, systematically searching the tents, the fire ring, and the off-duty men. "Where's Maddock?"

Brother Honesty's blue eyes grew warmer. The commander's unlikely friendship with the Marchlander had turned into a blessing of the Light. "Perhaps the picket lines? Shall I go and find him?"

Swift patted Honesty's shoulder. "Let's go together."

They walked side by side through the camp. The men greeted them respectfully as they passed, then returned to cleaning their gear or eating their meals. Morale remained high, the priest reflected, and not only because the mission was going as planned. "A well-fed army is a victorious army," Brother Honesty murmured. "I'd never before realized the truth of that old saying."

Swift nodded. "Those hunting dogs have more than earned their keep. I was a bit skeptical at first, but Maddock seemed so adamant—" He ran a hand through his white-blond hair, laughing. "Stubborn boy, but I'm glad I listened to him. Now, my men are stuffed full of good red meat."

Beyond beasts of burden, or food-producing livestock, civilized people had little use for animals. They considered creatures like dogs, monkeys, or birds of prey simply nuisances to dispose of. The Marchlanders, however, viewed them in a different fashion. Not only did they train these beasts to perform a variety of valuable services, but they lavished the animals with affection. It seemed eerily close to the foul entanglements of the Abomination, but the Hooded Order assured Brother Honesty of its distinction.

As commander and priest drew near, one of the captured Marchland horses lifted its head and whinnied. The rest of the picket turned to look at the approaching men.

Swift laughed. "The sentinel has spotted us."

Maddock came around from behind his mare, holding a brush in his hand. "Commander Swift. Brother Honesty." The youth's perpetually wary expression had disappeared as he traveled with them and now, after several months, he no longer exuded the air of a hunted animal. Intelligence and high spirits gleamed in his dark eyes, overlaid with a rigorous sense of self-discipline. "Forgive me, I didn't hear you coming."

Swift waved the apology away. "Tending your she-wolf, I see."

The roan mare snorted and tilted back her ears.

Maddock grinned. "Yes, sir."

"I watched the two of you during the drills today," Swift said. "You both seem to be getting the knack of mounted combat."

"Thank you, sir, but we still have trouble with that open-and-close figure."

"That's a tricky one for everybody. The secret is to shift your weight just as you go into the turn. That way—"

Brother Honesty stopped listening and retired a few steps, certain the commander and Maddock would lose themselves for a long time in talk of cavalry tactical maneuvering. It gave him the chance to mentally outline the next entry in his journal.

Velvet touched the priest's cheek, followed by a puff of warm air. Startled, Brother Honesty jerked his head to look. One of the Marchland horses stood with its nose just inches from his face. The priest's heart skipped into a faster tempo. If he moved or made a sound, the brute would undoubtedly bite him.

The horse regarded Honesty with large, fathomless eyes, then again brushed its nose against his cheek. Sheer surprise held Brother Honesty motionless. *So soft.* The horse lowered its nose to the man's hand and nudged at his fingers. Brother Honesty stared. *It wants me to stroke it!* He glanced toward the other two men, but they remained immersed in conversation. Cautiously, the priest slid his knuckles down the horse's muzzle, trying to avoid the damp nostrils. Beneath the soft hide, he felt solid muscle and the warmth of life. *Strange.*

The horse heaved a great breath, sounding for all the world like a human sighing in heartfelt relief. Reeling inwardly, Brother Honesty gazed at the horse. Animals possessed no emotions, no souls, no higher thoughts; yet this creature gave every evidence of craving affection. More than that, it occurred to him, the horse had attempted to communicate its desire with the innocent directness of a mute child.

Brother Honesty raised both hands to the horse's face and explored its contours, the unpadded bone beneath the sleek hide, the gliding muscles along the jaw.

Swift spoke quietly, "Brother Honesty, what are you doing?"

"Admiring a creation of the Light." Still stroking the horse, the priest turned to smile at the commander. "It's extraordinary."

Maddock sounded uneasy. "That's Juniper. He's not usually so friendly."

Swift grinned knowingly. "The good Brother has a way with unfriendly creatures. He's the only man I've ever known to gain the esteem of the Hooded Order."

Running his fingers down the thin blaze on the horse's nose, Brother Honesty chewed the inside of his cheek. "It doesn't make sense to me," he said finally. "One could argue that the beast is simply accustomed to being handled and was seeking the familiar. But since the handling usually involves the fitting of a bit and bridle, an unpleasant experience we can imagine, it doesn't seem likely that a thoughtless animal would beg for a human touch. Yet this horse very clearly did just that."

Maddock moved closer, stepping with a liquid grace that marked his every action. "I don't mean any disrespect to your beliefs, but I can't imagine what your home country must be like. Animals are our companions and helpers, and humans are the same to animals. The gods—or the Light—created them along with us and show humans no particular favor over the animals."

Brother Honesty raised his brows in surprise. "No particular favor? My child, we are heirs of the Light. We are the sons and daughters of its undying glory." He glanced at the commander for corroboration.

Swift nodded, but he had a peculiarly mischievous expression on his face.

Maddock sighed. "But we eat and sleep like animals. We mate and produce young. We are born, grow old, and die. How are we favored?"

"By reason of our souls, our higher understanding of our ultimate destiny."

Maddock chose his words carefully. "But animals have . . . souls . . . too. Or is the soul the same thing as the intellect?" He gestured helplessly. "If that's the case, then we're born without souls and gain them as our understanding increases."

Swift pressed the back of his hand to his lips, obviously enjoying the mild debate.

Brother Honesty found himself not only enjoying, but rejoicing in the Marchlander's earnest attempts to grapple with the truth. "My child, that is one theory."

Maddock glanced back and forth between the two men. "So

if our souls are in our intellects, can't a horse's soul be in its strength and speed? Can't a raven's soul be in its flight?"

Brother Honesty spread his hands. "The soul is more than physical aptitude. Otherwise, one might say that your soul resides in sword work."

Maddock's teeth flashed white as he grinned. "Perhaps it does."

Swift finally joined the discussion. "Animals are vessels of the Abomination," he said in a kindly tone. "We've explained that to you. How evil spreads. It's contagious."

The horse, Juniper, nudged Brother Honesty's shoulder, then nuzzled his ear.

The priest laughed and twisted away, a bit embarrassed by how pleasant the soft nose and warm breath felt against his skin. He found himself speaking to the brute as if to a small child. "Do you have something to add to our learned discourse?" He ran his hand down the blaze, thinking again how strange it seemed for an animal to seek human affection. A sudden thought occurred to him. "Perhaps goodness is contagious, too. Perhaps loving contact with humans permits a beast to grow a soul."

Swift made a noise of protest. "Good Brother, that's a rather . . . radical . . . speculation."

But the conviction took root and began to grow while Brother Honesty stroked Juniper's nose. He had become long accustomed to the Light leading him in unexpected directions. It regularly shattered his preconceptions, forcing his mind to expand in ways he never dreamed possible.

Swift cleared his throat. "Brother Honesty? Shall I have one of the Hooded Order scan you for infection?"

The priest lifted his gaze. Maddock and the commander stared at him in obvious dismay, and he abruptly wondered how long he had remained silent. "Commander, may I have leave to retire? I feel a need for prayer."

CHAPTER FOURTEEN

⟨❦⟩

A few days later, Maddock lay on his stomach amid the tall grasses decorating the edge of a small river. Wind rippled the tiny green forest, granting intermittent glimpses of the opposite bank and the dark mouth of a badger's den. Nearby, the camp settled into a careful silence that contrasted sharply with its usual morning bustle. This close to the fort of Radway Green, Commander Swift forbade any unnecessary noise. As Maddock understood it, that evening Brother Honesty and one of the Hooded Magicians would creep close to the fort to perform some sort of magical blessing.

Unaccustomed to idleness, Maddock pursed his lips. They would perform no drills so close to the fort, he had already groomed Little Sister to a fine burnish, and he could not talk to Brother Honesty because the priest attended a meeting in the commander's tent.

Maddock heard a soft step at his back, and a man spoke in a friendly tone. "What are you doing?"

Glad for the company, and thinking he recognized the soldier's voice, Maddock answered in a whisper. "Watching that badger den. It's so close to the river, I'm wondering if otters might live there."

"Hmm." The man sounded dubious, but he remained polite. "Wouldn't one expect to find . . . um . . . badgers living in a badger's den?"

"Of course." Maddock smiled without taking his eyes from the burrow. "I know it sounds strange, since badgers are so bad-tempered, but other creatures generally share their dens."

"Other creatures? Such as . . . other badgers?"

232

Maddock had to press his mouth into the crook of his arm to stifle his laughter. "Such as otters."

"Ah, yes." The grass rustled as the soldier crouched beside Maddock. "So you said."

"Usually it's foxes. Foxes, rabbits, owls, and sometimes ground squirrels."

"And don't they eat each other?"

Maddock remembered asking the same question as a child. "No. They're all friends."

The other man remained silent several moments. "You actually believe that."

Maddock twisted his head to look at the soldier. "Yes. I know—"

A Hooded Mage sat beside him, shrouded in black veils.

Deep cold suffused Maddock's blood. In an instant, his mind sorted through dozens of impulses fostered by training and instinct. He quelled them all, too self-disciplined to attack without a clear threat, too courteous to physically recoil. He remembered the battle in the beech grove, the ground shaking, and Ghan slipping lifelessly from his horse without taking a single blow. Maddock had later learned that the power of these magic-wielders tended to "overflow," ravaging whomever it touched. In fact, although the destructive power of one Mage alone could level a village, in battles where armies intermingled they required at least two. The second dampened or redirected excess magic from allies to enemies, just as it had to Ghan. Swift's soldiers gave the Hooded Magicians a wide berth. Maddock would have liked to do the same, but he did not wish to anger the creature and knew better than to show any sign of fear. He forced himself to keep talking. "I know it seems to contradict nature, but friendship does occur."

"Among animals?" The Mage chuckled. "Sounds like another component of Brother Honesty's new theology."

Maddock drew his brows down and studied the figure in black, noting the emblem of a skull on the Mage's shoulder. "Are you mocking the good Brother?" Irritation and aversion gained the upper hand.

"Not him. His ideas." Skull's tone turned indulgent. "There is a difference."

Maddock's lips thinned. "Aren't you under a vow of silence and secrecy?" he asked with heavy-handed sarcasm. "Please don't break it on my account."

Skull pushed back his hood and pulled off his mask. His long, dark hair lay fine and straight. His eyes looked large and expressive. "There? See? Not a monster." He shifted into a cross-legged position. "And I'm not saying anything to you that I haven't already said to Brother Honesty's face."

"All the same, I'd rather you wouldn't."

Skull presented Maddock with a strange smile. "The good Brother doesn't fear opinions that differ from his. You do, it seems."

"No."

"Really?" Skull lifted his chin. "Then you won't mind my saying I think animals are disgusting. They're furry amalgamations of hunger, lust, and the urge to defecate."

Maddock recognized a challenge when he heard one. He sat up slowly, centering himself in preparation for a verbal sparring match. "You don't believe animals possess spirits?"

"Of course they do. Everything has a 'soul,' for want of a better word. Every tree, every rock, every drop of water in that pretty little river, every blade of grass crushed beneath our backsides." Skull pulled off his gloves, revealing lean and elegant hands. "Knowledge of all souls is what gives me the power of magic."

Maddock tilted his head. "If you know about the souls of animals, how can you find them disgusting?"

Skull shrugged one shoulder. "Because they are. For example, those hunting dogs. They each have a soul, and yet they still eat their own vomit."

Maddock swallowed convulsively against a sudden unpleasant mental image.

"Is that not correct?" Skull raised his brows. "And while one moment a dog might lick his master's face, in the next instant it will lick its own—"

"But a dog doesn't know any better," Maddock interrupted.

"And I'm not convinced that a creature's worth should be measured by its sanitary habits."

"An excellent point. I concede that to you." Skull smiled. His eyes lit with obvious pleasure, as if he enjoyed the debate. "But my argument is that a creature's worth should not be measured by the possession of a soul. There is nothing particularly more important or special about a soul than a body."

"Except that the soul lives forever."

"Does it?"

Maddock verbally retreated, seeking more solid footing in the argument. "At least animals don't set out to deliberately do evil."

"True enough, I suppose. They don't label their actions good or evil, they merely obey instinct." Skull dropped his gaze. "Some may say I am evil. Would you agree with them?"

Maddock's mouth twitched. "I thought we were talking about animals."

"I'll take that as assent," Skull said quietly. "And yet I count Brother Honesty, who is unquestionably good, as my best and dearest friend. I would die to protect him from harm. Isn't that a strange thing for an evil man to say?"

Maddock drew breath to reply, then recalled his first real conversation with the priest. "There is darkness in light, and light in darkness."

Skull raised his head, lips parted.

Maddock sighed and spread his hands. "According to my people, I'm also evil. Because I've studied sword work and the ways of the warrior. It's all a matter of—" He broke off, shaking his head. "You say you find animals disgusting. Fine. But I disagree."

"Why?"

Maddock returned his attention to the badger's den. "Because there's so much more to them than their unseemly habits. When a lovely woman speaks to me, I don't dwell on the contents of her chamber pot."

Skull laughed. "Another excellent point."

From the shadowy entrance to the den, an otter thrust its peaked face into open air. It paused, sniffed intently, then squirted out of the tunnel and loped toward the riverbank.

With a thrill of triumph, Maddock ducked low in the grass. "Watch."

The clay riverbank sloped steeply toward the water. The otter flopped onto its belly and slid into the river like a sled on snow.

"Ah, yes," Skull murmured. "Very acrobatic."

Maddock grinned. "Wait."

The otter remained in the river for the space of three heartbeats. Then it launched itself from the water, galloped up the bank, and slid down the clay chute again.

Skull sounded intrigued. "What's it doing?"

"Playing."

Three more otters emerged from the den and also scooted down the slide.

Skull's tone turned patient. "That's not play. It's an instinctive urge to practice survival skills."

Maddock watched the creatures frolic and splash in the river, then chase each other down their slide. "Whatever you want to call it," he said. "It's entertaining."

"Yes," replied the Mage. "It is."

A fox slipped next from the den, its coat bright rust, its snout, ears, and legs black as soot. For a moment, it stood motionless, its nose lifted. Then it pattered down to the river, following a less precipitous path than the otters. The fox lapped water, its large ears in constant motion, and trotted back to the den. Just as it paused to enter, a common gray rabbit hopped outside. The two animals, hunter and prey, passed each other without a glance.

Trying to suppress his grin, Maddock turned to the Mage.

Skull stared, openmouthed.

Maddock raised his brows. "What sort of instinctive urge was that?"

"Amazing!" The Mage looked at Maddock. "These creatures have learned to band together for mutual protection."

"You could call it that. Or you could call it friendship." A new thought occurred to Maddock. "Someday soon, the Marchlands will be like that badger's den. All its different people living together in peace."

Skull regarded Maddock narrowly. "A strange thing for a warrior to say."

Everything is its own opposite. Maddock permitted himself to smile. "Not really."

❧

Kiarda reined in and dismounted from Snow Bell, the horse tossing her head and snorting her displeasure with the long ride. They had traveled all night, with the aid of the full moon. Though both stood exhausted, they did not have time for much of a rest. Surely someone had noticed they were missing by now.

Slender beech trees swayed in the dawn wind, leaves rattling, branches full against a sky brightening in increments. A lark warbled. Nearby, the brisk sweet waters of the river Coney rattled over stones. By all accounts, Kiarda had almost reached the spot where Vonora's hunting party had disappeared. Her mouth went dry with more than thirst. According to reports and rumors, she would soon find a place dubbed the Ash Pit, where the trees and grass had burned to nothing and even rocks had melted with the heat. The ground lay riven and thrown up in heaps, and the trees surrounding it leaned at crazy angles.

The folk of Dorlach Tor claimed Maddock and the Dark Court had destroyed the hunting party, but Kiarda wondered about the truth. He had not ravished her, and she now believed him innocent of any wrongdoing. Perhaps the gods themselves had acted to save him. *Have to find him. Can't breathe free until I atone.* She pictured him in all his wild beauty, and a bittersweet smile framed her dry lips.

Snow Bell nickered gently and aimed her little ears at the sound of running water. Jerked from her thoughts, Kiarda ran her hand down her mare's white nose. "I'm sorry, my lass. You're thirsty, aren't you?" She led the horse toward the Coney. "There should be a willow tree up ahead, leaning over the river. The bank is nice and low there."

Snow Bell swished her tail and regarded her mistress with calm, dark eyes.

Kiarda smiled as she trudged through the undergrowth, though her legs ached and her back felt as stiff as a granite slab. The Horsemaster, Cadder, had always claimed that the more one spoke to a Child of Hepona, the more it understood. "If I keep talking to you like this, by the time we find Maddock you'll be able to recite the heroic lineage of Dorlach Tor. That will surprise the—"

A carpet of green-and-pink foliage covered the undulating ground ahead. The trees slanted in myriad directions, as if holding the positions of a dance, and the Coney's restless voice gained a deeper music.

Startled silent, Kiarda stopped and stared. It looked beautiful, not the horrible and deathly Ash Pit of servants' tales.

Snow Bell nudged Kiarda with a wistful grunt.

Kiarda cleared her throat, her eyes wide. "Come on," she whispered. "But let's be careful. It could be enchanted."

Lush clover with fat, pink blossoms blanketed the broken ground. The willow still leaned from the bank, but it canopied a waterfall that plunged into a wide lagoon. Kiarda did not know whether to feel inspired or terrified. "Oh, Joyous Lord and Lady," she breathed. "I've never seen anything like it."

Snow Bell pulled toward the water.

Though still uncertain, Kiarda did not have the heart to deny her thirsty horse a drink. "Very well," she muttered. "But carefully now."

Slowly, they made their way to the Coney's edge, and the mare thrust her muzzle into the sparkling water. Lightning did not fall from the sky, nor did the ground open up to swallow them. Snow Bell drank her fill, sighed, and raised her head to dry her wet lips in Kiarda's hair.

Laughing, the young woman twisted out of reach, glad the mare still had the fettle to tease in spite of their long ride. "Oh, no, you don't, my fine lass. Save your high spirits for the road ahead."

Snow Bell vigorously shook her head, white mane and forelock flying, then gazed at her mistress with a merry light in her eyes.

Kiarda led the mare back to the clover. Curiously, she plucked a blossom and examined it. Pink petals, just opening for the morning, spread upward from a central stem. It appeared like any other she had ever seen. She sniffed it, then finally tasted it. "Seems safe."

Snow Bell snorted softly, as if in reply.

Kiarda pulled off the mare's tack and carried it beneath the leaning willow. They both needed to eat and rest before they could continue. She found the bread and cheese she had packed in her saddlebag, then stretched out on her stomach, propped up on her elbows, to watch the mare graze as she ate.

The lark sang again. A subtle breeze spread through the clover, carrying the wholesome sweetness of its scent. When she returned to Dorlach Tor, Kiarda mused, she would bring her parents to this place. Its beauty spoke of the loving hands of the gods, not the dire interference of the Dark Court. It was proof of Maddock's innocence and a mandate to continue her quest for his pardon.

As the sun broke over the horizon, Adan's hunch proved correct, to his relief. Kiarda's trail obviously led to the Ash Pit by the Coney. They had not lost her during the night.

Adan cued his mount to stop, then twisted to look over his shoulder at Bevin and Tynan. The healer's brown curls flew wild; the ribbon that normally held them had evidently blown off along the trail. Her plump face appeared pale under its coating of dirt, but her eyes carried a determined fire that evinced no trace of exhaustion. Tynan brought up the rear. Though more accustomed to long rides than Bevin, he seemed in much worse shape. His wide shoulders sagged. Fatigue and anxiety shadowed his eyes. Cat-Who-Bites-Priests poked his head out the neck of his linkmate's tunic.

From the trees ahead, a horse called a greeting. Adan's stallion flung up his head and whinnied a reply. His pulse suddenly jerking, Adan urged his mount forward. *Kiarda!* As they entered the beech clearing, Adan immediately spotted the future Lady of Dorlach Tor lying beside a partially uprooted tree. Other trunks sloped and pitched in random directions, like uneven teeth in a boar's shattered skull. The ground formed random humps and grooves. Adan feared the worst until he noticed how the mare stood untacked and knee-deep in clover.

With a cry of dismay, Kiarda rolled over and sat up.

Though comforted, Adan knew he had reached a difficult juncture. He pursued a new scheme, born during the midnight ride. He no longer intended to return Kiarda to Dorlach Tor immediately but rather to accompany her on her quest for a time. Not only would it delay the moment of the priests passing judgment, but it would give Kiarda a chance to see Tynan at his best. It would guarantee their marriage.

Adan pushed red-brown hair from his eyes. He had to strike just the right chord of pathos and loyalty, or Kiarda's pride would never permit her to agree. "My lady—" His throat closed, dry as dust from the long ride. It was a good touch, though unplanned. He coughed, then spoke in a gravelly whisper, "My lady, we were so worried."

Kiarda's face darkened. "What are you—?"

Adan dismounted. As his feet hit the ground, he staggered. The world seemed to spin, and he clutched the stirrup to keep his balance. His vertigo was unexpected, humiliating, and useful. Kiarda could always tell when he was exaggerating. He had learned it was best to manipulate her with the truth. "Sorry," Adan muttered, making no attempt to disguise his embarrassment. "Little more shaky than I thought."

Kiarda's expression changed from anger to alarm. She jumped to her feet and waded through the clover toward him. "Adan, are you all right?"

The spinning sensation grew worse, and a mist of perspiration gathered on Adan's upper lip. He clung to the saddle and forced himself to smile. "Funny. Was going to ask you that."

Bevin spoke up. "No, he's not all right!" Her voice contained an unusual impatience. "My Lord Adan has eaten nothing since yesterday at noon. He's worked hard and ridden far since then."

Kiarda put her hands on her hips. "I didn't ask him to come after me. I didn't ask any of you to—" She broke off with a sigh, then gestured wearily. "Tynan, don't just sit there. Help your brother."

Cheering inwardly, Adan clung to the stirrup and turned to

watch as Kiarda went to help Bevin dismount. The gods had blessed him; things were going better than planned.

Tynan gazed at Kiarda, six different kinds of anguish chasing over his perfect features. He glanced at his elder brother, and his lips parted in horrified worry.

A thrill of satisfaction surged through Adan. *Must look worse than I feel.*

Moving stiffly, Tynan flung himself from his horse and strode to Adan's side. "Almighty Hepona," he hissed. "You look fit to bury!"

Adan gripped Tynan's shoulders, keeping an eye on the women. "Listen to me," he rasped. "This may be your last chance to win Kiarda's hand."

"What do you—"

"Shut up!" Adan bent to speak in his brother's ear. "Whatever you think, whatever you feel, you keep it to yourself. Just agree with Kiarda. About everything."

"But—"

"Do it!"

Kiarda led Bevin forward, her arm around the healer's waist. "Over here," she murmured in a comforting tone. "Under this tree. I've got some food and water."

Bevin's voice still contained a note of impatience. "I'm fine, Kiarda. Built like an oak bucket. Stop treating me like a blown-glass figurine."

A secret warmth touched Adan's heart. *My kitchen lady.* He straightened abruptly, inducing a fresh round of dizziness, and whirled away from his brother. "I'll take care of the horses." He attempted to reach for his mount's reins, lost his balance, and began to fall.

Tynan caught Adan and yanked him upright. "Cut it out! Stop being so blasted heroic!"

Kiarda turned and narrowed her eyes. "He's right, Adan. Stop it." She gestured to her saddle pack on the ground. "I've got bread, cheese, and a flask of water. Tynan, you take care of Adan and Bevin. I'll take care of the horses."

For a moment, Tynan looked as if he would protest, then he nodded. "Yes, Kiarda."

Pleased, Adan allowed himself to be helped to the indicated tree. He settled on the cool grass and let his aching muscles relax. "Ah, that's nice."

Frowning, Tynan handed the water flask to Bevin, but he kept his eyes on Kiarda.

Bevin drank and passed the water to Adan.

Careful not to brush her fingers, Adan took it and also drank, very aware of the fact that her lips had touched the mouth of the flask an instant ago. The water washed the dust from the back of his throat and seemed to rinse away the last of his dizziness. Wiping his chin with the back of his hand, he offered the flask to Tynan.

His brother did not notice, his attention fixed on Kiarda as she walked by with the horses.

Adan cleared his throat. "Tynan. Thirsty?"

Cat-Who-Bites-Priests slipped from his refuge inside his linkmate's tunic. With a purring yawn, he stretched, then commenced to sharpen his claws on Tynan's knee.

The young man yelped and pushed the cat away. "Hey, what was that for? I didn't—"

The cat rubbed his face against the water flask.

Adan understood. "He's thirsty, even if you're not." He poured a bit of water into his cupped hand. "Here you go, my furry little brother."

Cat-Who-Bites-Priests sniffed the proffered refreshment, then began to drink and purr simultaneously.

Adan grinned. "Your whiskers tickle."

Tynan made an exasperated noise. "Adan," he whispered fiercely, "what's going on in that head of yours?"

"Hush!" Frantically, Adan turned to see if Kiarda had heard, but she stood beside the chattering river. He glanced back at Tynan and Bevin, wondering why the situation did not seem obvious to them as well. "We originally planned to bring her back before anyone noticed her absence. I think it's safe to say we failed in that."

Bevin nodded glumly. "I'd wager a search party is only an hour or two behind us."

Evidently satisfied, the cat wandered away from Adan and sat down to wash his face.

Adan wiped his damp hand on his trousers."We're going to get caught. It's inevitable."

Tynan sighed through his teeth. "Then why did you tell me not to argue with Kiarda?"

Adan tilted his head, gathering his patience. "Because you're an idiot."

Tynan glared. "Don't start—"

Adan flashed up his hand. "Do you want to marry Kiarda?"

"Of course! What kind of stupid question—?"

Adan punctuated his words by stabbing the air with his finger. "Then you'll have to stand by her. We all will. Like true and loyal friends."

Tynan drew his brows together. "But what about—?"

Trying to convey the importance of the situation, Adan gripped his brother's shoulder. "Do you want Kiarda to remember you as the man who helped drag her back to Dorlach Tor? Or as the man who loved her enough to stay true to her in spite of everything?"

Tynan jerked himself free. "But I do love her! I can't pretend to help her on this quest while—"

Adan struggled to keep his voice down. "I'm not asking you to pretend anything."

Tynan scrambled to his feet. "But you said—"

A dull ache formed behind Adan's eyes. "Just listen to me. All we have to do is—"

Kiarda interrupted. "—persuade me to let all three of you join my search."

Aghast, Adan whirled. Kiarda stood leaning against the tree trunk. No telling how much she had heard. Attempting to disarm her with humor, Adan pressed both hands against his heart and collapsed in facetious shock. "You scared me."

Kiarda smiled thinly. "Not nearly enough." She sauntered to her saddle pack, pulled out a loaf of bread, and tossed it to Bevin. "Here. You look hungry."

The healer hastily set the bread aside and climbed to her feet. "Kiarda. Please take us with you."

Adan kept his mouth shut, wildly praying for his brother to do the same. Bevin was their best hope now. *Be brave, my kitchen lady.*

Kiarda's gaze flicked from Bevin, to Tynan, and finally to Adan. She spoke gently. "No."

Bevin folded her arms. "You have to."

Kiarda lifted one brow. "Really?"

Bevin's mouth flexed indecisively, then hardened. "Yes. You do. It would be a different matter if you were only out to find Maddock. But you're not. You're searching for yourself."

A peculiar expression crossed Kiarda's face. For a moment, she seemed lost within a memory.

Adan found himself holding his breath.

Bevin stepped toward Kiarda with a dipping motion. "I can help you, if you let me. I can teach you to control the fox."

Kiarda spoke in an odd tone, "The spirit fox."

Bevin reached to her with both hands. "Please."

With a start, Kiarda seemed to return to herself. "No."

Tynan cleared his throat. "Then come back home with us. There isn't—" His voice suddenly shook, as if he fought back tears. "If you're not at Dorlach Tor, there isn't any reason for me to return."

Adan released his pent-up breath. *Well said, little brother.*

Kiarda shook her head. "I'm sorry. I can't go back. Not until I find Maddock and apologize."

Adan sighed. *Pathos and loyalty.* "Then we'll follow without your consent." He wearily hoisted himself to his feet and gestured at the three of them. "Dear lady, look at us. We're tired and dirty and starving, but we came after you because we love you." He pointed at the saddle pack in her hands. "You have food, clothing, and money. You're prepared for the journey. We're not. But if you ride off without us, we'll follow you anyway."

Kiarda froze, glaring, then her shoulders sagged. "That's not fair, Adan."

He replied with the simple truth. "Don't care. I love you too much."

Kiarda made a sound of disgust and turned away. "I don't

believe I'm saying this." She pointed toward the Coney. "I left your horses tied up over there. Better get them. We need to ride soon."

Tynan spoke unsteadily. "Kiarda. I love you, too."

Kiarda shook her head, muttering, and stalked off to catch her mare.

Bevin turned to Adan, her gray eyes shining with unmistakable admiration. "My lord, you're sneaky."

Adan felt a scorching blush rise to his cheeks. It suddenly occurred to him that the impromptu jaunt with Kiarda would allow him quite a bit of time with Bevin. "Why, thank you . . . my lady."

CHAPTER FIFTEEN

MADDOCK'S sword sliced air still dormant from the night. The first edge of sun teased the horizon, but the stars remained bright against a backdrop of dark sky scarcely tinged with pink. Cool air bathed the sweat on Maddock's arms, a comforting chill that reminded him of fall afternoons in Scratter Wood. He managed a smile at a memory that, scant weeks ago, would have driven him to tears. Along with the life he had left behind, he had grieved Gaer's death to its natural conclusion. The friendships he had since developed, the exhilarating sense of fellowship that acceptance brought, had granted peace to a soul in turmoil. Finally, he could envision the old Swordmaster as a blessed piece of his past rather than as a frozen outcast dying in lonely and horrible anguish.

Maddock continued to grin with a careless openness he once believed he could never again experience. Sword work was freedom. He savored the weight of the blade, the drag of air against honed steel, the musical whistle of its movement. The etched runes of Gaer's name flickered like spun silver through the starlight as Maddock whirled in a controlled arc, attuned to every sound, every motion. Though boldly committed to the maneuver, he could redirect it as fast as the thought of doing so, had learned to amend his next sequence to counter an opponent with the instinct the Swordmaster had described. *If only he were here to see me.* Maddock contented himself with fantasy: he imagined that a piece of Gaer's spirit lived on in the blade he had once wielded in battle.

Two shadows bobbed through the false dawn, headed toward the commander's tent. Alarmed, Maddock lowered his sword and darted toward them. Gradually, his vision carved enough detail from background to allow him to recognize them; Brother Honesty and the Hooded Mage had returned from their mission at Radway Green. Feeling foolish for worrying, Maddock skidded to a stop as the two disappeared inside the flap.

A soldier scrambled from the ground near Maddock's feet with the jerkiness of a startled colt. He glanced about with wild eyes, then focused on Maddock. He said something in their guttural language that the young man did not understand, accompanied by a sharp gesture that he did.

"Sorry," Maddock muttered, his accent mangling the foreign syllables.

Apparently realizing how ridiculous he must have looked, the soldier smiled sheepishly. His attention slid to the sword in Maddock's hand. "Spar?"

Why not? Maddock had to stop himself from laughing. Life had changed so much since the night he had battled Commander Swift, and all for the better. He no longer had to toss off the quiet coils of guilt that once assailed him whenever he so much as thought about the sword. His new brothers encouraged practices, and Commander Swift approved of his dedication to his weapon and his training. The commander had taken a personal interest in his tutelage; Maddock supposed because of his enthusiasm, since he never saw himself as particularly skilled. "Spar," Maddock repeated. "Yes." He sheathed his sword and waited while the other man located two practice weapons amid his gear.

Shortly, the soldier rose, passing one wooden *rattara* to Maddock and clutching the other in his right fist. Maddock crouched, squaring. His gaze slid to the commander's tent. In the instant his attention lay diverted, the soldier drove in with a hard thrust for Maddock's gut. Cursing his negligence, Maddock whipped up his practice sword. Wood crashed against wood, impact thrumming. Maddock proved stronger, slamming the other's *rattara* over his head. Maddock followed with a wild boring in that sent the other scrabbling for a defense. Again, Maddock's gaze strayed to the tent where Brother Honesty had disappeared, leaving his opponent enough time to straggle into a better position.

Only then, it occurred to Maddock that the priest had been moving stiffly, hands jerking in agitation. Something bothered the gentle Brother, which explained why Maddock found himself straining to keep his mind on the sword work he usually loved.

The soldier's *rattara* sang through the air. Maddock backstepped, barely sparing himself a bruising. Preoccupied, he halfheartedly parried and dodged several more attacks, rarely bothering to riposte. From the corner of his vision, he saw the flap of Swift's tent lift. Suddenly desperate for the liberty to confront the harried priest, Maddock changed his strategy. He charged his sparring partner with a frenzied flurry of wood. Caught off guard, the other man retreated. This time, Maddock pursued, scoring a touch against right thigh, then left neck in turn.

Head low, huddled into his threadbare cloak, Brother Honesty headed toward the rising sun and his tent.

Mad with impatience, Maddock bowed to the soldier. Together, they executed a short Dance of respect, the sequence not warming Maddock's blood, this one time. As soon as politeness allowed, he tossed back the *rattara* and hurried after his friend.

Branches crunched beneath Maddock's boots. He sprinted between tents, packs, and rousing soldiers without pausing for amenities. Shortly, he located the priest moving with the slow shuffle of a man in pain. Maddock raced to Brother Honesty's side, falling into step beside him. They walked this way for several paces, Brother Honesty staring at the ground and Maddock panting softly from exertion.

At length, Brother Honesty glanced over. He stiffened, genuinely startled by Maddock's presence. "Hello! I'm sorry, my child. I didn't notice you there."

Maddock raised his brows. "You couldn't hear me dashing about like a galloping stallion?" He added self-deprecatingly, "And huffing like one, too?"

Brother Honesty's head drooped again, and he seemed not to recognize the humor. "I'm sorry, my child. My mind is heavy."

It pained Maddock to see his friend sad, especially when the priest had rescued him from the same state on more than one occasion. "What's bothering you?"

"You wouldn't . . ." The priest sighed. "I mean, I can't explain . . ." He glanced at Maddock again, then inclined his head to a secluded patch of weeds near his tent. "I don't think Commander Swift will mind if we discuss it. You'll know soon enough, and it's better you understand the reasons for what we must do."

The sorrow in the priest's blue eyes impaled Maddock. He found himself wishing he could take the agony from the older man onto himself. He moved to the indicated area without speaking further. Unburdening was the first step toward solace, and he would not prolong Brother Honesty's discomfort. Finding a thick, rotting branch amid the dense growth of weeds, Maddock sat on it and gestured for his companion to do the same.

Brother Honesty did so, though whether coincidentally or because of Maddock's invitation, the young man could not tell. The priest seemed distant and preoccupied.

"We've spoken of the Abomination that afflicts the peoples of the Marchlands?"

Maddock shook his head, though the priest did not look at him to acknowledge the gesture. "I've overheard mention, but I wish you would explain it." He tried to sound encouraging, but he could not stop himself from sketching out a sign to ward off evil.

The priest seemed equally uncomfortable, shivering once, as if mere mention of the Abomination might bring it directly to them. "My child, it's a dirty and horrible thing, contagious and without cure."

Maddock tried to understand. "An illness? The healers—"

"—have no power against this," Brother Honesty finished sadly. "It's not like catarrh. It's a thing of evil, a magical pall of . . . of . . ." He struggled with words.

Understanding dawned with vicious clarity. Maddock found the word in his own language that Brother Honesty sought. "A curse." He found himself beset by sudden and unexpected relief. It explained so much that had seemed nonsensical: Kiarda's ravishing, the seventeen people whose slaying Vonora had blamed on him, the ephemeral creatures that had haunted the woodlands in the nights before he discovered his new brothers. *Dark Court.*

"A curse." Brother Honesty rolled his eyes toward the lightening sky in consideration. "This 'curse' means . . . ?"

Maddock returned to the priest's own description. "A magical pall of evil."

"Ah." Brother Honesty bobbed his head. "Curse. Exactly the word." His movement stilled suddenly, and he huddled deeper into his robe. "This curse, this Abomination, spreads from person to person like a dark and terrible fire. Once, it seemed certain that the only means to stop it was to destroy those who bore it and all who came in contact with them."

Maddock absorbed the words slowly, horror dislodging the misplaced sense of comfort. "What?" The word shocked from his throat. "You're not talking about—"

The priest's head lowered further, lost in the folds of his hood. "I am, my child."

Maddock had to finish. "Wholesale slaughter?"

Brother Honesty remained silent.

"Men of peace?" A worse thought seized Maddock. "Women and children?" He stared at the ragged edges of the priest's hood, wishing he could see the familiar gentle eyes. The agony that had glazed them moments before gained full meaning. "Surely there's another way."

As if guessing Maddock's thoughts, Brother Honesty swept down his hood. "We've tried blessing those around the victim with the grace of the One Light while a Mage destroys that piece of the Abomination."

"And?" Maddock grasped the rotted branch with trembling fingers, and chips of bark crumbled from the contact.

"It worked very well most places." Brother Honesty finally glanced toward Maddock, a glimmer of relief appearing amid the discomfort. "We've saved so many, praise the Light." He placed a sympathetic hand on Maddock's. "But we've suffered our second failure."

"Second?" Maddock's throat tightened. "The first?"

"Do not worry, my child." The priest's fingers closed around Maddock's, the grip warm and soothing. For a fleeting instant, Maddock relived a forgotten flash of memory, sitting on a deadfall with one pudgy toddler hand gripped in his father's callused fist. "They're unharmed. It was our first attempt, and Skull didn't know exactly how things should feel when we finished."

Maddock's eyes narrowed. He found the words difficult to follow.

Apparently reading his companion's discomfort, Brother Honesty turned to specifics. "This time, things went well, at first. I blessed the villagers, and Claw handled the magic. Then, just as we were preparing to leave, the Mage detected two signs of the curse not present earlier. Claw—'communicated,' shall we say?—that the first seemed warped and tangled. Then the second appeared, fully formed."

Maddock encouraged Brother Honesty with rapt attention. He knew nothing of the workings of magic, but the details enabled him to follow at a distant level and the need to focus on finding the proper words seemed to relieve the priest of some of that terrible anxiety.

"My child, that's almost exactly the way Skull described his findings at the first settlement. Claw could not offer an explanation. Commander Swift and I can only deduce that this twisted manifestation represents the leading edge of the curse." Brother Honesty released Maddock to emphasize his frustration with hand gestures. "The active agent of contagion. The very 'head' of the Abomination."

Maddock nodded briskly to indicate comprehension, worried the priest might continue seeking the best phrasing all day.

"If we can catch it in this one place and destroy it and all it's touching, we may finally fully eradicate the Abomination."

At what price? The priest's words seemed too simple, too obvious and certain to mean cold-blooded slaughter. Maddock clapped his chin between his hands, smelling the mildewed bark on his fingers. "Is this Abomination truly more horrible than slaying so many innocents?"

Brother Honesty did not hesitate, his nod grief-stricken but sure. "I'm afraid, my child, it is."

Realization struck like a million blows of a *rattara*. Only one thing Maddock knew met that description. *Almighty Hepona, they're not battling a creature of the Dark Court. They're after the Dark Court itself!* The idea left Maddock breathless, unable to speak.

The two men sat in a pensive silence neither could break. Gradually, both sought solace in prayer.

In disbelief, Skull lifted his gaze to Claw. *"What?"*

Now hidden from the uninitiated in the privacy of their shared tent, Claw cast off her hood and mask. "You heard me. More of that religious stuff about the Abomination." She smiled unpleasantly, green eyes gleaming. "Actually, I'm surprised you weren't eavesdropping on Brother Honesty's thoughts."

Skull's thin mouth tightened in a scowl. "Don't start—"

Interrupting, Claw laughed. "Things are finally about to get interesting. Honesty wants to purge the village."

Skull's irritation vanished into shock. "Purge?" he echoed, running his hands through his fine, black hair. "Did you tell him it isn't necessary?"

Claw found a leftover piece of stale bread from the previous day and bit into it ravenously. "No," she said with her mouth full. "Because it is."

Still lying on his bedroll, Wraith stretched his lanky frame. "Claw, don't eat that. There's fresh in the basket by the door."

Claw made a hungry noise, still chewing, and reached for the basket. "Purge is the only way."

Fighting for calm, Skull spoke in an even tone. "No, it isn't."

Claw pulled a crusty bannock from the basket. "Smells wonderful. I'm starving." She twisted a piece from the bread and stuffed it in her mouth. "Two manifestations. Appeared out of nowhere. And one was . . ." She gestured erratically. ". . . freakish. Ugly."

Wraith sat up, yanked a wineskin from beneath his pillow, and passed it to Claw. "And that's the Abomination?"

Claw hastily swallowed her mouthful. "Swift and Honesty think so."

"No," said Skull. "Impossible."

Claw uncorked the wineskin. "Doesn't matter what you call it. Does it?"

Glowering, Skull remained silent.

Claw took a generous gulp of wine then another bite of bread. "Telling you—" she paused to chew for a few moments, "—purge is the only way to make sure we wipe them out. I mean, you can't track them."

It was true. In spite of diligent practice, Skull lacked the required precision. "*I* can't," he said pointedly. "*You* can."

"Me?" Claw pretended to choke on her bread. "Are you mad? We don't have the time for that. And I can't spare the strength."

Skull narrowed his dark eyes. "Wraith could help you."

The youngest Mage assumed a considering air. "I suppose," he said. "But that would still be exhausting work, and we're pretty close to an enemy position. What if Swift needed us?"

Skull dropped his gaze, unwilling to concede the point.

Claw washed down her mouthful with another draught of wine. "Not only that. What if we did the tracking, and then still had to do the purge?"

Defeated, Skull closed his eyes. He needed Wraith or Claw rested and ready to draw upon all their resources so that one of them could dampen and redirect his power. An ordinary man with his foot poised over a swarm of ants could not pick an individual insect to trod upon. Skull possessed no more control over the raw energies of the sixth magic than that, and he would most certainly destroy Swift's men along with the enemy.

Wraith cleared his throat, and his voice took on a peculiar tone. "You seem reluctant to perform the purge."

"Do I?" Wearily, Skull deliberated upon his colleague's words. "Perhaps Brother Honesty's reverence for life is rubbing off on me."

"Hmmm." Claw sounded amused. "How odd. The good Brother is the one who wants the village annihilated."

Skull jerked his attention to Claw.

Claw raised her brows mischievously. "Yes?"

It was true. And what Honesty wanted was all that mattered to Skull. He reached for the wineskin, and a faint smile touched his lips. "Yes."

Clouds filled the early morning sky, glazing sunlight to a plane of pinkish-gray. The few beams that slipped through the gaps seemed to congregate on the mesh between the strike force's leather plates. In the middle of the leading rank, Maddock suffered a barrage of doubt and emotion. Excitement warred with terror and guilt; uncertainty prodded undirected shame. The armor perched like a stone across his shoulders, the odd mix of leather and mail hampering an arm accustomed to unencumbered strikes. The mingled odors of sweat and raw exhilaration formed a heady perfume he had come to associate with camaraderie. He belonged here, among the adopted brothers who would never turn on him like the people of his childhood so readily had. Yet he could not shake the realization that, in moments, he might destroy some of the very people with whom he had once shared a life.

Riding between two officers, at the lead as always, Commander Swift looked surprisingly nondescript. He wore the same armor combination as his men. The sorrel prancing and snorting its eagerness beneath him bore no colors, not even socks or blazes to mark it as special. A wood-framed, leather helmet hid the golden hair, and his bearing, though straight-backed and regal, matched many of his men's.

Little Sister fast-walked easily among the other horses, but her gait held a tight irregularity that revealed nervousness. Maddock forced his muscles to uncoil, patting the filly's speckled neck reassuringly. Cadder insisted the Children of Hepona could read human emotion better than any man and tended to echo the state of their riders. Maddock hoped that, if he could not control his own unsortable worries, he could at least try to spare his mount.

Swift called a halt, the command gliding down the wedge. Like a single, interconnected being, the men obeyed. Nestled on a mild slope, the village of Radway Green lay placid beyond a stone wall thick with moss and ferns. Rings of roads and cottages surrounded a central fort where an ancient and dignified Lady named Conna ruled with iron-fisted, but fair-minded, judgment. She had borne no children, but Cadder had often joked that during his childhood he had learned every horse fair of another orphan she had fostered. She had raised a score of gentle children, already outliving many, and had a strong-willed granddaughter groomed to succeed her. And now, it seemed, Swift and his men would finish what time and nature had not managed: the passage of Lady Conna.

Maddock closed his eyes, forcing away personal details. He tried to envision the Marchland village as those around him did: a clutch of strangers ravaged by the Dark Court's curse, a couple of hundred martyred for the cause of thousands more. The ethical question had plagued mankind for as long as civilization existed: it made sense to sacrifice a few innocents for the survival of the whole, but that did not make the task simple or even tolerable. Stane's words came to Maddock again: *That's what war is all about. Your blood, your opponents' blood, the blood of horses, and the blood of people you love. It is sheer butchery. . . .* The memory burned like poison, and its profound truth in this situation raised a wave of bitterness. His mind rejected the image, refusing to take counsel from the one who had stolen his joy and life, who had no doubt ordered his blameless father executed. Seeking composure, he repeated in a low mantra a phrase given to him by Brother Honesty for this very purpose: "Cleanse hatred with goodness and light. Cleanse hatred with goodness and light. Cleanse hatred . . ." He added emphatically, "I can do this."

Maddock opened his eyes. Around him, men sat steadfastly upon their horses, but their expressions revealed the same stress he felt. Though his brothers did not share his personal stake in the mission, they did not relish the prospect of shaking the blood of children from their blades.

Commander Swift drew his sword with a grand flourish intended to alert the three Hooded Magians stationed on the opposite side of the village. The soldiers in the wedge slumped, averting their eyes, some clamping their palms to their ears. Maddock mimicked the commander's composure, remaining rigidly in place, attention fixed on the village. Then, a low rumble shook the earth. The wall circling Radway Green trembled. The villagers glanced up from their many chores. Suddenly, the barrier shattered, flinging massive field stones like pebbles. Screams rose above the din of thumping rock, and the townsfolk fled like frightened rabbits.

"Charge!" Swift's command cut over the din. Little Sister tensed beneath Maddock, then thundered toward the village amid the wave of galloping horses. Maddock grasped the side of his saddle for balance, barely managing to free his sword before the roan sailed over the wreckage of Radway Green's once-grand wall.

Most of the citizens disappeared into the central fort, others cowering into closer buildings: cottages and sheds. A few of the men brandished picks, hoes, or axes. Most made only several frenzied sweeps to gain their families time before following them to shelter. Two dozen bodies littered streets bustling with normal activity only a moment earlier. Though he had not yet had a hand in the slaughter, Maddock suffered deep pangs of regret. His hand winched painfully around his hilt, and he avoided looking at any of the dead for fear he might recognize them.

Swift's voice rose again in command. "Retreat to the border!" The commander's eyes swept the fort as he wheeled his horse.

Arrows rained down upon the invaders, raggedly chaotic, as the men obeyed. The side of one shaft caromed off the helmet of the man beside Maddock, but no others came near him. Again, Little Sister flew over the wreckage of the wall, this time in the opposite direction. There, Swift directed his men to spread along the village border. Once more, he raised his sword to signal the Magicians, his soldiers remaining doggedly in place, though many demeanors revealed their contempt for and fear of the Hooded Order. Maddock's mind filled again with the image of Ghan's body sliding dead from his horse, a victim of magical overflow.

The outer ring of cottages exploded into fire. Shrieks rang through the air, accompanied by the abrupt roar of flame.

Startled, Maddock jerked every muscle. Little Sister became a tight ball of panic beneath him. "It's all right. It's all right." The Horsemaster's son stroked the filly's slick neck and forced himself to calm. It was not all right. Every hair on his arms rose as he imagined his own flesh charring, his own mouth screaming, clinging to Cadder as smoke and flame consumed them. Many men, women, and children had just lost their lives in a horrible instant of magic.

A second ring of cottages flared, then the third and last. Shapeless creatures stumbled from the wreckage, rolling in mindless anguish. Sheep bleated frantically in their pens, and cows huddled in the far corners of their pastures.

Arrows erupted from the fortress in uncoordinated volleys. Flight after flight grounded in a village now lost in billowing black flames. The acrid odor of fire mingled with burning thatch and meat, and Maddock's stomach roiled. Desperate knots of people bolted from the central fortress scant moments before it fragmented, flinging wreckage to the clouds. Thunder crashed against Maddock's ears. Colors flashed through the sky, bits of roof and furniture flung to heights once only the domain of birds. Cinders pattered to the ground like black hail, stinging the horses into kicking dances, leaving dark pinpoint scars on the soldiers' leather armor and helmets.

Maddock heard the commander's voice, the specifics of his words lost beneath the rumble of falling debris. A few dozen of Radway Green's citizens had managed to locate swords longstored. These charged the invaders with a doomed valor Maddock could not help admiring. Swift rode toward the closest knot, men trailing him. Nearer, Maddock raced toward the armed men and women of Radway Green. To his relief, he knew none of them, but their faces all held the same desperate courage and their movements a sure boldness. They had nothing left to lose.

Little Sister shied from a powerful sweep that opened the side of another horse. The animal collapsed, its rider trapped beneath it. The roan bucked and spun, attempting to run. Maddock cursed, fighting his mount. A villager's sword dipped toward the trapped man's throat.

"No!" Worried for his fellow, Maddock gave up the fight with the terrified filly. He leaped from the saddle and onto the villager, bearing the man down an instant before the blade met its mark. The sword lurched as the man tumbled, softening Maddock's fall and scoring a harmless slap against the side of the young man's cheek. Maddock rolled, the world whirling crazily, then came up in a ready crouch. He faced an arrow on the end of a drawn bow.

Maddock threw up his arm before terror fully stabbed through him. The shaft sped harmlessly past his shoulder, and his sword sliced the bow in half. He whirled to face the man he had knocked askew from horseback. The sword that had nearly killed

Maddock's fellow now plunged toward Maddock. He side-stepped, and the sword tapped off his mail. He returned a gut thrust that the other dodged. The man cut for Maddock's leg. Maddock attempted a parry, only to find the man's feint turned into a blazing rush for his head. He cringed, deliberately leaping backward to forestall the huntswoman behind him whose bow he had shattered. Instead, he tripped over her body, thudding to the ground with a heaviness that slammed pain through his spine and made him bite his tongue. The swordsman pursued. His blade plunged for Maddock's throat. The Horsemaster's son made a desperate twist. Steel grazed his neck, beading warm blood, then stabbed into the ground.

The time it took the man to jerk the sword free allowed Maddock to scramble to his feet. *Instinct*, Maddock reminded himself, dimly aware of the mounted crowd of soldiers. "Surrender!"

"Never!" The stranger sported a shock of brown hair and coarse features. About Stane's age, he had likely fought in many battles before the lie of the Joyous Reunion forced him to retire his sword. "Die, you blackguard." He charged Maddock with a bull's rush of fury.

Maddock parried a thrust for his abdomen, riposting with a high cut that found the groove between two ribs. The sword jarred through flesh, impact tingling through Maddock's hand. The man collapsed, wrenching Maddock's blade. It snapped with enough force to tear hilt and callus from the young man's palm. Blood geysered, splattering Maddock. The stranger's mouth opened, disgorging scarlet foam, and the dark eyes lay wide, glazed in death.

Maddock stood in wild shock, fingers aching, blood dripping from his hands. He had never expected human flesh to prove so unyielding, violent death to look quite so horrible. He sank to his knees, vomiting on grass strewn with stone and ash.

A hand gently clapped cloth to the shallow wound on Maddock's neck. He looked up to Swift's fresh-faced features and soft gray eyes. "I never believed the woman's claim that you killed seventeen people. If she could see you now, she would not doubt either." He crouched. "Your first kill?"

Maddock waited until he had full control of his gut before

wiping his mouth, taking control of the bandage, and facing his commander. "Second, sir," he admitted, clutching the rag against his wound. "But the first wasn't so . . . bloody." He did not know that for certain. He had killed Damas on the run, without bothering to look behind him, but he had neither the means nor wherewithal to explain that the differences had little to do with blood and more to do with the shock and depth of penetration.

Maddock rose to shaky legs, only then realizing several soldiers watched their exchange from horseback. Little Sister stood trembling at the edge of the forest near several other riderless horses. The haft of his sword lay in the dirt, stubbornly supporting the remaining half of blade. Blood filled the etched and scrolling letters, the final sequence of Gaer's name, the last symbol of Maddock's past destroyed by his own hand. Tears filled his eyes. He watched through a blur as two soldiers hauled his opponent to join a neat line of corpses. He removed the bandage and looked at the smear of scarlet, so insignificant compared to the handprint on the reverse and the puddle at his feet. "Where are the others, sir?" he managed.

Swift motioned toward the crumbling ruin of Radway Green proper and the curling gray plumes of smoke rising from the ashes. "Handling whatever remains. There's a group to the south taking down a last pocket of resistance. It's a few archers hunkered down in the woods."

Maddock headed toward the broken sword.

The commander stopped him with a touch. He spoke too softly for the others to hear, "Thank you for rescuing Cunning. Your courage, and your skill, are appreciated." He glanced eastward.

Warmed by the praise, Maddock followed the commander's gaze to a deadfall where the man who had become trapped beneath his steed steadied a massive splint on his leg.

"That she-wolf of yours was doing well in drills, but she wasn't quite ready for real battle."

Me either. Maddock nodded. "Yes, sir."

"Brave foemen should have the chance to die in battle, but that doesn't mean a warrior should forsake his own protections."

Maddock stared, understanding eluding him. It occurred to

him that Swift had had no reason to rush them into the town prior to the Hooded Magicians performing their dark magic. The commander had surely done so to allow those townsfolk who chose combat to die with valor rather than in flames. It also explained why no one had come directly to his aid while he fought the swordsman, though someone had handled the huntswoman at his back. "Protections, sir?" Maddock prodded.

"Armor. Horses." Commander Swift made a broad gesture to indicate none of his other men had dismounted. "Perhaps it's time to put a bridle on your horse. Or to choose another."

The commander had made an indisputable point, but Maddock could not discard the emotional ties to his filly. His body felt hot with exertion and shame. He could not abandon Little Sister now, not after what he had just observed, not after the part he had played in the destruction of an innocent village. "I'll work with her, sir," he promised.

The words seemed to appease the commander. "Very well. We took a few casualties, mostly horses. We'll need most of those extra mounts we took in the beech grove." He headed toward his sorrel.

"Sir."

Swift turned back to Maddock.

"There's likely a stable near the fort. If any of the horses survived, they could be blindfolded and led free."

The commander's brows rose, widening steely though remarkably youthful eyes. "Any animals found here must be put to the sword."

Surprised, Maddock stared. "Animals, too?"

From horseback, the soldiers shook their heads and whispered. Surely they questioned his concern for creatures after the tragically necessary murder of so many innocent people.

"By its very nature, the Abomination affects as many animals as humans." Commander Swift mounted and headed off to handle his other soldiers.

A soldier left the corpses and approached Maddock, offering the freshly polished sword of the man Maddock had bested. He said something in his language which contained the words "need" and "earned."

Maddock accepted the sword with a gesture of grace. "Thank you." It fit comfortably in his sheath.

The other retreated.

The side of Maddock's head ached, his stomach still felt queasy, and his gait remained unsteady. Muddle-headed from sorrow, he limped toward his mount.

CHAPTER SIXTEEN

K IARDA woke slowly to the scents of wood smoke, horses, and roasting trout. *Camp,* she thought with relief. *I'm safe.*

Bevin spoke from close at hand. "Kiarda? Can you hear me?"

"Yes." Kiarda opened her eyes but remained still. Intertwined branches filled her vision, sporting leaves as green as jade. Mulch cushioned the forest ground. Her cloak covered her naked body, and her head rested upon a folded saddlecloth. "I did it. I changed."

Bevin knelt beside Kiarda. "You didn't sleep nearly so long as usual, this time. Perhaps half an hour. Do you remember anything?"

Kiarda studied the canopy of leaves and tried to cast her thoughts back to the moments just before she awakened. "No, I—" A faint memory stirred of fox-time. "Wait. Yes. Smells, I believe." She recalled scenting more as a fox than as a human. "I could smell you and the boys and the cat, and I knew who you were though I couldn't think of your names." She drew her brows together, wondering how to explain. "I didn't have any words."

Bevin nodded, her gray eyes pensive. "That's an excellent start. Do you recall anything else?"

"Sorry." Kiarda glanced around for her clothes and caught another whiff of trout. Her stomach rumbled. "Is the fish ready?"

Bevin settled cross-legged on the ground, parked her chin on her fist, and regarded her friend silently.

"What?" Kiarda looked at the other young woman, waiting for an answer. "Did I say something wrong?"

"The fish."

"Pardon?" Then Kiarda remembered something else from fox-time, hunger and frustration. "I wanted some trout."

Bevin's somber expression opened in a sudden smile.

The full memory came pouring back, the tantalizing aroma, the cruel heat of the fire, the desperate circling to find a way to get at the tasty river fish. "I remember!" Jubilation pulled Kiarda to her feet with a whoop. "I remember! I tried to figure out how to get the trout."

Bevin laughed, slapping her knees. "That's right. I was afraid at one point that you'd burn your paws. You're quite a persistent fox."

"Stubborn," Kiarda corrected, grinning. She spotted her tunic and trousers folded up on the ground beside her boots, and stepped over to them. "I'm a stubborn vixen." She shook out her tunic and pulled it on. "So. Is the fish ready?"

"Should be." Bevin stood and went to the fire. "The boys ought to be back from Riverton soon. I suppose I can keep theirs warm."

Kiarda yanked on her trousers, still smiling. After a week of travel, Bevin had finally dropped the last of her formality and no longer referred to Tynan and Adan with their titles. "You can—if I don't eat their share. I'm starving."

"Ah, poor thing," Bevin replied with overstated sympathy. She picked up a fire-blackened stick and poked at the glowing coals. "Do you think they'll believe us if we tell them their fish flopped from the fire back into the river?"

"No." Kiarda sat down to put on her boots. "But what could they do about it?"

Bevin laughed. "Not only stubborn, but—"

"But greedy, as well."

"I wasn't going to say that," Bevin protested. "The word is 'devious.' A quality, as you well know, that I happen to admire."

"Oh, dear. You're beginning to sound like Adan. He's a bad influence." Kiarda pulled her bootlaces tight. "But I have to admit, you were right about the changing. And about remembering things during fox-time. I didn't think that was possible."

Bevin's cheeks turned pink, though Kiarda could not tell if the praise or the fire's warmth caused it. "Anything's possible in the realm of magic. Its laws not only permit the impossible, but at times demand it."

"Magic?" Kiarda straightened. "I don't have any magic."

"Perhaps it's more accurate to say that magic has you."

Kiarda studied her friend for a moment. "Does it still hurt? That you've lost your power?"

Bevin paid great attention to raking the clay-encrusted fish from the hot coals. "No." Her voice sounded strained.

Kiarda gestured helplessly. "If I could, I'd give you mine. I don't want it."

Bevin shrugged one shoulder. "Perhaps, some day, my magic will return."

Kiarda averted her gaze. *When roast trout swims.* "Of course," she said, trying to cover her pity with a comforting tone. "The gods are just."

"I'm serious," Bevin replied. "Sometimes, I feel like I could stretch out my hand and pluck it like an apple from a bough."

"Then why don't you try?" Kiarda could not fathom the healer's reluctance. "You might get your magic back!"

"Because I'm afraid."

Kiarda stared at Bevin. "Why?"

The healer sighed, keeping her gaze lowered upon her task. "Do you remember the day we lost little Lord Elrin? Everyone said the Dark Court assisted Maddock, but I'm positive it was just another magic-user, though he was using forbidden power. The sixth magic."

"But—"

"And he tried to destroy all the magic in Dorlach Tor. From healing powers to spirit-links. Couldn't you feel it? How something tried to rend you into separate pieces?"

Kiarda frowned. "No. I remember I had a terrible headache." She stood and walked to Bevin, crouched by the fire. "It had to be the Dark Court. What reason would any mortal have for doing such evil?"

Bevin glanced up, seeming startled. "What reason? Oh, please. You can't be that naive."

Kiarda shook her head, not wanting to believe that her baby brother had died for the sake of human ambition. "That doesn't make sense. If some madman wanted to be the only magic-user left in the Marchlands, he wouldn't have troubled with the spirit-linked. They wouldn't threaten him. And besides, they're blessed by the gods."

Bevin chewed her bottom lip. "Maybe. But from what I gathered when I resorted to the forbidden power, it didn't allow much control. It's like swinging a battering ram to knock on a cottage door. Our unknown enemy probably couldn't draw any distinction between different types of magic but could only will for the destruction of it all."

Kiarda picked up another stick, mulling the healer's words, and helped dig trout from the coals. "Then why did Byrta the Hunt-Keeper and Glovis the Blacksmith die? Why did everyone around Elrin fall senseless?"

"Not everyone around Elrin," Bevin said unsteadily. "Everyone around *me*. I was using the forbidden magic."

Kiarda maneuvered the steaming lump of hardened clay into the sand around the fire. "What do you mean?"

"The sixth magic overflows from the one who wields it. I tried to contain it, but it spilled over." Bevin blinked back tears and swallowed. "That's why it's forbidden. I would never have used it, but Sygil ordered me to. And I thought—" Tears welled up and rolled down her cheeks. "I thought I could save Elrin and Tynan. But I failed, and all those people died."

Horror shocked through Kiarda. The stick snapped in her hands. "You mean, if you hadn't fought back—?"

Bevin wiped her eyes on her sleeve. "Then only Tynan and Elrin would have died. And maybe . . . maybe you."

My parents could have died in the spillover. Kiarda lurched to her feet and paced away, hands flexing. "Why didn't you say anything before?"

Bevin's voiced carried unusual heat. "I tried, but no one listened to me. No one ever listens to me!"

Stung, Kiarda whirled. "That's not true."

"It is!" Bevin stood and put her hands on her hips. "No one looks past all this—this fat—to the spirit and mind within. No one takes me seriously. Except for Adan. Perhaps because he knows what it's like to be judged only by appearance."

Kiarda shook her head. "Bevin. *I* take you seriously."

"Not without an argument."

"What's that supposed to mean?"

"Just what I said!"

"But, Bevin-lass—" Kiarda clenched her hands in frustration, realizing her friend spoke the truth, and fought a peculiar impulse to laugh. "I argue with everyone. You've heard me fight with Ladayla about hairstyles and riding techniques. Why should I treat you any differently than I treat my sister?"

For a moment, Bevin stood utterly motionless. When she spoke, her voice was tight with pain. "Because I'm not your sister."

Kiarda tilted her head and said gently, "Now who's arguing?"

"I'm not—"

Kiarda crossed to the healer and laid her hands on the thick shoulders. "Some sisters are born to you, and some sisters you choose. I chose you."

Tears filled Bevin's gray eyes again, but this time she smiled. "Thank you. Because I—" She paused and sighed shakily. "Because I couldn't wish for a better sister than you."

A patternless sea of stalls stretched beneath the mile-long southern wall of the city of Riverton, a marketplace larger than any horse fair Tynan had ever seen. His gaze jerked from carpets to jewelry, from melons to salted fish to bales of dyed wool. The variety and abundance of the offered goods staggered him, and the cries of their sellers blended into an indecipherable cacophony with the conversation of meandering patrons. Heart pounding, feeling very much the provincial farm boy, Tynan dismounted.

Cat-of-the-Softest-Fur-and-Loudest-Purr poked his head from a saddle pack. Worried Dorlach Tor would hunt its missing children, and knowing Tynan and his link-mate enjoyed some fame in well-known songs, Bevin had altered the cat's appearance. Walnut juice stained his ears and nose a dark brown, and he wore a scrap of lace torn from the healer's petticoat around his neck. [[Don't forget me.]]

Tynan caressed his link-mate, then carefully unbuckled the

saddle pack and hung it over his shoulder so the cat rode against his chest. He wanted to say something comforting, but the words would not come. He glanced back at his brother.

Adan gave Tynan a reassuring wink and slid from his saddle. Mud covered the disfigured side of his face and begrimed his clothes, as if he had taken a fall. "How's my disguise?" he whispered. "Do you think I should have used a little walnut juice, too?"

Tynan's mouth felt too dry for speech. He shook his head.

Adan grinned, teeth flashing white. "It's overwhelming at first, I know. Just relax. You're not riding into battle."

Tynan nodded, remembering that Adan had traveled to Riverton several times in the past on business for Sarn Moor. "Don't know why I couldn't play the manservant," he whispered, though it had all been decided before they left camp. "You ought to be the one doing the talking."

"Not here to talk. Here to listen." Adan assumed the rough accent of a commoner. "Besides, one of these merchants might recognize me. Believe it or not, I have a memorable face, and these fellows never forget a customer."

Tynan scowled. He realized his nervousness made him surly, but he could not help himself. "Don't like leaving the girls back at camp."

"Better there than here, my lord," Adan said, not troubling to keep his voice down. "These southern men don't respect women the same as us. Paw at them like dogs, they do."

Tynan tightened his mouth. If he saw a man mistreating a woman, he would not be responsible for his actions. "Let's get this over with," he snapped. For Kiarda, he would mingle with ill-mannered rabble to seek information on a young man who could only have survived the woodland's winter with the help of the Dark Court. But Tynan didn't have to like it. "Come on."

The brothers walked into the marketplace, Tynan leading and Adan following with the horses. Every merchant seemed to speak in a clipped southern accent like Bevin's, haggling with customers or calling the virtues of their wares. Tynan passed stalls selling painted ceramics, fine tooled-leather tack, cages of rabbits, copper pots, fresh vegetables, perfumes, and wrought iron. An old man with a kindly face led a small herd of dairy goats between the stalls. Passersby would proffer a cup and for a copper, the old man would fill it with fresh goat milk. At every corner, pretty girls wearing scarlet dresses and roses in their hair sold bunches of fragrant heartsease.

As wondering admiration took over, Tynan slowly forgot his anxiety. He kept wishing Kiarda were there to see the sights or that he might find a small gift to take back for her.

Adan cleared his throat. "My lord, there's a likely-looking wineshop. Clean, leastways. And that's more than you can say for me."

Tynan glanced around. The shop appeared more like a tent stretched over a permanent wooden frame. Sober and respectably dressed men sat at the little tables in quiet conversation. "Thank you." Tynan looked over his shoulder. "Good man."

Straight-faced, Adan touched his forehead. "My lord."

Feeling self-conscious, Tynan entered the wineshop and sat down at an empty table. The other customers studied him for a moment with mild interest. He nodded politely, and they returned to their own business.

Cat-of-the-Softest-Fur-and-Loudest-Purr looked up from his refuge in the saddle pack. [[Put your money on the table.]]

"I know," Tynan muttered. He fished a small coin from the pouch at his belt and laid it in plain sight.

A serving maid with her hair tied back in a clean kerchief hurried to his table with a clay cup and a pitcher of wine. She dipped in a brief curtsy, not meeting the young man's gaze, poured the wine and set it on his table. Her face was pale and tear-stained, and she spoke in a tremulous whisper. "Will that be all, sir?"

Concern sparked Tynan into speaking without thought. "You've been weeping. What's the matter?" He glared around the shop. "Has someone ill-used you?"

The serving maid gave her head a startled shake. "Oh, no, sir. Nothing like that. We got word yesterday that my uncle died."

Tynan felt like a fool. He avoided looking toward Adan, who stood outside the tent with the horses. "I'm so sorry."

"Thank you, kindly." The maid curtsied again. "Silly of me to fuss. I haven't seen him since I was a baby. It's just that my poor papa—" Her voice broke off with a squeak. Fresh tears poured down her cheeks, and she hastily smeared them away with the back of her hand. "Poor Papa's so sad."

Deeply ashamed of himself, Tynan swallowed hard. "I'm sure you're a great comfort to your father."

Cat-of-the-Softest-Fur-and-Loudest-Purr jumped out of the saddle pack and onto the table. [[Don't cry,]] he meowed. [[I'm here. I'll make you happy.]]

The maid sniffed and laughed shakily. "Oh, you've got a kitty." She offered her fingers. "Is he friendly?"

"Too friendly."

The cat rubbed his chin against the maid's fingers, and she ran her hand down his back.

Tynan gripped the edge of the table, utterly trapped by the situation, forced to accept the touch of a stranger. He focused on the innocence of the maid's gesture and how stroking the cat seemed to ease her grief.

"You're a pretty kitty," she cooed, then glanced at the young man. "What's his name?"

Tynan tossed out the first thing that came to him. "Furry Purry."

His link-mate gave him a frosty stare. [[That is a dreadful name.]]

From outside, Adan snickered softly. Tynan refused to look in his direction.

The maid smiled wanly, still petting the cat. "My uncle lived in Radway Green. He was killed along with all those other poor folk."

Tynan had no idea what she meant. They had passed Radway Green only two days past. With Adan and Kiarda, he had approached at first light. Then, put off by the walls, they decided Riverton would prove friendlier. "That's a shame. What was it, an accident?"

The servant raised her brows in obvious surprise. "No, sir. Haven't you heard?"

Confused, Tynan shook his head. "I'm sorry. I've been on the road for some time."

"They fell on one another with . . . with . . ." Merely speaking of the forbidden objects clearly unnerved her. "S-swords. And bows, too. The priests think Conna died, then her heirs and blood relatives fell to fighting over the fort. The whole village got destroyed. Burned to the ground."

Shocked nearly dumb, Tynan struggled for a reply. "I'm sorry," he repeated, the words woefully inadequate. "A terrible loss."

"Yes, sir. Thank you, sir." She curtsied again, gave the cat a final pat, scooped up the coin, and hurried off to serve a new customer.

Dazed, Tynan reached for his wine cup. He raised it to his lips, then set it down without drinking. *An entire village. Gods above, what is the world coming to?* He shook his head to clear it. *The Joyous Reunion. The Divine Peace. This is impossible.*

Cat-of-the-Softest-Fur-and-Loudest-Purr hopped off the table onto his link-mate's lap. [[Furry Purry. Is that the best you could do?]]

Tynan ran his little finger between the cat's ears and down his back in silent apology.

[[Those men over there are talking about you.]] The cat blinked his eyes. [[They think you cheered up the serving maid, but I did that.]]

Tynan sipped his wine and grunted, wordlessly asking his link-mate to continue eavesdropping.

[[Now they're talking about Radway Green. The fellow with the red mustache just said it had to be the Dark Court. The people would never have done such a thing without 'direct and evil influence,' and nothing human could have caused such hurt.]] The cat twitched his tail. [[The other one said he won't go near the cursed place till the priests have blessed it a million times.]]

Dark Court. Shaken, Tynan looked at his brother.

Adan stood motionless between the horses, and his attention seemed fixed upon the newest customer.

Casually, Tynan allowed his gaze to sweep the tent. The newcomer sat two tables away, a well-favored man of indeterminate age with long silver hair. Slim and elegant, he wore brightly embroidered clothing in the style of the High Marches, though his

hawk-nosed face evinced foreign blood. In spite of Tynan's caution, the stranger caught the young man studying him.

Tynan's breath froze. He sensed it would prove unwise to
irritate the fellow.

The stranger simply smiled, however, and nodded courteously.

[[What's the matter?]] Cat-of-the-Softest-Fur-and-Loudest-
Purr peered over the edge of the table. [[Did someone threaten
us?]]

"Settle down," Tynan muttered. "Nothing to worry about."

The stranger stood and carried his wine cup to Tynan's table.
"Pardon me," he said in a friendly tone, "but I couldn't help noticing your feline companion. What an extraordinary creature."

Tynan feigned disinterest, taking another swallow of wine.
"Just a cat."

"May I join you?" the man asked politely, drawing a chair
close and sitting down before Tynan could reply. "His eyes are
most striking. It seems he understands every word I say."

The cat laid his ears flat. [[He knows who we are.]]

Pulse jumping, Tynan tossed back the rest of his wine.

The stranger continued in a calm, interested tone. "You're
from up north, aren't you? Ever been to Sarn Moor? One of Lady
Mona's five sons was gifted with a spirit-link to a cat, though I
suppose he's dead by now."

Tynan fought to control his breath, to keep his hands from
shaking. "Why's that?"

"Because all the spirit-linked are dying, just as all the magic-
users are losing their powers." The stranger regarded Tynan
steadily. "Those few who remain must stay careful and clever,
hiding their true natures, for an invisible threat stalks the Marchlands."

From the corner of his eye, Tynan saw Adan stir and tense.

The cat lashed his tail. [[Let's get away from here. Now!]]

Tynan kept his expression neutral. "Really?"

" 'A dark shadow hovers over mortal-kind. Almighty Hepona
has stretched forth her hand.' "

With an inward shiver, Tynan recognized the line from an old
song about warfare.

The cat climbed onto his shoulder. "Mow!"

At that moment, Adan stepped into the tent. He touched his forehead and cleared his throat deferentially, but his dark eyes glittered. "Your pardon, my lord, but you asked me to remind you of your appointment."

Tynan seized the opportunity. "Good man. Thank you." He stood, picked up his saddle pack, and nodded at the stranger. "Farewell." Heart pounding, he turned away and strode to his horse, glad to have his brother at his back.

⚜

Tynan stared into the campfire, sorting through the day's events. His link-mate lay curled in the nest formed by Tynan's crossed legs, also watching the flames. Adan bent over a piece of tack, attempting to clean it in the wavering light. Bevin had washed her hair and sat carefully combing out her damp curls. Sharpening her hunting knife, Kiarda slouched beside the healer.

Upon the boys' return from Riverton, Kiarda had insisted that they move camp. The stranger had known too much, she said, and she worried that he had been tracking them for Dorlach Tor.

Tynan raised his gaze from the dancing flames and looked at the healer. She had remained pinch-lipped and silent all evening. "Bevin?"

The healer lifted her head, her long hair glimmering in the firelight. "Who do *you* think he was? Is he the one who stole your power?"

"I don't know." Bevin sighed. "Probably not."

Kiarda glanced up. "How can you say that? Not that I'm arguing with you, but I thought you said you didn't know what the rogue magic-user looked like."

Bevin resumed combing her hair. "Not on the outside. I saw him from the inside. He's not without humor or compassion, but it's all overshadowed by a driving need to destroy." She paused and added in a reluctant tone, "He also believes absolutely in the rightness of his actions. He would not have given you that warning about the spirit-linked dying—he would have merely killed you. And from a safe distance."

Tynan ran his thumb knuckle along his bottom lip, trying to remember meeting the stranger at a horse fair. "He knew who we were. He did everything but call us by name." He turned to his brother. "I think he even recognized you."

Adan pulled his attention from the cheek piece of a bridle. "Ah?" His gaze went past Tynan to Bevin. "Pardon?"

Tynan followed the direction of Adan's stare. Firelight traced the curve of Bevin's face and turned her brown hair to gold. He noted with surprise that she almost looked pretty.

The cat shifted position on Tynan's lap, curling into a tighter ball. [[Our brother is in love with Bevin.]]

Thunderstruck, Tynan stared at his link-mate. "What did you say?"

Adan answered mildly. "I said: 'Pardon?' Which means: 'Please repeat what *you* said.' "

"No, I—"

Cat-of-the-Softest-Fur-and-Loudest-Purr covered his nose with the tip of his tail. [[And Bevin loves Adan. I think they should mate and have lots of kittens.]]

Scandalized, Tynan glared at the cat. "That's not nice!"

Adan sighed. "Little brother, has anyone ever told you how annoying you can be?"

"You have," Tynan snapped. "But, trust me, I'm far less annoying than ol' Furry Purry." He hoisted the cat off his lap and deposited him on the ground. "Go sit on someone else. I'm mad at you."

Ears laid back, the cat stalked away. [[And I'm mad at you. You yelled at me for nothing.]]

Adan gave an exasperated laugh. "Tynan-lad, I'm about to throw rocks!"

Kiarda glanced at Bevin. "Loons."

Tynan closed his eyes and drew a calming breath. "I was talking about the stranger," he said, picking up the lost thread of conversation. "I think he recognized you."

Adan shrugged. "Perhaps, but I don't guess so. I believe he just suspected who you were, and then only because that link-mate of yours doesn't know how to act like a normal cat."

Tynan's shoulders sagged. "True." He suddenly realized that

if they did not learn to hide the link, they would become a danger to Kiarda and the others. He picked up a stray twig and tossed it into the fire. "Furry Purry and I both need to practice acting normally."

At the edge of the camp, the cat sat with his back to everyone. [[My name is not Furry Purry.]]

Tynan's lips thinned, but he decided to start his practice immediately and pretend he could not hear his link-mate. He looked at Kiarda. "I'm sorry we didn't find any information on Maddock."

Kiarda smiled at Tynan. "You did your best."

Adan stirred. "Perhaps we learned something more critical to our survival: We're being tracked by someone far less benign than Lady Wylfre's Hunt-Keeper."

Bevin nodded, her brow puckering. "And we're walking straight into a war."

Tynan's gut went cold. "That's impossible."

Kiarda shrugged. "Why? Because the priests say so?"

Tynan had no answer to that. He gazed at Kiarda unhappily, wondering what he could say to make her abandon her futile quest. "Aren't you afraid?"

Kiarda tested the edge of her knife. "Of course. But I'm more afraid of living the rest of my life filled with regret."

Tynan stretched out his hand, trying to speak reasonably. "But you're putting yourself in terrible danger."

Kiarda lifted her chin, suddenly looking very much like her mother. "If what the stranger said was true, and I believe it is, then I'd be in even greater danger at Dorlach Tor. So would you and Bevin. Why give this unknown enemy a sitting target?"

Tilting his head, Adan assumed a considering air. "Why indeed? In fact, we ought to be posting a watch from now on. And we ought to pick up hunting bows for each of us, so we're all armed in some fashion."

Tynan stared around the ring in disbelief. "And we ought to return to Dorlach Tor where hundreds of armed people love Kiarda and would defend her against any threat!"

Kiarda set her jaw. "Not after what happened last time. I won't draw an attack upon my own folk."

Bevin regarded Tynan with a pitying expression. "There is no safe place."

A sudden chill seeped into Tynan's blood. He sat motionless, trying to fully comprehend the nightmare.

With a trilling cry, the cat trotted over to his link-mate and climbed into his lap. [[Don't worry. I'll protect our Kiarda. If anyone tries to hurt her, I'll scratch them!]]

Seeking comfort, Tynan stroked the cat's silky length. "I know," he whispered. "I know."

Adan stood up and stretched. "I volunteer for the first watch."

Kiarda nodded. "I'll take second."

Tynan bowed his head. He found himself desperately wishing that Lady Wylfre's people would find them. He would rather face the wrath of the priests than let Kiarda continue on the path to danger. It occurred to him that he could betray her, even though it meant she would never forgive him, never marry him. *Better than letting her die.*

Adan nudged his brother with his foot. "You'll take third, won't you?"

"Certainly." Tynan stood, lifting his link-mate. They planned to stop at another town in a day or two. There, he could surely find a temple where he could report them all to the priests. *Gods help me. I don't know what else to do.* "I'm going to bed."

⚜

Pain, and his link-mate's frantic cries, jolted Tynan awake.

[[Get up, get up!]] The cat sharpened his claws on Tynan's chest. [[Kiarda's gone!]]

The young man jerked upright and stared around the camp. Bevin and Adan stirred sleepily in their bedrolls, but he saw no sign of Kiarda. The overhead sky was growing pale with approaching dawn; but, in the trees all around them, the birds remained silent.

Wide awake, heart racing, Tynan scrambled to his feet. Kiarda's bow lay on the ground beside her empty clothes. "She turned into a fox!" *What if she couples with another fox?* A worse thought made even the first seem trivial. *What if the Dark Court catches her?* He whirled toward his brother. "Adan, get up! We've got to find her!"

A man spoke from behind Tynan. "Don't worry, my lord. She's safe."

Tynan spun.

Still dressed in elegantly embroidered clothing, the stranger from the wineshop strolled into their camp. He carried a limp bundle of red fur wrapped in a folded cloak.

Tynan clenched his fists, hearing Adan and Bevin scramble to their feet behind him. "What have you done to her?"

The hawk-nosed man raised his brows. "Nothing. She gobbled up all my bread and cheese, then fell asleep." He smiled, and his dark eyes crinkled in lines of kindly good humor. "I would never harm Lady Wylfre's daughter."

His scarred face as ominous as a thundercloud, Adan advanced upon the intruder. "Who in blazes are you?"

The stranger's smile turned wistful. "I didn't think you'd remember me, Lord Adan. You were only six when we last met. I used to serve as the Swordmaster of Dorlach Tor."

Adan stopped and studied the other man. "Gaer."

Breath laboring, Tynan stared. The name was a childhood memory, a lesson in what happened to those who disobeyed the will of Hernis and Hepona. He had to admit the fellow did not look like the monster of the priests' stories.

Kiarda-the-fox sighed contentedly and snuggled her nose into the crook of the Swordmaster's elbow.

Gaer looked back and forth between the two young men. "Lord Adan and Lord Tynan." His tone was an even blend of respect and affection, like that of a family retainer who had helped to raise them. "You have your mother's eyes." In a calm, assured manner, he carried the vixen to Bevin's bedroll and settled her among the blankets. "There you are, my lady." Then he turned and regarded them all with a bright smile. "Gorged, but safe and sound. An enviable state."

Adan gestured sharply. "Step away from her."

Gaer smoothly raised his hands. "Of course." He crossed to

the remains of the fire and crouched beside the ashes. "I won't hurt you. I'm here to help."

Bevin anxiously knelt beside the fox and examined her. "She's all right."

Tynan's breath came easier. He turned his attention to Gaer. "You've been tracking us."

The Swordmaster nodded, picked up a stick, and stirred the ashes. "Since your gathering at the Coney."

Adan moved to stand over him. "Why?"

A few coals flared sluggishly. Gaer fed them dead leaves. "To guard and protect the lot of you. Forgive me for saying this, my lord, but you're all just children." Tiny flames took hold of the fuel, and he blew on them to coax them to fuller life. "And also I want to help you find Maddock."

Aversion reared up within Tynan. "We don't want your help."

Gaer did not seem to take the least offense. "Don't you trust me, my lord?"

Tynan scowled. He positioned himself so that he and his brother flanked the intruder. "No."

The cat circled from behind, growling deep in his throat, and jumped onto his link-mate's shoulder. [[Tell him to go away.]]

Tynan narrowed his eyes. "Go away."

Gaer sighed. "Begging your pardon, my lord, but I'm afraid I can't do that. I'm going with you to the Low Marches."

Adan's voice turned ironic. "Oh, is that a fact? And I suppose we have no choice in the matter."

"No, my lord," Gaer said politely. "None whatsoever. Unless you kill me." He looked up at them. "I'm unarmed, at the moment. Your best chance would be to murder me now."

Tynan flexed his hands in frustration. "Don't tempt me."

Adan snorted. A slow, sour smile pulled his features steeply askew. "You've got it all figured out, haven't you? You know we won't kill an unarmed man. And you know we're not trained for combat, so we can't reasonably challenge you when you're carrying a weapon. We have to let you travel with us, since if we drive you off, you'll follow us in secret."

"Yes, my lord." Gaer shrugged apologetically. "Believe me, I wouldn't normally take such liberties. But where you're going, you'll need someone who can handle a sword."

Adan tilted his head. "I daresay."

Infuriated, Tynan glared at his brother. "Are you out of your mind? You can't let him come with us!" A new thought came to him, and he pointed at Gaer, sputtering. "He's an outlaw and an outcast. What if someone sees him with us and recognizes him? We're in enough trouble as it is. What will we tell the priests then?"

Adan's smile abruptly turned gentle. "The absolute truth: We're hostages."

CHAPTER SEVENTEEN

THE village of Tillsbury nestled among towering pine trees where the road forded the Rapid River. Neat, thatched cottages lined lanes of crushed rock, and the folk seemed well-fed and complacent. Like Riverton, it was a settlement of southern stock who ran their own affairs without the guidance of a Lady.

Riding in with his brother and the Swordmaster, Tynan observed signs of prosperity everywhere he looked. A flotilla of white swans patrolled the mill pond, and through the open doors of the village smithy he noted the workings of a foundry for casting large farm equipment. In a distant fashion, he realized he ought to feel more interested by what he saw; it might prove useful. But thoughts of betrayal weighted his heart.

Adan caught Tynan's eye. "Nice little town. They must be doing something right."

Glumly, Tynan nodded.

Adan raised one brow. "Miss your constant companion?"

Tynan forced himself to smile. He had left his link-mate with Kiarda, for safety and so he would know if trouble occurred at the camp. "I've never gone so far from him before." He searched the village lanes for a temple. Since Gaer held them virtual prisoners, only the priesthood could help. Tynan shielded his eyes from the summer sun. "Where's the marketplace?"

Gaer pointed toward a barn at the end of the lane. "There, my lord. They keep it under a roof." In the past few days of travel, Gaer had remained unfailingly polite and subservient, the model liege man. He obeyed their every order without hesitation, only refusing to leave them, and he treated Kiarda with a gallantry that bordered on worship. "The Tillsbury market is famous. It's open every day, rain or shine."

Adan whistled in admiration. "And all because they housed it in a barn."

"Yes, my lord. An elegantly simple solution."

Tynan tried to speak casually, "Where's the temple?"

"In the market, my lord." Gaer's tone went bland. "The priesthood of the Joyous Reunion takes strict safeguards to ensure the honesty of the merchants and the quality of the products."

Adan chuckled. "And I assume the priesthood also takes a percentage of the profits."

"Of course, my lord," Gaer replied smoothly. "A small administrative fee."

Tynan frowned, irritated without knowing why. "Well, it doesn't seem to hurt anyone." He gestured toward a bright garden where three curly-haired children romped with a dog. "The folk appear to be thriving."

"Yes, my lord. Allying oneself with the priesthood offers certain advantages."

Heat climbing to his face, Tynan glanced away. *Does he know what I plan to do?*

As they rode closer to the market, Tynan found the area around the barn filled with horses, wagons, and people. Like the people in Riverton, everyone spoke with the same clipped southern accent as Bevin. He found the quality of their speech comforting, even friendly, and reflected that the Divine Peace made it seem so. In his father's day, the folk of the High Marches had known the River People only as invading enemies. Tynan noted that Gaer possessed a slight accent, too, different from anything he had ever heard. "This may seem like a strange question, Gaer. But where are you from? Not from beyond the southern borders."

"No, my lord," Gaer answered readily. "I'm from beyond the eastern seas. There stretches a vast empire guarded by skilled armies and magic-wielders so powerful they could knock the sun from the sky."

Adan made an interested noise. "Why did you leave?"

"Because, my lord, the woman I loved married another man. It was either fall on my sword or travel."

The words echoed within Tynan. When Kiarda finally rejected

him outright, he wondered if he might travel. *Maybe I'll go east.* "Do you miss your home country?"

"Sometimes, my lord. The Imperial Court was beautiful, full of green lawns and fountains, a gathering place for the learned and gifted. And it was a country governed by reason and fair laws. Even the Emperor's name meant 'Justice.' " He smiled. "But now my home is in the Marchlands. All that I love dwells here."

A lump unexpectedly formed in Tynan's throat. He nodded, unable to speak.

They hitched their horses in the crowded yard outside the market. A superior breed, Adan's and Tynan's mounts jarred among the heavy farm horses, like polished jewels lying in gravel. Gaer's gelding, a mouse-brown saddle horse, was a fine animal; but he did not draw the same attention.

As the trio walked together toward the barn, Tynan cast a quick, uneasy glance over his shoulder. A farmer with a sun-burned face stopped loading his wagon and stared at the March-land stallions, a venal gleam in his eyes. Tynan's plan to turn them all in to the priesthood abruptly faltered. It was one thing to nobly surrender, but he could not bear to consider the shame of being captured. "Maybe this wasn't a good idea," Tynan muttered to his brother. "Even if Maddock passed through Tillsbury, which he probably didn't, no one would remember seeing him. Not only are we wasting our time, but we may be recognized."

Adan gave Tynan an elaborately patient smile. "True, on all accounts, but you're forgetting something: We need the supplies."

"But—"

Adan shook his head slightly. "Hush, now. Smile. We have to brazen it out. The girls are depending on us."

Tynan choked back his misgivings and followed Adan through the door.

Sliding shutters in the roof lay folded open, admitting streams of sunshine. Near the back of the barn, a full quarter of the floor space was devoted to a temple area. Enthroned images of Hernis and Hepona sat upon a raised dais surrounded by brackets of can-dles, and incense sweetened the air. Unlike the market at River-ton, the stalls formed neat and organized rows, with similar goods grouped together. Fresh produce, meats, and milled grains, all allotted a carefully defined section of the market; and each merchant did his or her best to outshout the others. The roar of mingled voices echoed among the roof timbers.

A growing anxiety made it difficult for Tynan to behave nonchalantly. He found himself glad and sorry that his link-mate had not come along. "Very tidy," he muttered. "Though a bit loud for my tastes."

Gaer pointed toward a table near the entrance, where a priest sat counting stacks of coins. "This way, my lords, to exchange our money. We may only make purchases with tokens issued by the priests."

Adan chuckled. "Very tidy, indeed."

As they headed for the table, Tynan noticed the red-faced farmer from the yard edge through the door. The farmer went straight to a merchant at a stall selling cornmeal and bent to whisper in his ear. Both men looked toward Tynan.

Pulse jumping, Tynan cleared his throat, covertly attempting to catch his companions' attention.

Apparently unaware, Gaer and Adan greeted the priest and began the transaction.

Tynan pretended to gaze in wonder around the market, trying to keep watch on the farmer. A gang of six rugged men were gathering around the cornmeal stall. Trying to look casual, he reached for Adan and tugged blindly at the closet hem.

Seeming to ignore Tynan's frantic pull on his cloak, Gaer answered some inquiry of the priest's, "Ah, no, Your Holiness. To Dorlach Tor in the north, and from there I ride to the Great Temple in Wray Valley." The Swordmaster paused and added delicately, "The High Priest has commissioned me to handle a . . . um . . . personal matter for him."

Startled, Tynan whipped around to look at the Swordmaster. Realizing he clutched a fold of the wrong man's clothing, he jerked back his hand as if burned. *What is he talking about?*

A redhead with a narrow face and shrewd blue eyes, the priest stroked his chin. "An arduous journey."

Gaer bowed. "Indeed, Your Holiness. But I comfort myself

with the assurance of a warm welcome at both destinations, from Lady Wylfre and from His Most Supreme Sanctity."

The priest raised one brow. "You move in exalted circles."

Gaer spread his hands and replied humbly, "Such is the rare luck, Your Holiness, of a bounty hunter."

Baffled, Tynan looked at his brother. Adan wore his accustomed expression of amused contempt laced with boredom.

The priest regarded the two young men and presented them with a self-satisfied smile. "And you, I presume, are only traveling as far as Dorlach Tor?"

Adan folded his arms and stared at the space over the priest's head. "That depends, Your Holiness. A lot may happen on the road."

The priest's smile turned thin. "You should consider yourself fortunate that your custodian shows so much courtesy toward your rank. Others, more concerned with merely collecting that rich reward, might not prove as gentle." He turned to the Swordmaster. "If you should require any assistance from me in this . . . personal matter . . . you need only ask."

Gaer bowed deeply. "Your Holiness is most kind."

Reward? Understanding flashed through Tynan. Gaer had led the priest to believe he had captured the brothers on behalf of the High Priest, and cagey Adan had grasped the game and played along. The cleverness of the tactic shocked Tynan. He had expected the Swordmaster to handle desperate situations only with violence.

Someone thumped Tynan's shoulder. He whirled.

The sunburned farmer and his cohort surrounded the money-changing table. "Riding a fancy horse, ain't you?"

Tynan raised his brows. "Pardon me?"

The farmer grinned, displaying strong, white teeth. "Steal it?"

"No!"

" 'Cause a messenger came through last week. Offered a lot of gold for a couple of laddies riding fancy horses."

The priest stood, his expression severe. "That's enough, my good man. I commend your vigilance, but their lordships are already in custody."

The farmer and his thick-necked friends looked crestfallen. "Begging your pardon, Holiness. We didn't know."

The priest enunciated each syllable, "Well, now you do."

The men shuffled away, casting reluctant glances back at Tynan and Adan.

The priest resumed his seat and looked up at Gaer. "My name is Jarric of Farn Tump. If you see fit, mention my cooperation in this matter to His Supreme Sanctity."

Gaer smiled. "You may be sure of it, Your Holiness."

The three men took a circuitous route back to camp, repeatedly doubling back and veering at odd angles to ensure no one followed them. Their mounts bore saddle packs stuffed with much-needed supplies.

Tynan found his feelings toward Gaer growing more cordial. "I don't understand, though, why Jarric believed you were a bounty hunter. He didn't look like the trusting sort."

Adan snorted. "He couldn't afford not to believe, little brother. Can you imagine what would happen to any priest who interfered with one of the High Priest's schemes? He'd be ten days dying."

"True, my lord," the Swordmaster replied. "And also, when I opened my money pouch, I 'accidentally' let him see a scroll with the High Priest's private seal." Gaer gave Tynan a self-effacing smile. "I owe my life to that scroll more times than I care to think about. Good thing no one ever demands to read it."

Tynan had to know. "What is it?"

"As I recall, my lord, it's a promissory note for a shipment of wine."

Adan stroked his mount's sleek neck. "When that farmer accosted Tynan, I feared we had a fight on our hands. I thought I'd finally see Dorlach Tor's infamous Swordmaster in action."

Gaer laughed, his dark eyes crinkling. "I hope I haven't disappointed you, my lord. Brute force makes very poor persuasion when used in excess. I've found it's best to employ violence only when diplomacy fails."

Coming from the outcast Swordmaster, few words could have surprised Tynan more, nor the realization that he might be starting to actually like this man. Kiarda had spoken the absolute truth when she decreed everything changed. But perhaps not all of it for the worse.

The next few days of travel passed in a surprising calm. The simple presence of a competent soldier in their midst seemed to quell their many fears about violence. On the fourth day after the men's visit to Tillsbury, they made camp far from human habitation near a clear river alive with salmon. Gigantic pine trees soared toward the flawless blue sky. Mountains edged the western horizon like a low bank of clouds.

Bevin sat alone on a rock distant from the camp, though still within sight of the others. She watched Kiarda build the fire ring, carefully placing each stone. Tynan stood hip deep in the river, trying to catch fish with his bare hands. His link-mate prowled the bank, presumably howling advice. On the soft ground beneath a pine, Gaer taught Adan a few basic moves for unarmed combat.

Bevin sighed and propped her chin on her fist. She found it increasingly difficult to ignore the restless stirrings of magic within her and increasingly painful to continue deceiving her friends. *I have no right to deny my help to them merely because it will put me in danger.*

With diligent practice, Kiarda was gaining more control over her link, now able to recall events from her "fox-time," as she termed it. She continued to exercise no influence over her vixen half, however, and suffered from a stronger feeling of being two separate entities. Bevin knew she could help Kiarda with the healing magic, help guide her through this strange emotional terrain. With her magic, Bevin also could help search for Maddock. If he had gone far, she could sense his general direction. If near, she could pinpoint his precise location. Furthermore, Tynan and his link-mate remained in peril from the rogue magic-user. Bevin could employ her magic to sense the approach of danger, perhaps even protect him. *I must do it. I have an obligation.*

Adan burst into laughter. Bevin turned her gaze to him. He was trying to emulate Gaer's stance: twisted sideways, narrow-based with flexed knees. The young man wobbled badly.

"An excellent first attempt, my lord," Gaer said. "Remember not to strain. Relax. Find your balance from within—"

With a startled squawk, Adan went sprawling headlong into the pine mast.

"—or," Gaer continued without pause, "collapse in a heap. That's always an option."

Still laughing, Adan rolled into a crouch and shook pine needles from his hair. "If you think that took talent, you ought to see me dance."

"I am certain, my lord, your dancing is a rare treat for the eyes."

Bevin smiled, feeling her face go warm. She never wearied of looking at Adan. Sometimes, when he met her gaze, she experienced such an expanding glow in her heart she felt as if she had swallowed the sun. She remembered how he appeared when viewed with the magical Sight, full of inner strength, hungry for love. *If I use my power again, I'll be able to see him as he truly is.*

Then, Bevin recalled the spring horse fair. She had as much as told Adan she had lost her magic, and he had felt sad for her. *I lied to him.* Bevin imagined his expression changing as she confessed her deception, pictured his hazel eyes widening with reproach and his lopsided smile fading. Tears threatened, stinging. Bevin bowed her head. *I don't know what to do.*

Approaching footsteps crunched on the gravel.

The healer swallowed and brushed her damp lashes.

Kiarda's voice filled with concern, "Hey? You all right?"

Bevin nodded and looked up, trying to smile. "Just thinking."

Kiarda sat down beside Bevin on the stone. Her red braids were fraying, and she wore a smudge of soot on her nose. "Thinking? 'Bout what?"

"Love."

"Yuck."

Bevin laughed in spite of herself.

"I hate love."

Pressing the back of her fingers against her lips to hide a foolish grin, Bevin shook her head. "How can you say that? You have a wonderful, brave, strong, beautiful man who adores you."

"You want him?" Kiarda asked hopefully and looked toward the river.

Bevin followed the direction of her glance. At that instant, Tynan made a swift lunge into the water. He reappeared a few moments later, sputtering and empty-handed.

Kiarda spoke in a more sympathetic tone. "Look at him. He tries so hard."

Bevin returned her attention to Kiarda. "Don't you care about him at all?"

"I love him intensely. But it's the same way I love Adan or Leith. Or you, for that matter." Kiarda sighed. "Try not to be disappointed, Bevin, but I don't want to marry you."

Bevin forced a smile. "I'm crushed."

Kiarda crossed her long legs and rested her hands on her knees. "Think Uncle Gaer would teach me how to fight?"

Uncertain if Kiarda were joking, Bevin peered at her. "No!"

"Why not?" Kiarda asked matter-of-factly. "He's teaching Adan."

"But Adan's a man." Bevin glanced toward the training area. Adan had assumed the tricky stance again but seemed to handle it better. Gaer tapped his thigh, murmuring a correction. "If Gaer touched you there, Tynan would reach down his throat and rip out—"

"He taught Maddock." Kiarda spoke as if offering an argument. "That's why Maddock went to Scratter Wood every few days. I'm amazed none of us figured it out."

"Kiarda—"

"I mean, just think about the way Maddock moved. Remember the way he walked? Gliding like silk over—"

Thoroughly confused, Bevin made an exasperated noise. "Wait. What are you talking about?"

Kiarda looked askance at her friend. "Love."

"What does Maddock have to do with—?" Realization hit. "Oh."

Kiarda's mouth and eyes went wide, as if the same understanding had struck her at the same instant. "Oh, gods."

Bevin lowered her voice. "Were you—" She paused, wondering if she ought to continue, then blurted, "Were you in love with Maddock?"

Kiarda shifted her shoulders in a motion not quite a shrug. "I don't know. Maybe. I just—" She spread her hands. "I just hated him so much when I thought he—" She swallowed. "And now I . . . keep remembering how—"

An exultant whoop came from the river. Bevin whirled.

Tynan splashed to the shore with a madly struggling salmon clasped in both arms. "Kiarda! Look! I caught one!"

Kiarda gave a breath of laughter that sounded like a stifled sob. "Dear, sweet loon."

Bevin slipped away from the campfire and wandered to the river's edge. Under the starlight, the water appeared black and fathomless. Its cheerful daytime babble had ceased, replaced by a deep roar. As Bevin watched the river surge past, she remembered the overwhelming strength of forbidden magic. The best part of herself lay in her power, and it had also become the source of her torment.

Adan spoke from behind her. "Lady, be careful."

Bevin startled violently and whipped around.

Adan stood tall against the night sky, framed by stars. "Sorry," he said. "I didn't mean to sneak up on you."

Bevin clutched the throat of her tunic and tried to calm her racing heart. "I didn't hear you. The river—"

"I'm sorry," Adan repeated. Like the water, his eyes seemed darker, containing unmeasured depths.

Bevin shivered.

"You're cold," Adan said gently. "Come back to the fire. It's dangerous for you out here."

"It's dangerous for me everywhere." Bevin twisted her face from Adan's unnerving gaze. "I have a confession to make, and it may upset you."

Adan's tone turned guarded. "Oh?"

"I—" Bevin's voice faded to a dry whisper. Her shivering grew more intense. "I've led you to believe—"

A warm, living weight landed on her shoulder. Tynan's linkmate stuck his nose in her ear, purring.

Bevin's heart labored under its double burden of fresh alarm and rising sorrow. "You scared me!"

Tynan called from the camp. "Furry Purry! Get back here!"

The cat meowed and patted Bevin's cheek, then stared at Adan.

"You hear that?" Adan said. "He thinks you ought to come back to the fire, too."

Bevin turned to Adan with difficulty. "Before we go, I need to—"

A silhouette against the dancing flames, Tynan stood and began to saunter toward them.

Adan called to his brother, "Don't bother. We're coming." Then, he sighed. "Lady, I fear if we don't return, they'll come to us, one at a time, until we're up to our elbows in friends, kinfolk, and fur-bearing creatures."

Defeated, Bevin bowed her head and started back to the fire.

Falling into step beside her, Adan cleared his throat. "What did you want to tell me?"

I love you. I'll always love you. Bevin folded her arms in a comforting self-hug. "I lied to you. About my magic."

Adan's voice was barely audible above the rushing roar of water. "You still have it? You never lost it?"

Bevin stopped and stared at him. "You knew?"

Adan smiled kindly. "I just pieced it together. You're not easy to read."

Bevin could scarcely take it in. "You don't hate me for lying to you?"

"Merciful gods, no!" Adan cried. "Far from it. I think you're extremely clever. If what Gaer says is true, then using your power could prove fatal." He tilted his head. "And besides, 'lying' is a rather strong term. 'Misled' is more accurate."

The cat on Bevin's shoulder meowed again and butted her cheek with his forehead.

Adan doesn't hate me. Waves of joy thrilled through Bevin's chest with every stroke of her heart. She resumed walking. "Thank you for understanding."

"Thank you for staying alive." Adan paused, then added in an odd tone, "But why apologize to me?"

"Because—" With a flash of panic, Bevin realized she did not know what to say. "Because at the horse fair you . . . you were so . . . so nice to me."

Adan chuckled. "Lady, as I recall, you were nice to me, too."

As they drew near the camp, Tynan strode out to meet them. "Well?" he demanded.

Adan shrugged broadly. "The river is still there."

Tynan did not seem to hear him. His attention fixed on his link-mate. "No. Absolutely not."

The cat jumped from Bevin's shoulder and stalked toward the fire.

Tynan made a noise of outrage. "You'll poop in my what?"

Kiarda and Gaer looked up in surprise.

The cat headed for Tynan's bedroll.

The young man hurried after his link-mate. "Don't you dare."

Kiarda glanced at Bevin. "What's going on?"

Fighting an impulse to giggle, the healer shook her head.

Adan returned to his spot by the fire and picked up another piece of salmon. "Sometimes, I'm extremely grateful I only hear half the conversation."

"No," Tynan protested. "No, we can't do that. It's not—"

Bevin settled beside Kiarda and began to consider how to make her announcement to the group. After revealing her secret to Adan, and getting such a gentle response, she no longer dreaded telling everyone.

Tynan sighed in exasperation. "Adan? Would you come here for a moment, please?"

Adan echoed his sigh, then smiled and got to his feet. "Excuse me, ladies." He popped the morsel of fish into his mouth and strolled over to his brother, licking his fingers. "What?"

With a backward glance toward the others, Tynan pulled Adan off into the trees.

Gaer raised his brows. "This could be interesting."

Kiarda laughed. "Or just silly. They're a matched set, you

know." She reached for another piece of fish. "Uncle Gaer, will you please teach me to fight?"

"I'd be honored, my lady," Gaer said without hesitation. "What did you have in mind?"

Bevin's lips parted in shock. "But—"

Kiarda gave her friend a triumphant smile, then turned toward the Swordmaster. "Nothing terribly involved. I'm just thinking that if we're riding into a war, I may be forced to defend myself at some point, and a bow is no good at close range."

"A valid concern, my lady." Gaer rubbed his chin with a considering air. "You must understand that it takes time and practice to become a proficient fighter. Your best strategy in any conflict would be to run. I could teach you a few kicks which would help you disable an enemy long enough to make an escape, should you find yourself grappling with an opponent."

Kiarda nodded. "That's all I'm asking, Uncle Gaer. Thank you."

Astonished, Bevin stared at the Swordmaster. "But . . . tradition . . . propriety. . . ." She gestured helplessly. "Can you really train her without touching her?"

Gaer looked both startled and reproachful. "I would never take unnecessary liberties."

Kiarda spoke soothingly, "Of course not." She looked at the healer. "It's permissible to touch in order to save a life, and I think that applies to self-defense training."

Relinquishing the argument, Bevin shrugged. "I don't care, really. They're your rules, not mine."

Adan left the cover of the trees, laughing and shaking his head. Tynan looked discomfited; the cat on his shoulder seemed pleased.

Kiarda raised her chin. "What's going on?"

In spite of his evident amusement, Adan's voice carried a note of strain. "Someone needs a lesson in reality."

Tynan twisted his fingers together. "Adan. Don't."

Adan pointed at Tynan. "You watch." He crossed to Bevin and sank to his hands and knees in front of her. Every line of his body bespoke a tightly coiled tension.

Bevin sat frozen, unable to speak, acutely aware that his face hovered mere inches from hers. His hair smelled warmly of pine resin, and his breath drifted across her cheek.

Adan gazed steadily into her eyes. "Bevin. I've been feeling this way for a long time now, and I think you ought to know. I love you."

At first, the words made no sense to Bevin. Then their meaning struck with a force that rivaled any magic, casting out her despair, healing the long-suffered wounds to her spirit, and charming away her ability to speak.

Adan smiled tenderly and turned to look at his brother. "You see?" His voice was raw with pain. "Some of us are doomed to live without love."

Aghast that he misunderstood her silence, Bevin did the only thing she could. She leaned forward and pressed her lips against the scars on his cheek in a fervent kiss.

Adan gasped and went rigid.

Bevin heard the protests and exclamations of the others. She knew she ought to pull away, but she could not. Made bold by the spell he cast, she leaned closer, nuzzling aside his fragrant hair to whisper in his ear. "And I love you."

Adan inhaled through his teeth, suddenly trembling. "Merciful gods!"

Thrilled by his reaction, Bevin sighed and whispered, "I never dared to dream of this."

Panting, Adan slowly turned his face toward hers. "Go ahead," he said hoarsely. "Dare."

Lost in desire, Bevin bent close to claim his lips.

At that moment, a small furry head inserted itself between them. "Meow?"

Bevin and Adan hastily separated.

Tynan laughed. "Yes, you're absolutely right." He put his hands on his hips, looking pleased. "They need to wait until they're married."

CHAPTER EIGHTEEN

S EVERAL days later, Bevin and her companions halted in a grassy clearing to rest and eat their noon meal. Now broad and rapid, the river thundered to their right, separating them from the main body of the Marchlands eastward. Far to the left, forested peaks thrust above the spires of fragrant pine.

Bevin patted her mare's glossy neck. "Easy, Buttercup. Steady, lass." She clambered awkwardly from the saddle. Though soft, the ground stung her toes. She loosed a startled hiss of pain, then glanced toward Adan to make certain he had not heard. He tended to fret over her slightest discomfort.

Adan had also dismounted; but he stood still, staring at a cluster of mountains ahead.

Recalling Adan's uncharacteristic silence during the morning ride, Bevin left her horse and approached him. "What's the matter?"

"Nothing." Adan turned and presented her with a wan smile. "Tired. That's all."

Bevin planted her fists on her hips and studied Adan. He looked glassy-eyed, with a peculiar tension around his mouth that distressed her. "Aren't you feeling well?"

Adan's gaze slid from Bevin, and his voice gained the humorous tone that signaled evasiveness. "Not as well as I'll feel after our wedding."

"And not as tired either, I'd warrant." Startled by her own boldness, Bevin felt her face go hot.

Adan blushed, too, though he also appeared pleased. "Tsk," he said primly. "I'm shocked."

Bevin glanced at the others. Kiarda was conferring with Tynan and Gaer about where to picket the horses. Satisfied they paid no attention, Bevin shifted closer to Adan and lowered her voice. "What's the matter?"

Adan twitched one shoulder in an abbreviated shrug, still not meeting Bevin's eyes. "Rotten headache. And I haven't slept much the last couple of nights."

Dream Cloud twisted his long neck and snuffed Bevin's hair, nickering curiously. She reached up to stroke his velvety nose while she scrutinized Adan. "I'm not going to stop asking until you give me a real answer. Tell me what's wrong."

"A little of everything." Adan finally looked at Bevin and, though he spoke lightly, his expression revealed desperation. "I'm getting scared."

That Adan admitted to fear of any kind sent a sudden shiver through Bevin. "Why?"

Adan tightened his lips, then aimed a pointed glance at Gaer. The Swordmaster remained near Kiarda, nodding deferentially as she indicated a place to stake the horses. As always, he appeared well-groomed, composed, polite: the model liege man. Kiarda trusted him completely, treating him more like family than a servant.

Skin prickling with a new sense of uneasiness, Bevin returned her attention to Adan and repeated her question. "Why?"

Casually, Adan fiddled with Dream Cloud's saddle girth, as if demonstrating a problem with the cinch. "We're too far north," he murmured. "I used to routinely travel on business for Sarn Moor, so I know the lay of the land around the Rapid River. And this isn't it."

Bevin's mouth went dry but she mirrored Adan's nonchalant manner, nodding calmly as if listening to a lesson about saddling a horse. They had been tracking the river north on Gaer's advice in order to strike a ford. "Where are we?"

"Not sure. I think we may be following the High Beck. If that's the case, then we ought to be getting close to home."

Bevin's gray eyes widened. "But—"

Tynan sauntered over, Furry Purry riding his shoulder. "All right, dear brother. Are you going to flirt, or are you going to help with the chores?"

Adan instantly assumed a wicked grin. "You mean I have a choice?"

Continuing to follow Adan's lead, for the moment hiding her misgivings, Bevin folded her arms and turned to Tynan. "Don't let that smile fool you. Adan isn't feeling well."

Tynan and the ginger tomcat exchanged significant glances, then both fixed their attention on Adan. "So that's why you've been so quiet this morning. We thought you were still mad because Furry Purry buried the rest of your supper in the sand for safekeeping."

Adan chuckled. "How could I be angry over such a loving gesture?"

Tynan tilted his head. "That's not what you said last night. You said if we—"

Foreseeing an extended and ultimately pointless quarrel, Bevin interrupted. "Tynan, tell me something. Do you trust Gaer?"

Tynan blinked, seeming disturbed by the question. "I'm not sure. Mostly."

Adan raised his brows, drawing his right eye into a tight squint. "Mostly?"

The younger man flung a look over his shoulder at Gaer, then cast an irritated glance at his brother. "I can only judge him by his actions," he said in a heated whisper. "He's helped us out of a bad spot, he works hard, and he's good to Kiarda. Considering that, I'm inclined to give him the benefit of the doubt. I mean, I can't believe all the stories I've heard about him."

Adan set his jaw stubbornly. "Why not?"

Tynan folded his arms. "Because I don't believe all the stories I've heard about you."

Wearily, Bevin shook her head. *So much for forestalling an argument.*

Adan's face darkened with a scowl. "What stories?"

Tynan stepped back, as if regretting his words. "Never mind."

Adan advanced. "What stories?"

Leaving Gaer, Kiarda entered the fray. "What's going on?"

The two brothers stood silent, glaring at each other.

Bevin pinched the bridge of her nose. Her eyes burned, and

she wondered if she might be getting a headache as well. "Nothing, really. You know how they bicker."

Kiarda's brows lowered as she regarded the men; her hands flexed in and out of fists, a sure warning of decaying patience. "We're all tired and hungry. The sooner we tend the horses, the sooner we can get some food in our bellies."

As if agreeing, Tynan nodded and began to turn. Then he paused, lifting his chin in defiance, and looked at Adan. "There's a rumor that you stole Lady Tassi's hunting horn. But I don't believe it."

Adan's mouth twitched sardonically. "The horn does not belong to Tassi. It's the birthright of the Hunt-Keeper of Sarn Moor." He paused, clearly measuring Tynan's reaction. "And yes. I stole it."

Aghast, Bevin stared. "What?"

Kiarda snorted. "Oh, Adan. You needn't embroider the facts. You only put the horn out of Tassi's reach to protect your Hunt-Keeper's rights. That's hardly theft."

Tynan gazed at Kiarda, his brown eyes filled with horror. "I don't believe this! How can you—?" He gestured helplessly. "You knew? All this time?"

Kiarda frowned. "What of it? I know a lot of things."

"But—"

Kiarda whirled, heading back toward the horses. "Come on. It's not fair to make Uncle Gaer do all the work."

Her heart pounding, Bevin glanced at the brothers. Tynan's handsome face openly displayed all his anguish and fury. Though more guarded, Adan's expression betrayed a hint of inner pain. Bevin struggled for words to disperse the storm of emotion around her and found nothing. She started after Kiarda.

Adan's voice turned raw. "Bevin."

She turned.

The oldest brother of Sarn Moor regarded Bevin earnestly. "Are you angry with me?"

"No." Then Bevin wondered what she did feel. "But I'm beginning to think we all carry too many secrets. Perhaps we would travel lighter without them."

Tynan cleared his throat. "Well-spoken, Bevin." He crossed

to her mount and collected the mare's reins. "I'll take care of Buttercup for you."

Bevin smiled weakly. "Thank you."

Tynan's eyes softened with obvious affection. "A pleasure. Anything for my future sister."

Feeling obscurely ashamed of herself, Bevin watched Tynan lead the mare away, then turned to Adan. "So what shall we do?"

Adan's shoulders slumped. "I don't know."

Bevin chewed her lower lip for a moment. "You ought to tell Kiarda."

"Thought about it," Adan said. "But would she listen?"

"Probably. She's not Tassi."

Adan laughed humorlessly. "True." He slipped his hand under the cheek piece of Dream Cloud's bridle, then hesitated, gazing at Bevin. "Are you sure you're not angry?"

"Adan—"

"Because I'd die if I lost you."

Touched, Bevin blinked back sudden tears. "I love you. I shall always love you. And if you make me kiss you again, the others will never give us a moment alone."

Adan's scarred visage relaxed. "Again, true." He led the stallion forward. "Come on, lad."

Lost in an inner tumult of worry and doubt, Bevin followed Adan with her eyes as he moved to join the others. She had wounded him, she realized, and she would do anything to prevent it from happening a second time. Without another thought, she invoked the magic within her.

Familiar power suffused Bevin's spirit with a warmth like sunshine. The sky seemed suddenly brighter, the smell of pine more subtle and intense. Bevin drew and released a deep breath. "Yes," she whispered. "Oh, yes." She looked at Adan. Once again she saw him clearly, his strong sense of responsibility, his arrogance, and the combination of pain and pride that served as the foundation of his humor. All virtues and flaws woven together into the unique tapestry that was Lord Adan of Sarn Moor.

Adan stripped off his stallion's saddle, then turned toward Bevin as if she had called his name. Affection poured from his gaze, coupled with a healthy carnal desire. The fact that he wanted her seemed like a miracle, and the realization took Bevin's breath away. For a long moment, she could only gaze at him in rapt contemplation.

Adan smiled. "Yes?" he called. "Did you want something, my love?"

Want to eat you alive. Bevin resisted the urge to run into Adan's arms. "No," she said. "Just looking."

Adan flushed and shook his head. "Tsk." He resumed his work.

With effort, Bevin turned her attention to the others. Tynan still struggled with anger and confusion, a victim of his own sweet nature. The link between himself and the cat gleamed like a silver chain, so plainly obvious it seemed strange to recall she could not see it without magic. Kiarda's link remained blurry, but her personal qualities burned like a beacon. Her capacity for love, her desire for justice, and her implacable will shone as clearly as Bevin remembered. Bracing herself, the healer looked at Gaer. She found a complex mass of inner wounds, indomitable strength, and infinite self-discipline. She saw unmistakable shadows of secrecy, but Gaer's concern for his young charges was indisputable. Relieved that the Swordmaster intended no harm, she sighed and let the tension drain from her tired shoulders.

With renewed mental clarity, Bevin reviewed their entire journey. It occurred to her that every member of their party pursued a different quest and each fled separate dangers, yet they were all bound to each other and, somehow, to the larger events of the Marchlands. She could find Maddock for Kiarda, sending out a seeking thread of magic that would traverse the interconnected web of all living things. It might take hours or days for the echo to return to her, and she would have to keep her power alive to receive it, but she had to take the risk. All their fates had become inseparably linked.

Miserably silent, Tynan sat apart from the others with his arms folded. *Adan's a thief. And Kiarda knew.* The thoughts revolved through his head like the refrain of a song. *Kiarda knew and didn't care.*

The future Lady of Dorlach Tor reclined on her cloak, listening attentively while Gaer related a story about her parents' courtship. Bevin sat with her feet demurely tucked to one side, nibbling a piece of spicy jerked venison. Adan also lay on his cloak, with a cold cloth over his eyes, dozing. He claimed to have a headache. Tynan doubted it.

Furry Purry did not share his link-mate's mood. Hunkered near Kiarda's feet, he cheerfully gobbled up Adan's share of the hard-boiled eggs. [[Good,]] he nattered, licking his whiskers. [[Eggs are good.]]

Tynan did not know which troubled him most, Adan's dishonesty or the others' blithe acceptance of it. He also could not decide what to make of the questions raised about Gaer. Though an outlaw and an outcast, the Swordmaster had provided protection and guidance, without which their journey might well have spiraled into a constant flight from one peril to the next. *I want to trust him.*

Oblivious to Tynan's torment, Kiarda leaned toward Gaer, her face shining. "So Father challenged Lord Brunil to a fistfight?"

Gaer nodded. "Just as you said, my lady. A fight for the honor of Lady Wylfre's love." His gaze turned inward upon the memory, and a fond smile played over his lips. "Everyone knew Lord Stane had no way of winning. He possessed neither the strength, the weight, nor the reach of Lord Brunil."

Kiarda lifted her chin triumphantly. "But Father won anyway."

Gaer's grin deepened. "No, my lady, I'm afraid he did not. Lord Brunil repeatedly knocked him into the mud and called for him to admit defeat. Each time, Lord Stane got back up, a little muddier and a little bloodier, and refused to quit the fight."

Kiarda blinked. "Oh." Then one corner of her mouth crooked up. "Sounds like my father. When he believes he's right, he never surrenders."

Still seated, Gaer bowed from the waist in a manner both lighthearted and respectful. "Quite so, my lady. And it was this very quality that your mother, the Dark Flame of Dorlach Tor, most cherished."

Still dwelling upon his brother's dishonesty and his betrothed's acceptance of it, Tynan spoke without thinking. "Tell me, Kiarda. What quality do you most cherish?"

Kiarda turned to Tynan, brows raised. "Pardon?"

Tynan's stomach lurched. He drew a hasty breath to apologize, then realized he was not the least bit sorry. "Truthfulness? Integrity? Or the ability to pick pockets?"

Adan gave a grunt of laughter and pulled the cloth off his eyes. "I wondered when you would mention that again. You've been sitting there stewing all this time. Haven't you?"

A rare fury seized Tynan in a heated grip. "What of it? You obviously don't care what I think."

Kiarda's gaze softened, and she tilted her head. "I'm sorry you're distressed, my love, but you don't know the whole story."

Tynan shook his head tightly. "Adan confessed that he stole Lady Tassi's—"

Adan propped himself up on his elbows. "Not Tassi's horn," he said patiently. "Janna's. The horn belongs to Janna the Hunt-Keeper. She begged me to reclaim it and put it in a safe place."

Kiarda added, "Adan merely put it out of Tassi's reach. Somewhere she couldn't search."

Adan grinned. "My trousers."

Tynan regarded his brother coldly. "That isn't funny."

Adan did not appear chastened. "Only temporarily. It's in my pack right now, wrapped in an old cloak. Go look, if you want."

Tynan folded his arms. "No, thank you."

Adan reclined again and closed his eyes. "I had to do it, Tynan. Tassi was going to give the horn to her uncle Drez."

"Lady Tassi would not do that!"

Kiarda sighed. "My love—"

Tynan gestured furiously. "From the very beginning, Adan found fault with everything Lady Tassi said and did. He hounded her constantly, criticized her, mocked her, showed her no respect, no—"

Adan rolled his head wearily. "Tassi was unfit for the Ladyship. She—"

"So you say." Tynan found himself trembling, and he struggled to steady his hands. "But I think you were just jealous of her. You had grown to think of yourself as the ruler of Sarn Moor."

Adan spoke in a mild tone. "True."

Kiarda's face hardened. "Tynan, be quiet. You don't know what you're saying."

"But he—"

Kiarda abruptly rose to her feet and glared down at Tynan. "Tassi entrapped Culan into marriage. Understand? Her father and brothers found them in bed together. Adan had to agree to the wedding, or Tassi's family would have stoned Culan to death."

Deeply shocked, Tynan could not think past Kiarda's anger. Then, slowly, the sense of her words penetrated. "Stone . . . Culan . . . to death?"

Furry Purry lifted his head from the crumbled bits of egg. [[What did you say? Did someone kill Culan?]]

Confusion, doubt, and rage robbed Tynan of the ability to speak. He sat still, his hands lying limp and nerveless on his lap.

[[No!]] Furry Purry pattered to Adan, jumped on his chest, and peered into his face. [[Say it isn't true!]]

Adan ran his hand down the cat's sleek back. "What's the matter, my whiskery little brother? Have we upset you?"

[[Culan!]]

Unwillingly comforted by the secondhand sensation of Adan's touch, Tynan felt his tension ease. "It's all right, Furry Purry. Culan's unharmed."

The cat raised his amber eyes. [[Then what's happening?]]

Tynan sighed and wiped his sweating hands on his trousers. He became aware of the others watching him. Bevin's round face had turned white and anxious, Gaer looked compassionate, and Kiarda still appeared furious. "What's happening?" he repeated slowly. "A good question."

The cat abandoned Adan and ran to his link-mate. [[Tell me.]]

Tynan drew a breath, then paused, sorting through his emotions, choosing his words with care. "I feel as if the people I love don't respect me. That they hide things from me, then become impatient with my ignorance. And that they only tell me the whole truth when they want to punish me."

Kiarda scowled. "That's ridiculous."

"Is it?" Trying to ignore the trembling in his knees, Tynan shifted the cat to his shoulder and climbed to his feet. "Then let's see how you feel when it happens to you."

Kiarda smiled grimly and knotted her hands into fists. "Go ahead."

Tynan tossed a glance at his older brother. "Adan doesn't trust Gaer." He returned his attention to Kiarda. "Did you know *that?*"

Something flickered in Kiarda's eyes. She spoke in a tone that demanded explanation. "Adan?"

Adan sighed and sat up. For a moment he studied his brother with a sour expression, then he accosted the Swordmaster. "Simple question: What is the name of the river we've been following?"

Gaer lowered his face. His mouth tightened with what appeared to be both stoic surrender and the stifled urge to laugh. Then he turned his bright gaze to Adan. "My lord?"

Silently, Adan raised his brows and widened his eyes in a brittle parody of a child waiting to hear a bedtime story.

Gaer chuckled and touched his forehead in a gesture of deference. "The name of the river, my lord, would be the High Beck."

A chill invaded Tynan. He had not wished to give credence to Adan's suspicions. "Gaer, you lied to us. You said it was the Rapid River."

Adan snorted. "No, he didn't. He just didn't correct us when we called it by the wrong name."

Tynan swallowed hard, glaring at the Swordmaster. *A lie is a lie.*

Rubbing her chin with her thumb knuckle, Kiarda paced away, then turned back. "I knew it was the High Beck."

Tynan jerked his attention to his betrothed. "What?"

Gaer's expression showed no surprise, but his slight accent abruptly deepened. "My lady?"

Kiarda regarded him solemnly. "I surmised that you had another reason for leading us this far north, besides striking the ford."

Tynan found his voice. "And you just let him do it?"

Kiarda did not take her eyes from the Swordmaster. "I knew, Uncle Gaer, you would tell me your purpose when the time was right." She crouched to look him in the face. "I followed where you led because I trust you."

"My lady—" Gaer's voice shook. "You honor me."

Adan yawned. "Touching. Quite. Please forgive me for asking, but where in the blazes are we going?"

Gaer folded his hands on his lap. "Radway Green."

Tynan made a strangled noise of protest. "That's madness! Radway Green was attacked scant days after we passed by. It's tainted. . . ." He made a broad gesture to ward off evil.

"Tainted, yes. But not by the Dark Court." Gaer did not look up. "My lords, my lady, those gifted with magic have lost their powers, and the spirit-linked are dying. I know what these things are: the opening attacks of an invasion force from beyond the sea."

Kiarda resumed pacing. "And you wish to go to Radway Green to . . . investigate?"

Gaer searched for words. "Destroying a village is not a standard tactic, my lady, especially not this early in the campaign. I hoped to learn something of their plans by examining the site."

Shocked and unwilling to believe, sick of the whole situation, Tynan made shooing motions. "Good. Fine. Go."

Kiarda paused, tilting her head. "But Uncle Gaer, surely there are other responsible parties, folk with memories of war, who have already gone to Radway Green? Must we meddle in the investigations of the priests and the local landholders?"

Gaer spread his hands. "Those are appropriate questions, my lady. But those authorities do not possesses knowledge of Imperial war strategies. I do."

Kiarda focused on the mountains to the north. "Are you asking me, Uncle Gaer, to quit my search for Maddock?"

"No, my lady. I want to find him, too." Gaer paused, then added softly, "I ask only that you set aside your quest for a short time. Indulge an old man."

Kiarda stood motionless, her eyes on the distant horizon.

Tynan tensed. *Don't do it. He's lived among the Dark Court for years. Could be a trap.*

Bevin cleared her throat and glanced timidly at every face. "I think we should go, Kiarda. We may be all that stands between the Marchlands and disaster."

Adan flexed his mouth into a grimace of dissatisfaction. "I agree. The destruction of Radway Green may not have been due to the machinations of a mysterious, invisible army. But then again—" He broke off with a shrug.

Tynan gazed in entreaty at Kiarda, waiting for her to turn to him for advice.

Kiarda sighed. "Very well. We'll go to Radway Green."

Bitterness engulfed Tynan. He turned, blinking back tears, and strode blindly away from the group.

Still riding Tynan's shoulder, Furry Purry stuck his nose in his link-mate's ear. [[What's wrong?]]

Tynan whispered through gritted teeth. "She should have asked me what I thought."

Furry Purry gently curled his tail around Tynan's neck. [[She didn't ask the others.]]

"I'm not like the others." Tynan forced himself to walk faster over the grassy hummocks. "I'm her betrothed. Kiarda ought to ask me what I think."

The cat swished his tail in a stroking motion against his link-mate's back. [[Well, then go tell her that.]]

Tynan found himself standing on the edge of a steep bank overlooking the river. He watched the muddy water surge by, thinking about how he had believed, incorrectly, that they followed the Rapid River. Tassi's love for Culan, Gaer's loyalty, Adan's integrity; he had been mistaken about them all. "No," he said unsteadily. "I can't. What if I'm wrong?" His brown eyes filled with tears, and he bowed his head. *What if she doesn't love me after all?*

The cleansing finished, Brother Honesty carefully wrapped up the Ewer in its protective silks. He felt whole and calm, his soul still enraptured by the glory of the One Light.

After the attack on Radway Green, Commander Swift had led the strike force into the mountains to allow the alarm to die down. Approaching the critical stage, their mission increasingly depended upon secrecy. More importantly, to the priest's mind, they all needed to undergo a period of quarantine and purification after exposure to the Abomination. Set within an inspiring grove of soaring pines, the camp took on the air of a woodland temple. When the soldiers were not at drill or on duty, they participated in prayer and ritual bathing.

Brother Honesty laid the Ewer in its trunk, aware of the awed gazes of the soldiers around him. His status had changed much since their arrival in the Marchlands; it pleased the Light to exalt a humble priest, making him an adviser to the Supreme Commander and the confidant of Hooded Magicians.

At the edge of the camp, enshrouded in a ball of impenetrable black smoke, Skull, Claw, and Wraith had withdrawn to perform rituals of their own. Every few moments, the air above the ball curdled, as if from rising heat. Most of the men took care to keep the priest between them and the Magicians, seeming to assume he offered protection from those random flashes of magic which could kill a man in slow agony. Brother Honesty pitied their fear. As Claw had once explained to him, rather impatiently, the power only killed when a Mage employed it for destruction. The backlash of spells of silence and the creation of illusions were harmless by comparison, merely causing muscle cramps or withering the nearby vegetation. The priest wished he could allay the soldiers' anxiety, but the Magicians' secrets were not his to tell.

Brother Honesty turned and found the commander standing at his elbow. Swift's gray eyes looked somber, and his youthful face wore an unreadable expression. "Brother? A moment of your time?"

The priest nodded serenely. "Of course, Commander."

Wordlessly, Swift laid a hand on Brother Honesty's shoulder and escorted him toward the ball of darkness.

Close up, the air smelled singed and bitter. Puddles dampened the ground, their surfaces shimmering with splashes of oily purple and greenish-blue. A sound floated from an indeterminate source, whining and sputtering like a roasting animal carcass.

Amused, Brother Honesty suspected Claw of providing the repellent details. She enjoyed scaring the men.

Swift glanced around, obviously checking to ensure they were not overheard, then spoke in a low murmur. "This isn't right."

"Pardon?"

Swift's features tightened with worry, and he inclined his head toward the Magicians. "I've never seen them act like this before. I don't know what they're doing."

Brother Honesty's round eyes softened with understanding. "My child, may I remind you they have never before engaged in holy work?"

The commander drew a breath, then seemed to change his mind about his intended words. "Well, yes." His brow cleared. "Yes, of course, you're right. It's just that I gave them no orders. What could they be doing?"

Brother Honesty studied the ball of smoke, remembering that the Hooded Magians inside could see out clearly. "Would you like me to check on them? Just peek in to find out if they're all right?"

"No, I only—" Swift gripped the priest's shoulders and peered at him. "You can do that? They'll permit it?"

Brother Honesty blew out his cheeks. "I'm not sure. I can try."

Still gazing at him, Commander Swift slowly shook his head. "You never fail to surprise me, Brother. I wish I had half your courage."

Uncomfortable with the praise, the priest looked at the ground. Entering the ball would likely prove no more dangerous than walking into a tent, but that secret was also not his to share. "Any virtue I have is a gift from the One Light."

"You're too modest."

Smiling shyly, Brother Honesty slipped from the other man's grasp and turned toward the magic. "Let's see if they'll let me in."

"Brother—"

He raised his hand calmly. "But I want to go. I'm curious now." Moving at a casual pace, he approached the smoke-filled ball. *Skull? If I'm doing something wrong, please stop me.* Nothing changed. Forcing himself not to hesitate, Brother Honesty stepped into the blackness.

The smoke vanished. Skull, Wraith, and Claw perched on a blanket, hoods thrown back, faces unveiled.

Dark-eyed Skull turned his head and smiled, then touched his lips in a signal for quiet.

Brother Honesty grinned in return and folded his arms, preparing to wait.

Claw sat cross-legged in the middle of the blanket, eyes closed, hands raised to the level of her shoulders with her palms up. Her hair fell over her forehead in a scribble of curls, her face rapt and tranquil.

Wraith crouched beside her, all knees and elbows. His gaze fixed on Claw with unwavering intensity, and the obvious effort of concentration lent his horsy features unprecedented intelligence.

No sound filtered in from the camp. Outside, Swift walked all the way around the bubble. The commander did not appear happy, and the priest wondered if he ought to step out immediately.

Skull shook his head and gently gestured for the priest to stand still.

Brother Honesty froze, not wishing to disturb the Magicians' efforts.

Minutes passed. The priest slipped into a meditative state, filling the silence with blessed memories of his novitiate at the Prime Temple and the days of fasting and prayer.

Finally, Claw sighed and stirred, her features collapsing into lines of exhaustion. "Got it," she said. She leaned into Wraith and laid her head on his shoulder. "So tired."

Wraith slipped his arms around her and chastely kissed the top of her head. "Rest."

"Sorry to make you wait, good Brother." Skull patted an empty spot on the blanket. "Please join us."

The priest settled on the indicated place. "Commander Swift was concerned for you."

Skull raised one brow. "Concerned? You mean suspicious."

" 's hard," Claw said, speech slurring with evident weariness. "Far 'way. Delicate work. Needed shielding. Levels—" She waved a hand in an erratic gesture. "Levels 'pon levels."

Brother Honesty looked blankly at Wraith.

The Mage's wide mouth flexed in an apologetic smile. "We sensed a seeking spell working its way toward us. Someone is trying to find our friend, Maddock."

A chill formed in Brother Honesty's stomach. "Could you stop it?"

Claw appeared to be falling asleep, but she made a derisive noise.

"No," Skull said with kindly patience. "We were more interested in who sent it."

The cold spread to Brother Honesty's extremities. "But they must mean the boy harm!"

Skull shrugged. "Immaterial. We traced the path of the—"

Wraith's head jerked up. "We?"

Skull sighed. "Claw traced it back to its source, with Wraith shielding her. A difficult process for those of us who wield the sixth magic."

Wraith shook back his lank hair and smiled proudly. "But we found her, Brother. Our missing Mage, Bevin. She's about four days from our camp, and she's got a spirit-link with her."

Brother Honesty folded his icy hands together. "The Abomination."

Claw stirred and raised her head. "Two. There were two links, one only partially formed."

Wraith stroked his long chin. "Well, now that you mention it, I also thought I detected a second one not yet wholly formed, but I wasn't sure. Everything buzzed and echoed so much inside that shield."

Numb with dread, Brother Honesty sat motionless. The demon of the Abomination was proving too strong for them. It would continue to spread and grow, contaminating everyone it touched.

Skull turned to Brother Honesty, his brows raised earnestly. "Please, Brother. Stop torturing yourself. I can't bear it."

The priest gazed at Skull. "But what are we going to do?"

Claw grunted and sat up, as if irritation lent her strength. "Same as always. Move in close and attack."

Skull frowned at her. "It's not that simple. You can't—"

Wraith interrupted with a rude noise. "Yes, it is. Yes, we can."

"Right," Claw said. "Just sever the links and drain the magic. No different than the others."

Skull shook his head. "Bevin is not like the others. If she gets inside your mind and learns how—"

Claw snorted.

"—learns how to manipulate the greater resonances—"

"Impossible."

"Takes years to learn that. She won't—"

Skull punctuated his vehement words by stabbing the air with his index finger. "She could reduce our entire strike force to crisp, black ashes without breaking a sweat!"

Brother Honesty sucked in his bottom lip. They always talked over and around each other, and sometimes he found it difficult to keep up with the conversation.

Wraith spread his hands. "Well, if you're afraid of Bevin, I'll go."

Skull's fine brows drew together. "You're not listening to me. She's not like us. She can wield all five of the lesser powers. If she—"

"Bevin will never even know I'm coming."

"You can't afford overconfidence. If she—"

Wraith narrowed his eyes and regarded Skull with intensity.

Skull stiffened, as if insulted. "That has nothing to do with it!"

Wraith spoke quietly. "I think it does. You hear the thoughts of others, and it weakens your resolve. You're too sensitive."

Skull's response was silent glowering.

Distressed, Brother Honesty cleared his throat. "Please, my children. I think we're losing sight of our mission."

Claw smiled sourly. "The good Brother's right. Let's stop arguing and start killing."

Brother Honesty recoiled at her words. "Cleansing the Abomination."

Claw waved dismissively. "Same thing."

Wraith turned to the priest and gave him a look of undisguised pity. "Don't worry, Brother. We'll fix your demon-whatsis."

Wracked by doubt, Brother Honesty shook his head. "But I don't—"

Skull pointed to something outside the sphere of darkness. "Commander Swift looks terribly anxious."

The priest glanced over his shoulder. Swift had drawn his sword, and he stood staring toward their invisible debate.

Skull continued, "Perhaps, good Brother, you might return to him and relay our discovery? He'll probably wish to send a detachment out immediately."

"Yes. Of course." Brother Honesty climbed to his feet, then paused, looking down at the Magicians. In spite of their dreadful power, they were simply people, flawed and full of conflict. It was a testament to the glory of the One Light that they championed the battle against the Abomination. He raised his hand in benediction, ring flashing. "May the Light shine upon you, and from within you, my children. You are heirs to its triumph."

"Triumph," Claw repeated with unpleasant relish. "Lovely. We like to win."

Skull shook his head and glanced away.

Wraith's expression of pity deepened. "Shouldn't waste your time on us, Brother." He glanced around at his colleagues. "We know what we are. And it has nothing to do with the Light."

CHAPTER NINETEEN

E VEN after a week, Radway Green still stank of death. Ravens swept the dusky sky over the ruined tower and hopped among the stones of fallen cottages. The once proud walls lay in piles of rubble; incongruously, the gateway still stood. Upon the wooden planks of one gate, in red paint, someone had scrawled the horns of Hernis, a crescent-shaped symbol which served as both a warning and a ward against evil.

Shocked out of his personal sorrow, Tynan stared in rising horror at what remained of the ancient and prosperous holding. Beneath him, his mount shifted and began to tremble. "Easy, lad," he muttered, stroking Storm Cloud's sweaty neck. "Nothing to worry about." His words rang hollow. Tynan twisted in his saddle to look at the others.

Pale and teary, Bevin also attempted to comfort her agitated mount. Kiarda's expression was remote and unreadable. Adan's scarred features contorted in anguish. He sought his younger brother's gaze, and Tynan could read the thought that burned in Adan's mind: *This could have been Sarn Moor.*

Tynan forgot his days-old anger. He urged his stallion close and silently clasped Adan's shoulder. *I'm sorry.*

Gaer dismounted and dropped his reins, leaving his gelding to wait for him, and paced forward. He studied the ground, the surrounding forest, and the ravaged village. Tynan watched him, wondering what details the armsman's experienced eye read from the landscape.

Perched on his link-mate's shoulder, Furry Purry stuck his nose in Tynan's ear. [[He's afraid. I can smell it.]]

Thoroughly disquieted, Tynan compressed his lips. *Almighty Hepona.*

Kiarda also dismounted. "Uncle Gaer?"

The Swordmaster turned. Though he did not look fearful, his lean face did not convey its usual composure. His keen eyes glinted with anger and a strange excitement. "My lady?"

"Who did this?" Kiarda asked. "It wasn't a band of southern raiders, was it?"

Gaer shook his head. "No, my lady. Someone much worse, much more dangerous."

Pushed by an urge to stay protectively near Kiarda, Tynan climbed down from Storm Cloud. "You're absolutely certain it wasn't the Dark Court?"

"Yes, my lord." Gaer returned to them, his boots scuffing through cinders and broken rock. "Only a Mage of the Hooded Order could have done this."

Kiarda tilted her head. "Hooded Order? What's that?"

"Wielders of evil magic." Gaer's attention turned inward, as if lost in a memory. "Once they were the blight of a kingdom across the eastern sea, until a wise and powerful emperor harnessed their strength. Now they travel with the Imperial armies, aiding in the defense of their homeland."

Adan spoke up, his voice shaking with barely controlled rage. "Defense? How could Lady Conna and her folk be a threat to an empire across the sea?"

"It would seem, my lord," Gaer said softly, "that the current emperor has turned his hand to conquest. I have long feared this development."

Tynan broke out in a cold sweat, imagining the Marchlands trampled beneath an invincible horde of soldiers. "We have to do something! Warn someone!"

Kiarda released a long, shuddering breath and looked at him. "I agree. But how? Who will believe us?"

"I—" Tynan stopped. Kiarda could be right. The doctrine of the Divine Peace had become so firmly entrenched it seemed just possible no one would listen—even to the future Lord and Lady of Dorlach Tor. Worse, the priesthood might declare them outcast along with Gaer. "We'll find proof."

Adan made a derisive noise and swung off Dream Cloud's back. "Radway Green is proof enough, and they're ignoring that.

You can't make people see, little brother, when they choose to be blind."

With uncharacteristic abruptness, Gaer whirled and strode from the group. His head hung, as if searching the burned-off grass, but Tynan could not help wondering if Gaer grieved for lost time and the foolishness of those he had tried to help.

With a trilling purr, the tomcat jumped down from Tynan's shoulder and trotted after Gaer. [[Leave this to me. I'll sort things out.]]

Tynan drew a breath to call his link-mate back, then decided it would harm nothing for Furry Purry to follow the Swordmaster.

Kiarda sighed. "I think Uncle Gaer is distraught. I've never seen him like this."

Adan crossed to hold the head of Bevin's restive mare. "Settle down, Buttercup," he scolded gently. "That's a good lass."

Bevin dismounted carefully; but when her feet hit the ground, she grimaced. "Ouch. I'll never get used to the way it makes my toes sting." She glanced toward Gaer's retreating figure, then looked at the others. "He's worried about us."

Kiarda frowned thoughtfully. "Maybe. But I suspect he rather wishes he weren't burdened with us. Otherwise, he could track this evil Mage himself."

A sudden thought came to Tynan. " 'A kingdom across the eastern sea.' " He looked at his brother. "Remember? That's where Gaer said he came from."

Adan nodded, his scarred visage tight. "That's right. And something about a choice between falling on his sword or traveling."

Tynan's heart picked up tempo. "But don't you see? The magic-user comes from his homeland. These invaders are Gaer's own people."

Kiarda's lips parted in an expression of shock and the beginning of anger. "But surely . . . you're not suggesting . . ."

Tynan shrugged uneasily. "I don't know. He doesn't make sense to me. He never did."

Bevin spoke with rare force. "I don't believe Gaer's part of any plot against the Marchlands. But he's anxious, that's for certain; maybe he's afraid we'll turn on him when we learn the truth about his origin." Her brow puckered. "He's so full of sorrow."

"Sorrow—?" Adan tilted his head and studied Bevin quizzically. "How do you know that?"

Bevin returned his gaze calmly. "How do you think?"

Tynan swallowed hard. *Magic.*

The realization evidently hit Adan at the same instant, and his tone became pleading. "Bevin, no. Don't do it."

Bevin smiled gently. "Too late."

Kiarda glanced back and forth between them. "What are you talking about?"

Bevin drew a breath to reply.

Adan spoke first, his voice taut with anguish. "Bevin's using magic."

For a moment, Kiarda stood motionless. Then her eyes darkened with worry, and she laid her hands on the healer's shoulders. "Bevin-lass, is this wise?"

"It's necessary." Bevin appeared unusually confident. "Refraining from magic was causing more problems than it solved."

Adan shook his head. "It's too dangerous, my love. What if that evil Mage finds you?"

Bevin shrugged. "There are other dangers more immediate than him." She looked pointedly at Tynan, then Kiarda. "We can't afford to get divided, to doubt each other. I can help settle our differences."

Tynan felt sick with guilt. *My fault.* "Bevin, it's not worth your life."

"Don't be silly," Bevin said. "I don't intend to die."

"Look at Radway Green." Adan jabbed a hand toward the standing arch. "The magic-user who did that, my love, also wants to steal your power. He can sense you now, right? You've just lit a signal fire."

Bevin nodded equitably. "He also wants to kill Tynan and Kiarda, all the spirit-linked, for his own mad reasons."

Frowning, Kiarda sharpened her tone. "So you've made it easy for him to find us?"

"I've made it possible to sense his approach. To shield you and Tynan from his attack. And to fight back."

Adan's voice cracked. "By putting yourself in danger?"

"Why not?" Bevin spread her hands. "Why should I be the only one exempt from risk?"

Tynan turned away, throat aching with the threat of tears. "Because," he said unsteadily, "I want you to be my sister someday. Please don't—"

A thin, wailing cry floated over the ruins of Radway Green. [[Here!]] Furry Purry called. [[I found something!]]

Tynan felt his heart skip, then quicken. He dropped his reins and ran toward his link-mate's voice.

The tomcat circled a clump of sod, his tail bristling. [[Hurry!]]

Gaer reached the excited animal first and fell to one knee. Heart still pounding with borrowed emotion from his link-mate, Tynan reached the spot. "What is it?"

Furry Purry clawed at the ground, flinging dirt. [[A sword!]]

"I'm not sure, my lord." Gaer pulled his dagger and used it to cautiously raise a length of shattered metal from the burned grass. "It appears to be part of a sword. Of Marchland make, judging from the—" He broke off with a gasp.

Tynan crouched beside the other man. "What?"

The others arrived as Gaer grasped the hilt and tugged the fragment completely free of the sod. "This sword—" His accent thickened. "Lord Kyll had it made for me as a gift."

Kiarda knelt for a closer look. "Grandfather Kyll?"

"Yes, my lady." Gaer studied the damaged blade, tilting it to catch the dying rays of the sun. An inscription glinted. "See there? My name."

The tomcat jumped onto Tynan's shoulder. [[I knew it was important. But what's it doing here?]]

Tynan cleared his throat. "How did it get here?"

"I have no idea, my lord."

Kiarda lifted her eyes from the sword. "Maddock."

Tynan stared at her. "But—"

A tortured light filled Kiarda's eyes. "He took it from Dorlach Tor when he escaped." She abruptly rose and turned away, gazing toward the ruins. "Maddock must have been at Radway Green when it was attacked." She stiffened, her next words emerging in a stilted whisper, "He's dead."

"No," Bevin said vacantly.

Tynan jerked his attention to the healer.

Bevin still crouched on the grass, staring at the broken blade through narrowed, gray eyes. "No," she repeated dreamily. "The path to him is now clear."

Clearly worried, Adan stretched out his hand, but stopped short of touching his betrothed. "Bevin? My love?"

As if awakening from sleep, she blinked and looked at her companions. "Maddock is alive." Brushing the grass from her trousers, she stood and pointed toward the mountains to the northeast. "He's that way."

Kiarda whirled, her expression haunted, and whispered something under her breath.

The ravens wheeled and cawed in the darkening sky. Tynan shivered. It was said the birds could sense impending death. *Maybe they're waiting for us.*

❦

Uncertain what had awakened him, Gaer rolled to a crouch, eyes sifting shadows, ears desperately attuned. Dappled by glimmers of moonlight through branches, Adan sat watch between a pair of beeches stunted by the shade of colossal pines. A blanket hung from his shoulders, and dark hair fell over his lowered forehead. Tynan slept on his back, breaths labored by the tomcat flopped heavily across his chest. Kiarda and Bevin curled together, sharing their blankets. The coals of the dinner fire cast their faces in a healthy, reddish glow.

Adan's head swiveled toward Gaer. "What?" he whispered in alarm.

Politely, Gaer waved the younger man silent and gave his silver hair a short, brisk toss. A distant rustle of brush caught his attention, so short and gentle he wondered if he had truly heard it.

Adan rose, gaze jerked in the direction from which the sound had come.

Impression confirmed, Gaer stood and headed for the fire. Its light would draw unwanted notice. Before he reached it, Bevin sat up suddenly, wrenching the blankets from Kiarda who shivered in her sleep.

"Please, be still," Gaer whispered. "We might go unseen."

"No," Bevin hissed. As darkness replaced the glow of the dying campfire, her face looked positively green. "Magic—"

Clouds oozed over the few gaps in the foliage overhead, leaving no light but the dense scarlet of the coals. Tynan gasped, and the cat rolled from his chest with a howl of pain.

"No!" Bevin launched herself past Gaer, the Swordmaster's agile backstep rescuing both from a collision. Seizing Tynan's hand, she plopped to the ground beside him and dragged the cat into her lap.

Kiarda scrambled to her feet. "What's going on?" she slurred loudly, caught between sleep and outrage.

Thunder boomed, drowning out Gaer's mannerly plea for quiet. He kicked mulch over the fire, plunging them into near-total blackness.

"Not again." Bevin panted, as if she had run for miles rather than only dove across a camp.

Gaer followed the swish of Kiarda's clothing as she moved toward Bevin. "Magic-wielder?" the future Lady asked.

"Yes. Forbidden magic. He's targeting Tynan's link."

The cat loosed a keening wail of terror.

Gaer drew his sword, frantically seeking some light on which to ground his vision. The darkness ceased working to their advantage in the midst of so much noise. "Limit sounds to the necessary," he commanded. "Please."

Tynan muttered something that silenced the cat.

Kiarda screamed, drawing Gaer immediately to her side.

Bevin's linens rasped as she shifted. "My lady, here. I can shield you, too."

Kiarda stumbled into Gaer, and he caught her blindly. She sagged against him. "Head . . . feels like . . . shattering."

Gaer hauled Kiarda to Bevin, surrendering her to the healer's free hand. *Forbidden magic.* Alarm struck through the Swordmaster. He gritted his teeth, grounding his courage, trying not to consider the power of the Hooded Order. To do so might paralyze him. "Where is he?"

Bevin's voice emerged in a frightened squeak. "Not far. Straight south. He's not alone." She made a wordless sound of terror. "Hurry. He's found me. Can't shield much . . ." Her voice collapsed into a sharp intake of breath. "Hurry!"

"My lord, please watch over them." Gaer did not pause for Adan's confirmation before plunging into the foliage southward.

Branches tore Gaer's arms, and vines clawed at his feet. Another clap of thunder rang out, deafening all sound for several moments after it faded. Lights fluttered and winked like flames through the forest. Though its unnaturalness chilled him, he appreciated the glimpses of vision it provided. A scream at his back spiraled worry and rage through him. He quickened his pace, dodging around trees and floundering through brush, forced to backtrack when a copse of brambles grew too thick to penetrate. Face scratched and bleeding, arms stinging with buried nettles, he chose another route. Galvanized by Bevin's anxiety, he fought through a clump of juniper and tumbled into a clearing.

The fall saved Gaer. A sword swished over his head, and he seized the wielder's ankle as he rolled. The man fell to the ground. Gaer surged upward. A quick cut opened the man's throat. Warm blood splattered Gaer's hilt, and he allowed momentum to take his opponent down. A magical flash glinted from steel flying toward Gaer's face. He spun, his blade tearing flesh. The other sword retreated, and Gaer assessed the situation in the instant it disappeared. In the center of the clearing, a figure swathed in black hovered beside a robed man who appeared unarmed. Two more charged Gaer. An axe in one's hand swept toward his head. Then the light failed.

Gaer sprang backward, swerving beneath the axe's fall. Dodging around the warriors, he launched himself for the floating Mage.

Someone shouted a warning in the language of the Empire. Words from Gaer's past erupted from memory: *To touch a Hooded Mage means instant death.* Tensed for an explosion of fire and pain, he plunged his blade deep into the dark figure. The sword lurched through the muscles just below the left shoulder blade. Gaer dragged it down and out with all of his strength. The hooded figure managed a single scream, then toppled to the dirt. Gaer ducked as he jerked his blade free, certain he would find both warriors on top of him. Yet, as the clouds unraveled from the sky, he found the two had barely moved from where the last flash of magic had revealed them. Either they had not followed his attack or they feared the Mage too much to approach, even to defend him. The robed man dropped to his knees beside the Mage, pawing at his clothing, no threat to Gaer . . . at least for the moment.

The axeman charged Gaer. He caught the attack on his sword, impact aching through his arms. Staggered, he barely extracted his sword in time to riposte. His blade sped gracefully for the axeman's neck as he swerved from the path of the other soldier's low cut. The tip of Gaer's sword carved flesh. Then, agony slammed against his leg. He plummeted before he realized he was hit. The sword trailed him, speeding toward his chest. Gaer forced himself to roll. The blade tore his sleeve and sliced a line of agony along his forearm. Protecting his head, he weaved his sword in half-blind chaos intended only to gain him space. The soldier retreated.

Gaer attempted to stand, but his injured leg buckled and agony howled through it. As he sank to one knee, he found the axeman also on the ground, hands clenched to his neck, blood seeping between his fingers. The swordsman stood over Gaer, driving his blade toward the older man's heart. Triumph blazed in his eyes.

Gaer surged upward. Parrying the blade aside, he slashed open the other man's side. The man grunted in agony, then collapsed, slamming into Gaer, who was already off-balance. Fire seemed to sear the wound. Gaer tumbled, his opponent on top of him. Pinned, he struggled frantically, anticipating death from the axman or the one who attended the Mage. A shadow fell over Gaer. He twisted, freeing his sword arm, prepared to fight to his last breath.

"It's me." Tynan's voice had never sounded so welcome.

The ginger tom rubbed across Gaer's face, fur tickling. Tynan placed his fingers beneath the corpse, Kiarda and Bevin scrambling into positions to assist.

"Careful, my lord, my lady," Gaer said.

Without reply, the three hefted the body. Gaer scooted loose, rescuing them from the need to fully move the corpse. The axman no longer lay where he had fallen. Gaer forced himself to stand, favoring his aching leg, gaze flickering over the clearing. The creature of the Hooded Order still lay where it had fallen. The hood had fallen from its head, revealing youthful male features. *Human?* Gaer stared. The robed man knelt at the Mage's side, cradling the head against his robes, sobbing. His fingers twined through the Mage's long sandy hair, and a diamond identifying him as a priest of the One Light caught the starlight at intervals. Adan stood over them, one of the dead men's swords in his hand. Three bodies lay still in the clearing. Gaer saw no sign of the axman and suspected he had fled. With a wound as severe as he had taken, it seemed unlikely he would return to attack them soon.

Bevin stepped in front of Gaer. "You're hurt."

"Thank you for your concern." Gaer bowed awkwardly. "I'll be fine." Stress intensified his accent, and he did not pull away when she cupped the leg wound in her hands. Within moments, the pain softened to a dull throbbing, and he could bear weight. He pulled away before she could fuss over the tear in his forearm or the bramble scratches. They did not bother him enough for her to worry over them when only an untrained civilian guarded their living enemy. Besides, her touch, though allowed by its nature, would agitate the others.

To Gaer's surprise, Bevin turned her attention to the bleeding swordsmen. "Bevin-lass, what are you doing?"

"Tending wounds." Bevin did not bother to look up, but crouched beside one of the soldiers.

Gaer shook his head but did not interfere.

Adan spoke the words on Gaer's mind. "My love, if you find any of them alive, promise me you'll let us know before doing anything that might make them competent for another battle."

Bevin did not bother to answer, but her expression mingled grief and worry with irritation.

Tenderhearted, but not stupid. Eased by the exchange, sword still in his grip, Gaer turned his attention to the Mage and his companion. As he headed toward them, the cat streaked past. Boldly approaching the stranger, the animal clambered onto the Mage's corpse and cuffed the living man's face with a gentle paw. "Mow! Meee-yow!"

The man turned his face upward. Mouse brown hair fell around grief-stricken features, and mild blue eyes blurred by tears studied the ginger tomcat. "What's this?"

"Cat," Tynan warned. "Get away from there."

Ignoring his link-mate, Furry Purry ground his soft face against the stranger's.

"I don't care . . ." Tynan started.

Gaer dropped a warning hand to Tynan's shoulder. "My lord." When the young man looked his way, Gaer made a silent plea for caution. Apparently, the excitement of the moment had caused Tynan to forget the necessary secrecy and revert to the relationship he had known since birth.

The stranger stiffened and skittered backward, dropping the head he had so tenderly cradled. The Mage's neck snapped backward, and he flopped to the dirt. "Abomination."

Confused by what seemed like an abrupt change of heart, Gaer stared from the priest to the Mage several times. Men had called those of the Hooded Order worse, yet it made no sense that the robed one had only just now realized the nature of his companion. "Who are you?" he finally demanded in the tongue of the Marchlanders.

The priest used the same language. "I am Brother Honesty." Though unsteady from fear, his voice seemed remarkably gentle for one who faced, alone, a group of armed foemen. "And you are called?"

It seemed an odd time and circumstance for such an exchange, yet Gaer saw no harm in it. "Gaer."

The priest wiped his eyes with the back of one sleeve, a movement that caused Adan to tense and move the sword nearer. Gaer noted with alarm that the young lord had drawn close enough that any man with combat training could overpower him and take the weapon. The priest, however, did not seem to notice.

"Gaer," he repeated, brightening slightly. "Where I come from, that means—"

"—I know what it means." Gaer cut off Brother Honesty before he could finish with "Sorrowing." He had chosen the name deliberately when he had arrived in the Marchlands still filled with loss, and it had become more appropriate with time. "Why did your . . ." He looked deliberately at the Mage. ". . . 'people' attack us."

Rebuffed, the cat stalked back to Tynan, tail low. Gaer noted with relief that Kiarda and the young man remained safely behind him. Bevin still examined the soldiers.

"I'm sorry, my child." Brother Honesty pressed his hands together, still crouched near the Hooded Mage. "I am not at liberty to speak of that."

Gaer's eyes widened. He appreciated the priest's courage and loyalty, if not his evasiveness. "Would the realization that we can kill you at any time make you more talkative?"

"My child, that death is inevitable, and I do not fear it. The Realm of Light awaits me."

Adan glanced at Gaer, his expression uncomfortable.

Tynan said, "You're not going to kill him." His voice broke, "Are you?"

Gaer lowered his sword. "No, my lord." He examined the stranger from the mild features to the patched robe, to the threadbare sandals. Only one thing seemed out of place. Gaer focused on the bright green ribbon on the priest's sleeve. "A priest who is also a soldier?"

At the word "priest," murmurs suffused Gaer's companions. Even Bevin looked over.

Brother Honesty's eyes crinkled in confusion. Then, tracking Gaer's gaze, he tugged at the ribbon of rank. "Honorary."

"Ah." Gaer glanced around the clearing, trying to make sense of what he saw. A priest of the Light mourned the loss of a creature of darkness, while a Marchland healer attended accompanying soldiers who had attempted to slaughter her companions and herself. For the moment, nothing made sense, and his next course of action seemed anything but obvious. Perhaps matters would clear with sleep, and the priest might prove more eager to talk.

Without taking his eyes from the man in front of him, he called to Tynan. "My lord, if I might have some rope." He would rather have fetched it himself but worried for Adan's safety alone with a stranger.

Tynan headed toward the packs. Divining Gaer's purpose at once, Brother Honesty said softly, "You need not bind me. I won't try to escape."

Gaer studied the priest in silence.

"I swear it by the grace of the One Light."

Gaer nodded. "Thank you, my lord, but I won't need the rope after all."

Tynan stopped, clearly taken aback. Adan cleared his throat. "Are you sure that's wise, Gaer? He is a . . . well . . ." He shook his head, uncertain. "Is he really a priest?"

Brother Honesty answered for Gaer. "A servant of the One Light, my child."

Keyed by Brother Honesty's voice and ancient terminology, memory assaulted Gaer. He saw the setting sun kindle fiery highlights through Graceful's dark hair as she left him, long legs carrying her swiftly from sight. He squinted, trying to clear his head of a ghost of remembrance long banished. "Priests of the Empire are not like those here. They listen without judgment. They guide instead of punish, teach with word and action rather than cruelty. Find goodness in that most evil." He dropped his regard to the Mage.

Brother Honesty said softly, "Even the Hooded Order is a creation of the One Light."

Gaer finished, "A priest of the One Light would not break a vow so sworn."

Brother Honesty nodded.

Bevin returned to Kiarda's side. "All dead," she announced, head respectfully bowed.

"My lords, my ladies." Gaer bowed to each in turn. "If you would like to resume your sleep, Brother Honesty and I will tend to the bodies."

Adan studied the weapon in his hands as if for the first time. He rounded up his companions, heading back into the brush.

Brother Honesty knelt at the Hooded Mage's side. And began to pray.

Eyes stinging, old tears glued to his cheeks, the reek of friends' blood haunting his nostrils, Brother Honesty sought solace in a sleep that eluded him. Cold wind swayed the needled branches high overhead, and pinecones pattered irregularly to the forest floor. Night insects clicked a regular, high-pitched chorus. On watch, Tynan whispered occasional soft observations to his cat while the breathing of the others filled the clearing with familiar camp noises.

These sounds barely penetrated Brother Honesty's grief. Though he had not died, his life ended the moment the paw of the Abomination brushed his cheek. Touched by its contagion, by the very leading edge of its spread, he could never return to his people. His vow not to attempt escape had become easy in comparison. The enormity of that realization washed over him once more, and he clapped his hands over his face. Fresh tears trickled through his fingers.

As the night wore on, terror and sorrow gave way to honest questioning. Brother Honesty could not understand why the One Light had exposed him to the Abomination. Poor Wraith had died opposing the demon, so his place in the Realm of Light was assured, but Brother Honesty's soul was in grave peril. *Why infect Your servant with the Abomination and deprive the remaining soldiers of the vessel of Your succor?* The tears stopped as Brother Honesty moved beyond fear to pondering those dilemmas. Eventually, the One Light would bring him to the answers, but not without intense thought and fierce self-scrutiny.

Rolling into prayer position, Brother Honesty caught glimpses of his new, unwilling companions. Gaer slept on his side at the base of a pine. The girls sprawled on their backs beneath shared blankets. Adan curled into a tense ball on his bedroll, looking uneasy even in sleep. Brother Honesty examined Tynan last. The young man paced between his companions, the cat clutched against his chest and his angular features pinched into a pained expression.

Sensing Tynan's anxiety, Brother Honesty slipped naturally into his role as consoler. For the moment, he did not care that he faced the vehicle of transmission for a profanity forcing the slaughter of thousands of innocents. A youth was tormented and needed the support of the One Light—and the gentle assistance he could accord in its name. Brother Honesty waited until Tynan's trek brought him near. "My child."

Tynan froze. His head swiveled toward the priest.

"My child." Brother Honesty kept his voice low so as not to awaken the others. "You seem troubled. Would you like to talk?"

Tynan's brown eyes narrowed in suspicion. His fingers twitched around the cat. "I'm not freeing you."

Brother Honesty spread his hands. The gesture usually displayed a lack of weaponry, but it served as an indication of innocence as well. "I have no intention of breaking my vow. I just thought you might want to talk."

"Well, I don't." Tynan folded his free hand sullenly across the other.

The cat made a noise low in his throat.

Tynan frowned at the animal, then looked up through a curtain of dark hair that had slid into his eyes with the movement. "Are you . . ." he started uncomfortably. ". . . are you really a . . . a priest?"

"A servant of the One Light." Brother Honesty held out a hand to Tynan, the offer surprising even himself. Once touched, he found he no longer feared the Abomination.

Tynan did not reach for the proffered hand, but he remained in place. "You're not like any priest I've ever known." The sentence emerged like an accusation.

Brother Honesty recalled the words of the headmaster as he prepared for his journey with the advance force: *The priests of savages are savage.* He sought a gentler description. "Your priests believe respect lies in fear and repentance in pain."

Tynan stroked the tomcat with nervous motions. "And you?"

Brother Honesty obliged, "That respect is earned and fear

only taken. That pain causes anger, and violence begets violence. Repentance comes only with gently guided understanding."

"You truly believe that?"

"My child, it is simple truth."

Tynan sighed, staring at his feet. Brother Honesty studied the soft dark hair falling over features bright with youth and potential. The large eyes and obvious uncertainty made him appear childlike, anything but the demonic entity he represented. "Violence begets violence."

"Yes."

Tynan raised his head, revealing his straight brow and strong chin, a handsome and regal contrast to the image of infantile innocence. "There, our priests would agree with you."

Brother Honesty raised his brows to indicate his interest in listening, though Tynan's point ran counter to his own.

Tynan pursed his lips, as if trying to decide whether to trust the priest with his concerns. The cat meowed, clambering from Tynan's arms to his left shoulder, then arranging himself around the young man's neck. "Gaer was outcast because he refused to denounce his warrior ways and give up his sword training. Yet . . ." Tynan winced. He had apparently come to the matter that bothered him. "Yet, when your people attacked us, I was glad he had joined us. Glad that he killed—" He broke off with a grimace, obviously recognizing the cruelty of his words to Brother Honesty.

Emotional pain stabbed Brother Honesty, but he hid his own discomfort to address Tynan's. "Competence, by itself, is no sin, my child. Knowing violence is not the same as using it."

Tynan stared. "Our priests would claim otherwise."

Brother Honesty opened his expression. "And your experience?"

Tynan glanced at the cat, then back to Brother Honesty. His words came slowly, full of self-realization. "Gaer could have resorted to violence several times but used words instead. He didn't fight until we were attacked and our lives were at stake. And then . . ." His breath caught, and he mumbled the rest. ". . . I was . . . glad . . . even though people . . ." He trailed off.

Tynan's difficulty speaking made his concern utterly clear.

Brother Honesty found the comforting tenfold harder for needing to justify the deaths of his own friends. "My child, it's always upsetting to change lifelong doctrine."

Tynan nodded, then whispered, "Everything's changed."

Brother Honesty listened.

"The Joyous Reunion." Tynan shook his head. "If it ever existed, it's gone now. I'm starting to rely on, even to like, a man I've learned to despise since . . ." He paused. ". . . as long as I can remember, anyway. And I'm not even sure about my duties and boons to Lady Tassi—"

"Lady Tassi?" Brother Honesty encouraged.

Tynan waved the topic aside. "It would take too long to explain."

"I don't mind," Brother Honesty said. "I'm not sleeping anyway, and it's a gift from the One Light to have the station and opportunity to help others work through their problems."

"You *have* helped." Tynan's voice contained new strength. "You've helped a lot, thank you. I just need time alone to think."

As do I, Brother Honesty admitted. It frightened him to discover he liked Tynan, an innocent victim of a terrible plague. Deep in his soul, he knew that feeling had a reason and that the One Light attempted to reveal a purpose for its priest's recent predicament.

The ginger tom slid from Tynan's shoulders and bounded to the ground. Marching to Brother Honesty, he rubbed against the priest's shins. The small body brushed warmly against him, and fur tickled through his leggings.

Surprised, Brother Honesty back-stepped. "What's it doing?"

Tynan explained with obvious reluctance. "He wants you to pet him."

"Pet?"

"To stroke his back."

Brother Honesty crouched and held out a hand, only to find his fingers shaking. He steeled himself, remembering the horse who had nuzzled him at the camp.

The cat arched to meet Brother Honesty, gliding smoothly beneath his palm to assure full contact from neck to tail. Circling, the tabby butted beneath the priest's hand for another pass, emitting a deep, rumbling sound.

Brother Honesty jerked away. "It's growling at me."

Tynan laughed, the light sound like music after expressing such weighty worries. "He's not growling. He's purring. Don't you have cats where you come from?"

"No." Brother Honesty did not know whether he spoke truth. "At least, I've never seen one. We don't . . . um . . . allow animals to walk freely among us." He watched the cat sit, studying him with wide, amber eyes. The animal did not ruffle his fur, did not appear angry or dangerous.

Tentatively, Brother Honesty moved back into his position. He ran a hand from the cat's head to the base of his tail, eliciting another purr. "Why does it do that?"

"Purr?"

"Yes."

"It's a cat's way of saying it likes something."

Brother Honesty dropped to his haunches, reclaiming his hand. "It likes me stroking it? You're certain?"

"He likes almost anyone stroking him." Tynan added carefully, "Most cats do."

"How queer." Brother Honesty ran a hand through the soft fur again. It felt strangely nice, soothing in its own way.

Tynan shrugged. "Not queer at all. Not if you've seen cats act that way your whole life."

Brother Honesty's own words returned to haunt him: *It's always upsetting to change lifelong doctrine.* He knew it would be better to wait until Tynan raised the subject, but curiosity won the battle against propriety. "Does that make up for the rest?"

Raw puzzlement crept over Tynan's features. "The rest?"

Brother Honesty swallowed, hating to remind the young man of his affliction. "Sharing the fouler, brutish things. The instinctive actions. The dirty parts of a beast's existence."

Tynan stared, dark eyes wide with offense.

The realization he had affronted one he had intended to aid struck Brother Honesty an agonizing blow. "I'm so sorry, my child. I didn't mean to hurt you."

Tynan found his voice. "I'm more surprised than hurt. Animals are graceful, beautiful inventions of the gods and beloved by their creators. They can do things we can only dream of: fly, survive in the depths of water, balance on a string, live through a fall that would shatter our bones, to name a few." He shook his head with the frustrated sorrow of a priest unable to offer hope to a soul in despair. "You obviously know about the spirit-link, so I'll stop trying to hide it. It was a birth gift from the gods, a blessing I'm grateful for every day of my life."

Grateful. Brother Honesty blinked, his turn to lose his ability for speech. "Again, my child, my humblest apologies for offending." In that moment, his mission became blazingly clear. The One Light had entrusted to him a task every bit the blessing Tynan claimed for his link. Now forever cast among these unfortunates, he would dedicate what little remained of his life to work with those stricken with the curse, to guide them toward enlightenment and redemption before Swift's troops became forced to end their lives. Brother Honesty gathered the ginger tomcat into his arms. *It begins.*

CHAPTER TWENTY

A FTERNOON sunlight straggled through the forest canopy, dappling the tents with tree shadows and tossing glimmers from armor and swords. Men milled through the camp, tending horses and hounds, sharpening weapons, or chattering in small groups. Pleasantly exhausted and hungry after sword practice, Maddock settled beside the cook fire and reached for a fresh loaf of bread. Cunning, his injured leg still in a splint, eased to the ground beside the Horsemaster's son, grunting a little in pain. A grimace accentuated his weathered features and crooked nose.

Maddock gave his brother-in-arms a sympathetic glance, mentally picking through his limited vocabulary of simple verbs and his larger store of expletives. "Hurts?"

"Yes." Cunning grinned ruefully, using the simplified speech pattern that assisted Maddock. "I like."

Maddock passed him the bread, not sure he understood. "You like . . . hurts?"

Cunning made a comic face. "Yes. Hurts . . . good. Dead . . . bad. Damn bad." He clapped Maddock's shoulder. "I no like dead. Yes?"

Maddock smiled in return, warmed by the soldier's attempt to joke. "Yes. Damn yes."

Cunning broke into good-natured laughter.

Maddock reached for another loaf of bread.

A clap of thunder exploded over the camp.

Maddock lunged to his feet, ears ringing. Horses screamed from the picket lines, and a soldier yelped an oath. In the center of the camp, Commander Swift dashed out of his tent and studied the cloudless sky.

A vaguely familiar voice shouted, "Damn you!"

Maddock whirled toward the sound.

Black robes in disarray, Skull strode through the camp, gaining speed with each step. "You ran?" His hood flew back, revealing his narrow face twisted with fury. "You ran? You—you bastard!"

Lips parted in surprise, Maddock looked at Cunning for an explanation, but the soldier cringed with his hands shielding his eyes. The young man glanced around camp and saw the others also averting their faces. Only at that moment did he remember that no one was supposed to see the Hooded Order. With a shrug, Maddock started after the black-robed figure. "Skull! What's going on?"

The Mage did not pause or answer as he charged toward the boundary. Soldiers in his path scattered like rabbits, but he did not spare them a glance. Commander Swift stepped in front of the Mage and held up his hand. "Stop."

Skull's mouth worked, shaping silent words, but he obeyed.

The commander's expression turned stern. "Explain."

Skull pointed toward the edge of camp and spoke in a low, choked whisper. Commander Swift whirled and rapped out a string of orders to the men nearby, who ran in the direction Skull indicated.

Wild with curiosity and growing anxiety, Maddock looked for anyone who could fill in the details.

The third Mage, Claw, hovered near his elbow like a drift of black smoke.

Forgetting he was supposed to be afraid of the Hooded Order, Maddock spread his hands. "What's going on?"

Claw's cowled head swung toward him.

Maddock's skin prickled. At his feet, the ground opened up in a mouth wide enough to swallow a horse. The young man skipped backward. The mouth developed cracked lips, which peeled back from yellow and broken fangs in a burst of guttural laughter. "You speak to me, little one?" it asked in the tongue of the Marchlands, its voice deep and monstrous. "You wish me to answer your petty questions?"

For a moment, Maddock stared at the apparition, thinking of

the Dark Court. Then he looked at Claw. "Yes," he said calmly. "If you please."

The mouth growled softly. "I cannot," it said in a grudging tone. "I know no more than you. Only that it concerns Brother Honesty's mission." The mouth folded in upon itself and disappeared.

Alarmed, Maddock jerked his attention to where Commander Swift still faced Skull. "Brother Honesty?" Abruptly remembering his manners, he turned and presented Claw with a quick bow. "Thank you."

The Mage folded its gloved hands into its sleeves and bowed in return.

Maddock started toward the commander, hoping he was not breaking military protocol but too worried about Brother Honesty to restrain himself.

Swift glanced at the Horsemaster's son as he approached. "Maddock."

Skull turned. In his large, dark eyes Maddock read fury and bone-shattering grief. "Friendship ran."

His words made no immediate sense. Then, Maddock recalled that Friendship was one of the soldiers sent with Brother Honesty.

Skull's long-fingered hands crushed the air in front of him as if curling around a throat. "One of the Marchlanders had a sword and knew how to use it. He killed Wraith. Killed Virtue and Courage. And that bastard, Friendship, crawled away and left Brother Honesty alone and unprotected."

Distressed and confused, Maddock shook his head. "How do you know that?"

"Because—" Skull paused and seemed to struggle for control. "Because I can read thoughts. Sometimes. And Friendship just got close enough for me to pick up." Again, he pointed away from camp. "He's about fifty yards in that direction, dying from blood loss."

Commander Swift rounded on the Mage. "Friendship's wounded? Why didn't you say that from the start?"

Skull gestured savagely. "Because it doesn't matter! One way or another, he's dead!"

Swift turned on his heel, snapping out more orders. As the men hurried to obey, the camp came alive with activity. The commander whirled on the Horsemaster's son. "Maddock."

The young man jerked to attention. "Yes, sir?"

Swift thrust a finger toward Skull. "He's under arrest. Keep him in camp. If he tries to leave or attempts to work magic, kill him."

Maddock nodded and drew his sword. "Yes, sir."

The commander shot Skull a flinty glance. "I'll deal with you later." He turned and headed off toward Friendship, with two swordsmen following.

Gripping his hilt in both hands, Maddock fixed his gaze on Skull. He wondered if he stood a chance against the Hooded Mage.

Skull's voice was tired-sounding, used up. "No. You don't. Your orders are impossible to obey."

"Don't be too sure."

Skull sighed. "Let's not engage in a pointless argument."

Maddock frowned but nodded. "Do you think Brother Honesty's all right?"

Skull slid his hands into his long, fine hair. "No. I think he's dead."

Pain lanced Maddock's heart. "You don't know that."

"It's a logical assumption. He had no weapon, would not even try to defend himself. Do you really think his intended victims might spare him?"

Choking on welling grief, Maddock clenched his jaw.

Skull regarded the young man coldly. "Just how many of your people carry swords? I thought it was forbidden."

Maddock thought about Lord Stane and the desperate villagers of Radway Green. "Some of—" He paused and cleared his throat. "Some of the older men remember their war training."

Skull did not seem to hear him. "I would have died to save him, you know. I should have been with Brother Honesty. Not Wraith."

Though Maddock felt the same, he groped for solace and understanding. "But now he's with the One Light."

Skull's narrow features tightened. "I don't believe in the One Light. I don't believe in the Abomination."

But—"

"I believed in Brother Honesty." Skull looked at the sky and closed his eyes. "Now . . . there is nothing. Nothing."

Maddock abruptly shivered, warned by instinct, and raised his sword.

With a swish of black robes, Claw darted under the blade. The Mage snatched a fistful of Skull's robes, jerked him off-balance, and delivered a cracking right cross to his jaw.

Skull sprawled sidelong to the ground and lay still.

Maddock whirled toward Claw and found this Mage's hood had also fallen back. She shook curly hair from her face and regarded him fiercely. "Well? Think I was just going to stand there? You were both about to do something stupid."

"You—" Maddock's sword arm sagged. "You're a woman."

Claw's eyes glinted. "That's right, pony-boy."

Skull rolled to his back and moaned.

Claw set her foot on his throat. "Behave yourself, or I'll get rough."

The fallen Mage opened his eyes and gingerly flexed his jaw.

Claw looked down at Skull. "Is it broken?"

Skull's voice was husky. "Don't think so."

"Pity."

Maddock forced his tightened muscles to relax. Taking a wary step back, he glanced around at the other men in camp. The few who dared to look in their direction wore grim expressions, and the young man considered what the loss of Brother Honesty meant to the mission. Without the priest, they had no hope of battling the Abomination.

Skull looked at Maddock, his eyes dull. "Nothing," he whispered. "Nothing."

⌘

Maddock perched uncomfortably on a folding stool in the commander's tent while Swift paced with his hands clasped behind his back. "He was still alive when Friendship escaped. If the

Marchlanders didn't kill Brother Honesty, what would they do with him?"

Maddock tried to put himself in the place of the group of strangers with whom the priest had gone to deal. "Depends on who was hurt and how much they wanted revenge for the attack."

Swift made a thoughtful noise. "Would they question him? Put him to torture?"

Maddock recoiled. "No!"

Swift paused and raised his fair brows. "Really?"

The young man drew a steadying breath. "Not themselves," he said reluctantly. "They would probably take him to their Lady. And if he didn't answer her questions, then the priests of the Joyous Reunion would—" A horrid image sprang to mind of gentle Brother Honesty flayed by the whip.

Swift nodded and resumed his restless prowl around the tent. "The good Brother would resist to his death rather than talk, I'm certain of it. But we need him alive."

Maddock's heart lightened at the thought of rescuing Brother Honesty. "It was only a small group, traveling the backcountry, wasn't it? We could ride out and take them, sir, before they made their way to the nearest fort."

"Except that they have a powerful magic-wielder with them, not to mention the Abomination." Swift tilted his head as he paced. "The attack on Radway Green was risky enough. We can't afford to completely imperil our mission." He turned on one heel, striding in the opposite direction. "We were sent to establish forward supply bases and to garner what allies we could to blunt the expansion of the lords of the south—until we ran into the Abomination. We have to retain whatever's left of our secrecy."

A sudden thought struck Maddock. "Then only send one man out, sir."

"One man?"

"Me."

Swift stopped and gave the Horsemaster's son a measuring stare.

Maddock struggled to marshal his reasons. "I'm a pretty good tracker. I could find the target group, see if Brother Honesty's still alive. And if I'm caught, they won't be suspicious of me."

Swift continued to study him silently.

"Please, sir. Let me try."

The commander looked away. "On one condition: That you do not attempt to make contact with the group. I can't afford to lose you to the Abomination. Simply assess the situation from a distance and return to make your report."

Maddock drew a breath.

"Think before you answer," Swift said quietly. "If you discover that Brother Honesty's a prisoner, you must not attempt to rescue him yourself. Understand?"

Maddock rose to his feet. "Yes, sir. Understood, sir."

Swift finally turned, and a smile softened his youthful face. "Good man. I know I can trust you."

Maddock straightened his shoulders. "Thank you, sir. I won't fail you."

❧

Tynan sat on the bank of the Coney and watched its clean, vigorous waters tumble past, ferrying bark chips, leaves, and pinecones in its current. Sarn Moor lay only a few days' travel to the east, and the young man ached with homesickness. He longed to see his brothers again, to walk the rooms of the House and converse with folk he had known since childhood. The summer horse fair would begin any day, and Tynan wanted to stroll, hobbled to Kiarda, through crowds of kin and romping children. The danger of the Mage from across the sea seemed dilute and distant, despite the vivid images of death anchored in memory. Strengthened by nearness and nostalgia, ties of blood seemed enough. They already planned to go to Sarn Moor. Their warnings might go unappreciated and unheeded, but they owed it to their families to try to rescue them from their own folly. He glanced over his shoulder at the camp.

Among the trees, Gaer instructed Adan in a point of swordsmanship. Bevin groomed Buttercup where she grazed among the other horses, clearly trying to create a bond where it would probably never exist. A well-mannered "teacher" horse would better suit the healer's level of competence. Buttercup needed a rider who would take control. Kiarda was gone, roaming the woods in fox-shape, which bothered Tynan more than anything. Logically, he understood Bevin's arguments: that Kiarda had gained enough control to avoid another coupling, that their enemies would never recognize her in this form, and that she needed occasional time alone to fully command and dominate the fox's instincts. Emotionally, however, he hovered on a razor's edge of panic.

Pleasure tingled through Tynan suddenly, raw and glaring contrast to the terror and aching in his heart. *Cat, what are you doing?* Tynan glanced around for his link-mate as rapture trembled through him in coarse waves. He found Brother Honesty perched on an overhang downriver, staring into the water with the same intensity as Tynan. His hands stroked something unseen in the crook of his crossed legs, dislodging a storm of orange-and-white hairs. Tynan started to rise, then settled back into position. The more insistent he grew about moving the cat, the more determined the animal would become about staying. He knew Furry Purry, who now referred to himself as Cat-Who-Conquers-Mages, would tire of the game now that he had apparently won over Brother Honesty's affection. The tabby always preferred attention from people who disliked cats.

⁓❦⁓

Perched on a high bank overlooking the Coney, Brother Honesty reveled in the patterns of light shimmering from the rushing waters, so like the bright glitters thrown by the diamond in his ring. Stroking the ginger tom's warm fur brought a comfort he would not have believed possible when he had bounced in a weathered saddle that poorly fit the swaybacked packhorse. Even moments ago, the soreness of his backside would have taken precedence over any other feeling. Now, the threading of his fingers through silken fur and the gentle curve of muscle beneath became an almost sensual pleasure. The cat's obvious delight only added to the strange experience.

Near Brother Honesty's left foot, movement stirred the

gravel. Gingerly, Furry Purry stepped from his lap to explore this new abstraction. The priest watched as the animal approached the area with cautious precision. The cat had nearly reached the spot when a green frog freckled with black jumped toward the water. Furry Purry crouched, watching, still except for a white tip of tail that flopped like a dying snake in the crush of brown grasses.

Brother Honesty brushed shed hairs from his robe.

Suddenly, Furry Purry pounced, gliding like a bird before landing lightly on the edge of the overhang. The frog shot through his paws, plummeting into the river with a tiny splash. An instant later, the bank crumbled beneath the cat, and he toppled over the side amidst a gritty shower of dirt.

Shocked to his feet, Brother Honesty scrambled toward the edge just as the orange body struck the water with a yowl of terror. Almost in concert, Tynan screamed. A wave fountained from the impact, droplets stinging Brother Honesty's face. The cat bobbed to the surface, desperately paddling.

Without thought, Brother Honesty leaped over the side of the overhang to the lower, graveled bank. The water swept Furry Purry downstream, spinning him in wild, helpless circles. The burble of the river drowned the details of Tynan's shouts and muted the voices of his companions to a frantic hubbub. Brother Honesty charged ahead of the current, debris crunching beneath his sandals, wildly scanning the river for a solution. The water became a gray blur of movement. Trees shot past, seemingly endless bars of brown. Then, he found a large branch wedged in the waters nearly from bank to bank, slimy with trapped water weeds and debris. Veering toward it, he finally dared to look back. The cat spiraled toward him, paws chopping madly through the current.

Hold on! Brother Honesty sprang for the jam. His foot came down hard on a jagged stone. Pain shot through his ankle. Balance lost, he stumbled, momentum carrying him toward the wedged branch. He plunged to the ground, gravel stamping bruises across his chest. A twig abraded his cheek, missing his eye by a finger's breadth. He half-crawled, half-staggered onto the bottleneck, wildly hoping it could support his weight. Bleary-eyed, he sought the cat. He found nothing but surging water. "Cat?" The roar of the river drowned his call. "Cat!"

A tiny form bobbed toward him, no longer fighting the current. Bracing his feet, Brother Honesty leaned as far out over the racing waters as he dared. The cat swirled toward him. His heart quickened as it approached, now three body lengths from him, then two, one. Abruptly, the cat disappeared beneath the surface.

Tynan's shriek came from nearer than Brother Honesty expected. A clamor of voices followed. He heard footsteps slam down onto the nearby gravel of the bank.

Without bothering to see who had nearly reached him, Brother Honesty launched himself from the snag to a spot just downriver from where he'd last seen the cat. Water closed around him, a thick, cold hindrance. He groped blindly through the depths, covering as much area as possible, worried the ginger tomcat might tumble past without his knowledge. His hand struck something solid and fuzzy, knocking it askew. He dove for the object. His chest struck the surface, splattering water and grit into his eyes. His hands closed over the limp and furry body as his legs glided upward. Caught by the river, he struggled to right himself without daring to release his burden. The current claimed his head unexpectedly, and he choked water into his lungs. Gasping and sputtering, he raised the cat and tried to kick to the surface. The river proved stronger. Without hands, he could not battle it. Reluctantly, he prepared to release the animal.

At that moment, strong hands wrested the cat from Brother Honesty's grip. Freed, the priest churned with his hands. Limbs from the snag tore at his skin, and his fingers glided through trapped sludge. His robe wound into the branches, holding him under. He kicked wildly, wrestling the current. Then, more hands had him, and Adan's placid voice filled Brother Honesty's hearing. "Easy. I've got you. It's all right." He guided the priest's grip to solid boughs.

Brother Honesty wrapped his hands around the bark, noticing the numbing chill only as his upper body consistently contacted the air. Adan meticulously freed the priest's robe from the branches. On the upper bank, Tynan paced and wrung his hands, talking incessantly to the still, furry bundle wrapped in Gaer's cloak. The Swordmaster planted himself between the young man and the water as if he worried that Tynan might throw himself into the river as well. Bevin knelt over the creature, stroking it with her hands and, presumably, her magic.

Brother Honesty studied his own hands. They trembled, the fingers pale, almost blue, with cold. A whiter band of skin encircled the finger where the diamond of the One Light had once sparkled. Horror shivered through him. *Lost.* He could not help groping for an answer. Perhaps the Light had stripped him of his priesthood for placing the life of a filthy-habited animal above his own. *I should have let the cat die, should have rescued Tynan from his curse.* Guilt prickled the edges of his consciousness. The priest glanced toward the frantic young man stalking the upper bank and realized something which banished that discomfort for a worse one. If Furry Purry fell into the river tomorrow, he would do nothing different.

Adan held out his arms. Brother Honesty leaned toward his benefactor, allowing the oldest brother of Sarn Moor to heft him, dripping, from the snag. He wrapped his own cloak around the priest. "Thank you . . . Brother."

"My child." Brother Honesty huddled into the proffered cloak, trembling with cold. "It is *I* who should thank *you.*"

"No." Adan placed an arm around Brother Honesty and helped him up the graveled bank. "If you saved that cat, you also rescued my brother."

"I . . . I don't understand." In his own mind, the priest could see only the opposite, that allowing the cat to die might have released Tynan from his bestial ties to the Abomination.

"Wait here just a moment, please." Adan dashed over to Tynan and the others.

Unable to hear their exchange, Brother Honesty pulled Adan's cloak more tightly around himself. And waited. Mercifully, the cold stole his attention from brooding. Tonight, he would have much to think about. In the meantime, he wanted nothing but to warm himself before his senses surrendered to the chill. Shivers wracked him until his teeth rattled together.

Leaving the others to tend to the spirit-linked, Adan herded Brother Honesty back toward the camp and the fire. "Have you never heard of couples so devoted that when one dies the other suicides? Or withers away with grief? Have you never seen a parent throw himself on a child's pyre?"

Unable to think clearly, Brother Honesty could not fathom the purpose of Adan's questions. "I saw such a thing not too long ago, my child. An elderly husband and wife married longer than forty years. When she died, he deliberately followed her." Brother Honesty locked his gaze on the cheery red flame dancing between the trees. Soon, he would enjoy its warmth. "Suicide grieves the One Light."

"I'm not asking you to condone it." Adan guided Brother Honesty into the clearing, and the horses whinnied a greeting. "Only to understand it. The bond between the spirit-linked is as strong and loving as the longest human relationship. If that cat had drowned, it is unlikely we could have stopped Tynan from killing himself for long." He winced, and pain flashed through his eyes.

Even as Brother Honesty hustled to sit on a deadfall drawn near the fire, he did not miss Adan's discomfort. Clearly, the young man had observed something similarly ugly. "One of the darker parts of the Abomination." Despite his words, he suffered a strange sensation of closeness to Tynan and the cat. The young lord should feel grateful, and perhaps he did, but Brother Honesty found himself awash with a sense of gratitude to them that bordered on indebtedness. He could not fathom its source. "Surely now you understand why we want to save others from exposure to it."

Adan grimaced, then said patiently, "Spirit-links don't work that way. People are born with the gift you call abominable. They don't catch it like the pox."

The fire's warmth proved even more welcome than Brother Honesty anticipated. He shifted closer. "So the cat will live?"

"Bevin believes she can save it."

Brother Honesty allowed a tight-lipped nod, still uncertain what he thought about the matter. All of his experience and knowledge told him he would have done the world a favor had he allowed the cat, and even Tynan, to die. Yet, he could not banish the feeling of ultimate goodness that comes of rescuing another human from death.

Adan dipped his head to study the priest's face. "You successfully risked your life to save a man. But you don't look too happy about it."

Brother Honesty lowered his head further, out of Adan's new line of sight. True to his name, he spoke the truth, though he knew it would hurt. "I'm not certain I did the right thing."

Adan jerked upright. "Saving my brother was not the right thing?"

Brother Honesty sighed, wishing he had the words to overcome a lifetime of ignorant savagery. He would likely never convince Adan of the danger the Abomination posed to his world and his people, could only try to protect him from it. All their lives, the Marchlanders believed in their gods and their so-called gifts. He could not overcome their lack of knowledge in a single speech. He stared at his left hand, without its flashing diamond for the first time since his novitiate. He felt naked without it. "I like Tynan, but . . ." He trailed off with a shake of his head, seeking a way to explain without trivializing the young man's existence. A remembered detail fueled his argument. "My child, if this Abomination . . . this gift from your gods . . . is not contagious, how do you explain Lady Kiarda's budding link?"

Adan sighed, clearly as frustrated as Brother Honesty by his inability to make his position clear. "As I've told you several times, her link started at the time of her birth in a fort too far from Sarn Moor to allow the easy spread of disease—"

Brother Honesty raised his head and spread his hands, rescuing Adan from the need for further repetition. The argument had grown very familiar and very old. "Let me make sure I understand. Lady Kiarda's link actually began at birth but didn't manifest until a year or so ago."

"It would seem that way."

"She thought she was going mad. She suffered memory losses, discovered herself to be with child, accused an innocent retainer of ravishment, denied a true friendship, then gave birth to deformed and stillborn twins."

A nod.

"And this is a blessing? Of your gods?"

Adan sighed. "Kiarda's situation is unique. Her link was damaged."

Brother Honesty continued to press. "And your gods . . . allowed this to happen?"

The dark brows rose suddenly. Adan seemed startled. "Why not? They allow all sorts of terrible things to happen." He tapped the scarred half of his face. "You think I was born this way? If I asked you why your all-powerful One Light permitted this disfigurement, what would you tell me?"

Brother Honesty's soft blue eyes gleamed with obvious pleasure. "I would ask you what good had come of it."

Adan's voice gained a hint of anger. "What good?"

The priest slipped his hands up his sleeves. "Did you become stronger? Did you learn ways of making people see past your appearance, of overcoming obstacles? Did you learn skills to compensate for a lack of personal allure?"

Adan smiled sourly. "Had to, didn't I?"

Brother Honesty tilted his head. "And so tell me, my child. What good has come of Lady Kiarda's damaged link?"

Tynan's voice broke in, "What's that supposed to mean?"

Brother Honesty whipped his head toward the sound.

Tynan strode to the fire, the tomcat soaked but alive in his arms. "It's a miracle that Kiarda's link didn't break, that she didn't die moments after her birth." He arranged the cat in front of the fire. "Kiarda's alive. That's a great goodness."

The argument, though strong, skirted the issue.

Bevin and Gaer gathered gear.

Recovering from his startlement, Brother Honesty pressed, refusing to weaken his point by stopping just because one of the main objects of it arrived. "Is it such a goodness, my child? Isn't she, at this moment, imprisoned in animal form, at the mercy of base instincts?"

Tynan moved to stand over the priest. "Why base? Why not noble? After all, people are animals, too."

The priest shook his head. "Last night, your cat was catching and eating crickets. Did you share in that experience?"

Tynan shrugged. "Of course."

"And did you, my child, enjoy the savor of insects?"

Tynan winced. "As long as I didn't think about it too much, yes. They taste a bit like beef liver."

Adan chuckled. "How delicious."

Tynan shook his head with obvious impatience. "Simply finding something distasteful doesn't make it evil. But you claim the spirit-link is evil."

"The Abomination is a vile corruption that grows and spreads, devouring everything it touches." The customary words left Brother Honesty's mouth without need for thought.

Tynan lifted his hand, attention on the ginger tom rolling in the dirt to place his belly toward the fire. "Spirit-links don't spread. In fact, they're rare. They've occurred among us for as far back as anyone can remember. If they're so contagious, why isn't everyone in the Marchlands linked to an animal?"

Why indeed? Tynan had an undeniable point, though Brother Honesty found himself thinking of other diseases that cycled, seeming to disappear for seasons or years then ravishing hundreds of people in months. Brother Honesty caught himself studying Tynan with the fondness of a father, still unable to escape the weird and invisible bond that had formed between them since the moment he discovered he had saved, not just the life of a cat, but of a young man as well. But, when he withdrew his gaze, it fell upon his empty finger.

Following the priest's attention with what seemed like astounding insight, Adan spoke quietly. "Is it because you lost your priesthood ring that you think your god does not approve of your actions?"

Brother Honesty would not lie. "My child, the One Light speaks to me in unusual ways."

Adan rose. "Then, perhaps you can explain this." He thrust a hand into his pocket, then emerged with the ring in his outstretched palm. Its encounter with the Coney seemed not to have damaged it at all. In fact, it seemed to shine more brightly for the washing.

"Where . . ." Brother Honesty latched his awareness on the ring, joy adding internal heat to the drying warmth of the fire. ". . . where did you find it?"

Adan dragged out the suspense, pacing several steps before whirling to face Brother Honesty. "On the paw of . . ." he jabbed a finger toward Furry Purry, ". . . your so-called creature of the Abomination."

Tynan started to speak, silenced by Adan's sudden glare. Gaer raised a hand to cover a conspiratorial smile. Bevin's expression turned quizzical, but she did not ruin Adan's farce.

Mostly unaccustomed to deceit, Brother Honesty missed the cues. *A miracle. An undeniable sign.* He could not imagine any logical or physical way that such a thing might have happened. The One Light must have played a part, and the message seemed irrefutable.

Gaer dropped the last pack onto the pile. "We're here until Lady Kiarda returns. Might I suggest a nap? Better to push on well rested."

Brother Honesty followed the Swordmaster's gaze to Tynan. Wrinkles lined the youth's mouth, his skin had turned sickly pale and his eyes looked peaked. His link–mate's ordeal had clearly affected him. "A good idea," the priest said, though he knew he could not sleep. He had too much to think about.

⋘⧏⋙

Crouched in the hollow of a rotting tree trunk, the vixen studied the strange man. He did not come from the safe-warm-food place, though like those other men, he smelled of horses and woodsmoke. He was sitting on the ground, eating bread. The vixen licked her teeth. She liked bread.

The man did not move. Warily, the vixen crept from her hiding place, holding her bushy tail low. If she sneaked close enough, she might find crumbs. The other men always let crumbs fall.

The man turned and met her gaze. The vixen froze. Images, sounds, and feelings flashed through her: memories of walking on two legs, using hands, speaking. She knew this man.

Maddock's dark eyes brightened, and he slowly extended a hand. "Hello, little lass."

Kiarda could not move. The past surged through her, sweeping away the previous year's pain and returning her to a lifetime of love. She wanted to say his name but could only emit a high-pitched whine.

Maddock chuckled softly. "Don't be afraid. I won't hurt you." He broke off a piece of bread and held it out to her. "Here, my lass. Hungry?"

Kiarda longed to run to him, hold him tightly, and weep into his neck. *I'm sorry. I'm so sorry. It was all my fault.*

Maddock's black hair hung longer than she recalled, falling past his shoulders like midnight transformed to silk. His fine features had grown more weathered and he bore a new scar on his chin, but his eyes were the same, still reflecting a spirit as wild and pure as mountain wind. Smiling, Maddock broke a smaller piece off the bread and tossed it to her. "Here, my lass. Eat it. It's good."

Only at that moment did Kiarda fully realize she wore a fox's shape. Her own identity remained clear to her, but she also maintained awareness of her spirit-link, the animal portion of herself. The fox-half was confused and anxious, and keenly interested in the bit of food that lay in the dirt. Kiarda sent the creature soothing thoughts and permitted the fox to move to the tidbit. Keeping her eyes on Maddock, she gobbled up the bread.

Maddock laughed under his breath and spoke in a caressing tone. "You like that, don't you?" He again held out the bread. "Here's more, if you want, my lass."

Kiarda thought her heart would break. [[Maddock. Maddock, it's me. Kiarda.]]

"Come, come, don't cry. I won't hurt you. I would never hurt such a pretty little lady."

[[I know. I was wrong about you. We all were.]]

With unconscious sensuality, Maddock pressed the wad of bread to his lips and mouthed it, pretending to eat it. Then he held it out toward her again. "Delicious," he said in a coaxing voice. "Have some more."

The vixen wanted the offered tidbit, but the young woman within her resisted the impropriety. The resulting conflict weakened the tenuous unity of her identity. Kiarda felt her hold on the fox-shape begin to slip. *No! I can't shift now!*

"Come on," Maddock teased gently. "I know you want it."

Desperate to keep her animal form, Kiarda slowly padded toward Maddock. Trying not to think about how close she stood to him, or how near his fingers were to her mouth, she began to nibble the bread.

"Good lass," Maddock murmured, his breath stirring warmly in her ears. His free hand stole toward the white fur at her throat. "Will you let me stroke you?"

Kiarda shied from his touch, knowing she would lose all control.

"No?" Maddock laughed indulgently. "Well, quite right. 'Tisn't proper. Forgive me, little lady."

Kiarda's hold on the fox-shape became even more shaky. Alarmed, she backed away. She had to leave him, or the unthinkable would occur. [[I'm sorry, Maddock. I can't stay.]]

"Don't go," Maddock begged softly. "I didn't mean to frighten you."

Heart aching, Kiarda hesitated. Her vision blurred, and she thought, at first, her eyes had filled with tears. Then, with horror, she realized the change had begun. [[No!]]

❦

Kiarda awakened slowly. First, she became aware of lying prone on the ground. Then, she realized a blanket covered her. *Thank the gods. I made it back to camp.*

Someone stirred nearby. Kiarda raised her head and brushed auburn hair from her eyes. "Bevin?"

Maddock stood a few yards away with his back to her. He spoke in a thick voice, "Are you covered?"

Sick with shame and despair, Kiarda sat up and wrapped the blanket around herself. "Yes."

Maddock turned cautiously, then stood motionless, regarding her with an unreadable expression.

"I didn't—" Tears stung. "I didn't mean for it to happen this way."

Maddock finally moved, looking away from her to the surrounding woods. "What are you doing out here?"

"I—" Kiarda swallowed. "I was looking for you. To tell you—to beg you—to forgive me."

Maddock lowered his black brows. "Forgive you?"

Kiarda's hands twisted in her lap. She had rehearsed this moment in her mind for weeks, planning exactly what to say. Now that the moment had come, she could not recall a word of it. "Last winter. When you found me—"

Maddock's voice turned harsh. "I saved your life."

Wounded by his tone, Kiarda nodded, one tear trickling down her cheek. He had a perfect right to be angry. "Yes, I know."

"I saved your life," Maddock repeated implacably. "And you destroyed mine!"

Kiarda gazed at Maddock helplessly, unable to speak.

Maddock folded his arms. "And you can stop weeping. It doesn't fool me."

Kiarda sniffed and wiped her cheek, but more tears began to roll. "I'm not trying to fool you. Everything that happened was a terrible mistake, everything was—" Her voice shook uncontrollably, and she paused to regain some measure of composure. "I have a strange spirit-link that makes me change into a fox. It started to manifest last winter, but I didn't know what was happening. I couldn't remember—"

Maddock turned away. "And so you accused me of—"

"No!" Kiarda blurted. "I didn't accuse you. The healers, my parents, told me what you did." She amended. "What they *thought* you did. And I had nothing else to believe."

Maddock swept his hand through the air in a furious gesture. "I would never have harmed you!" He whirled to glare at her. "I loved you, Kiarda! I loved you so much I—" He broke off abruptly, shaking his head. "But I kept my place. It wasn't proper for the Horsemaster's son to yearn for the future Lady."

"You loved me?" Kiarda repeated faintly. She felt as if a shaft of light had pierced her heart, the sweet joy and the searing pain indistinguishable. "Why didn't you ever tell me?"

Maddock's tone went bitter. "Would it have done any good?"

"Yes." Kiarda found herself laughing shakily. "It would have changed everything."

Maddock's mouth tightened. "Really? How? Would you have married me, and come to live in the stables?"

Kiarda wiped her cheeks and took a steadying breath. "No, I would have married you and made you future Lord of Dorlach Tor."

Maddock made an impatient noise. "You mock me."

"No."

Maddock stiffened. "My lady, your parents would never have given their consent."

Kiarda blinked in surprise. "Do you think I have their consent to be out scouring the Marchlands?" She stood up, holding the blanket in place. "Maddock, you know how stubborn I can be. Do you really suppose I'd let anyone or anything stop me from marrying you?"

Maddock reddened, the anger draining from his expression, and he stepped back. "Kiarda—"

She could not lift her gaze from him, drinking in the way he moved, the way light struck his hair, the flash of unspoken thought in his eyes. "Maddock, I'm so sorry for everything. Come home with me to Dorlach Tor. We'll find a way to —"

Maddock spoke with sudden gentleness. "No."

"But I need your forgiveness. I need—"

"No," Maddock said, smiling sadly. "Too much has changed."

Stricken, Kiarda fought to keep her voice steady. "And so . . . this is it? This is how it ends?"

"Yes." Maddock tilted his head. "I've learned to face the consequences of my actions. You should, too."

Kiarda recoiled. "Why else do you think I'm out here, looking for you?"

Maddock turned, then paused without looking back. "Keep the blanket. I'll sleep in my cloak."

"Maddock!"

"Go home, Kiarda." Maddock strode off into the trees and was gone.

Kiarda clutched the blanket to her. "Home," she whispered. Bread crumbs lay on the ground at her feet, broken and soiled. She tried to weep, but her tears, now summoned, failed her. Nothing remained but to do as he said. And return home.

CHAPTER TWENTY-ONE

S ORROW weighted Kiarda's shoulders like a lead mantle, and each of Snow Bell's solid hooffalls seemed to drag her deeper into despair. Maddock's words cycled endlessly through her memory: "I've learned to face the consequences of my actions. You should, too." The events of the last few months haunted her ever more strongly as they rode past familiar landmarks on the route to Sarn Moor: the babies she had hated, then cherished and lost; the man she had desired and destroyed; the mangled spirit bond that would leave her forever incomplete and longing.

Maddock's revelation, that he had loved her, too, struck a blow as devastating as any of the horrors that now seemed to define Kiarda's life. She pictured his wild mane of black hair, dark eyes full of unbridled spirit, and the lithe, well-muscled frame. Recent experience seemed to have turned his proud, wild nature coarse, bitter, and spiteful. And she had no one to blame but herself. *Oh, Maddock. I'm so sorry.* She could not stop dreaming about how differently things might have turned out had she only guessed his feelings for her, had she only expressed hers for him, had she only known of the damaged link. *If . . . if . . . if . . . I've learned to face the consequences of my actions. You should, too.*

Kiarda's companions gave up trying to draw her from her dark considerations as the Great House of Sarn Moor became intermittently visible through gaps in the foliage. Occasionally, an excited roar reached their ears, a crowd's response to a clever or dangerous trick or an unexpectedly high price paid for a horse or its training. Memories of past horse fairs flooded Kiarda's mind. She had always preferred the summer ones: cool breezes fluttering through her hair, drying sweat; fresh juices she missed during the colder months; the sweet hint of *sprirranin*, a rare spice that grew only in late spring, in the cakes. For a moment, she imagined herself strolling through the streets of Sarn Moor, horse sweat in her nostrils and a hobble clenched tightly in her fist. She tried to picture Tynan at the other end, but her mind conjured images only of Maddock.

Tynan had gone as quiet and sullen as his betrothed, hands twitching in clear agitation. The cat perched on Storm Cloud's withers, a paw across the saddlebow for support. Though surely Gaer worried for his reception, the urbane Swordmaster appeared composed. The wind fluttered his silver hair into streamers, and his posture remained elegantly poised. Brother Honesty rode the packhorse, hunched over withers made prominent by its swayed back, and glanced from one companion to another in obvious distress. He had neither the time, position, nor means to address their sorrows, and that clearly grieved him. Bevin and Adan conversed softly at the back of the group.

Gradually, the sounds of the horse fair grew clearer. Children squealed with unabashed glee. Men and women laughed, and merchants competed for attention in loud superlatives that carried into the woodlands. Occasionally, a horse snort or whinny reached them. Gaer's horse, Mannered, answered with a sudden trumpet that shocked Kiarda from her thoughts. The Swordmaster reined, then bowed suavely from his saddle, first to Kiarda, then Tynan, and lastly Adan. "My lady. My lords. I believe we'll meet enough hostility without prisoners, no matter how pleasant and gently handled."

Every eye turned to Brother Honesty, who seemed unruffled by the abrupt attention. He ran a dirty-nailed hand through his mouse brown hair. "I will stay where you ask until you or others come for me."

Silence followed Brother Honesty's vow.

Gaer dismounted. "My lady?"

Fully jarred from her thoughts, Kiarda jerked toward Gaer, only to find him studying her mildly. "I don't—I mean I . . ." She trailed off, considering the situation. "I'm certain no amount of questioning will break Brother Honesty's silence on matters of his people, and I see no reason to subject him to our priests." Recollection of the priest's brutality to her father flared Kiarda's nostrils. Brother Honesty's knowledge might prove invaluable, but she refused to obtain cooperation through torture. She paused, feeling generous toward the helpful and willing prisoner who had saved Tynan's life. "What if we just . . . released him?"

Gaer performed a beautiful gesture of deference and turned his gaze to Tynan who stared off toward Sarn Moor, apparently oblivious to the conversation. The cat had moved to his leg, and he stroked the striped fur absently. The Swordmaster edged his head back to Kiarda. "Were you seeking *my* opinion, my lady?"

The query forced Kiarda to realize she should practice allowing her future husband some say in matters of import. "Yes, Gaer, I was."

"Thank you, my lady." The armsman bowed. "I think, perhaps, we should discuss Brother Honesty's disposition privately." He inclined his head toward a copse of low bushes.

Still startlingly cooperative, Brother Honesty nodded. "It seems easier for me to move than all of you." He clambered stiffly from the packhorse, passing the reins to Gaer. Then, without a backward glance, he edged beyond hearing range, though still within their sight.

Gaer waited barely a moment before speaking. "My lady, we may need Brother Honesty to convince Culan and Lord Stane of the existence of this enemy."

"Indeed." Adan's scarred features twisted in a dubious expression. He deferred to Gaer's superior knowledge of their enemy, phrasing his concern into a question. "Couldn't we also use him as a hostage, to bargain with his people?"

"Probably not, my lord. A priest would have little or no status among Imperial forces."

Finally attentive, Tynan raised a different sort of argument. "Surely their army has moved by now. What if he can't survive long enough to find them?"

Bevin massaged a thigh that surely ached from the ride. "The Mages might be able to track him. . . ."

"It seems to me," Adan added, "that Brother Honesty could determine whether or not he could find his people for himself."

Now Gaer seemed lost in consideration.

Certain the armsman would have something significant to say, Kiarda pressed. "Gaer? Your thoughts, please."

Gaer stroked Mannered's side. "My lady, I believe Brother Honesty's time with us has had an effect on him. I'm sure we could sway him toward a peaceful solution. If he *can* find his people, he could pave the way for a parley."

Tynan pounced on the contradiction, "But you said priests had no power among Imperial forces."

"No official power, my lord," Gaer agreed. "But they're always good talkers. He couldn't barter for them, probably wouldn't work as a hostage, but he just might get them to listen. *Before* they attack."

Adan nodded. "And, if he does have a way to find his people, it might be worth secretly following him."

"My lord, an excellent idea." Gaer expertly applied the compliment before expressing his concerns. "It would have to be done with very small numbers and in a cautious manner by the right person, to keep from worsening rather than assisting the situation."

As the conversation reached its natural conclusion, attention gravitated to Kiarda, who desperately wished for some way to guess the future. "You've made this very difficult. Especially when the one I trust most in this matter has argued both sides."

Gaer cringed, then executed a bow even more formal than usual. "My apologies, my lady. It's not a straightforward situation with an evident solution." Surely he realized she wanted him to make the decision, but propriety would not allow it. "If you do choose to release him, I would advise that you elicit his current opinion on our people and the spirit-link. He can only spur peace if he truly believes in it."

"What if he lies?" Tynan glanced toward the copse.

"My lord," Gaer said. "I don't believe he can."

Waiting only until Brother Honesty glanced their way, Kiarda gestured him to them. As he trotted back, she studied his blue eyes and mild features, hoping for a clue. "We were wondering . . . how you feel about us . . . about the spirit-link . . . now."

Brother Honesty did not hesitate. "The One Light has caused our paths to cross for a reason." His gaze fell to the diamond on his finger. "Long ago, a wise friend called the spirit-link a harmless oddity, but I dismissed him as ignorant. I look forward to the day I have the opportunity to apologize."

Kiarda lowered her head. *Better to hope he accepts your apology.* She shook off a thought that could only cloud her judgment now. Hoping her original idea had been divinely inspired, she said, "You're free."

"Free?" Brother Honesty repeated, as if incapable of understanding the word. "But—" He glanced at Tynan, then shook his head. "Thank you, Lady Kiarda." Moving to the side of Bevin's horse, he clasped her foot, an impropriety he could not understand. She stiffened, sending her horse into a wary sidestep that rescued her from the priest's gentle touch. "Bevin, you have more strength, more integrity than anyone I've ever met. Please . . ." His tone turned almost pleading, "Please, don't let circumstance push you to darkness."

"I'll try," Bevin promised. "But you must entreat your people to turn from it as well."

"I will."

Gaer inclined his head toward Sarn Moor. "We should go now."

Adan dismounted, then moved to Bevin's horse to assist her. Cued by his brother, Tynan hurried to do the same for Kiarda. She did not wait for him but sprang to the ground and seized Snow Bell's bridle. "Let's go." She headed toward the village, the others trailing.

Adan spoke from behind Kiarda. "Bevin and I have been talking. We think it would be best to split up. Tynan, Bevin, and I will try to rouse Sarn Moor. You and Gaer find your parents."

The strategy made sense to Kiarda. To seek out one family before the other would cause insult. Furthermore, Bevin could protect Tynan should the need arise, and Gaer could shield her, at least from physical threats. Should she need magical defenses, Bevin would find her. "Sounds good. Let's do it."

The road to the village swerved, suddenly revealing it in vivid detail. The flags of myriad Marchland towns, villages, and steadings flew from the Great House, snapping in the summer wind. Tight rows of stands lined the main street, and gaily dressed people thronged the yards and roadways near the entrance. Two men hunched beneath a brown blanket, one sporting a yarn tail and the other inside a crafted horse head with soulful dark eyes. They danced, legs high-kicking while spectators clapped and shouted. Children ran, giggling, between the adults. Several courting couples marched proudly at either end of hobbles or stared at one another with coquettish fascination.

It was not until the brothers and Bevin headed into the crowd that a child spotted Kiarda and Gaer. Tugging on her mother's skirt, she indicated the two swords at the man's belt with an exaggerated gesture. The woman followed the child's motion, expression first congenial, then abruptly openmouthed with shock.

Gaer spoke softly, "I think it best to remind you, my lady. I might not be well-received."

Really? Kiarda kept the sarcasm to herself. Gaer would not appreciate it. "You belong with my family, Uncle Gaer. I'm sure my father will welcome you back."

"If you say so, my lady." Gaer did not sound convinced, but he would never argue with Kiarda. "Just, please, prepare yourself for the possibility of trouble."

The crowd parted around them as they walked through Sarn Moor's main street. Even the merchants stopped hawking their wares to stare at the pair. Everywhere they went, the happy noises died to nervous whispers, yet no one dared to stop them. Then, gradually, the crowd sorted itself out. The women and children disappeared behind a growing contingent of men. At length, Kiarda found the burly Sarn Moorian blacksmith in her path, side by side with Dorlach Tor's cooper, Iaian. She sidestepped to pass, only to find Gaer and herself surrounded. The Swordmaster flicked Mannered's reins over the bay's neck and wiped his hands casually on his trousers.

From Kiarda's left, the Stablemaster, Tormaigh, spoke. "My lady, your parents have worried desperately for you. Please step aside so we can take you to them and deal with the outcast."

Kiarda remained in place. "Gaer and I would speak to my parents together if you would only move aside and show us the way."

Murmurs followed, nothing Kiarda could sort. Gaer remained quietly at her side, but one hand found his hilt and the other hovered near the spare sword he had claimed from their enemies. That gesture, though not openly violent, stirred a sea of hostile and horrified glares. The only word Kiarda could make out was "blasphemy."

"Outcast," Tormaigh shouted over the hubbub. "You have disobeyed the terms of your sentence. Leave at once, or we will be forced to put you to death."

The threat stabbed Kiarda like a blade. She glanced worriedly at Gaer who seemed distinctly and oddly unconcerned. "I'm not leaving," he said. "So do as you must, young man."

Tormaigh's confidence evaporated into stammering. "I—I didn't mean myself—I mean I, who—?"

"I'll do it." A woman's voice cut clearly over the others, and the Hunt-Keeper, Gaina, stepped from behind the men. Shrugging her bow from one lithe shoulder, she reached for an arrow.

Gaer tensed, grip closing over his hilt.

"Wait!" Kiarda plunged between Gaer and Gaina, trusting their self-control too much to worry for her life. "You can't put a man to death without an order. I command you to put aside that bow!"

"She can if that man poses a threat to our people." Stane's commanding tone carried, and Kiarda sought her father amid the gathering. "I applaud your courage, Gaina. And I support it. If Gaer makes a move toward anyone, shoot him; but be careful not to harm my daughter."

Men stepped aside and returned, creating temporary paths in a wave that revealed Stane's every movement. Finally, he stepped in front of Sarn Moor's blacksmith. His blond hair lay in fine disarray, and his blue eyes glittered above the familiar small, well-defined features. His look softened as his attention fell upon Kiarda, and he made a slight motion toward her that seemed unconscious. "Kiarda, thank the gods you're not hurt." He turned to Gaer, and his jaw clenched. "Release my daughter and go. You're not welcome here."

"My lord, your daughter does not answer to me." Gaer raised his hands to demonstrate Kiarda's freedom. "But I will not go. Not until I've spoken my piece."

"We will not listen to the words of an outlaw."

"My lord," Gaer executed a flourishing bow, incongruous with his next words. "You leave me no choice but to make you listen." With unmistakable intention, he reached for the extra sword.

"My lord?" Gaina said. Kiarda heard the scrape of arrow against bow stave as the Hunt-Keeper drew.

Stane raised a stalling hand, gaze locked on Gaer.

Desperate, Kiarda grabbed Gaer's arm, blindly repositioning to foil Gaina's aim.

A collective gasp passed through the crowd.

Kiarda seized on their shock, raising the hand locked to Gaer's wrist. "Father, an army from across the sea devastated Radway Green. Gaer worries they might attack us next. He just wants to explain."

Now that Kiarda had the full attention of the gathered people, she addressed the detail that had gained her the opportunity to speak. "What's wrong? Haven't you ever seen a girl with her grandfather?" Though she usually called him "uncle," the spoken relationship fit better. He had always treated Wylfre as a favorite daughter.

"He's not your grandfather," Stane finally managed, though the more significant matter still hung in the air.

"He is," Kiarda insisted. "Closer than any of my blood." She released Gaer's arm. "There's no impropriety to a girl touching her grandfather."

"My lady, if I may," Gaer said softly.

Kiarda quieted to allow him to speak.

Gaer cleared his throat. "My lord, you will need this." He flung the spare sword to the ground at Stane's feet.

"My lord?" Gaina questioned more loudly.

Stane waved dismissively at the Hunt-Keeper. "Hold your fire." He made no attempt to retrieve the sword. "The priests told us the folk of Radway Green fell to bickering over the ascension of Conna's heir, that they abandoned the Divine Peace and fell victim to one another and the gods' retribution."

Gaer mulled Stane's words several moments, which was several moments longer than Kiarda believed necessary. "With all respect, my lord, I am certain the priests believe they speak the truth. But we've visited Radway Green. This was not the work of gods, but of men."

Stane paused nearly as long. "How do you know that?"

Kiarda clasped her hands together, hardly daring to hope. That her father asked for clarification, rather than dismissing Gaer's claim outright, suggested a willingness to listen objectively. Finally, it seemed, the priests' scourges might cost them Stane's loyalty.

"I know the stylings of the Empire, my lord." Gaer added with distaste, "and the work of the Hooded Order."

Doubtful frowns formed on many faces, and the majority of the men shook their heads. They would need more persuading than their leader.

Kiarda believed she held the key piece of information. "An army of strangers speaking a language I don't understand attacked us, including a magic-user wielding dark spells like the one that killed Elrin and the others."

Skepticism gave way to alarm. Stane's lips parted, though no sound emerged.

"If not for Uncle Gaer," Kiarda finished, "we would have died. He saved our lives." Suddenly, she fully understood why Gaer had not initially wished to release Brother Honesty. His presence alone might help convince them she spoke truth.

But Stane, at least, needed nothing further. Bending, he reached for the sword at his feet. His fingers closed over the hilt as if of their own will, and determination set his features. The crowd watched in silence as he approached Gaer.

Ignoring the bared steel, the Swordmaster knelt in front of the Lord of Dorlach Tor. It was a grand display of trust that brought tears to Stane's eyes. "Rise, old friend," he whispered, then choked out, "I've missed you."

The instant Gaer obeyed, Stane caught him into an embrace. Tears streamed from the Lord's eyes, sorrow long hidden behind a veil of righteous anger and layers of doctrine based on falsehood.

As Kiarda watched the display, she found her own vision blurred by tears. *If only forgiveness could be that easy for Maddock and me.* She shook the thought away. Gaer had much to teach, the men much to remember. And precious little time.

c⚬‰⚬

With Tynan and Bevin at his heels, Adan charged through the throng in Sarn Moor's streets, attention locked on the Great House to the exclusion of buildings and people familiar since childhood. He allowed nothing to distract him, refusing to acknowledge friends and relatives who attempted to question his disappearance or celebrate his return. After he had warned Culan of the invading army and assisted in mustering a defense force, he would apologize for his brusqueness to the survivors.

Even Tynan's touch did not draw Adan from his mission; though, a moment later, the impropriety of Bevin's gentle hand on his wrist did. He stopped, whirling toward her.

Bevin released Adan the instant he turned. Sandy curls fell in disarray around features flushed with exertion. "Furry Purry went after catmint someone practically waved in his face."

"Let him—" Adan started, but Bevin shook her head.

"I need them together to protect them."

With a sigh, Adan turned to return the way they had come, scanning the crowd for his brother and the fuzzy nuisance linked to him.

Bevin shoved Adan toward the Great House, and a homely woman in lace stared, bug-eyed, at the indiscretion. "You go on. I'll take care of Tynan."

But who will take care of you, my love, Adan started to protest, concerned that someone had deliberately separated him from his brother.

"The Mage is dangerously near. Go!"

Bevin's words had the opposite effect on Adan. He froze. "The enemy—"

"Go!" Bevin practically shouted. "I'm the only one who can handle the Mage. I'm of no use against the soldiers."

Despising his need, Adan obeyed, plunging back into the masses as he called a final warning. "My love, catch up as soon as you can." He did not await an answer.

Now Adan's inability to return the greetings of companions and cousins shifted from guilty discomfort to irritation. He wanted to flail through them, to trample those who delayed him, not caring whom he injured in the process. The moments they stole from his mission might mean the difference between life and death for too many innocents. *Bevin, do your best.*

The moment of distraction sent Adan careening into a massive man dressed in a dark cloak and reeking of alcohol. The impact hurled Adan backward, and he stumbled into someone behind him. Balance now wholly lost, he slammed, bottom first, to the cobbles. Pain shot up his spine, and he mumbled apologies in the general direction of those he had wronged. He started to rise.

A hand clamped to Adan's forearm. He glanced up to see who had chosen to assist him and now recognized Tassi's older brother, Rian. Light brown eyes studied him from beneath high-ridged brows, and a sneer twisted his thin lips. "Well, looky here," he slurred. "Look who dared to come back." His grip tensed painfully.

Adan tried to jerk away, but Rian's grip followed his motion, tightening further, fingers bruising and nails gouging flesh. He now realized the man behind him was Tassi's cousin, Vychan. His brother, Cyneath, stood in the shadows of the alley between the miller's home and business.

Sudden terror flashed through Adan. "Hey!"

Rian thrust Adan into the alley.

Adan stumbled, assailed by abrupt desperation. He swung wildly as the others converged on him. More fingers latched onto his arms, dragging him, kicking and swearing, from the main road. They all stank of too much ale.

"Quiet," Rian hissed. When Adan did not instantly obey, he plunged a fist into the young lord's face.

Pain exploded through Adan's cheek, and he drew a gasping breath. Momentum hurled him backward, into Cyneath's arms. Fear flared to outrage. "How dare you—"

"Where's the horn, Adan?" Rian demanded.

Adan staggered to his feet. "You're drunk." Infuriated by their manhandling, he would rather die than tell them.

Vychan seized Adan's pack and tore it open while his brother and cousin pinned Adan between them. Clothes spilled free. Foodstuffs, toiletries, linens, and silk tumbled into the mud.

Adan seethed, trying to recall Gaer's teachings. Abruptly, he stomped on Rian's foot.

Rian snapped out an oath, releasing Adan's arm. The eldest brother of Sarn Moor made a desperate leap for his things. Cyneath kicked him as he moved. Agony flashed through his leg. He collapsed onto his belongings, skidding wildly through filth. He rolled, only to find Rian on top of him, coarse features scarlet with rage. "I'll kill you, you ugly blackguard!" His fingers closed around Adan's throat.

Air disappeared. Adan bucked, knocking Rian askew. Before he could escape, the others dove for his limbs. Cyneath seized an arm. Vychan dropped the mangled pack, leaping for his legs. Adan caught him a kick in the chest that sent him sprawling. He slammed his unfettered fist against the back of Rian's head. Rian's forehead crashed into Adan's, sparking white-hot flashes of light. The fingers loosened around Adan's windpipe, and he gasped in a trickle of warm air. Then, a boot slammed against his ear. Vision fled, leaving a splotch of eerie darkness in its wake. Adan attempted a surge to his feet. His face bashed into Rian's again, and both sank backward.

"Where's the horn?" Vychan demanded. A foot hammered Adan's groin. His gut spasmed, and remaining breath dashed from his lungs. He could not have answered had he wanted to do so.

Tynan's voice rang over the threats. "He doesn't have it."

Rian's body disappeared from Adan's, and a blurry glimpse of the alley returned to the young lord's sight. Tynan and Bevin stood at the alley's entrance, the cat perched on his link-mate's shoulder. On his knees, Rian rocked beside Adan, hands clamped to his nose. The cousins stood between him and Tynan, both now facing the new threat.

The cat shifted as Tynan continued, "I have Tassi's horn." It was a bald-faced lie, the last thing Adan ever expected from Tynan.

What are you doing, little brother? Taking advantage of the moment of surprise, Adan buried his fist in Rian's face. Tassi's brother slumped silently to the muddy tatters of Adan's belongings. Leaping to his feet, he charged Vychan.

Vychan whirled as Adan reached him, swinging a broad

roundhouse for Adan's face. Adan ducked. Hooking a leg around the massive cousin's, he tossed him easily to the ground. *Thanks, Gaer.* He did not have long to savor the triumph. With a bull below of fury, Cyneath sprang for Adan.

Adan backpedaled furiously. His foot came down on the Hunt-Keeper's horn, still wrapped in one of his fouled and shabby cloaks. Pitched backward, he plummeted to the ground with an impact that jarred his teeth together. He bit his tongue, tasting blood, then tensed for the slam of Cyneath on top of him.

Tynan's link-mate launched himself at the larger man, yowling, spitting, and clawing. Cyneath screamed, dropping away from Adan to attend the demon animal ripping at his head. Then Tynan caught the man a blow that sent him tumbling into the mud as well.

Adan caught the cat as he sprang free of the grounded man. "Thanks, my furry little brother."

Bevin gasped.

Head ringing, gut aching, Adan snatched up the bundled horn. "What's wrong, my love?"

"There're two Magicians," Bevin announced. "I can't—" She broke off, the same realization surely striking her and Adan simultaneously.

"You must. No one else has magic to assist."

Bevin nodded, determination filling gray eyes that turned as hard as mountain stone. "I need high ground."

Adan did not question. "The upper balcony of the Great House?"

Bevin shook her head. "No time for that. I need someplace open that won't require discussion and convincing."

"The prominence?" Tynan suggested an overhang that served as a favorite play place in their youth, even as the same thought came to Adan.

Rian moaned. Adan glanced toward him, then at Vychan who rose but did not attempt another assault. "You two go. I'll rally Culan." He took a dizzy step toward the Great House, cursing the dull anguish still plaguing spine, gut, and face. *And hope it's not too late.*

Adan watched Tynan and Bevin scurry toward the prominence as he limped toward the Great House of Sarn Moor.

Wind whipped Bevin's sandy ringlets into tangles, and she clutched Tynan's hand like a lifeline. She could feel his desperate boil of emotion as a strange harmony to her own. Terror and dread mingled with determination, the cat's consciousness inseparably entwined with his link-mate's. Always before, they had seemed inhumanly close. Now, they impressed her magically-enhanced senses as a single entity eternally bound, and a depthless comfort accompanied their newfound oneness. She only wished she could share their solace.

The sorcery of the Hooded Magicians crushed toward her in searching bursts. They knew she had come among those gathered for the horse fair, but they had not yet located her amid the celebrants. She had selected her position to assist them, a high point of solitude that separated her essence fully from the crowd's. Their dark magic did not allow for finesse. Should they attempt to slaughter her, they would surely take hundreds of nearby innocents with her. Now, they could face her alone, her only regret the need to drag Tynan into the fray. Had she left him among the others, he would serve equally as a focus for their destruction. *Come and get me, Evil Ones.*

As if in answer, the prickles of magic found Bevin. She felt them study her, fighting the urge to flee in abject terror. No legend of the Dark Court seemed half so horrible as the forces that flowed over and around her now. She suppressed horrified shivers, walling emotion into a deep pocket of her being. She stood stalwart, delivering an outward appearance of unshakable competence. Perversely, the exploration seemed strangely tentative for users of the dark power. At least one of the magic-wielders worried about Bevin's abilities. Her bluff, it seemed, had fooled him. Under less dangerous circumstances, Bevin would have laughed.

Soldiers massed around the borders of Sarn Moor. She could feel their eagerness, their excitement, and their fear. In scant moments, the battle would begin, whether or not Adan managed to convince Lord Culan and Lady Tassi, whether or not Kiarda and Gaer had won over Lord Stane, whether or not the folk of the Marchlands mustered against their enemy. Soon, the swords of the Empire would flash against the people she loved. One way or another, she would protect them from the Hooded Order. And hope men too long at peace could handle the Empire's swords.

Leading Little Sister, Maddock had followed Kiarda's fox tracks to hoof and foot marks in the silt near the Coney, including the unmistakable prints of Brother Honesty's threadbare sandals. The arrangement confused Maddock, and he interpreted as best he could. Kiarda claimed she did not have her parents' permission to seek him, yet she traveled with at least one man who had not wholly forgotten how to fight. That suggested Stane's influence. Likely, the Lord of Dorlach Tor had arranged Kiarda's companions, in secret so as not to arouse her ire and defiance. And, as Skull had claimed, a powerful magic-wielder accompanied her as well, the only explanation for Brother Honesty's apparent willingness to remain among them without evidence of physical restraint.

Maddock had read all of that from traces left around the river, before following the horse sign east, toward Sarn Moor. Every step drew him nearer to his childhood, sparking flashes of memory. He had loved the broad streets of Sarn Moor, the brilliant colors of its flag, the giggling games of tag he had once played in its stables during the horse fairs that had brought his father there. When youth had obviated the need to consider rank, he had shared his rare toys and secrets with Adan and Culan. He had never worried that they had more than he did, only reveled in the chance to play with their marbles, dice, and figurines—especially the horses.

Trees bobbed past Maddock as he crept along the roadside, trailing hoofprints in the soft, summer dirt of the road to Sarn Moor. Head down, he found himself frequently shaking ragged clumps of black hair from his forehead and eyes. It needed cutting. The sweet musk of horses twined to him with the breeze, bringing a new round of recollection: the sting of sweat against the normal nicks and cuts that accompanied hard work, the power of an errant stallion rearing against the training harness, and Cadder's calm voice cutting over terrified whinnies. Nothing had ever seemed to ruffle the aging Horsemaster; his least cooperative charges, human and animal, suffered only his firm and loving guidance.

Ice suddenly filled the pit of Maddock's stomach, driving away happier memories. His father was dead, killed either by grief over his son's alleged crime or the lady's order of execution. As Maddock came upon the site where Brother Honesty's sandal tracks diverged from the hoofprints, grief paralyzed him. He stood, gaze trained without comprehension on the information the ground revealed to him. He had known of his father's death for weeks, had cried himself to sleep more than once. Yet the rigors of sword training and living among soldiers had distracted him by day. His life in Dorlach Tor seemed centuries ago, another man, another world, another existence. As the game-calls of children and the shouts of men drifted over the rattle of wind through leaves and the diminishing burble of the Coney, the young Maddock returned to haunt him.

Father. Maddock managed a single shaky step, Cadder's face perfectly preserved in his memory. *Father!* A whiff of spice drifted to his nose, accompanied by a sudden rush of bitterness and anger. "Stane." *You stole my life, my joys, my father! And all of it, a lie.* Hatred burned like the hottest of Dark Court fires.

As if to give a target to Maddock's rage, Stane's familiar voice disrupted his thoughts. "Maddock?"

Maddock stiffened, jerking his head toward Sarn Moor. The Lord of Dorlach Tor stood alone on the path, apparently following the hoofprints in the opposite direction. Maddock blinked, shaking his head to clear it. Surely, his own desire for revenge had conjured this hallucination; only the gods could have blessed him with such an opportunity.

Stane took another step toward the young man. "Is that you, Maddock?" He wore stained leathers, and the sword at his left hip looked incongruous. The voice remained steady, absolute, and certain.

He's stalking Brother Honesty! Suddenly, Maddock did not care whether he faced reality or a vaporous creation of the Dark Court. The man he had once trusted, who had killed his father and Gaer, first breaking them with lies; who had torn Maddock from his one chance at true love and turned his life to hopeless shambles; who was planning to slaughter the finest man remaining in his life, now stood in front him. Alone and unguarded. Maddock drew his sword and charged.

Stane barely threw up a defense in time. Their blades slammed together with a clang that echoed. Pain thrummed through Maddock's fingers, but it thrilled him as well. Illusion would not hurt.

"Maddock, please," Stane tried. "I only—"

Maddock cut for Stane's abdomen. "I hate you, you fiend."

Stane dodged the strike, bearing in with one of his own. "I'm sorry, I—"

"Too late." Maddock wove a wild flurry of steel that forced Stane into desperate retreat. "Too little."

"We . . ." Stane stepped backward. ". . . could . . ." He evaded a crazed jab. ". . . discuss . . ."

"There's nothing to discuss!" Maddock thrust, only to find himself leaping aside to avoid a slice that wove through his own frenzied assault. "You ruined everything!" The understanding behind those simple words turned Maddock's vision to a red plane of fury. Diving beneath Stane's sword, he drove a muscled shoulder into the older man's gut.

Breath dashed from him, Stane managed no further words. He staggered.

Maddock pressed his advantage, deliberately driving Stane toward a rotting stump beside the path.

At that moment, familiar war howls echoed from Sarn Moor, followed by a ragged frenzy of screams.

"No," Stane sobbed. Distracted, he missed his footing, boot heel stabbing down on the side of the stump. He scrabbled for balance, sword and arm flailing, then collapsed.

Torn between dread and triumph, Maddock swooped down on his grounded enemy. His sword rose for the killing strike.

"Maddock, what are you doing!" Panic raised a voice from Maddock's childhood half an octave.

Though unused to hearing his father's tone so dense with emotion, Maddock recognized it. He froze, whirling, forgetting about the enemy now at his unprotected back.

Cadder stood on the path, white hair clotted with chips of bark, dark eyes wide with sorrow and outrage. He looked beyond Maddock. "My lord, please. There must be—"

Maddock did not allow his father to finish. Dropping the sword, he hurled himself into Cadder's arms.

Accustomed to horses, Cadder caught his son easily, without giving a step of ground. The embrace felt so warm, so perfect and real to Maddock, he refused to let go, to speak, to move for fear it would all melt into Dark Court-inspired illusion. Then, suddenly, a third man joined the embrace, surely Stane. Anger banished beneath a rush of confusion, Maddock found himself unable to care. "What's going on?" the youth finally managed.

Stane stepped back, eyes toward Sarn Moor, though the forest fully blocked his vision. "Almighty Hepona."

Cadder continued to clutch his son's arm, as though he feared to lose it again. He addressed Stane, however. "My lord, Gaer said I'd find you if I took this road. I didn't expect . . ." He changed tacks suddenly. "Maddock is innocent. Please don't kill—"

Stane raised his hand to silence the Horsemaster. It was his life Cadder's sudden appearance had saved, not Maddock's. "No one's killing anyone." The shrieks wafting from Sarn Moor told otherwise. He whirled on the Horsemaster's son. "Maddock, can you stop this?"

"I—I don't know." Nothing made sense to Maddock.

Stane continued, "Gaer said another man rode with them. A priest. If I could find this Brother Honesty, he might have some influence over the army."

The pieces started to fit now. Gaer was alive. He and Stane had reconciled, and the Swordmaster believed the Lord of Dorlach Tor best suited to convincing Brother Honesty. Or perhaps, he wished to protect his lord by sending him from the main conflict on a pretext. Many things still jarred, but those details could wait until after they averted a war. Maddock sorted his memories of Commander Swift's strategy. He looked over the village, toward the mountains, pursing his lips. "I think I can help, but I want one thing in exchange." He did not await confirmation but snatched up his sword and headed after Brother Honesty.

"Maddock," Cadder snapped, clearly horrified by his son taking advantage of his lord's desperation.

An explosion rocked the southeast corner of Sarn Moor. Red flames soared upward, capering like demons, trailing plumes of tarry smoke. Screams erupted from the village.

Stane hurried after Maddock. "Anything."

The ever-changing emotions marching through Maddock left him trembling. He spoke while he still maintained control, "I want Kiarda's hand."

Cadder gasped, fingers locking painfully to Maddock's forearm.

Stane took the words in surprisingly easy stride. "If you help stop this war, and she'll have you, I won't stand in your way." He did not have to add, *But Tynan might.*

❧

Driven to one knee by the force of the Hooded Magians' attack, Bevin clutched Tynan and wept. "No!" With magically-enhanced senses, she choked on distant ash and cursed her weakness; a blast had claimed a piece of Sarn Moor. The five magics allowed her to protect Tynan; but, eventually, her strength would trickle away, leaving her nothing. Without an offense, she could only hope her protections outlasted the rabid assaults of the Magicians. Every scream pounded through her like a blade. Every death she could not prevent drove another tear from her eyes.

Tynan clung, or perhaps it was the cat. Bevin could no longer separate the two. They remained with her, a single, silent entity worried about distracting her from her work. Her presence alone kept them alive, though the Magicians no longer focused on them. She sensed no unusual distress from Kiarda either. She worried for her life, and those of loved ones; but the Magicians did not seem to be targeting the links. In fact, one seemed only to dampen the backlash of the other, sparing the Empire's soldiers. But the strength of the other was proving more than enough.

Bevin rose, feeling tattered and wrung. Little remained of her cracked and battered shieldings. Soon they would crumble, admitting the howling fury of unstoppable destruction. Groaning at the effort, she set to repairing her handiwork one last time.

Weapons flashing, horses snorting and prancing, Swift's soldiers boiled through Sarn Moor's streets, howling battle cries that echoed between the shops and cottages like the wails of the Dark Court. Hysterical citizens ran, screaming, from the assault. Pockets remained behind, soldiers who had hastily gathered lumber axes and picks, scythes and utility knives, and a few ancient swords bundled away for safekeeping.

When Maddock caught up to Brother Honesty, he talked the priest onto Little Sister, behind him, while Cadder and Stane mounted horses who had lost their riders to the battle. "Where's the commander?"

Brother Honesty pointed toward the thick of the battle where sunlight glinted from Swift's familiar helmet.

"Let's go!" Maddock charged into the fray without thinking, father and lord at his sides. Once among the Empire's men, the two desperately risked their lives, yet neither hesitated. Steel clanged around them, and shouts of defiance accompanied screams of pain. Maddock rushed through in wild despair, his mission true insanity. He had faced down Lord Stane, a man who had trusted his family for generations. He would not find the high commander of the Imperial forces so easy to convince.

Maddock rode in a strange fog that admitted little, afraid to contemplate the fate of those who rode with him. Battle frenzy seemed a distant abstraction, the combatants ghostly illusions in the pale context of dream. He searched for some thread on which to ground his reason, some emotion or need to drive him to action, but found himself only hoping wildly that the four of them somehow reached Swift without challenge. Apparently, the direction and boldness of their approach, coupled with their lack of harm to the Empire's men, allowed Swift's warriors to accept them without question. Then he caught direct sight of the commander, leading his men in a hacking and slashing assault upon Stane's warriors.

In a moment, the feelings that had evaded Maddock descended on him in a dizzying rush: love and hatred, desire and need, morality and evil. *Why?* The world seemed lost, incapable of logic. Both sides seemed right—and both desperately wrong. "Commander Swift!" he shouted.

Several heads turned toward Maddock then. Their gazes found him and Brother Honesty, also Stane and Cadder. They stopped fighting, surrounding their commander protectively.

"Maddock, not now!" Uncharacteristic anger filled Swift's voice. Engaged in a battle with a weaver who also happened to be a veteran, he did not turn.

Another soldier said something in the language of the Empire, filled with curses against Maddock's ignorance.

"Buidhe, step down!" Stane told the weaver, who backed away, trying to disengage.

Once safely free of attack, Swift whirled, his men crushing between him and further danger. His gaze went directly to Stane. "Who are you?"

Though it seemed an impossible place for introductions, Maddock saw no other choice. "Sir, this is Lord Stane, master of Dorlach Tor. He wants to talk peace."

Commander Swift glared at Maddock. "This is not an appropriate time or place for parley." He glanced about to ascertain that his men kept the Marchlanders at bay while they spoke. Some mounted like the invaders and others on foot, the Marchland warriors retreated, heeding Stane's order to Buidhe. He gave his own men a "defensive pause" command, then returned his attention to Maddock and Lord Stane. "I'm afraid peace is not an option. Your people have been exposed to an abominable plague. The only hope for the innocents of your world, and our own, is for all of you to die." He made a broad gesture to indicate Sarn Moor, then glanced at Brother Honesty.

Lord Stane shook his head. "What sort of plague is this? The one that drained the magic of our healers and slaughtered our blessed spirit-linked?''

"One unspeakably horrible. Best you never know the details."

Stane shifted on his horse but did not draw his weapon. "Do we not have the right to know what fate is worse than the slaughter of our women and children?''

Commander Swift drew a deep breath, then loosed it slowly. "The locking of human souls with animal." He shuddered, awaiting a similar response from Stane and Cadder that never came.

The Lord of Dorlach Tor shook aside yellow hair, brows high in a request for more details.

Brother Honesty broke in then, his voice gentle compared to leaders accustomed to others' obedience. "Commander, it seems we've made a mistake."

Swift's nostrils flared, but he looked at the priest.

"The spirit-link is not the contagious abomination we once believed."

The spirit-link? Maddock stared, shocked to discover the detail that, had he known it earlier, could have spared Radway Green and those who had thus far died in this battle.

"They've influenced you, Brother."

"No!" Maddock could not help shouting, earning a sudden glare from Swift. "He's right, sir. The spirit-link is not catchable." Tears filled his eyes at the thought of lives lost for his ignorance. Had he only known, he might have saved so many. "And there's nothing horrible about it."

"I *am* influenced," Brother Honesty admitted. "But through experience only, not force or magic. It was Skull who first told me that linking a human soul to that of an animal is merely a quirky bit of magic, not a danger. Then I did not believe him. Now, I know better."

Commander Swift remained silent several moments, studying the priest.

Lord Stane broke the hush. "At least give us a chance to discuss it."

Thunder boomed over the village. Flame gouted from the south side of Sarn Moor, igniting thatch-roofed cottages in a savage wave. Commander Swift stiffened. "Brother Honesty, stop the Magicians!'' He pointed northward, then reined his horse in a circle so tight it reared, shouting commands to his men to halt the fighting.

Maddock spun Little Sister in the indicated direction and galloped toward the border, Brother Honesty clutching his waist.

Suddenly, Gaer appeared at his side.

"Master!" Maddock shouted over relayed orders and persistent screams.

"I'm going to help you stop those Magicians," Gaer said, waving his sword. "Whatever it takes."

❧

Bevin's consciousness wavered, and she struggled against the black void that would mean the end, not only to her power but to the folk of the horse fair as well. She understood the strategy of her enemies. They would wait only until the Empire's forces retreated, then they would overwhelm her faltering shields with a destruction that would level the town of Sarn Moor. Tynan's steadying arms barely held Bevin aloft; she could no longer feel his touch. Her head ached in time to her heartbeat, and all vision disappeared. Drained of emotion, she fought with blind devotion, hopelessness beckoning her with a blessed oblivion she scarcely managed to refuse. "It's over," she whispered.

"No!" Tynan shook Bevin. "Don't give up!"

Can't fight anymore. Bevin gathered the vitality remaining in body and soul. Magical sight revealed the two Magicians, male and female, already prepared to celebrate their victory. In a moment, even this last strength would wash from Bevin, leaving her an empty shell and them in total control. Her world, everyone in it, would dissolve into a brilliant flash of agony while she watched helplessly, desperately hopeless.

"No!" Tynan shouted again.

Another voice rose over Tynan's. "Give me the horn, you little weasel! Give it to me!" Pushed, Tynan slammed against Bevin, then something pulled him relentlessly from her protection.

"Tassi!" Tynan screamed. "No—!"

The healer urgently tightened her grasp. "Stop! Get away!

You'll ruin everything!" The effort of speaking cost too much. Unconsciousness threatened. As Bevin fought the darkness, instinctive anger welled up in her, lending her the strength for one last action. The sources of magic filled her mind's eye, the five encircling powers flinging jeweled highlights as they cascaded upward, the last falling, dark and braided, deeply sinister.

Tassi shouted, "Impudent bitch!"

Within the frenzied depths of the magics, Bevin saw the faces of the Magicians, laughing, as ugly as Tassi's voice, so much closer yet distant, lacking in comparative significance. Within the clear waters she saw the folk of Dorlach Tor, the people she had come to love and respect, the world that had become so much hers. *Adan.* Her course suddenly became horrifyingly clear. *I love you.* She dove for the dark entwining of the central magic, despising herself as much as the desperation that drove her to it. *And I'm sorry.*

Tassi's hand crashed against Bevin's jaw. "Just who do you think you're speaking to?"

Though staggered, Bevin felt nothing. Light crashed through Sarn Moor's sky, so brilliant it struck down reality. White-hot lightning split the heavens, howling toward the Hooded Order. The backlash splashed from Bevin like a tornado, command fully lost to the Lady of Sarn Moor's assault. Auras in rainbow colors surrounded Tynan and Tassi in a multicolored rush of power with a beauty so raw it defined ugliness instead. Screams erupted in a thousand voices. The cat yowled, the very voice of destruction. Self-hatred coursed through Bevin, accompanied by unexpected smugness. Then, the last of her awareness fled, replaced by utter darkness.

⳹⌘⳦

Gaer clung to his pitching mount, feeling its massive muscles tense and bulge beneath him, cursing his lack of control. Maddock also managed to remain on Little Sister's back, though she bore no saddle. Brother Honesty tumbled, rolling from the path of the frenzied horses as the ground stilled back to its normal conformation. Gaer's bay gelding ceased bucking, though its sinews remained bunched, its eyes rolled backward in suspicion.

Maddock dismounted to assist Brother Honesty, and Little Sister shied from the young man's hold. Gaer kicked his horse toward her, but it resisted moving even a step nearer the smoking ruin of forest ahead. "We're going to have to walk the rest of the way," Gaer announced.

Maddock glanced at his restless filly and nodded. Releasing her, he assisted Brother Honesty to his feet. "Are you all right?"

"Fine, my child." Brother Honesty brushed dirt from his robe. Despite his claim, his voice emerged with teary hesitation.

Gaer's fingers blanched around his sword as he moved cautiously toward the patch of shattered pine that had once hidden the Magicians of the Hooded Order. Scattered rocks and dirt clods ringed the periphery, blown there by the same force that had quaked the ground and terrified the horses. A dense blanket of crisp, green leaves covered the ground, the branches above nearly bare. As the Swordmaster approached with wary caution, something stirred. A black-robed figure rose dizzily from the wreckage, cowl thrown back and packed with bracken. Long hair as dark as Maddock's, singed and snarled with leaves, fell around a narrow face that held a grimace of pain.

Gaer raised his sword to finish the creature.

"No!" Brother Honesty hurled himself between the two, knocking the unsteady Mage sprawling.

Gaer held his position, turning the priest a dangerous glare. "Out of my way, Honesty. There's only one way to deal with this evil."

Brother Honesty did not move. "My child, do not fall prey to the same error that nearly caused us to destroy your people. Like the spirit-linked, the Hooded Order are also vessels of the One Light."

"*Mistakes* of the One Light," Gaer corrected, but he did lower his weapon. "This thing must, at least, be restrained."

"I will take responsibility for Skull," Brother Honesty promised.

The Mage spoke, voice shaky, "I could listen to you discuss my disposition all day, but Claw needs our help." Frantically, he pawed through the debris, then glanced abruptly up at Gaer. "Worry more for Bevin and those with her. The sixth magic is new to her, against her nature. I'm alive because something disrupted her, but the power can't be diminished. The excess had to go somewhere."

Gaer had heard of the horror of Hooded Magicians' backlash. His disgust for the creatures intensified. "Maddock—"

"I'm on my way." Maddock scrambled toward Little Sister. Brother Honesty continued to dig through the fallen branches.

"Bevin's on an overhang," Skull directed. "North side of town." He turned on Gaer then. "Battle's over, Swordmaster. Slay me now, and it will be murder."

"I've found her," Brother Honesty announced, almost disappearing into the pile of green leaves he had constructed.

Her? Gaer shifted, staring down at an oval face partially obscured by black ringlets. Something familiar struck him about her features. Shock stole his words. *It couldn't be.* He pressed the curls from her cheeks.

At his touch, the Mage stirred. The green eyes fell open, glazed with death.

Gaer straggled backward. "Graceful?"

"Honor?" Claw spoke Gaer's given name. "I didn't want—" Her voice faded.

Torn between love and revulsion, Gaer hefted the Mage from her bed of leaves. She did not assist, dead weight cradled in his arms. "What didn't you want, Graceful? What didn't you want?"

Skull broke in softly, "She didn't want to hurt you. She didn't want to lie, but when the magic called, she had no choice but to go."

Gaer held up a forestalling hand. "Let *her* speak."

"Those *are* her words." Skull knelt beside Gaer. "But she won't ever speak them."

No pulse drummed against Gaer's fingers. He wanted to cry, but the tears would not come. He had buried Graceful more than two decades ago. He wondered why she had shared these details of her past with Skull.

"She didn't. I read minds," the surviving Mage explained.

"She also would have told you that we called her Claw, but she secretly called herself *'Gaer,'* Sorrowing." He lifted one brow. "Odd coincidence, isn't it, Gaer?"

The Swordmaster lowered Graceful's corpse to the ground. "Call me Honor."

Epilogue

K IARDA followed Bevin and Skull through the corridors of Sarn Moor's Great House, scarcely recognizing the gaily colored wall weavings she had loved in her youth. No longer hooded, the Mage huddled into his dark cloak, raven hair spilling over the collar. Years of training to hide his identity had been undone by the woman he now looked to as a teacher, by circumstance and by the understanding of Claw's sacrifice. Reviled, those of the Hooded Order had had no choice but to conceal their identities to allow themselves any kind of life in their other guise. Once, he had shared his secret with Brother Honesty and, now, with everyone.

Kiarda, too, had found a new beginning—the chance to marry the man she had so long loved and turn Maddock into the future Lord of Dorlach Tor. But sorrow kept all joy at bay. She had not yet given him an answer, though she knew it heaped more pain on a life she had cruelly and wrongfully shattered. The one person in the whole world she did not wish to hurt now nervously awaited the response he deserved. The answer seemed obvious, yet Kiarda endured a depression leagues deeper than grief over the deaths of two dozen, including her cousin Tynan and Lady Tassi.

Bevin opened the door to her quarters, ushering her companions through it. The instant the panel opened, the yowls of the damned devastated her hearing. The ginger tomcat lay on his side in a wicker cage, refusing all food and water. The agony in his cry went even beyond Kiarda's own.

Skull glided inside, hovering beside the wretched animal. The tabby fur lay matted and dull, the nose bloody from repeated bashings against the container, the claws tattered and peeling.

Tears flooded Kiarda's eyes, blurring the animal to a limp ball of orange. "Oh, you poor darling. Poor, poor darling." She reached for the latch, stopped by Bevin's hand.

"No, Kiarda. If you free him, he'll kill himself."

Skull explained further. "They found him hurling himself between soldiers, desperately trying to die. He's refused all food and drink. He would have pounded himself to pieces on that cage if he hadn't become too exhausted to fight."

Too exhausted to fight. Kiarda felt a kinship with the animal that flared into understanding. "I know how he feels," she said softly. "Empty. Lacking. As if parts of himself were missing. Even—"

"—the greatest pleasures of the world lack meaning." Skull finished Kiarda's sentence.

"Yes," Kiarda said, no longer surprised by his talent.

"You feel the same way."

"Yes." Kiarda swallowed hard. "Perhaps it would be best to let him . . . die." Now that she identified with the animal, the words became even more painful.

"Or," Bevin said. "Perhaps we could heal both of you."

"Heal . . . ?" Kiarda dared to hope. She latched her gaze on Bevin. "You can help?" The room came into focus, the canopied bed, the chiseled chest of drawers, the woolen rug hugging her bare toes.

"I believe," Bevin said slowly, measuring her every word on Kiarda, "that with Skull's assistance . . ."

He nodded.

". . . I can secure the broken ends of the links."

Kiarda blinked, trying to comprehend the details. "The broken ends?" She shook her head while both magic-wielders watched her intently. Her eyes widened, and she returned Bevin's stare. "You mean link me and Furry Purry?"

"Why not?" Bevin said, tone almost pleading.

"Why not?" Kiarda repeated aloud. She looked at the cat, ribs showing through heaving flanks. She managed her first smile in days. "He would have to agree, too." Kiarda meant that she would not force such a thing against the animal's will, but Bevin revealed the deeper truth of Kiarda's words.

"Success would require cooperation from both sides."

Kiarda felt the first deep stirrings which suggested joy had not wholly died within her. "You have mine, at least." A thousand questions descended on her at once. "Would he become a fox?"

"Nothing like this has ever been done before." Bevin shrugged. "If I had to guess, I'd say he'll remain himself but develop some foxlike tendencies." She looked at Kiarda's red-blonde hair. "Perhaps some of the coloring." She cleared her throat and glanced at Skull, who nodded again. "And you might find yourself with some of the mannerisms and thoughts of Tynan. Could you live with that?"

Kiarda thought of her cousin, his sweet, almost naive kindness, and the tears left her eyes to course along her cheeks. She sobbed out, "I would consider that the greatest honor of all."

"You sit." Bevin indicated a chair. "Skull and I will do all the work." She lowered her head, murmuring, "But first, we have to ask Furry Purry."

The cat staggered to its paws. "Ee-arr-rra!" it managed. "Eeee-aaarr-rrra!"

"I think we have an answer," Skull said with a laugh.

The air around Kiarda seemed to tingle, then the cat's cry gained a new dimension. [[Tell them my name's not Furry Purry. It's Cat-Who-Links-With-Cousins.]]

Depression fled like a vapor. "I'll tell them," Kiarda promised.

cᵍₒ

Kiarda ran the brush over Blood Rage's shoulder in slow, smooth strokes. Grooming her father's old stallion calmed her, helped her to think.

Soft sounds filled the horse tent, the swish of a tail, the crunch of oats, a robin in the tree overhead. Three stable hands sat in the grass outside the door, quietly discussing how to mend an antique bridle. Cat-Who-Links-With-Cousins slept, curled in a ball of orange fur, on Blood Rage's glossy rump. Kiarda cherished the contemplative hush, so very different than the whirlwind of noise and activity in Sarn Moor's Great House.

Filled with desperate sorrow over Tassi's death, Culan had eagerly surrendered his title to Adan. More recently, Culan had spoken of joining the priesthood to aid in its reform. Though still grieving himself, the new Lord of Sarn Moor had thrown himself into rebuilding the shattered village, working to put his people's lives back together. Bevin was never far from his side and her gentle nature had won over Sarn Moor's folk, who already deferred to her as their Lady. A constant stream of brick-layers, carpenters, and merchants filled the road, mingling with a tide of political emissaries.

Kiarda's mother and father were closeted every day with Commander Swift and representatives of the Marchland clans, hammering out a peace treaty. Kiarda had sat in on some of the sessions and found them interesting and reassuring. All parties wanted an accord, but making the practical arrangements was time-consuming and exhausting. *Rather like planning a wedding.*

Kiarda's tranquil mood faltered. She paused with the brush in midair and sighed.

Cat-Who-Links-With-Cousins opened one eye and twitched his whiskers. [[What's wrong?]]

With every passing day, as the broken spirit-links continued to heal and meld together, the cat demonstrated an increasing number of Tynan's traits, as well as foxlike characteristics. His voice in her head was Tynan's.

Kiarda smiled weakly and spoke in a low murmur pitched for her link-mate's ears. "The usual."

The tomcat rose and stretched. [[Maddock?]]

"Yes." Kiarda raked her fingers through the brush, cleaning the horsehair from it. She had not yet found the nerve to approach the Horsemaster's son about marriage. "I don't know what to do."

Cat-Who-Links-With-Cousins padded toward Kiarda, up the length of the stallion's spine. [[Pet me.]]

Kiarda grinned in spite of herself, setting the brush on an overturned bucket. "And will that help matters?"

[[As far as I'm concerned.]] The cat jumped from Blood Rage, settled into his link-mate's waiting arms, and broke into a rumbling purr. [[Ah, yes. See? Much better.]]

Kiarda kissed him between the ears. "Incorrigible flirt."

[[I am Cat-Who-Knows-Best.]]

"You are Cat-Full-of-Poop."

The stable hands outside broke into a round of respectful greetings, and a shadow loomed in the tent's doorway. Blood Rage twisted his head to look, snorting.

Kiarda turned.

Maddock hesitated, seeming blinded by the tent's gloom. "My lady?"

As Kiarda's gaze traveled over him, she noted that he wore a new set of hunting leathers with high boots and close-fitting trousers. A sword hung from his belt.

Maddock tilted his head, and his hair slid over his eyes. "Is this a bad time?"

The tomcat butted Kiarda's chin with his forehead. [[Say something.]]

Quivering with love and desire, Kiarda tried to find words. She was glad he had not cut his hair; she decided she liked it long. "Looks good."

"Pardon?"

Kiarda felt her face grow hot. "I mean the time—looks good—and not—not—" She shrugged helplessly. "You know. Not bad."

The cat prompted her. [[Come in.]]

"Please," Kiarda blurted. "Come in."

Maddock's expression relaxed a bit. "Thank you." He strolled toward her, moving with easy grace. "Nice and cool in here."

Kiarda swallowed hard and nodded, sweat trickling down her sides beneath her tunic. "Yes."

Blood Rage pricked up his ears and extended his nose toward the young man, nickering softly.

Maddock's eyes suddenly sparkled. "Hello, old friend. Remember me?" He stroked the stallion's gray muzzle and looked at Kiarda. "Some things haven't changed."

Kiarda nodded again and found it took tremendous effort to make herself stop.

"I mean," Maddock continued, "that you're still the most beautiful woman I've ever seen. With or without sweet mash in your hair."

"What?" Kiarda groped for the braid on her shoulder and found it wet and sticky. "Eyew!"

Blood Rage snorted mischievously and shook his head.

[[Oh, yes.]] Cat-Who-Knows-Best yawned. [[Meant to tell you earlier. Horse drooled all over your hair.]]

Lips clamped together, as if suppressing a smile, Maddock crossed to an equipment rack, found a clean tack cloth, and held it out to her. "Here."

Kiarda returned the tomcat to Blood Rage's back, then accepted the rag from Maddock, very much aware of how close their fingers came to touching. "Thanks."

"My pleasure." Maddock glanced through the tent's doorway toward the Great House. "Actually, my lady, Bevin asked me to come find you. She was hoping you'd help with her wedding plans."

Kiarda's hands shook as she wiped her hair. "I suppose."

Maddock chuckled. "Bevin says that besides fare for the guests, she plans to make a special treat for just her and Adan on their honeymoon. A sweet-twist."

"But that's for courting couples."

Maddock cleared his throat. "Yes. Well. She says they'll each take one end of the twist . . . and eat their way to the middle."

Unbidden, the thought of doing that with Maddock flew through Kiarda's mind. Her blush turned scalding. "Wonder if Bevin would agree to make two sweet-twists."

Maddock tilted his head. "Two?"

Kiarda could not take her eyes off him. "After all, there're going to be two weddings."

For a long moment, Maddock gazed at Kiarda, motionless. Then, he whispered, " 'Yarda . . . did you just consent to marry me?"

Maddock spoke with such love, such longing and tenderness, that Kiarda's lingering doubts vanished. She recalled all their suffering of the past year; all the losses, the transformations, the grief, at last redeemed by what stayed constant. "Yes, I want to marry you," she murmured. "I love you. I always have. I always will.

"That will never change."

APPENDIX

Ladayla: the third child of Lady Wylfre of Dorlach Tor; a girl
Leith: the second child of Lady Wylfre of Dorlach Tor; a boy
Lis: one of Kiarda's three maids
Maddock: Cadder's son
Mona: the Lady of Sarn Moor; Lady Wylfre's cousin
Oric: Tynan's steward while in Dorlach Tor
Rian: Tassi's older brother
Rina: one of Kiarda's three maids
Stane: the Lord of Dorlach Tor
Sygil: an aging healer in Dorlach Tor
Tassi: Culan's wife; the Lady of Sarn Moor
Threv: a childhood friend of Maddock who drowned
Tormaigh: the Stablemaster of Dorlach Tor
Tynan: the thirdborn of Lady Mona's five sons
Vecco: a high priest from Egas Cairn
Vernon: a southern king
Vonora: Anra's granddaughter; Byrta's daughter; Damas' twin
Vychan: Tassi's cousin
Wylfre: the Lady of Dorlach Tor
Yasly: the head cook in Dorlach Tor
Yos: Mona's brother-in-law

PEOPLE OF THE EMPIRE

Claw: a Mage of the Hooded Order
Courage: a soldier
Cunning: a soldier
Friendship: a soldier
Graceful: Gaer's once-betrothed
Honesty: a priest of the One Light
Honor: Gaer's birthname
Justice: the Emperor
Skull: a Mage of the Hooded Order
Swift: the commander
Trust: a field officer
Valor: an officer

Virtue: a soldier
Wraith: a Mage of the Hooded Order

PLACES

The Coney: a river
Dorlach Tor: a fort
The Empire: a country across the eastern sea
Ewyas Skarrd: a fort
Farn Tump: a fort
The High Beck: a river
The High Marches: the northern Marchlands
The Low Marches: the southern Marchlands
The Northern Wastes: the polar north
Radway Green: a fort
The Rapid River: a river
Riverton: a river city
Sarn Moor: a fort
Tillsbury: a river city
Wray Valley: site of a conclusive battle in which the Marchlanders and River people formed an alliance to defend against Vernon. Later became the temple headquarters for the priesthood of the Joyous Reunion.

EMPIRE WORDS

rattara: a wooden practice sword

MARCHLAND WORDS

dorlach: an ancient term for a quiver of arrows
sprirranin: a sweet spice that grows only in late spring and does not keep well

Religious Concepts

The Dark Court: evil spirits

The Divine Peace: the prophesied peace that will result from the
Joyous Reunion

Hepona: the Marchland goddess of battle

Hernis: the Marchland god of the hunt and the harvest

The Joyous Reunion: the prophecied time when Hepona and Hernis marry, after which all blood feud, war, and arranged marriages will forever end.

The Light Court: capricious spirits

The One Light: deity of the Empire